Jeff Stuart spent twenty
years in the esoteric w
Executive of a comp
Governments in over 100
He travelled extensively,
of the world, such as Cen
Africa, and Central America, dealing exclusively with Governments at Presidential and Ministerial level, and with their respective security forces. He witnessed first-hand the extraordinary role banknotes (especially) played in those states, and realised the dangerous potential for de-stabilisation implicit in the business in the hands of the unscrupulous.

THE M€N WHO BOUGHT THE WORLD

THE M€N WHO BOUGHT THE WORLD

by

JEFF STUART

HAMILTON CO. PUBLISHERS LTD.
LONDON

Paperback ISBN 1 901668 83 5

Publisher

HAMILTON & Co. Publishers Ltd
10 Stratton Street
Mayfair
London

For my wife, Margaret Mary, for all her love, devotion, tolerance and understanding

FOREWORD

The following story is “fiction”. At least, it is as it was written.

But all the locations are genuine, as are all the organisations, all the technology referred to, and all the machinery, methods and suppliers used in banknote printing. The associated statistics are also genuine.

This scenario could occur: There is nothing to stop it. It only needs one determined rogue Government, or State Security printing Works, or privately-owned High Security Printer, to make it happen. It is really as easy as that.

All the characters are, of course, fictional. Nothing else is necessarily so.

Jeff Stuart

THE MEN WHO BOUGHT THE WORLD

£$£

Chapter One

There is a very small but elegant office in the Lowenstrasse in the small but elegant city of Zurich in Switzerland, which houses, very discreetly, the secretariat of possibly the most powerful club in the world. "Discreetly" is perhaps far too mild a word. "Secretively" is more apposite.

Secrecy is at the heart of the organisation and every member of it. The organization, and its members, live, breathe, eat, drink, and think secrecy and they sell it.

Only a handful of people in the world know of the existence of this club. Just the members, all Governments and whatever security forces they surround themselves with, and a few major companies who deal, discreetly of course, with the members of the club, but who can never be members themselves and then there are the world's Central Bank governors, and one or two of their staff. In all, this is probably only about a thousand people out of the 5 billion walking the earth.

All the members of this club are implacably hostile to each other. Not personally, but on behalf of the organizations they represent. None would rush to save another from a firing squad, be it in Tajikistan, Haiti or Iraq, if that meant more benefit to their organisation. They would be more likely to buy the bullets.

But, every year without fail the Secretariat in the small office in the Lowenstrasse organize a meeting, always held in the most sumptuous hotel in some great city, or a grand mansion or chateau near such city, which every member attends. They go with their wives or their girlfriends and perhaps one or two of their closest colleagues, and for a few days they behave like old friends at a reunion. They are immaculately polite to each other, they share the finest repasts prepared by the most renowned chefs in that particular country together, drink the most expensive champagne together, and the wines, visit art galleries together, have private dinner parties at the smartest restaurants and swell the coffers of a dozen interpreting companies in each selected country for they have no common language. They greet each other with manufactured joy, great firm handshakes, kiss each others' wives and/or girlfriends, meet steady friendly gaze for gaze, each one trying to prevent their free hand gripping the others' throat.

This organisation, this club, is the A. I. I. F. The Association Internationale des Impremeurs Feduciaires. These men are the only people in the world who can print their own money. They can also print anyone else's money, everyone else's money. In fact, there is no money on earth that they can't print. They print the money for 200 of the 251 countries in the world. Their aim is to print it all

There are 15 of these men.

£$£

Chapter Two

The world turns, economies operate, and countries survive, because people believe in little scraps of paper with smudges of ink on them. If they didn't, and disastrously at times they haven't, what is known as order, perhaps civilisation, in such countries teeters on the brink of collapse. The haunting sepia footage of decent hard-working Germans collecting their salaries, wages, pensions in wheelbarrows in the Weimar Republic in 1923 are familiar to all. The National Socialist Party, which clawed its way to the pinnacle of power over those mountains of virtually worthless banknotes, made sure of that. It was precious material for the propaganda machine of Reich minister Goebels to convince Germans that they needed the New Order. In 1991, in the beautiful, desecrated, raped and looted nation of Zaire, on an avenue in Kinshasa the capital, the Avenue de Aviatours, re-named by the locals "Wall Street", banknotes were bought and sold by the "brick". That is, a thousand banknotes, still shrink-wrapped, just as they were delivered by foreign printers, in denomination of up to 1,000,000 or even 5,000,000 "Zaires", the nation's legal currency. The local traders got them straight from the airport as they were flown in by President Mobutu Seso Seso Seko to pay his Palace Guard, Security Forces and Army. They were obtained through the usual corrupt "officials", before they'd even got to the Banque du Zaire. A 1m Zaire note was supposedly worth $333, at the "official exchange rate" of approximately 3000 Zaires to the $. No one believed it. The actual rate on the street was a fraction of that, but even then the notes were far too high in denomination, more than the vast majority of the population earned in a year. When the 5m Zaire notes were introduced in 1991 and paid to the soldiers, the shopkeepers of Kinshasa finally rebelled and refused to accept them.

They'd had enough. They had reached the stage when they simply didn't believe in the paper money. Three hundred people died in the ensuing carnage as the soldiers vented their frustrations "in the normal way." When Marshall of the Soviet Air Force Dudeyev, who declared himself the first President of independent Chechenya, had his own banknote printed by the British company De La Rue, and smuggled them into his little land-locked country through the already independent Baltic state of Estonia, where he'd been stationed and still had many friends in high places, it led to two gruesome murders in London of his agents who'd arranged it all and signalled the beginning of a war in which tens of thousands were killed and maimed, the Russian Federation almost brought to its knees in impotent rage, and nearly led to the fall of President Yeltsin.

There is a legion of such stories. The world turns on these little scraps of paper. They are the greatest and most consistently successful, confidence trick foisted upon mankind. But they work, because men accept them.

In 1993 in Somalia, the abortive attempt by the USA, in the guise of the UN, to impose order amongst the war-lords of that benighted state and save a starving population after the collapse of the puppet government of Said Barre, made an awful situation appalling. He'd survived and prospered by playing West against East. The country disintegrated when he was ousted because neither West nor East were interested in playing his game, or rather their games, any more, and dead Americans joined dead Somalis on the dirty, dusty streets of Mogadisliu. Yet, a few hundred miles to the north, in the town of Hergeisa, where only one building remained standing amidst a Hiroshima-type landscape, and that was used as an hotel where westerners who cared or dared venture there washed in tanks in the street, the power of paper money as a vital unifying force was recognised. A determined man named Ergal, the leader of the main Northern faction, assuming the "Presidency of Somaliland" was negotiating with another British company, Harrisons, to print banknotes for his Government and, with their introduction, help to establish a "nation state" with its own identity. At first, all he had to pay for these was to offer a barter deal with 40,000 sheep or Somali camels, highly-prized as the best in Africa, especially in Egypt. Against all the odds he succeeded. He sold the sheep to Saudi Arabia and paid in cash for his banknotes. In the whole of that area of the Horn of Africa they are still the accepted currency, a nation coalescing around them.

In Moscow, where the "Mafia" run everything from the best hotels, the prostitutes, the drugs, the extortion rackets, half of the banks, a lot of the businesses, and the taxis, roubles churned out by the billions each year by the two State Printing Works, the Gosnaks, in Moscow and Perm, count for nothing. US dollars are the currency of Moscow. From the Aerostar Hotel to the Ukraine Station at the end of Leninsky Prospekt a taxi ride costs $8. It takes about three minutes. It is more than the average Muscovite earns in a day. On the tram, which follows the same route it costs one Rouble. In 1993 there were 1500 Roubles to the dollar. Russians didn't believe in Roubles any more.

In South-East Asia, in countries the US tried to "bomb back to the Stone Age", Vietnam, Laos, Cambodia, only US dollars count. The fact that they are mainly counterfeits, printed in Hong Kong, is immaterial. These pieces of paper are accepted, the economy works because of that acceptance, and the world turns. The same applies to Central Asia, in Tajikistan, Turkmenistan, Uzbekistan, Kazakhstan. Counterfeited by a privately owned printer in Turkey.

As long as "the people" accept the pieces of paper as payment for goods or services, those pieces of paper are "currency". If they don't, there is anarchy.

£$£

Chapter Three

Banknote printing is a curious mix of art, craft, technology and manufacturing printing process, and an obsession with security, both within the document itself, during the process of its production, around that process and around the finished articles. It demands the collective co-ordinated talents of paper-makers, ink technologists, artists, designers, metallurgists, printing and plate-making experts, and security experts. The same demands are required for other security documents such as traveller's cheques, passports, Bearer Securities (Bonds), motor vehicle tax discs, I.D. cards, even high-class store vouchers and a range of other products, but banknotes remain the most special, the most emotive. To most people, the idea, the lure, of endless stacks of $100 bills or £50 notes, crisp and shrink-wrapped in 1000-per-packet blocks, only about the size of half a house-brick, is fascinating. There is an almost primordial pleasure in handling them, carelessly throwing from hand to hand $100,000 or £50,000. In actuality, it is probably Travellers Cheques which present the most beguiling spectacle of pecuniary attraction. One thousand $1000 cheques stack neatly into a box no bigger than the average video recorder, $1,000,000 in the palm of the hand. They're also virtually untraceable and most easily negotiable. By the time the number is reconciled the exchange is Iong gone and a Bond, just one piece of paper looking like a graduation certificate with, say, 10 "coupons" stuck on the side of it, can be worth $1000,000, each coupon one-tenth of that and exchangeable with no questions asked, on simple presentation at a bank. Highly regarded by the masters of organised crime for their anonymity. There was a mugging in London in 1990 when a perfectly normal briefcase was stolen from a city messenger strolling, unaccompanied, to a delivery. It contained nearly

£400 million pounds worth of Bonds. Even a genuine, blank, British passport (or German, or American etc.) can be sold for between £3000 and £20,000 to an aspiring Bangladeshi, Indian, or any other African Asian, Nigerian or any other Black African or Hong Kong Chinese to escape their particular lot in countries popular only with tourists and arms dealers.

But banknotes still retain their overwhelming attraction. All the different and varying alternatives to them, from cheques to chargecards to smart cards and electronic banking have not stopped their continuing popularity due to their enduring convenience in the last hundred years. The volume of banknotes produced rises inexorably by at least 5% per annum world-wide, notwithstanding World Wars, recessions, slumps, demonetisations and not even taking into account the massive "blip" caused by the dismemberment of the former Soviet Union, when 14 countries previously using the Rouble all decided they wanted their own currency.

A fascinating statistic was revealed in the 1980's when the U.S. Government, in that country renowned for its obsession with new technology, gadgets and gimmicks, undertook a study aimed at determining whether they should increase the capacity of their massive State Printing Works, The Bureau of Engraving and Printing in Washington D.C., connected to the White House itself by underground tunnels large enough to house a small railway (much used by Franklin D. Roosevelt during World War II), which prints all the U.S. currency and stamps. They discovered that whilst 95% of fiduciary transactions by value were non-currency, 95% of transactions by volume were in currency. It was simple, nobody goes to buy a newspaper, or a cigar or a box of matches, a beer, or pays for a taxi with a plastic card or a cheque of some kind. The discovery led them to replicate the huge Washington organisation in Fort Worth, sister city of Dallas, Texas to continue to meet demand.

The basic characteristics, the fundamentals of all

modern banknotes, their printing and security features, emanate from a scientific study authorised in pre-Victorian England in 1818 after a series of serious counterfeiting scares rocked the City and the Bank of the then most powerful country on earth. British scientists and engineers were regarded in awe around the world, so it was to them that the Bank turned. The Old Lady of Threadneedle Street ordered the finances of the richest country in the world and guaranteed financial rectitude and legitimacy to the people of nations far flung across the earth, more than a third of the population of that earth, behind the pink tailcoats and the top hats of the "receptionists" in the marbled hall of the Bank of England, where footsteps echoed over vaults containing the world's largest gold reserves. Grave men, important men who knew they were important, had had their self-assured, comfortable complacency shaken by crafty entrepreneurs who'd realised how easy it was, after the Bank "went off gold" during the "Restriction Period" (the war with the French was severely stretching the Government's resources) and issued paper money for the first time in low denominations of £1 and £2, to counterfeit these notes in one or two of the hundreds of print-shops which flourished in the great city. "Common folk", previously only accustomed to using coins, were now handling vast sums of paper currency. Something had to be done! There was an outcry and demands for an immediate increase in the security of such notes. The Bank asked for proposals and suggestions from all quarters. The Royal Society was called upon. Its illustrious member, Sir Joseph Banks (of Captain Cook's voyages fame) got involved. There were in fact 400 replies to the Bank's request for "inimitable" notes. The most impressive, and the one which still dominates banknote printing to this day was from the Society of Arts (it had not yet been awarded the appellation of "Royal") in April 1818. Their report contained three key elements:

(a) "Hand-made" paper containing a watermark.
(b) Black ink.

(c) Simple design.

The paper was not to be ordinary paper made from wood-pulp, but from cotton fibres, combed cotton or "rag" as it came to be known, steel or copper engravings were to be used, executed by hand and then printed by the intaglio process whereby the ink rests in the grooves cut into the metal by the engraver which would thus, when transferred to paper, be raised above the surface of the paper creating three-dimensional relief and lines with a tactile feel. Where the engravings are deeper the ink is thicker and vice versa. These light and dark effects created by bold broad deep engraved lines or those which barely scratch the surface produced the three-dimensional relief which, when viewed under the light, would be markedly different from the conventional printing processes, which were mainly the oldest, letterpress, and litho which was as yet in its infancy at that time. These measures, the tactility and the fact that, if genuine, the ink would rub off the note when "scrubbed" against a piece of white paper, were adopted as the essential basic elements of banknote and security printing. So, the Society's proposals were accepted and the modem banknote was born. These are still the basic elements of all banknotes.

In the intervening 170 years of course many refinements and additional security features have been added, but all are still dependent on these basic foundations. Watermarks and numbering of individual banknotes were introduced,.The numbering increased in sophistication until it developed into vertical as well as horizontal formats, then went further 'til the individual figures in a sequence were of different sizes and colours. Multi-colour printing in general as extra background security was rapidly developed. Security "threads" were introduced into the paper itself, and "planchettes" (little dots of coloured paper incorporated at the paper-making stage) and coloured fibres used for the same purposes. Reactive chemicals to prevent any attempted alteration, ink manufacturers developed inks which contained reactive dyes, soluble in water, pigments which fluoresced in U.V. light or produced different tones under infra-red radiation, magnetic or electrically conducting ink which could be "read" using special equipment, optically variable inks which changed colour depending on the angle they're held to the light. In the 1980's holograms and kinograms were produced, to be incorporated into banknotes as they are on credit cards. These and many other devices have been added to the banknote printers' "architectural portfolio" to create "mansions" on the "foundations" so solidly laid so long ago.

All because those little scraps of paper with smudges of ink on them make the world turn.

£$£

Chapter Four

There are 251 countries in the world. Fifty-one of these, mostly the major countries, but surprisingly not all of them, have their own State Printing Works. Within these organisations money is printed to the exact orders of the Central Bank. In this way the money supply within the nation is controlled. The Americans have the Bureau of Engraving and Printing in Washington and Fort Worth,.The Russians the two giant "Gosnaks" in Moscow and Perm (the old Communist regime spared no expense where security and control were concerned). The British have the Bank of England Printing Works in Debden in North London, a huge and impressive edifice tucked away in those pleasant suburbs with the discreetness which is so uniquely British. The Swedes have a whole town dedicated to security paper making and printing, Tumba Bruk, probably the oldest State Printing Works in the world (the Swedes were the first in the West to adopt the Chinese idea of paper money, and accomplished it with Scandinavian thoroughness). The Germans have their Bundesdruckerie, the Dutch their Staatsdruckerei, the Japanese their Japanese Printing Bureau. The Chinese print away in Beijing, and the Indians, desperately short of paper currency, have two huge plants and are building two others whilst in the meantime they have ordered vast quantities of back-up notes from a couple of the privately-owned banknote printers. The Zimbabweans have their "State Printing Works", the now privately owned Fidelity Press, built with the connivance of the Germans during Rhodesian "U.D.l." and the so-called "sanctions".

There are some surprising omissions. The Canadians, members of the G7 group of nations, have their currency printed by two private security printers, Canadian Banknote Company and British American Banknote Company, both based in the capital, Ottawa. The Portuguese, members of the E.U., have an elaborate system whereby banknotes are part-printed abroad then finished in that country, because they had a security scare in the late 1920's which virtually brought their currency down and led to the (innocent) demise of a fine old British High Security Printing company, Waterlows. (another story.)

Then there are the 15 members of the A.I.I.F. who print for everyone else .

All these organisations and companies, in the interest and pursuit of complete security, are supplied by an astonishingly small band of machinery and materials suppliers.

Three companies dominate the world of such suppliers, two of which are, not coincidentally, based in the lovely city of Lausanne in Switzerland, and the other in the rural backwater of Overton in Hampshire in England.

De La Rue Giori are the major machinery suppliers, from the C.A.D. systems, to plate making to printing machinery. They control 75% of the world's banknote printing machinery. De La Rue Plc, the largest privately-owned security printing company in the world, immensely rich from the pickings they made from the carcass of the old British Empire and de-colonisation after which most, for instance, of the poor African countries decided to stay with the "devil they knew" rather than sail into uncharted waters, bought 50% of Giori in the mid-sixties and thereby gained a pre-dominance, and healthy profit, which makes them the envy of the world's other privately-owned security printers. They own the patents on the extensive range of machinery used in security printing developed by Reno Giori (real name Cohen, Jewish, saved from the Holocaust by Italians who didn't share their German master's racist obsessions during the war, and who ended up in Switzerland, again, another story, worth the telling.) The Bank of England retain patents on bespoke machinery but they're out of date and would only be used in an emergency. The Americans have tried desperately to develop their own, largely unsuccessfully, and the Japanese have done so in their own inimitable way through the only rival to De La Rue-Giori, Komori Machinery Ltd.

In 1994, under the very eyes of the British Tory Government, supposedly so committed to anti-monopolistic dogma, this same company, De La Rue, gained control by acquisition of the second of the three major suppliers, Portals, the security and banknote paper makers. Three hundred years old and once partly owned by the Bank of England, who are one of their main customers. It was a hard-fought take-over contest. The two companies were roughly the same size, but De La Rue won. With the exception of the USA, China and Russia, who all insist on using their own paper, they now control over 80% of the paper used for banknote printing throughout the world, by privately owned companies or State Printing Works.

The third company is Sicpa, based in Lausanne like Giori. They produce over 80% of the ink used by all security-printing companies. They're immensely successful. Even their "pool" car is, traditionally, a dark green Rolls Royce which will pick customers up from Geneva Airport to transport them to the quiet luxury of the 1,ausanne Palace Hotel before the obligatory visit to their impressive factories (one of which, Fid-Ink, is a joint venture with De La Rue - a neat example of corporate incest) before lunch or dinner at La Gironde, reputedly one of the finest restaurants in the world, where the cheese-board boasts 121 choices, many rare Swiss mountain goat varieties. They own factories in 12 major countries in the world, including the U.S.A., where they provide the ink which is used to produce the U.S. banknotes.

This, in brief, and with many omissions, is the esoteric world of security print. This is the world which contained the seeds of it's own destruction, and the possible destabilisation of every country on earth, without violence, without armies, or I.B.M.'s, or chemical weapons, or nuclear submarines, or spies, or anything else. Just a simple deduction by a handful of men who wanted power and wealth beyond imagination. And no one knew it was even happening. No Security Services, not even the CIA, the FSP (successor to the KGB), Interpol, MI5 or MI6, the SIS, any of the military establishments, the bankers, the politicians. No one. Until it was almost too late…

£$£

Chapter Five

John Dilworth's alarm went off at 4.30 am. As he was jerked into consciousness by it he thought of a comment Elvis Presley once made of a beautiful woman he met in Las Vegas, "She's enough to raise the dead". That's what that bloody clock was. It had been a leaving present from the last company he ran and it was good. It was so piercing it frightened the birds, badgers and foxes early in the morning around his pleasant home in the small village in the trees in the countryside in the hills 35 miles west of London when it went off.

Vanessa, wearing her white lace nightgown, the one she looked lovely in, hardly stirred. Her soft, thick blonde hair tumbled down the pillow as he almost leapt up, in his usual way, nearly fell over the suit-holder and pilot's case he'd packed the previous night and headed for the en-suite shower room. The hot water streamed over him as he slowly became fully-conscious, gathering his thoughts as he lathered himself with Imperial Leather soap, looked for the shampoo but couldn't find it so washed his hair with soap, remembered the "crack" he'd had at the village pub the night before with the lads and the two over-large whiskies he'd downed as he watched the late news, to Vanessa's disapproval, before hitting the sack at 12.30. She was right, he drank too much, but it never stopped him rising to what ever challenge the next day brought and he kept bringing home the bacon to keep them in their comfortable middle-class lifestyle didn't he? Still, as he was going away for who-knew-how-long he felt guilty again about not spending all last evening with her.

His driver was coming at 5.30 am., so the early-morning ablutions had to be dispensed with quickly. Vanessa still didn't move as he checked his passports (two, for obvious reasons. Some countries still wouldn't accept you if you had a South African stamp prior to a certain date in them, and an Israeli stamp was difficult in many countries and he wasn't certain where he was going to end up this time. He kept them carefully separate.) Then he checked his document case. He had everything. He stroked his wife's hair. She murmured "So long JD" (even his kids called him that often).

"Love you Ness," he said, stroked her hair and the nape of her neck again with genuine tenderness, then went downstairs with all his kit for a bowl of cereal and a coffee. He really did wish he'd spent the evening with Vanessa, the kids were all grown up and away, so they'd have had the house to themselves.

Dawn was breaking, the birds were in full song, as "old" Ron (He was only 10 years older than JD!) arrived exactly on time as usual to take him to the airport. The hedges along his drive were covered with a crochet of spider's webs and there was the still silence of early morning all around as he threw his gear into the boot of the Jaguar XJ6 and climbed in to greet Ron and listen to the last of the BBC World Service News on Radio Four. He wondered, as they sped through the village and then the beautiful leafy countryside of the Chiltern Hills on their way to Heathrow Airport what the bloody hell he was doing all this for. His salary, of course. Christ, he thought, there must be an easier way to make money. Maybe he should join the "General Staff' of the huge conglomerate he worked for, those people who'd never had a "proper" job but just read everyone else's' budgets and corporate plans and reports and felt wonderfully, smugly clever if they found a flaw in them, their "superiority" established again and their day's work done. Flaws, his mind meandered again, as it often did. If there was ever a flawed character, it was his, he thought. His flaws were more like the tectonic plates which broke up continents and caused upheavals like the Himalayas and the Andes. But no, he knew he couldn't work at HQ, he had to be at the "front-line", in amongst the muck and bullets, doing something useful, constructive. He vaguely remembered a statistic about accountants, which most of the staff at HQ had the honour to be. The Japanese economy was ten times bigger than the British and they only had one-tenth the number of accountants. We'd taken to accountants like the Americans had taken to lawyers, he thought, Wonder who can do the most damage? Accountants, he decided. They could screw up huge companies, lawyers usually only screwed individuals.

He was 48 years old, tall broad-shouldered, a little over-weight, although he trained regularly he'd inexorably gained weight after stopping playing rugby at 44 and he ate too much, drank too much and smoked too many cigars, though he was always on a diet. Didn't he always eat low-fat crisps? He flipped down the sun visor to look in the mirror and bring some order to his thick dark hair, now streaked with grey. Some men, he mused, have it dyed like this to make them look distinguished. If he'd been vain enough he'd have bought some Grecian 2000 but he was no more than normally vain, and anyway, with a wife like his who attracted men like bees to a rose garden he didn't need to be. Vanessa was tall, athletically built, certainly not fashionably slim, with laughing eyes and a great figure. He fancied her himself every time he saw her, especially when he came home from one of his trips. She always came to the airport to meet him. And they'd been married for 25 years. She always did something special for him when he returned, pleated skirts, suspenders, stockings, high-heels, always demurely cloaked in one of her smart coats of course. It was the lightning cure for jet lag. He really did wish he'd stayed in last night.

The M25 London Orbital motorway was busy even at 6 am. He listened as Ron told him about his latest little Jack Russell terrier, the last one having bolted and nearly made it all the way across the M40. He was a good bloke, JD thought, salt of the earth, and he watched the boring flatlands of the Heathrow approach pass him by as the black Jaguar purred towards Terminal One. He noticed again that colours only appeared as the light intensified. Cows materialised from the mist in one or two fields like gravestones from the fog in a cheap horror film. God, it was an ugly landscape. What must tourists think when they first venture out of Heathrow? They should line both sides of every road leading to and from the airport with giant advertising hoardings for six or seven miles, or make the tourists use coaches with blacked out windows, or the underground. He wondered what the day would bring, and however many other days he'd be away. You never knew with the Chief.

At Island 73 in the terminal he met his old friend and colleague, Frederick Ian Thomas, "Fit" to everyone who knew him. Sixty-six years old, now a "consultant" with the company. He'd fought with the Gurkhas in the Malaysian "Emergency", seconded from the Seaforth Highlanders. He often joked about coming from Ealing, ending up in a Scottish regiment and then finally becoming a Subudar with the Gurkhas.

He'd retired twice, at 60 and 65, collected his gifts, then carried on! Some cynics in the company thought he was only aiming for the third set of retirement presents.

Fit looked good for his age. Always tanned, from hours on the golf course, and almost a lifetime of travelling in temperate and tropical climes. Just above medium height, good build, no excess weight. He ate and drank sensibly, in moderation, wherever he was. Urbane was a word coined in English to describe him. The perfect salesman, the most agreeable companion. Unflappable, confident, even-tempered, superb at his job, certain in any company, in any situation. His ready smile and keen humour, laced with cynical wit, masked completely the never-mentioned pain and heartbreak of his life, the loss of his only child at the age of 15 in a road accident. Few knew of it. He didn't speak of it, only to those closest to him, and then only to rejoice in the pleasure of having such a son for those 15 years. His wife, Veronica, just a couple of years older than him, was the same. No one who met her could guess at the tragedy which lay behind her delightful persona. Still elegant, still lovely in fact at 69, she and Fit became JD and Vanessa's closest friends over the sixteen years the men worked together. Their working relationship had never impinged on that friendship. JD flirted outrageously with Ronni. Ness and Fit told them they wished they'd get on with it and run away together, then they could enjoy a civilised life together left behind with the money and the houses.

They greeted each other warmly.

“Christ, JD! You look as though you've been on the thrash all night, or Vanessa’s given you a night to remember. You're too old for that, I keep telling you.”

“Well, she'd have been safe with you. Mind you, she might have looked after you, she's a big supporter of “Help the Aged”.

“ Bugger off.”

Nothing had changed. The conversation took off smoothly from where they'd left off when they'd arrived back from Dar-es-Salaam two weeks earlier.

Normally they would have met in the British Airways Executive Club Lounge, which is air-side at Terminal One, and poured themselves a large scotch even at that time in the morning when everyone else was more sensibly drinking coffee and eating biscuits and who would have looked at them askance, with disdain. But they'd travelled together to so many unsavoury places that they'd always felt it better to set off in this way. It counteracted foreign germs they assured each other.

But this time they were at Island 73 to check in and be transported to the Executive jet side of the terminal, so it was going to be a “dry” morning. They joked about it then, after the preliminaries were over, they walked airside and climbed into the BAA courtesy car which took them over to the far side of the airport and the small lounge which handled private flights. They said little, often when they were travelling they said nothing for long periods. Silence is only tolerable amongst people who know each other well.

The private executive jet side of Terminal One is one of the areas where the British Government greets visiting VIP'S. It is simply but elegantly furnished. This morning, in the thin early morning sunlight, there was very little going on. They sat in the lounge alone, apart from BAA staff who quietly fussed over them and offered them coffee, and waited for the Chief.

"Where the hell are we going?" Fit asked JD.

"Buggered if I know. I just got a call from HQ to meet the Chief here at 6.30 am. Talking to his secretary I got the impression it's Uganda or Zaire. You up-to-date with your injections?"

"I've got so many needle marks in my arms that if we're going to L.A. or Edinburgh the police'll arrest me for being a junkie."

"Yeah. I'm the same. How many malaria tablets you got?" He unbuttoned his double-breasted suit, reached into his pilot's case, pulled out his toilet bag and searched through it until he found the containers.

The two men solemnly took out their Avoclar and Paludrin and counted them. The young female staff watched, amused. Two oldish men counting pills.

"We're OK. We'll swap some." JD pulled out his sheaf of photocopied "World Digest" notes covering every country in Africa from Mozambique to the North African littoral. "Want to read any?"

"No. I never remember the statistics anyway. I'll leave that to you. You're the boss. You're better at bullshitting."

"Thanks," said JD dryly, and started reading the first sheet. Malawi. Capital no longer Blantyre, now Lilongwe on the Zomba Plateau. Pity, he liked Blantyre, the Mount Soche Hotel, the steak restaurant opposite. Airport now Lilongwe, not Chileka. He remembered Chileka well, with the golden cockroaches running like a narrow stream of shimmering water up the corners in the gent's toilet.

His thoughts were interrupted by a slight commotion at the front glass doors. Two security men who were "chauffeurs" came in carrying light baggage followed by a tall, good-looking, "stately" (no other word for it) man who could have been 55 or 65 (he was actually 68) immaculately dressed as usual, who headed towards them grinning.

"Morning boys." JD inwardly smiled, no one had called him a "boy" for 20 years, except the Chief

Brandon "Chief" Spencer was a good 6ft 4in. He owned the tailors which made his Saville Row suits because they'd had a little cash-flow problem 15 years before, and he liked their exquisite workmanship, their dedication to perfection, so he bought them. He was like that. He appreciated people who knew their job. He appreciated JD and Fit. He knew their faults, they weren't hard to discern! But they were professionals, capable of getting on with the high and low of any society in any land, he'd observed at first hand. They were almost a couple of rogues, not quite perhaps, but they could "do the business".

He was universally known as "Chief" by Presidents, Prime Ministers, his pilots, his colleagues, secretaries. He'd built up an "empire" in Africa, the Middle East, India, South-East Asia and Latin America in mines, agriculture, hotels, tourism, property development, computer and motors' franchises. He even owned newspapers in three continents. He'd called it simply InTraCon Ltd., now Plc. (International Trading Conglomerate.) He now wielded the power of an immense company with a turnover of £17 billion p.a. It had taken 30 years. He only wished she could have been here to see it come to such splendid fruition. She'd been gone 20 years now. She'd have loved it. No one had given him more support in the early pioneering days. He was glad she'd experienced some of the riches, but she'd never seen the two boys grow up to be the mature and intelligent men they were now, running the mining side and the hotels. He'd achieved it all through charm. He could charm the leaves off the trees as well as the birds. He was conscious of being one of the last of the great "tycoons". Armand Hammer, Jimmie Goldsmith, Maxwell, Getty, Gulbenkien, all dead. All ruthless in their own way. He believed charm was more effective, when laced with just a touch of the steel of a Panzer division and the deadly accuracy of an Exocet.

JD and Fit stood up and shook hands

"Good morning, Chief. How are you?"

"Fine. I'm so sorry I'm a little late. I had to take a call from the Foreign Secretary just as I was setting, out." They knew he wasn't name-dropping. British business abroad on the scale of his was of serious interest to whatever Government of the day. "Hope you've been looked after. So good to see you both again." His diction was perfect. JD could never help thinking it was just like that of those 1930's British film stars, with their cut-glass accents, but delivered with a drawling lilt which was almost mesmeric.

As it was his executive jet they were flying out on it obviously mattered little what time he arrived.

They were both accustomed to travelling with him, so they knew now there'd be no time to finish the coffee. They picked up their bags, handed their passports to the drivers/security men and moved after him through the lounge to the airside door. Their passports would join them later, on the plane. The pilot and co-pilot were waiting for them outside and walked with them to the plane. The former was a large but very fit-looking genial German in his thirties named Anton and the latter a Texan called Pierre (He'd told JD once, in the Ibex restaurant of the Norfolk hotel in Nairobi that his mother had fallen in love with the name after hearing a Chuck Berry song about a Cajun wedding -- it goes to show you never can tell, JD had said.) The Chief, with his perpetual sense of humour, called them "The French Team". It puzzled the German.

JD caught up with the Chief.

"Chief, we're all jabbed up and packed for the duration but it was a bit of a rush and we've not arranged visas and..."

"Don't worry, JD," the Chief cut in. "All arranged." He gestured towards the small boarding steps leading into the G4. "After you."

"No, you first, Chief."

This little ritual took place every time they used the aircraft. It was his form of courtesy. Like "punctuality is the politeness of Kings" thought JD.

The Chief hopped up the steps like a twenty year old. Anton and Pierre acted as a sort of "grecting party" at the foot of the steps, and the stewardess, Anna-Greta, kissed them all as they got on board. She was already preparing tea, coffee and soft drinks. Attractive, she'd worked with the Chief for twenty years, and all that had changed was an almost imperceptible thickening of the waist.

The Gulfstream Four is the "Rolls Royce" of executive jets. Currently selling at £30m~plus they can seat over 20 people in a conventional internal layout. But this was not conventionally laid-out. It was luxuriously appointed. When you climbed on board, with the flight cabin on your left, you turned right and moved through Anna-Greta's galley, equipped for the type of people the Chief entertained regularly. The movers and shifters of political life, from four continents, and corporate guests accustomed to similar luxury. At the head of the galley, immediately next to the flight cabin there was a steel locker which contained two AKM's (successor to the AK47), two Charter Arms Bulldog .44 Special five-shot models with three-inch barrels (easily carried in a pocket), and two Heckler and Koch VP70 semi-automatics. All legal. The aircraft went to some strange places, the pilots had a secondary function as well as their main one.

Once through the galley the cabin opened up to two large "armchairs" on the right-hand side, bigger than normal first-class seats, facing each other separated by a table. The Chief always used the seat "facing front" and whoever he wanted to talk to, or "grill", sat opposite with their "backs to the engine" (as JD's grandmother always described such seats on a railway train, he remembered fondly.) On the left was a long "settee" which could comfortably seat three and doubled as a bed, then two more armchairs and table on the left, another settee opposite, and two more armchairs.

Beyond that there was an opulently furnished toilet, shower cubicle and vanity unit with gold-plated taps and, finally the baggage cabin.

The Chief travelled in style. In building and maintaining his "empire" he did little else but travel. So who could blame him?

After the preliminaries were over, coffee and sparkling mineral water served and held safely in the built-in beaker-holders in the beautifully veneered panels which also contained, beside each seat, the cellular phones which ensured that the aircraft was never out of touch with anywhere, they taxied and took off.

Executive jets, especially the G4, perform like powerful military aircraft. short take-off, steep climb, nothing like a conventional airliner. They were very soon at 40,00Oft. well above other "civilian" traffic, cruising at 500 mph. They had a range of 6,000 miles. The temperature outside, the cabin display told the passengers, was -40C. The visual display, with its almost computer-game symbol of an aircraft, showed them slowly turning east and south and heading for Europe.

JD and Fit settled at the back, in shirtsleeves now. You were always better, as you were with Royalty, well away, they'd decided long ago, only responding when you were called upon by the Chief. Until then, keep out of the way.

They were thinking of starting a game of Crib, and then the call came.

"Boys, come and sit up here." He waved them forward.

They were both mature and intelligent men. They'd done a lot, seen a lot (too much, perhaps). They'd been successful in their own ways. But, if anyone had asked them, they'd admit they held this man in some awe. He'd achieved so much, had such a sharp mind (razor-sharp, they often thought). Talking to him could be a pleasure, an, entertainment, or an ordeal. If he wasn't in the mood to be a raconteur it could turn into the "Third Degree". They went forward.

"How's your wife and children. JD? I do hope all is well

and yours, Fit?" the conversation took on it's usual courteous complexion. They chatted amicably. How were his sons? Had he seen the reports in the F.T. of the estimates of oil reserves in Kazakhstan? What did he think of the new Government'? What did they think of the new Government?

They were approaching the Swiss Alps before JD managed to get his first question in.

"You wouldn't like to tell us where the hell we're going Chief, would you?" He was grinning as he said it.

"Oh, I thought you knew. Have you not been briefed?" He feigned surprise, but his eyes twinkled. "We're going to Uganda, to Entebbe, to meet President Kirikulu at State House. Luke's meeting us there."

They'd not been briefed because no-one knew, at the Company's HQ in the heart of the City of London where the Chief was flying off to. There they just did what he told them to do, happy to collect generous salaries and share options and keep their jobs while he ran the whole damned shooting match. At the mention of Luke JD and Fit exchanged glances. He was a "fixer", a close relation of a certain African president who seemed to know everyone of importance on that continent, spoke six languages (English being the poorest, they rather sourly suspected from his communications, written and spoken). Many Africans, the world's best linguists they thought, were so adept. It was amazing, and he usually meant a lot of work for them.

"Then I'm going to Mombassa. There's a hotel for sale they want me to look at. I think it's in the wrong position, but tourism's burgeoning there you know. But they're also having a lot of trouble with armed bandits. Anyway, you're not coming with *me* there." He smiled. "I want you to meet the President, I'll be with you, and then I've a special project I want you to look at. The people involved will be at Entebbe, Luke's arranged it. I'll tell you about it when we get there, but if you'll excuse me please, I must get a couple of hours sleep. I only got back from Mexico in the early hours and I've not had a wink yet. Do you mind?" His studied politeness impressed them yet again.

Mind? They were out of the "hot seats" like a shot. The Chief called Anna-Greta. She prepared his bed on the large settee and he was asleep within seconds.

They mused a little over what the "special project" could be, and who the "people involved" were, agreed they couldn't crack that puzzle so they played Crib, using an A4 pad as a crib board. Fit was exasperated because JD couldn't remember the rules again. It had been like that all over bloody Africa. He might be reasonably intelligent, but you'd never play Bridge with him as a partner he thought. JD concurred wholeheartedly. He couldn't even remember how to play Monopoly. It was one of the many things Vanessa got irritated about. She said his mind only ever retained what he thought was important, and she complained that didn't include what "most normal people" thought.

The G4 hit the Nile Delta. It was now going to follow the ancient river (of life, to so many countries, for thousands of years) almost to its origins. It was a physical guide marker on the around leading to Sudan, Kenya, Uganda, almost to their very destination, Entebbe. With the Chief asleep, Anna-Greta got a six-pack of Heineken from her secret store and they sipped their way to the "heart of darkness".

£$£

Chapter Six

When you land at Entebbe, at the new terminal building, the first thing you notice is the old terminal building. The comical (though not to his own poor oppressed people) dictator Idi Amin "Dada" was so enraged by the success of the Israeli commandos in rescuing the hostages he'd so blatantly contrived to keep in the hands of the Islamic fundamentalists when they hi-jacked the El-AI airliner in 1976, that he'd ordered the complete closure of the old terminal, the scene of his humiliation, and built a new one on the other side of the runway. The old one stared at you hollow-eyed across the tarmac, a seedy decaying shell of a monument to cruelty, hubris, shame and stupidity.

When they landed it was being "refurbished." Painters were still sloshing emulsion on the walls. It was the landing point for a bevy of African bankers, the conference of the AIB, the African Investment Bank. The Government, knowing how "precious" each delegate thought they were, had made sure that friendly efficient Ugandan officials, all female, would usher them all through the VIP section of the terminal - still being painted, so there was the usual "African" problem of every one of the nearly 400 delegates all trying to get through, to be processed, in the small VIP section. It was a matter of status. They were stuck in the queue. The rest of the airport was empty.

The official cars picked them up. They drove through the bedraggled streets of Entebbe, where the fishermen lived who could no longer make a living out of lake Victoria because of the voracious pike lately introduced into the lake which had decimated fish stocks, and out along the road to State House. JD thought idly, why don't they catch the pike. . ?

They went through the usual "road blocks" manned by

soldiers in shabby, tattered uniforms, sweat beading on their foreheads, some no older than 15, maybe even 14. JD always thought there was nothing more dangerous in the world than a 14-year-old boy with an AK-47. He was more frightened than you, his eyes pale with fear, his hands trembling, but he had the gun.

During the short drive the Chief gave them a very quick briefing on who they were about to meet as well as the President, and where they were going. They looked at each other. Sitting in the back, the Chief couldn't see them. Fit rolled his eyes, JD raised an eyebrow. This could be an unusual trip.

State House nestles in rising, beautiful gardens, verdant with the perfumed plants of the tropics, trees, bushes, walls, colonnades woven together with a heavy lace-work of bougainvillaea adding colour to colour everywhere in every corner. A Van Gogh dream for a visitor or observer, it would have been a nightmare for Vincent if he'd ever been faced with the impossible challenge of capturing it on canvas. Even if he'd captured the colours, what about that pervading perfume, how to capture that in oils? Or the way the blue-grey African sky nuzzled into the trees at the edges of the gardens? It is situated on a slight hill. It's a "snap-shot" of what the British brought to so many colonies. A charming, but relatively small Palladian mansion, straight out of Buckinghamshire or Hampshire. Set down amongst the humid and tropical vegetation of Central Africa, with elegant porticos and beyond them, cool, shaded rooms furnished in the manner of Downing Street or the finest gentlemen's club in London, Whites perhaps, or the old Pall Mall club, now the home of the Institute of Directors, where mahogany, leather, gilt, silver and chintz blended to create an atmosphere of quiet, calm reflection and sumptuousness.

The one slightly different detail was a convoy of six military trucks, headed and tailed by APCs sporting Pintle-mounted 12.7 mm M2 machine guns. All the trucks were filled with the President's personal protection unit looking bored and resentful in the hot sun as the air-conditioned

Mercedes pulled into the space at the front entrance.

"Cadillacs." JD nodded towards the APC closest to them.

"Cadillacs? I didn't know they made army kit. Bugger me!" Fit was staring, but the guard, smartly out-fitted, tough-looking, stared back, so he quickly turned his attention to following the Chief and JD.

In the centre of the column was the President's own armoured Mercedes four-wheel-drive. JD reflected momentarily on opportunities lost by the UK motor industry, and the arms dealers, in Africa.

Luke was there at the front entrance, standing in the shade, ebullient as ever, bounding around in an off-white lightweight suit. His shirt and teeth positively shone in the sun as he left the shade to greet them. If I was black, JD fleetingly ruminated, I'd never wear anything but white shirts. They look so damned smart, and ours grey.

"Chief! It's good to see you!" He embraced the Chief awkwardly, for JD and Fit only a nod and a limp handshake. "It's all arranged. The President will see you in 10 minutes! Come in, come in." He'd obviously appropriated State House in the way he did any room or office wherever he went, but never more blatantly than he did in his own country. There he was a surrogate for the President himself like Bormann or Himmler for Hitler thought JD. His accent was an approximation of English. He shepherded the Chief into the beautiful spacious reception room, French windows open at both ends to allow some waft of air through the room. Large and comfortable sofas loosely spread around, occasional tables and ornaments, the odd bust here and there, magnificent carpets covering parts of the polished parquet floor, grave and dignified portraits festooned every wall. All white men, JD noted, who'd played some part in the colonisation and then the running of the country, the "Pearl of Africa", the one Churchill suggested as a "homeland" for the Jewish nation. They all settled in comfort to wait.

The birdsong sweetened the air, but almost drowned in

the piercing collective whine of the cicadas sounding like a jet engine undergoing tests in a maintenance hangar. The Chief lay back relaxed after an animated exchange with Luke in Swahili. Fit sat in an armchair and almost immediately started to doze. (He always did that. He didn't have to make conversation or answer any question then. Leave that to JD. He was the boss. He was paid for it.) JD sat on the edge of his seat, so as to be ever alert, aware. The Chief paid his salary, he might start asking questions.

The minutes passed by - ten, thirty, Luke got more agitated, the Chief got more patient, knowing Africa. It was always like this. Fit dozed, JD fidgeted.

After an hour, not long by African "waiting-for-Presidents" (or other senior officials) standards, Luke obviously couldn't sit any longer. His body always radiated nervous energy and enthusiastic tension. He leapt up, with a thin film of perspiration on his forehead and cheeks.

"Do you think they'll give us lunch?" His brows were furrowed, his eyes seemed a little frightened.

The Chief, still settled back and resting in his armchair, hands stretched in front of him, fingertips together under his chin, responded in that languorous drawl.

"Luke, they bloody well should do, at least a sandwich. We gave them £6m for their uniforms before they took over." Luke laughed nervously, but couldn't sit down. He'd arranged this and the Chief was waiting.

Fit dozed on. JD remained on the edge of his seat, keeping awake, trying to look intelligent. The guards looked even more bored and resentful. So this is Africa, JD thought again. He remembered W. C. Field's gravestone legend, "I'd rather be here than in Philadelphia." He started composing one of his own, about Africa. Fit, the old hand who'd been through this many times, woke up once, looked out at the armoured column, and muttered to JD.

"Christ, I was thinking of going for a stroll, but I think that lot would probably eat me." He closed his eyes again. Two more hours passed. Luke paced, Fit dozed on, JD engaged the Chief in small talk and reminiscences about

Uganda. The Chief reminisced himself. He had some great stories.

£$£

Chapter Seven

The heavy mahogany door on their left opened, and an immaculately dressed officer entered. By the darkness of his skin it was obvious he was an indigenous Bagandan, and his accent, as immaculate as his uniform, marked him out clearly as Sandhurst-trained. He had that distinctive inimitable Sandhurst intonation and speech pattern, sparing in its delivery so as to avoid any misunderstandings.

"Mr. Spencer, Gentlemen, the President offers his apologies for the delay. Important and pressing matters had to be dispensed with. He would much like you to join him now." His speech was also virtually accent less, another Sandhurst success thought JD. He gestured towards the door, smiling, very erect, shoes and buttons glistening. JD saw from his insignia that he was a Colonel. They all stood up, Fit woke up and stood up, Luke shut up and they followed the Chief as he followed the Colonel.

Beyond the door was a corridor about 30ft long leading to another door flanked by two smart sentries who snapped to attention, then the one on the left opened the door for the Colonel and the guests. They climbed a polished wooden staircase into a large but unpretentious office lined with books and portraits and mounted gifts the President had obviously received, all tastefully displayed.

President Kirikulu was a Ugandan patriot and a Pan-African of a rare kind. He'd travelled south in the past to Mozambique to fight with Samora Machel in the long liberation struggle against the Portuguese, and then returned to his own country to do the same. He'd fought a long guerrilla war against men who were little more than warlords. He'd been a loyal member of Yoweri Musaveni's forces, and had remained one of his staunchest supporters. Now he was President, and he was determined to make

Musaveni's progressive economic reforms even more successful. He'd continued the enlightened and democratic policies of the previous government, but the armed convoy was unfortunately still necessary. There were still members of the old regimes who wanted him out of the way. He was a rarity in a continent of corrupt dictators.

He was an honest man who was trying to do what was best for his country. A country which had been racked by internecine wars, brutal tyranny and “Slim's Disease” - known to all Ugandans long before “Aids” became a frightening feature of western life. The Ugandans knew the ancient, pre-20th century, sexual fertility rituals, still practised in the rural areas of their country and Rwanda, Burundi and Zaire, which had caused the transfer of the disease from animal kingdom to Homo Sapiens, but it was too late now. All the President and the Administration could do was deal with the consequences as humanely as possible, and complete the re-building of the economy to allow them to pay for such care. He was an economist, like many well-educated Africans he had more than one degree, and a good soldier and he'd made a good President. He also had a sense of humour. He rose from his desk as they entered.

“Chief! It's good to see you. How are you? Luke, and you? Mr. Dilworth, Mr. Thomas, come, come.” He shook hands with JD and Fit, slapped Luke on the back and put his arm round the Chief and guided him to the large leather chair beside his desk. The others sat in smaller chairs in front of the desk.

“Gentlemen, I'm so sorry. I apologise for the delay. Come with me to Kampala, I'm leaving soon, as soon as we're through here, and I'll give you lunch and we can talk some more.”

“No, no Mr. President. We can't inflict ourselves on you. You're too busy. We wish only a few minutes of your time.” The Chief had slid into super-sales/charm mode JD thought and anyway, he's got to get to Mombassa!

The President had gone back behind his desk now and they were all seated. There was an elephant's tusk mounted in silver on the left- hand side of the huge desk and a bank of telephones on the right, the flag of Uganda stood proudly behind the desk, American style, flanked by photo-portraits of former President Musaveni, Kirikulu himself and to JD's surprise, the Queen. The Colonel stood by the door at the back of the room until the President motioned him to sit in the hardback chair next to the only entrance.

"The two other gentlemen waiting to see you are in the annexe downstairs, or probably on the terrace by now in the fresh air if they've any sense. But first, what is it you've come to do me for this time Chief. Tell me." He grinned broadly, this was a pleasant interlude in an otherwise fraught day.

The President laughed, the Chief laughed. Everyone in the room laughed. Luke passed on his President's good wishes, the Chief launched into a sales spiel about tourism and hotels. JD wished he'd been one of Dalton's salesmen. (or persons as they had to be called these days. JD remembered one female trades union official who'd objected to the term "man-hole cover." Fit wondered why he'd lost at crib again, and let them get on with it.)

"Now you know Mr. Dilworth and Mr. Thomas. They represent, in fact JD runs, our security printing operation, Dalton and Sons Ltd. Fit is our most experienced Sales Director. They have a presentation for you. They can do all your security print for much less than you're paying your present suppliers. We'll guarantee that. You know you've been paying far too much for ages."

The President smiled his ready smile again.

"But of course, Chief, we're Africans! You colonialists have always exploited us."

The Chief raised his hands in mock horror, but there was a twinkle in his eye when he replied with equally mock indignation.

"Mr. President. I've never exploited you."

"No, to be fair, Chief, not in that way you haven't. You just own a third of the damned country!"

They laughed as they sparred. Politics against business. In the end even though it might be a long time coming, business always won.

"But look, my colleagues, JD and Fit," he'd fallen into the familiar now, but the President understood, "give them a chance to quote, Mr. President. Don't stay tied, please, to the old colonial printers the Crown Agents used to provide." Before the President could reply, the Chief suddenly went on to say, "Or we could build you a plant to do your own. All of it. Then you'll be independent, free. JD has the proposals with him." He gestured nonchalantly towards JD.

Christ, he is good, thought JD. In the midst of the myriad deals he's pulling down he's remembered I once told him, years ago, that I always carry four or five "General Security Printing Plant" plans. They could be used as the foundation stone for any country in the world which wanted to build such a plant, extrapolated accordingly. The Chief often surprised him like this. JD supposed that's why he'd achieved so much in life. He was always on the ball and had a phenomenal memory.

JD snapped into action, took a slim folder out of his document case which was nestling in his pilot's bag, and half rose to walk to the desk to give it to the President, who held his hand up, palm forward in a "stop" sign.

"No, no, JD." He didn't say Mr. Dilworth. He'd picked up on that immediately. "I don't need it. I'm not a Nkrumah! We can't justify such expenditure. But I would like some really competitive quotes from you for all else we buy abroad. You know how poor we are, yet we spend six or seven million pounds sterling on currency, passports, I.D. cards, Customs documents, postage stamps etc. Every year, we'd like to reduce that. Reduce it by 20% for us and I can pay for another 200 medical centres around the country, and afford to keep them running, every year. You look a little surprised by that Mr. Dilworth. Don't be. Consider, to build a centre using local craftsmen and materials only costs about a thousand pounds. Basic equipment, for these aren't like European clinics you know, will cost about £3000 per centre, sterilisation equipment, sterile disposable hypodermics, dressings, water supply with heating facilities, diesel generators etc. You save us 20% on £6m and we can set those 200 centres up for £800,000 sterling, and still have £600,000 left to start recruiting doctors and nurses. I reckon we need 50 doctors and 100 nurses. Many Ugandans train as doctors in your country, in America and other countries in Europe. Many want to help their country. They're young, they're idealists, but by our standards anyway they'll be very well paid, £10,000 per year. They can live like kings here on that! And the nurses would be well paid too, £1000 per annum. Each team will look after four health centres, geographically convenient. Our poor people in the countryside should then have a visit to their local health centre at least once a week, something unheard of in our country and that, Mr. Dilworth, is only with one year's savings. Think of how you could improve on that as the savings are made each year."

JD was already feeling personally guilty about all the poor Ugandans who couldn't get medical treatment.

The President had been leaning forward, gesticulating animatedly, his eyes alive. He made it sound like a campaign speech in a general Election. JD knew from his biog. that he was a very intelligent man with excellent academic qualifications who spoke six languages, English, French, Portuguese, Swahili and two Ugandan languages, but his English pronunciation had all the charmingly idiosyncratic inflections found all over the sub-Saharan continent in former British colonies. Year became "Yah", Dilworth, "Deel-wath", JD, "Jay-di". The President sat back in the big swivel chair. JD had remained standing respectfully at the corner of the desk holding the plant presentation against his diaphragm with one hand, playing with the corner of it with the other. The Chief and Fit both made a move as if to speak, but this was his pitch. He was a second in front of them.

"Mr. President, after the way you've put this into context I assure you that our company will come back to you with detailed estimates as soon as possible. Our target will be 20% reductions across the board. You know we think you've been taken advantage of in the past by your other suppliers. We believe your country has been taken advantage of since independence. We will endeavour to put that right, and still make a profit for ourselves!"

The President was pleased. He trusted Brandon Spencer and JD's last comment led him to believe he could trust this man. He'd spent a long time as a Minister, and then as President, listening to smooth white businessmen pretending to be philanthropists who so wanted to help Uganda. If he did nothing else today he'd done Ugandans some good. "The first thing," JD went on, "is for you to issue instructions to release details of your orders and their costs for this last year, perhaps two if possible. If you'll fax them to us, to me personally, I'll ensure you get a reply within a week." He knew that was a tall order, practically speaking, but it was a vital step to keep the ball rolling. In Africa strange things could happen even to a President's instruction as it filtered down the line. People with vested interests in maintaining the status quo in order to maintain the standard of living they and their relatives had grown accustomed to, got hold of it and discovered the plethora of reasons why it couldn't be carried out, some of them dreamt up by the incumbent white suppliers who had people who specialised in doing just that. They did themselves. He also knew it would be hellishly difficult to reduce prices by a full 20%, even though the other suppliers had a swathe of costs hidden in their prices to cover corruption payments, and he had little doubt that, whatever the President instructed, "considerations" would be required at a few levels in the administration and the Bank, the Postal Service and any other department involved. Kirikulu wasn't corrupt. He was probably the only President in black Africa who wasn't. JD admired him for it. The Chief and Fit believed the same about him. But, unknown to him, (or perhaps it wasn't, but he needed them) most of the members of his Government and the Civil Service were. As bad as the rest of Africa. Unlike the others, though, it wasn't sanctioned by the President and he didn't get a cut. Poor bastard! JD felt genuinely sorry for him. He was working grindingly hard to rebuild a country and raise standards in every sphere. He wondered how long it would be before the system, and the realisation that he was surrounded by men who seemed to be growing rich and African fat, ground him down and broke him, and he started receiving his "consideration." The endemic, wearying, morale-sapping corruption smothering Africa like a stinking over-ripe Camembaert was the main reason he hated the place. He wasn't a full-time natural salesman like the Chief or Fit. He could adopt a persona for a limited period of time, just enough time to get in and out, get an order, but then disgust, anger and hopelessness overcame him, and he could eat no more shit in front of the smarmy, greedy, ruthless politicians and their cronies, who were often torturing people in the basement when you were smiling and drinking coffee on the 24th floor. That's when he had to get out. He knew the whole world was corrupt, well, almost all of it. He could think of only about 20 countries where corruption wasn't endemic. But somehow it seemed worst in Africa, with all the other horrors raddling the continent, wars, genocide, famine, disease, appalling crime statistics, a crumbling (if not crumbled) infrastructure in every country except perhaps South Africa. Even that was struggling now, and the stupid, bigoted Boers and their savage church had done for the blacks in that country, and in Africa, what Hitler managed to do for the Jews. They'd treated them so awfully that all civilised nations didn't feel able, worthy, to criticise the apparent faults and abhorrent deeds which were perpetrated by them when they got hold of the reigns of power themselves. What made it worse was that everyone in "the West", amongst the "G7" nations, in the EU, in all the damned organisations like the World Bank and the IMF, knew about the corruption. All anyone ever did was lament about it, withhold the odd loan here and there. No one did anything about it. There was too much money to be made out of the continent. Only in the countries where the Government had completely collapsed were strong measures taken. That was because a country without an effective Government couldn't organise repayments. In many African countries most of their export incomes earned from all they really had to offer the world, raw materials/commodities, simply went to pay off loan interest to western banks. They were caught in a perfect trap. They kept paying, then had no money left to improve anything and, then they had to borrow more, to improve anything. It was heart breaking.

"JD," the Chief's voice interrupted his thought process. Meandering again! "That's excellent. It would he so good if you could do that." He'd shifted round in his chair to listen and to speak to JD. Now he turned to face the President again. "Mr. President, do you think it would be possible for the Colonel to take Mr. Dilworth and Mr. Thomas to our friends?"

"Of course, they'll be out on the terrace." The President motioned to the Colonel who stepped forward smartly as JD and Fit rose. The President stood also, and proferred his hand. They both shook it warmly as the President said "Thank you for coming. I look forward to your communication. The Colonel will ensure you get the prices you want. I hope to see you again very soon."

"Good luck in all you're doing, for your country Mr. President," JD said, in that quaint stilted language, half embarrassed, half unctuous, that one tends to slip into in the presence of power.

Fit followed him and smilingly said, "But I hope you make some time to play golf sir. If not, next time I'll bring you a hand-held golf video game like the one I gave to the President of Zambia a few years ago. You can play it at Cabinet meetings."

The President laughed spontaneously. "You do that, Mr. Thomas. You do that. I'll hold you to that."

The Chief remained seated. "I'll join you in a few minutes gentlemen."

They followed the Colonel. As they walked he said to them, "Gentlemen, I will prepare the documents you want immediately on my return to Kampala. We leave immediately the President and Mr. Spencer have completed their discussions. The information will be with you within four days. I'll fax it to you." He sounded efficient and business-like but extremely courteous simultaneously. He didn't waste a word.

JD passed a business card to him and said, "Send it to my private fax Colonel, if you would please. The number's on there."

"Of course sir."

They retraced their steps, crossed the large cool reception room and stepped through the pure white net drapes which graced the open French windows, acting as a shield to the heat and a man-made spider's web for the myriad of things that fly in the little town that sits almost perfectly on the Equator on the banks of Lake Victoria, not so far from the once mysterious source of the White Nile.

£$£

Chapter Eight

The two men sitting at the large round white table on the terrace were wearing full military uniform. Their only concession to the heat of the almost noonday sun was that they'd taken their peaked caps off. These lay side-by-side on the table, out-glittering each other with gold badges and braid. The table parasol hung unopened. In front of them was a tray containing a coffee set which had obviously been used. Both had an exotic multi-coloured fruit cocktail drink in a tall glass decorated with fresh fruit at their hand. A white-clad middle-aged waiter stood respectfully against the bright flowers and trailing creepers adorning a small wall, awaiting any further requests. The air, though humid, was heavy with the perfumes of a well-kept African garden.

They turned in anticipation as the Colonel, JD and Fit stepped onto the terrace, and began to rise from their seats.

The Colonel snapped briskly to attention and saluted. Both men returned the salute rather casually, their eyes concentrating on JD and Fit.

"General Belazir, General Osman. May I introduce Mr. John Dilworth, Chief Executive of Dalton and Sons Ltd and Mr. Frederick Thomas, Overseas Sales Director of the company." The Colonel relaxed from his military stance and gestured gracefully to each in turn with his right hand, then swivelling back to the Generals with a slight incline of the head held his left hand out to indicate their identity as he said, "General Belazir of the Great Socialist Peoples Libyan Arab Jamahiraya Army," (impressive, thought JD, he knows his stuff) identifying the smaller and stockier of the two men, "and General Osman, of the Army of the Jamhirayat-es-Sudan."

They all shook hands. Belazir was in his early fifties, about 5ft 6in, broad but somewhat overweight, quite dark-skinned for a Libyan, with thick wavy hair which reminded

JD of nothing more than the Pacific rollers sweeping onto the Revelcadaro Beach in Acapulco. Osman was tall, over 6ft, slim, with the paler almost golden tanned skin of the Northern Sudanese. He was fine-featured, with dark eyes and a carefully trimmed sculpted moustache and beard. He looked athletic and his light sand-coloured uniform was immaculate, contrasting with Belazir's, which would have been immaculate if he'd lost 30 lbs.

General Belazir was smiling broadly, two gold teeth glinting in the equatorial sun almost completing the line of buttons, which ran up his tunic. He waved them to the table.

"Please, come, join us." They all sat down. The Colonel stepped towards them.

"Gentlemen, before I leave you, can I order you coffee, or a fruit cocktail, or anything else?" He stressed the "anything" for obvious reasons.

JD and Fit had an easy understanding. They never ordered alcohol in the company of Moslems. (Fit was fed up with JD telling him the story of how that was Churchill's mistake when he met King Saud during the war. He'd drunk and smoked. Roosevelt hadn't, and the Americans got the oil deal. Christ, that boy's head was full of disparate rubbish!) Fit said they'd love coffee and fruit juice. The Colonel motioned the waiter with no more than a glance and gave instructions softly but firmly in Swahili.

He thanked them, saluted perfectly again, and disappeared through the white drapes of the French windows like an actor leaving the stage.

They sat down. JD would have taken his jacket off, as would Fit, but they knew they'd better wait for the Chief. Like all the officials they'd met in Africa, he didn't seem to feel the heat and always dressed formally.

"It's a pleasure to meet you. I hope you hadn't been waiting long. The President was very busy when we arrived." JD addressed them both. General Osman replied, "No. Don't worry. We came in by military transport, plane of course, from Khartoum, we arrived an hour before you did, but we brought plenty of work with us." He nodded towards two document cases tying on the table. "We heard you arrive, but knew you had to see His Excellency first."

JD noted a distinct American accent in Osman's cultured voice. A contrast to Belazir's good, but quite heavily-accented English. He found out from subsequent conversation that Belazir had done some training in Britain in the early Sixties but only for a short three months, and had then perfected his English liasing with the 14/20th King's Hussars when they were based in Benghazi. Osman had studied in the U.S. at Princeton. He was the scion of one of Sudan's richest merchant families, and his specially tailored uniform was matched by the flawless skin of the affluent, and his manicured hands looked as if they'd never even touched money in case it was grubby, in the physical sense, that is.

More pleasantries passed between them, then the coffee and drinks arrived. They thanked the waiter, but Fit waved him away "We'll pour our own, my friend." The waiter backed off looking afraid and unsure. He obviously thought it was his duty to do it. He didn't want to get into trouble. The Bwana's had a strange habit of changing their minds.

Fit was pouring the second cup when the President stepped onto the terrace, followed by the Chief and Luke. They all rose.

"Gentlemen, I hope you're comfortable. Don't hesitate to step into the reception room out of this sun." He looked at the waiter. "Nelson will make sure you have whatever you want, including some lunch." Nelson, bright-eyed and grinning for the first time, delighted that the President remembered his name because State House, Entebbe, was only used occasionally, Kampala being the home of the permanent staff, snapped, "Yessah!" in Ugandan English.

"I'm about to take a quiet drive to Kampala," the President said dryly, eyes twinkling, "accompanied by a few friends. They still think Amin Dada is lurking in the bushes. I keep telling them he's beside a pool in the General's country!" He nodded towards Belazir.

The General laughed and put his hands up, palms facing

the President, fingers spread, in mock surrender.

"I'm dropping the Chief off at the airport, so I'll take my leave. Thank you for coming, Mr. Dilworth, Mr. Thomas." They returned the thanks simultaneously. "General Belazir, General Osman. Please take my greetings and best wishes back to your Presidents, and all my other friends in Libya and Sudan. I hope your business together goes well."

He turned to the Chief. "I'm sure you want a few words. I'll meet you at the car. Mine's the one in the middle, without a cannon," he laughed.

The Chief obviously knew the generals. They simply shook hands, as did Luke, who was especially friendly with General Osman, half embracing him. JD guessed they'd known each other for some time. Same age, roughly, too. It was probably Luke who'd set up the meeting in the first place, although he knew the Chief was on good terms with the Libyan Head of State.

"Well boys, good luck to you. I'll leave you to discuss all the details. The plane will be back for you in about four hours. You should be able to get to Khartoum in time for dinner, and a good night's sleep. The Captain is then flying back to Mombassa, and we'll pick you up tomorrow morning about 8a.m and all fly to Libya together. Couldn't be easier, could it?" He was grinning. "I have to fly to Germany then, but General Belazir has already arranged a scheduled flight home for you." JD and Fit wondered just when that would be.

Another round of handshakes and pleasantries, then the four of them were on their own. They ordered a light lunch, chosen by the generals. Fruit, nuts, goats' cheese and tomatoes, with a little olive oil, and bottled water. Nelson disappeared through the small side door.

"Has Chief Spencer told you what we're interested in?" It was Belazir who switched the conversation immediately to business.

"Yes, very briefly. You want a plant to enable you to do your own Security Printing. I have a general proposal here if .." He was reaching for the document case in the pilot's bag.

"No, don't bother now, Mr. Dilworth. We'll discuss it in detail in Libya in more secure surroundings. Not that this isn't secure," he added, quickly glancing around, "but I'd like one or two other people in on the discussions, so I don't want you to have to keep repeating yourselves. Please, let's enjoy the day. I suspect none of us ever have a few hours when we do virtually nothing in our normal lives. Let's stroll through the gardens."

It all sounded perfectly normal to JD.

"Of course. Do you mind if we take our jackets off, General? General Osman?"

"No. No. Please do. For Sadiq and I this is quite cool of course!" The Generals were both smiling in a tolerant but slightly amused way at the two slightly damp Britons. JD was almost "glowing", Fit was more comfortable in the heat, with his almost permanent tan, but there was a faint film on his forehead. They were glad to shed their jackets.

They moved off the terrace into the extensive carefully tended luscious gardens. Out of the lee of the house they saw soldiers standing casually in pairs, at strategic points around the perimeter, on guard duty. They were watched from all sides. They were obviously free to roam the gardens and the State House Reception Rooms, but it was doubtful they could stray out of those restricted areas. They understood that perfectly.

As they strolled in the languid air enjoying the physical senses of sight and smell, they exchanged information about each other. The two Generals were very open, very friendly. They'd known each other for quite a few years, thrown together when the Libyan army was trying to regain a huge swathe of territory in the south of the country which had been annexed by Chad with French and U.S. backing, and which was still the subject of dispute, and still guarded by the Chadian puppet government of the French, and the French Foreign Legion. ("Still shown on all maps," said Belazir with some intensity, "as a disputed area"). Unknown to most people (and of little interest, thought the Britons) the two Islamic Republics had co-operated, especially when the French "stuck their oar in" (Belazir's English was littered with such familiar vernacular expressions: he must have spent a long time with the soldiers at Benghazi mused JD). JD's favourite reading matter was probably military history and geopolitics, so the conversation genuinely interested him.

"I know you weren't happy with the imposition of Habre as President by the French, the U.S and the O.A.U., but I thought the Leader," (he knew all Libyans called their Head of State that: it seemed to please Belazir), "had personally met him and made peace and the ceasefire has held successfully. We all know the French are only interested in the uranium they're sure is there, but how the heck did you get across the desert to help, General Osman?"

"You are well informed, Mr. Dilworth." Both Generals were impressed. Fit was amused. JD could have told Manstein, Montgomery or Montcalme about their own battles, and where they'd gone wrong if he'd had a few sherberts .

"Ah. Mr. Dilworth, we "fuzzy-wuzzies" are used to fighting in the desert. Even your Mr. Churchill said so after he'd taken that little river cruise with General Kitchener." Osman was half-laughing. He may have been educated in the States, but he too was very familiar with English.

"No, seriously, it's an extremely remote area. Its nearest point, Chad I mean, is 600 miles, 900km, from Omdurman-Khartoum." JD always bracketed the two cities together, they were only separated by the Nile, and joined by the bridge.

"Yes, it was a tough operation logistically. We're the largest country in Africa, one of the largest in the world. Most of our country is extremely inhospitable, from barren desert to impassable swamp. Bit like the States!" He laughed again. Both men laughed easily. JD and Fit were beginning to feel comfortable, to like these men.

"But we have a major highway running clean through our country. It's called the Nile! What we did was provide armoured support, and personnel carriers, trucks and material to the extreme Northeast of what the French call Chad. General Belazir could only use Ouri, in the centre of the disputed area, and Aozou in the west as concentration points. They had to watch the Kourizo Pass and to ensure the French didn't occupy the heights of Kegueur 'Ferbi. If they'd done that, he would have been out-flanked and cut off."

JD was trying to picture the area in his mind. Apart from Omdurman the nearest he'd been to it was Ndjamena, the Capital of Chad, and that was 1200kms away, about 750 miles.

"We moved armour and personnel by river and road from Omdurman to El Khandaq and El Debba, used the military airfield and Libya's transport planes to get a lot across to El Atruii Oasis, where we'd made a temporary landing field. The rest we drove across the Jebel Abyed Plateau. That was some journey! And, Mr. Dilworth, no one knew what we were doing. Not even the Americans with their satellites. They simply didn't expect anybody in the middle of the Sahara. Perhaps just a few Sudanese playing war games!"

He was obviously proud of the role they'd played. He should have been, thought JD. Getting armour across there was bloody good going. If they'd concentrated such effort on John Garang's Christian rebels in the south they'd have soon crushed them. Well, no, tanks aren't much use in jungle and swamp.

General Belazir interrupted his meandering thoughts.

"We were very very grateful for General Osman securing our left flank and we've been friends and comrades in arms and Islam since. We were both on the Military Mission to this country," he waved his hand at the garden, "when President Musaveni built the precious bridges with the Islamic North." JD knew he was referring to their two respective countries, which had sometimes been more than tacit supporters of Idi Amin, their fellow Moslem, and various Islamic rebels over the past few years.

Lunch arrived. JD told them his story, office boy to Chief Executive, they liked that. Islam was a very democratic religion, all were equal before Allah; and Fit entranced them with stories of Malaya, the jungle, the Ghurkhas and their Kukris. The Generals agreed - they'd hate to fight in a jungle. Not being able to see the enemy, air cover almost useless, armour the same and all that disease, monsoons, rain, leeches.

The time slipped pleasantly by. They were still sipping coffee when they were interrupted by the Colonel stepping smartly on to the terrace. It was attention and salute time again.

"Generals, gentlemen. Your crew are back. They have called as arranged from Entebbe Airport and await you. The same driver and limousine are waiting for you at the front, and will take you back to the airport. An invitation is extended to you to join the flight." He addressed the latter invitation to the Generals. They readily accepted. Much more attractive than a transport plane.

They thanked the Colonel. They'd expected him to go with the President but he was obviously a fixture here. He told them it had been a pleasure to be of service to them.

"Bet he says that to all the girls," murmured Fit to JD.

When they got to Entebbe the Captain, Anton, met them in the VIP lounge.

"Plans have changed," he said, serious and business-like as always, but with a look of wry amusement. "We're flying you straight to Libya, missing Khartoum. You'll have tomorrow for the business, and then the Chief wants to meet you in Nairobi the following morning, at the Norfolk for a debriefing. He's not going to Germany now, he's going south again. We'll get you a flight from Nairobi home. General Belazir, the Chief asked me to ask you whether you'd do him the very great favour of getting Mr. Dilworth and Mr. Thomas back to Nairobi in time to meet him?"

"Of course. Leave that to me Captain." He was expansive, anything for his dear old friend the Chief.

"OK gentlemen?" The Captain was already putting his

cap on and turning to head for the aircraft.

"Of course," they said. They'd been through all this before. It could all change again mid-flight. Fit had once ended up in India when he'd set off for Zambia.

They were airborne within 30 minutes. The Generals were obviously impressed with the G4. As Belazir said, it was First-class-plus, and they could smoke anytime, anywhere! A bit better than the Tupelov transport they'd arrived in, he teased Osman.

Fit asked whether they were landing at Tripoli, and Belazir explained that Sirte Military Airfield was their destination. "Roughly between Tripoli and Benghazi."

"It will be dark when we get there, and we've arranged for you to stay in a special Government Guest House a few miles away, so you won't see much, but we're meeting back in the Base tomorrow morning. There are special facilities there so you'll see it all then. It's quite impressive. Although, as foreigners, and infidels, we may have to blindfold you." General Osman laughed and smiled his concurrence.

After coffee and soft drinks and bowls of fruit and nuts were served, JD and Fit excused themselves, saying they'd spend the time on the flight completing the "General Presentation" so that it was "customised" for Libya. They had the laptop and printer to enable them to do that. It would be a useful start to their meeting.

"As you wish, of course, gentlemen. But don't go to too much trouble. I think what you will learn tomorrow will give you much else to think about. General Osman and I have much we can discuss and prepare also, regarding this and other business. We have, according to the Captain, another four hours flying time, so we all might as well make use of it, mightn't we. Anyway," he said mischievously, "we've all had too much relaxation today than is good for the soul. But I would say again, don't do too much work on your papers because, when all our team meets tomorrow, our plans and requirements may surprise you."

"Thanks, General, but don't worry, what we're doing is making sure that what we have here," he tapped the pilot's case, "will serve as a foundation for whatever you want."

Both Generals nodded and murmured agreement.

JD and Fit went to the back, set up the Toshiba 11OCS lap-top and the Hewlett-Packard Desk Jet 400 printer, spread two copies of the general presentation around the table, altered and printed out a new title page so that it read "The Great Socialist People's Libyan Arab Jamahiraya Security Printing Plant", read through the documents again, for the fiftieth time each probably, to familiarise themselves once more for anything that might come up the following day (it always impressed people when the answers rolled off the tongue without reference to papers), then settled back to discreetly read the newspapers they'd both bought at Heathrow. They'd achieved their usual. They'd made friends with the "customers", they'd found out what they could, they'd hopefully entertained and rather impressed the Generals. Now they wanted a break and they were sure, from many past experiences, so did the Generals. There was no point over-doing attention. It became cloying and annoying. Less experienced salesmen always had that painful lesson to learn.

It was the first time they'd been alone since they'd met the Generals.

"What do you think?" JD valued Fit's judgements of people. His own tended to be too "hearty", too optimistic. He always sought the best in people, as in situations. If he'd been buried in crap up to his neck he'd have told everybody who'd listen that his head was free. It led to him often being let down, but he couldn't help it. It was his nature, and the positive approach was often motivational. "I like them both."

"Yes, I do, especially Osman. He's an idealist, isn't he? You know, wants to do right by his country, building the future, that crap. Wonder what he's doing with Belazir on this though?" He answered himself. "Never mind, we'll find that out tomorrow. Belazir, well he seems all right. Friendly enough. Very friendly in fact. But he's seen some stuff, JD. He's been at the top since '69. There's been some heavy stuff gone down since then, some nasties. Have you seen his eyes? Small, black almost beady. Would you trust him?"

"Christ! You sound like my Grandma. She never liked or trusted James Mason 'cos he trapped that woman's fingers in a piano by slamming the lid, or Richard Widmark who pushed that cripple downstairs in a wheelchair! It didn't matter how many times I argued with her that they were only doing it in films, that it was part of the script, the plot, she said they must be like that or they couldn't play the parts so well. And anyway, she always said, look at their eyes! Now you're doing it! Mind you, you're nearly as bloody old as she was."

"No, no. I'm not. I like them. I've already said so. I think we can trust them. It certainly sounds interesting, eh'? We can't but gain if we go along with it all anyway, can we?"

They'd leave the Generals well alone for the rest of the flight. If they'd heard what they were discussing they may not have felt the same way.

£$£

Chapter Nine

They spoke in Arabic, that beautiful poetic language rich in precise hyperbole, satisfying to the speaker, harsh on the ears of the non-Arab listener. They were born more than a thousand miles apart, about the distance from Berlin to Moscow (a journey which takes the traveller through two time and at least five language zones) but conversed in the same tongue. In writing, they could have communicated with people from the Atlantic to the Urals, with people on the other side of the world, living around the Java, Banda, Sulu and South China Seas. It was a religious heritage and culture of which they were both fiercely proud. Osman was a younger, more idealistic believer in a pan-Arabic union founded, of course, in the one true religion, Islam.

Belazir had been, all those years ago, one of al-Khaddafi's advisers to the Revolution Command Council after the bloodless coup they were all so proud of in 1969. Almost the first thing they proposed was Union with Egypt and Syria, and later on Syria and Chad. None of it had happened. He was getting older, and not a little jaundiced now, he had to admit to himself. If God had decreed it, it would have come about. But they hadn't done badly. State Socialism and the teachings of the Koran had created a country where the annual GDP of $30bn shook down as about $9000 per head of population, not bad. One of the best in the Arab world, one of the best in the Islamic world, even including Malaysia and Indonesia. They'd done a good job. The outside world didn't understand it, but the people had a say. He'd like to see the U.S. President, or any European President or Prime Minister, being harangued at a People's Committee held in a large auditorium or the open air like the Leader often was. And it was all televised, not edited! His patience was legendary. Belazir had seen him in Misurata have to leave his seat and calm an old lady who was on about hospitals, “Mother, Mother, I hear you. It will be looked into. Calm yourself, please, in the name of Allah.”

He couldn't see Richard Nixon, Lyndon Johnson, Margaret Thatcher, Francois Mitterand or old Kohl in front of an angry crowd trying to explain their policies face to face. The most they did was speak to orchestrated party rallies, conferences and conventions. And they thought they were democratic. His thoughts were interrupted.

“Youssef, now that the plans have changed and we're not over-nighting in Khartoum I've worked out a new little agenda. Tell me what you think.”

Osman slipped out of his tunic a long slim blue leather-bound pad and placed it on the table. Belazir absent-mindedly noted that, incongruously, it was embossed “Drummonds, Admiralty Arch, London. Royal Bank of Scotland.” They didn't have a branch in Omdurman, did they? Sadiq carried on.

“By the time we get to Sirte it'll be at least 9 pm. I'm presuming they're staying, we're staying, at the Guest House?”

“Of course.”

“Well, that's another 20, 25 minutes drive. If we have coffee and refreshments we can still retire by 11 p.m and have an early start to the meeting, say 9 am., after a good breakfast. I also presume the Governor is already in Sirte. (Belazir nodded.) I don't know about you, but I'm sleeping for another couple of hours after morning prayers! I'm knackered! Do you realise we've been on the move for over 24 hours now?”

“Don't tell me, I'm an old man now.”

“No, Youssef, no you're not. You're in your prime!”

“Prime? Do you know I'm 56? Life expectancy for males in Libya is 57!”

“That's 10 years longer than the Sudan, my friend and I'm already 39. Eight years to go, by God's will.”

“Sadiq, don't worry. I think the statistics include all the poor people. That distorts things. If God wants the average to be 57, or 47, he permits many more poor people, so the balance is struck, and we, the affluent, can live much longer. I'm sure of this. I've thought about it."

"Youssef, if you were a Roman Catholic the Pope would excommunicate you!" Osman was laughing, "Let's get down and sort this out, you old Jinn, this is my brief agenda:

1. Meeting with the Governor, General Saif, and all the team at 9 am. We spend the whole morning on setting out the background to our plans, what we want, and then let a question and answer session develop: we'll have to encourage that, you know what I mean?

2. Break for lunch at 1.30 pm. Let Saif take everybody but the Governor back to the Guest House.

3. Tour the installation. Just those parts, of course, they'll have to see. That will take a couple of hours.

4. Re-convene with the Governor and Saif."

He noticed Belazir looking quizzical. "It's necessary, Youssef, remember, Saif, as Head of Internal Security has got to sort out control of all communications from now on. He's in it totally. He'd be better sitting in on everything. He thinks like a policeman, a secret policeman, so he doesn't think much at all, so he's not going to say much or be disruptive, but he needs to be up to speed at all times with everything from now on."

Belazir held his right hand up, "I agree, I agree."

5. "Break for refreshments at about 6 pm. The Governor and Saif can go their own way. After that, let the Englishmen have a wash and brush-up, meet again, give them all the plans and drawings they need, only those they need at this stage, the space they will have at their disposal, final discussions about timing of responses, how and who to

contact, the nature of the contract we'll sign. We'll do all this together. Perhaps we shouldn't let Saif go. Perhaps he should stay with us for this part? Yes, I think he should and then we should be loading them on to the plane you're going to organise now. While you're doing that you need to prepare the Governor and Mahmoud Saif about the change of plans and us arriving tonight and not tomorrow morning from Khartoum." He picked up the satellite phone from it's elegantly concealed holder in the side-facia of the seat, and held it out to Belazir, eyebrows raised and half-smiling. "Then it's back to the Guest House for us and a long and well-deserved sleep!"

"How I admire the energy of youth," Belazir said with a hint of sarcastic resignation. "Let me get my phone numbers." He reached for his slim document case. He never put anything in his tunic pockets. It spoiled the smooth line he liked so much, which he knew made him look slimmer and more distinguished. It was worth having his uniforms tailored in Rome.

Osman excused himself and went aft to the bathroom. JD and Fit spotted him coming and slid their newspapers to one side and pored over their presentations. They nodded and smiled to him as the General passed. They stayed in earnest concentration on the business until he returned to his seat.

"They're reading their newspapers," Osman said. Belazir chuckled.

"I've made all the re-arrangetnents. Through Mahmoud Saif. As Head of Libyan Internal Security it doesn't seem unusual for him to set up a temporary HQ at the Sirte base. That's what he's done, a bit ahead of time, he's on the ball."

"Excellent. What about the other six delegations?" Osman still had his notebook and pen out.

"They're all set up, no need to alter them. We'll start Saturday morning. We have the whole weekend, and it will give us a day of rest Thursday, then a refresher on the Sabbath before the meetings. They've all confirmed they're attending to Mahmoud. He's arranged for a helicopter from

Tarabulus." (He used the Libyan name for Tripoli).

"Did they have any trouble getting here? I mean, Libya?"

"No, the Italians came through Malta, their American friends with them, the Palestinians flew from Damascus, the other Americans were on a historic visit to Carthage. Clever, that one, eh? The Latin Americans came through Madrid, and the Chinese through Bahrein. The trickiest were the Irish, they were probably under surveillance. They did Shannon, New York, Athens, Cairo, Tarabulus."

"So, now it is in the hands of God and us." Osman looked serious.

"And them." Belazir almost imperceptibly inclined his head towards JD and Fit.

They were both up to the leader page.

£$£

Chapter Ten

Anna-Greta entered the cabin from the galley. By this time all four men were lying back in their seats, relaxed or dozing. The only sound was the steady, almost soporific drone of the quiet jet engines.

"Gentlemen, we'll be landing in 10 minutes. The Captain asked me to remind you to take everything with you. We're going straight to Mombassa after re-fuelling at Khartoum. General, anything you want delivering there? Any Orders of the Day?" She laughed at her little joke, as Osman did. She knew how to make men feel flattered by a little attention.

They all put their papers away, sat back and looked out into the black night. There was no sign of human habitation, no lights anywhere to be seen on either side of the aircraft. In fact, apart from the falling sensation in the stomach caused by the steep descent of the powerful jet, there was nothing to indicate they were landing.

Then Fit pointed wordlessly. JD turned and peered through the window. Three lines of lights, tapering towards the tail, seemed to be snaking silently, steadily towards them at an angle of about 30 degrees. No other lights showed. Only those obviously on the runway. The G4 was nearly down.

They hit the floor with a thud. Obviously a steep descent. The engines soared urgently to high crescendo, like Pavarotti hitting a high A. Without seat belts those facing forward were thrown forward a little, the others pressed into the back of their seats. JD knew what Anton was doing. He loved this jet and it's power and performance. He never failed to tell anyone who'd listen that it was the "Rolls-Royce" of jets. Rolls-Royce RB183.03 Tay Turbofan engines, 25647 kg of thrust, cruising speed 908 Kph., he was demonstrating its power and versatility. "It's almost capable of VSTOL," he'd say excitedly as he explained the joy of the job he loved to do. "When I land I save as much time as possible - and that's mainly taxiing. The shorter the better. I have the brakes on the highest automatic setting, I close the throttles, operate reverse to maximum (that's when you hear the babies scream), then I whap up the spoilers to the higher setting which dumps all the lift off the top of the wings, and, Ve Stop! Ve Germans are gut at ze flying!" He was always taking the piss. "Ah!" JD would say, "a fun-hun! Your father bombed our town hall!" Anton was a great companion when he was on the "Tusker White Cap" beers, and he didn't have to fly for 15 or more hours.

"Christ!" Fit said, "Anton's in a hurry again! Better get off before he takes off again!"

They moved through the galley in single file. Anna-Greta had unfolded the small staircase through the fuselage door, and was standing waiting to say farewell. Anton came out to shake hands, and Pierre called out his goodbyes from the flight cabin.

"Probably see you the day after tomorrow in Nairobi," Anton said to JD and Fit.

"We'll have a drink in the Delamere Terrace at the Norfolk."

"We won't, I'm flying to Malawi, remember? Catch you next time."

The night air was cool. Now that they'd stepped off the plane and out of the glow of the interior lights they could see that they weren't in pitch-blackness. There was a pale moon, as huge as it can only be in the desert. It couldn't be the same one that apologetically appeared over Europe. The night was tomb-silent. They could sense that instinctively even with the whining roar of the jet engines behind them. The Captain and Anna-Greta stood silhouetted in the doorway, waiting. In the distance there was just distinguishable the huge dense black shape of a rectangular building. The Generals were looking expectantly towards it. Far over to the left there was a smaller structure, unidentifiable. No other features could be made out. Flatness, blackness, surrounded them. As their eyes grew more accustomed to the darkness they noticed a solitary light in the larger building, and a much fainter one on or in the smaller structure. The lights were obviously hooded, so it was the light they cast which was discernible, not the source.

"It's like Arthur C. Clark's bloody black monolith on the dark side of the moon," Fit said out of the side of his mouth. JD laughed.

Two more lights, like searchlights, pierced the darkness suddenly, pointing straight at them. They moved, but it was difficult to tell properly because they were moving directly towards them. There was no sound other than the jet engines, but it was a car, travelling at speed. Within seconds they could see it. A large dark Mercedes. With a final, "Bye," the door to the jet closed. The car pulled sideways, braking hard, and stopped 20 yards away from them. They walked towards it as the doors opened. The jet engine's whining moved up a scale and the G4 taxied away from them, already beginning a smooth arc ready for take-off in the direction from whence they'd come.

The two men emerging from the car were in uniform. It was difficult to see much in the darkness, with just a faint wash of moonlight and the backdrop of the car's interior lights, but they looked in their mid-forties. Their uniforms were darker than Belazir's and Osman's, which were both light sand-coloured. Both men saluted Belazir.

"Let me introduce General Mahmoud Saif and Colonel Ahmed Anan, both of the Libyan Internal Security Force." He spoke only to JD and Fit. It was obvious Osman knew both men from the exchanged smiles and nods.

Handshakes all round. General Saif spoke in English, heavily accented, "Please gentlemen, get in."

Belazir waved JD, Fit and Osman into the back seat. He shook his head and motioned Saif to take the front passenger seat. The Colonel was driving, for himself he pulled down a jump seat from the back of the front seat. JD immediately offered to use it. The General would have none of it.

"You're guests in my country."

They only drove to the 'black monolith'. It turned out to be a very large dark building, two or three stories high, it was hard to tell. There were no windows, and the only door the Britons could see gave little clue to its scale. But it was a huge double-door, probably 12ft high with large wooden ornately carved handles from what they could see, but that wasn't much in the muted glow of the single hooded light. The Colonel jumped out and saluted, a few words of Arabic were exchanged. General Saif slid into the driver's seat, Belazir got out and into the passenger seat and they nosed their way into the night towards the other building with its faint light.

"He's stationed here," Belazir said, obviously referring to the Colonel.

In less than a minute the powerful headlights on full beam picked out the other 'building'. It wasn't a building. It was a giant gate, in the form of an arch, with a simple single crash bar across it. It stood incongruously in isolation. JD and Fit could see no walls connected to the towers of the gate. How odd. There was movement under the cold light. They could see now there were at least three sentries. It was a small guardhouse, built onto the side of the gate. The soldier who stepped out of the open door saluted in a sloppy fashion, the barrier was already rising automatically, the two other sentries stood as the car, hardly slowing down, sped through.

Then they were on what looked like a brand new road, gleaming white lines picked out by the headlights. Nothing could be seen either side. They drove in silence, but not an awkward one, just the quiet of men who've spent hours talking to each other, so have little else to say, and who are tired.

Belazir broke the silence as a blaze of lights suddenly came into view as they crested a small hill after about 20 minutes. The lights were very close.

"Mr. Dilworth, Mr. Thomas. You'll be glad to know this is your hotel for the night."

"Looks big, General. Which hotel is it? I mean, you know, which chain, Hilton, Marriott, Sheraton?"

Belazir laughed, and they could see Osman smiling in the light now flooding into the car in something like a stroboscopic effect as they passed through well-lit avenues of trees, including many palms.

"None of them! This is the Hotel Libya! You'll be impressed. We built it for the OAU Conference in the late Eighties when we held the Presidency. It's totally secure. You're in the grounds now, over 70 acres. As good as any of the hotels you name. Better, you get personal service, and it's never crowded!"

He was obviously proud of the place, JD thought. It wouldn't occur to him to question the viability or sense of putting up such a bloody great building for non-commercial purposes. It reminded him of the huge "Guest Houses" in the former Soviet Union, especially in the Central Asian Republics. They were often situated right next to the Presidential Residences, sometimes even in their vast landscaped grounds, palaces of luxury for the "comrades" who looked after the interests of the "comrades" outside the grounds, who lived in one or two-roomed wooden houses with their hens and lambs and goats.

He was still thinking like this when they stepped inside, into the "Reception". It was pleasantly affluent and crowded. It seemed to double as a non-alcoholic bar and meeting room. The westemers raised some curious interest, but after their passports were taken, they declined the offer of drinks or refreshments and retired to their large and pleasant rooms. Both had been provided with juices, water and fruit. They shared a fresh orange juice together in Fit's room, bemoaned the lack of a good scotch or gin, then hit the sack. Fit, the better early riser, promised to wake JD at 7.30 am. Belazir had briefed them, they were leaving at 8.30

am. for the meeting. He'd left them with the remark, "I think you'll find tomorrow very, very interesting, and mutually beneficial."

They liked the sound of that. They slept well.

£$£

Chapter Eleven

Even at 8.30 am. it was hot. The bright morning sun glinted off the East and South-facing windows of the uninspiring modern complex. The three black Mercedes started to pull away from the entrance. The road and the walk-ways were soaking wet, and the air had smelt so fresh when they'd first stepped outside. Automatic sprinklers were gently showering every tree, bush, plant and blade of grass wherever they looked in the extensive gardens. The earth was satiating its thirst, birds were singing, and the only other sound was the water rippling across the leaves and the luscious dripping which itself seemed to cool the air. Few humans were about.

JD and Fit were in the first car, with General Belazir. They recognised Osman and Saif in the second, with someone else they didn't recognise. Likewise the two men in the third car were unknown to them. This morning, all the cars had military drivers looking smart in lightweight uniforms.

"That's a very impressive hotel, or conference centre, General." Fit spoke from the back seat, not meaning a word of it. It was soul-less and tasteless.

"Yes. Thank you. We built it, as I told you, for the OAU conference. It's used a lot still. Mainly for Government and Military Conferences, and we let the oil companies use it. We charge them a very high price!" He laughed out loud, with a hint of a sneer in his voice.

"I'll bet you do!"

The General grunted what was obviously an order to the driver. He responded crisply and flicked the air conditioning on. They'd both noticed the brusque manner in which the General addressed his fellow Libyans. His authorative mien induced something akin to fear. They were glad they were

British and guests.

As the car pulled round the plaza and out into the road they could see for the first time that they were on the edge of a sizeable town. The road they were on led away from it. It was brand new, as it had looked in the headlights the previous night, and was almost arrow-straight. Within a couple of minutes of leaving the grounds and gardens, as they passed over the small hill, the landscape swiftly gave way to nondescript scrub, stone and sand, virtually flat and featureless in every direction. There was a scattering of small farms not far from the road, and goats wandered freely from one isolated green-grey bush or clump of foliage to another. There was nothing else on the road. The landscape became desert, sandy stone-coloured, and flat, uninteresting, parched, within a couple of kilometres. Then there were no buildings, no people, no goats, nothing to look at, just the straight road, the sun and the horizon.

JD broke the short silence.

"This air-conditioning is superb, General. It certainly looks hot and arid out there. It's hard to believe the Romans called this the garden of Africa! They exported masses of corn, timber, and olives from here back to Italy. Look at it now. It must be difficult for you."

Fit looked at him. Where did he get such crap from?

"Again, Mr. Dilworth, well-informed."

JD felt smug. He liked impressing people.

The General continued. "You know, humans have mainly caused the desertificationby over-farming, deforestation, letting the irrigation systems fall into ruin. It wasn't just the Romans, though they milked the country. The Byzantines recovered the situation a little, but the main problems were caused by the neglect during the long Ottoman Empire. When the Italians tried to revive things in the 20th century it was too far-gone. But we have extensive plans. We can get the water. There is no shortage. In a few years this desert, the Sirte desert, will be agricultural land again."

JD knew what he was talking about. The plan to tap the huge natural water reservoirs under the deserts. The Sahara virtually floated on water. It was extremely controversial. The supply was not replenishable. No one knew what would happen if the reservoirs were drained. More, worse, desertification? Huge "dust-bowl" settlements, artificially created, with no hope when the water ran out? It was very high-risk. He knew the Libyans were. . . . .

The General interrupted his thoughts. He and Fit leaned forward a little to hear. The General was speaking to the windscreen, he hadn't turned. His voice had taken on an "official" tone.

"Gentlemen. We're now 8 or 9 kilometres from a top-secret military base. Our most secret. Even the Americans don't know what we have here, although they patrol us twice a day by satellite, and we have regular visits from our old friends the spy planes. They know, everyone knows, of course, that there is a military airfield here. Not something you can hide, even in a desert! But, you know, they've still never figured out, as far as our intelligence tells us, why we inexplicably made the Tarabulus-Benghazi coastal motorway eight lanes in the by-pass round Sirte. For six miles! Well, it would take 747s, the Space Shuttle, Galaxies anything!" He chuckled.

He was obviously enjoying his peroration and warming to his subject.

"You've just stayed on the outskirts of the coastal town of Sirte. Remember when Reagan ordered the unlawful shooting down of two of our jets in 1989 and the world wondered why we hardly reacted? The reason we didn't make more of an issue about what we considered an appalling act of aggression was that we wanted to draw as little attention as possible to what you're about to see. The jets were based here, the base is about 50 km from Sirte, half way to Mabruk. It's in this desert of Sirte. Not only is it our most secret base, it is our biggest and, and here is the vital point, it is all underground. Apart from the airfield, of course, even we couldn't do that!"

He paused, for a little effect. Then he said, simply but proudly, "It is the headquarters of our nuclear defence system."

He noticed JD's look of surprise in the rear-view mirror. "You didn't know we had one, eh, Mr. Dilworth? We have no nuclear weapons, but we don't trust the Americans. Any country which will bomb a capital like Tarabulus, completely disregarding civilian casualties, in a fit of blind hatred over our Leader, will stop at nothing. We fear the Americans and their blood lust. They wouldn't hesitate to use nuclear devices on us if they got their chance. After all, we're not the same colour or religion as they, so we can't be as important, can we? We're not even the same colour as the poor slaves they use to do most of their front-line fighting."

His voice had become intense again, and harsher with bitterness. It was obviously politic not to strenuously argue the American case at that precise moment. He visibly relaxed a little and returned to his theme.

"It is probably the best, and the biggest, in the world. We know, for instance, that it is five times bigger than Nato Strategic Strike Command HQ in the Chiltern Hills near High Wycombe which has Europe's biggest nuclear bunker, conveniently situated very near Chequers, your Prime Minister's country home, and where the C. in C. of U.K. Air is based." Again he paused. "I suppose the Naval Chiefs will be at sea and the Army in the middle of the land battle anyway if there was a war. The leaders of every nation must be protected, of course."

His tone was now smoothly sarcastic. In the mirror JD could see his dark eyes glinting, half-mockingly but humorously too it seemed. He pressed on swiftly, reverting, to his "official" tone.

"We believe it is even bigger than any site in the USA. It is completely bombproof. You will see. We have made it the headquarters of all our armed forces. You probably already know."

They didn't. The Chief hadn't mentioned it in his briefing. "I am the Commander-in-Chief of all land and air forces, under the Leader, of course." He added the last comment very hurriedly. "You may wonder, gentlemen, why I'm telling you all this." (JD's mind flashed back to all the old films he'd seen. Because we're never going to get out alive! He suppressed a smile, and tried to be a serious businessman again) "There are five good reasons:

1. We know the very nature of your business is secrecy.

2. We trust the Chief, Mr. Spencer. As does the Leader. So we trust you.

3. You are soon going to be privy to the most secret plans of our government--- and those of our Arab brothers.

4. This base, the Sirte base, is central to our plans, and so are you.

5. This base is where the work you do for us is to be based. So, you have to see it.

"I'm not being deliberately mysterious. It will all be clearer to you very soon. But we are very close, only four or five kilometres away, so let me give you first a little advanced information about who you will meet this day."

Before he could say anything else the air was violently assaulted with a thunderous roar which completely obliterated all other sound. The car vibrated as two fighter planes, Mig. 25s, "Foxbats", one on each side of the car, blasted past, almost at ground level, certainly not more than 40ft. They looked as if they were missiles launched from imaginary wings on the Mercedes, thought JD. They headed straight down the straight road.

"They're going home. We'll soon join them." The General paused only momentarily to let the reverberations fade away then carried on the briefing in a business-like tone. "Generals Osman and Saif will be there, you already know them. The Governor of the Central Bank of Libya, Mr. Celal Dajani, will complete our "team". Representing Syria there is Mr. Wael Murad, from Palestine Mousa el-

Assad; Jordan, Khalid Rudeinah; Lebanon, Bachir Riarchi; Iraq, Abdul Abu Routisi, Iran; Fayed Khosmenjani."

"Well! That's some gathering, General. Are we -?" JD got no further. The General turned in his seat, looked at them both and grinned. He held up his left hand, knuckles facing them, fingers outstretched. When he spoke he was almost laughing.

"Gentlemen, I know, I know. I can feel waves of your Western curiosity and impatience. Relax, be patient. In this next few hours all your questions will be answered, I assure you," he turned back, and waved an arm at the windscreen. "Look. We are there."

It was a slight exaggeration. On the horizon, centred bang on the road, as if the arrow of the road had thudded into the heart of whatever it was, they saw a small shape and a larger one behind it. To the right, a cloud of dust hung in the air. From their vantage point it looked un-moving.

At 140 km per hour along the smooth surface of the straight road the shapes quickly became discernible, and they could see the dust wasn't still, but billowing, spiralling and settling. It was the gatehouse, and the big dark building, the monolith. The dust was raised by the landing Migs, and they'd disappeared in it. Where to?

£$£

Chapter Twelve

The gate looked even more incongruous in the daylight, alone in the scruffy desert, which was the colour of the bottom of a well-used ashtray sprinkled with a little sand. Two wires stretched out on either side of it into the distance as far as the eye could see, supported by no other visible means. It looked to Fit like nothing more than a scene from a Roman triumph immediately after a battle, when victorious Legionnaires were gleefully tearing vanquished foes apart by tying each leg to a horse and riding them in opposite directions. JD was certain that somewhere, carved on it in cuneiform, he'd find the name “Ozymandias”.

It was an archway, probably 40 feet high, rendered brick, with the rendering in need of another coat of paint. Across the roadway running between it was a red and white pole with broken wire mesh hanging beneath it. Three guards stood in a rough approximation of attention, with what looked like AK-49s sloped to arms. A fourth guard stood inside the small guardhouse, obviously at the barrier control. Their uniforms, sand-brown, looked rather dirty and worn, JD noticed, as did their boots. He also noticed they were all older men, probably late thirties, obviously not conscripts. Of course, he thought, they wouldn't be at HQ.

The General barely saluted as the barrier rose, and the car sped towards the “monolith”. The tarmac road ended at the gate. They were now on a vast stretch of concrete, which swept all round the monolith and merged with the huge runway which stretched out into the desert, disappearing in the distance. There appeared to be nothing else around; until one looked more carefully. On every side, within the wires, there were small flat-topped humps, like raised square manholes, only a foot or 18in. high, stretched in regular lines and situated approximately 20 metres apart.

The tops were solid. There was some kind of grating around the sides; air ducts, concluded JD.

The car stopped at the entrance they'd seen the previous night. It was the only entrance as far as they could see. There were no windows. It was huge. Just stuck there unannounced, in the midst of the desert. The other cars pulled up behind. The drivers of all the cars leapt out and opened the doors then stood to attention. The General didn't acknowledge anyone, just waved to JD and Fit to follow him through the impressive double-door entrance. Inside, there was just a small low-ceilinged room where red-jacketed young men, almost boys, were waiting, in what seemed like trepidation, holding trays of small glasses with mineral water and cordials, which they offered in greeting. The General seemingly snarled at them and they backed off hastily. He probably just said, "No thanks," but spoken Arabic could sound harsh and marvellously militaristic, like German and Japanese. The language to bark orders in. JD was meandering again. What a bloody great door - for such an insignificant room.

The next door, simple and normal-sized, repeated the surprise, in reverse. It opened into a vast hall. It obviously occupied almost all the space in the "monolith". Equally obviously, it was the reason the building was there, alone in the desert. It seemed as big as a football field. In size and height it reminded JD of the atrium of the Acapulco Princess Hotel, all nine floors of it. In decor it reminded him of the toilet of a seedy London West-End pub. It was painted a sickly yellow, more like buttermilk soiled with the dust and scum of a few years. It was surrounded on three sides by sofas, with the occasional armchair, three or four deep. They were all in exquisitely appalling taste: White, off-white, red, black, red and black, white and black. JD and Fit looked at each other, simultaneously registering the same facial expression, corners of their lips pulled down slightly, eyebrows raised slightly. Just enough so no one could see them. They would, of course, enthuse about how impressive the "room" was in oleaginous salesmen mode. It was like a second-hand sale of late Sixties furniture bought from the cheapest of cheap furniture outlets, and even those only lines which couldn't sell even in the poorest areas. This was furniture which wouldn't be looted in a riot.

On the fourth side of the room there was an enormous black "throne". It wasn't leather either. Above it was a giant eagle, (or was it a Phoenix?) also black, probably 12ft high, 15ft wingspan. This was obviously a huge traditional Arab "Majlis" room, where the Sheikh, Sultan or king met his subjects in person to listen to their complaints, petitions, pleas or poems of praise. It didn't take much imagination to guess who occupied the black throne.

They followed the General quickly across the polished parquet flooring to the only other door they could see in the vast hall, directly opposite.

They stepped from kitsch modern Arabic decor in the worst of taste into what looked like a Hollywood film-set for a sci-fi film. They looked at each other again, impressed this time. They were in a room about 25ft high. Its dimensions were approximately 100ft. by 50ft. The floor, ceiling, and walls were metal of some sort. They looked like satin-finish stainless steel. There were no features at all in the room, apart from row after row of small indented lights in the ceiling and, curiously, similar indentations in every wall but these displayed no sign of lights. Next to the doors, which were distinguishable from the walls only because of the lack of indentations, was the faint outline of a panel, little more than a "tracing" on the satin finish, mainly obvious again because it lacked any indentations. There was just one aperture, only about 2mm in diameter in the otherwise flawless surface of the "panel". All the party were now in the room. The doors seemed to close automatically, with a just perceptible thud and muffled metallic click. The General took what appeared to be a silver pen from his inside pocket. It wasn't a pen. He unsheathed it. It reminded JD of the shaft of a micrometer, but much slimmer. It was obviously a pre-programmed electromagnetic "key" he guessed. He found out later he was almost right. It also contained a tiny activating laser and a miniaturised "smart chip". The General slid the "key" into the "key-hole".

Nothing happened. Or nothing seemed to happen. Then JD and Fit realised, not through any external visible sign or clue, but from that internal mechanism in the human body and brain, which is almost a sixth sense, that they were descending. Rather swiftly. But there was no vibration, no noise, nothing to indicate movement in the large room. It was one great elevator. It was impressive.

The door opened. They all stepped out into a brightly lit corridor. It was actually the space between two metallic partitions about 100ft apart. The ceiling or roof was again 25ft high at least, and was identical to that in the elevator, metallic, sunken lights. The air was fresh, cool and clean though they were obviously underground in the military base, perhaps the bunker. The corridor seemed endless, and featureless. There weren't even the now familiar indentations in the walls, but after they'd walked about 25 yards JD noticed the same faint lines "traced" on the metal, obviously indicating doors. By the side of each door was the same small "key-hole".

The General stopped at the second such door, and inserted his key. It slid open to reveal a large conference room. It was decorated normally, with no metal visible. There was a table to seat 24, floor thickly carpeted, the far wall was lined with a long low unit the top of which was full of glasses, trays, hobs, coffee pots, bottles of mineral water and cordial. Two red-jacketed waiters were in attendance, positioned at each end of the unit. They didn't move. Neither did the men they were to meet.

The General immediately took his position at the head of the table. He motioned JD and Fit to join him on his left and General Osman moved to Belazir's right. JD saw there were small name cards propped against the pair of tumblers in front of each seat, as were small pads, pens and pencils. The General waved his arm in an expansive welcoming gesture.

"Please sit, gentlemen."

He did so himself.

"Let me introduce everyone to Mr. Dilworth and Mr. Thomas of Dalton and Sons Ltd. You know why they're here. You all know each other of course."

He proceeded with the introductions. JD and Fit were grateful he'd given them the run-down in the car, and each scribbled the names down. JD scrawled a rectangle first on his pad and placed the names as they were seated round the table. Clever bugger, thought Fit, glancing at it.

The general snarled at the waiters, who poured and placed thick black coffee in traditional small Arabic cups before each person, then put mineral water and other drinks in clusters, with openers, at strategically convenient places on the long table. They returned to their positions.

The General addressed JD and Fit. "The coffee will be served continuously. If you want none, just "waggle" your cup." He laughed himself, as they did, at his use of the vernacular English word and his demonstration of a "waggle" with his right hand. They both retorted that yes, they were familiar with the custom. The General went on, addressing everyone now.

"The waiters speak no word of English. Believe me. That's why they were chosen. We will speak English for the meeting, please gentlemen. You can speak freely."

The air in the room remained cool and fresh. JD reckoned the temperature to be about 72 degrees, about the same as a good air-conditioned hotel. It was comfortable, even wearing a jacket and tie. Apart from the three generals, everyone was wearing jacket and tie.

General Belazir leaned forward, hands clasped, resting on the table in front of him. He spoke without notes.

"Thank you for coming, all of you. You know why we're here, but we thought it vital that you meet our friends from Dalton and Sons personally, and that they meet us. You all know their parent company, and most of you know the Chief of that company, Mr. Brandon Spencer. He it is who has introduced Daltons and our friends to us. I have not briefed Mr. Dilworth or Mr. Thomas about our plans. They presumed initially we were here to talk about a Libyan Security Printing Plant. I now propose to explain our whole plan to them, to reveal the full extent of it. But first, has anyone any questions or comments?"

There was a general shaking of heads and negative murmurings. JD thought everyone looked comfortable, relaxed. They, for certain, knew what was coming. He was very interested. The General leaned back, but kept his hands palms downwards on the polished table, slightly raised with just fingertips in contact with the wood. The posture of a concert pianist. He spoke quietly.

"I have to perhaps bore you a little, Mr. Dilworth and Mr. Thomas. I'm sorry." They simultaneously raised their hands and inclined their heads in gestures of acceptance and understanding. "This story really starts back in 1970, in this country, after our revolution in 1969. The Revolution Command Council, of which I was not part, but in which, if I may say without being immodest, I always played a major role as adviser to the Leader, The Council was fervently Pan-Arab, believing it to be the only way forward for the tragically fragmented Arab world, reeling from the assaults of the US Imperialist-backed Zionism", He sounded as if reading from a well-rehearsed script on auto-cue, but learnt, and perhaps meant, from the heart. "So we proposed a union, a sacred union with Syria and Egypt, our two Arab brother-nations most oppressed by the Zionists. We had the money. They had the people, combined population 62m and the military wherewithal, the "clout" as you would say." He smiled, and continued, "It came, unfortunately, to nothing. We tried again with Syria in 1980, and in 1981 with Chad. Nothing. The Leader was not only Pan-Arabist, but also wanted to "cleanse" Africa of Western corruption." He looked at them, squarely. "I'm sure you've read his Green Book. He proposes a democratic Socialist Islamic state from here to Zaire. It is natural. It transcends the artificial boundaries imposed by the colonialists. The Americans and the French have prevented it. Egypt, from Sadat onwards, little more than American pawns, and Tunisia and Algeria,

French fiefdoms, have played into the same hands." His tone had turned sour, slightly bitter. He paused for a few seconds, and then he brightened up noticeably.

"However, we have learned from you Europeans! You were very clever, you understood the frail weakness of human nature so well. You must be glad we Muslims gave back to you Plato, Socrates and Aristotle after your Christian Dark-Ages! Within a few years of killing each other with a savagery unprecedented in human history, you were planning political unification! Admirable! Astounding! Your best brains drove this. You, they, were wise enough to appeal not to a common European heritage, as we tried to appeal to a common Arab heritage, but to that seedy unpleasant side of life, economics, employment, survival, greed, which touches everybody's heart and pocket and family. You started with a trading organisation, treaty. The European Coal and Steel Community, 1951. It arose out of the Schuman Plan, 1950. It's aim: to make war impossible because of inextricably inter-twined economic links between old, no, I mean new, enemies. Our aim was the same, amongst Arabs. But we wanted to make war possible against the Zionists who'd stolen the land from the Palestinians, with the massive backing of the Americans. The Palestinians were poor, and ill equipped. It was time to do something!"

His voice had become charged again. He paused again. His tone reverted to a gentle and reasonable argument.

"We have learned from you. What we are now proposing, pursuing, is an economic union. Because of the violent trauma of war and the hatred it left in so many hearts, it has taken you over 50 years to reach your present state. A union, inviolably linked, with common economic purpose and common political and philosophical policies, even a common currency, the Euro. We--," he gestured with his right hand slowly round the table, "propose to now commence working towards union by adopting the latter. A common Arab currency. We've already agreed it. It will be the precursor to an economic union and finally, a political union of all Arabs, Islamic states. We will introduce a new world order, and help all those poor states your western governments and banks have trapped, held and exploited in economic feudalism almost, if not slavery." He was sitting bolt upright now, with his hands clenched in fists, knuckles downwards, his body tense. He visibly relaxed only after what seemed like minutes but was probably only seconds. The intensity left his eyes, his body. He stopped looking straight ahead. He looked at JD and Fit. All eyes round the table followed his. His look softened even more. He opened his hands, palms upwards, towards them, in the universal gesture of friendship, openness.

"Of course, I, we, don't blame you personally," he laughed a sharp, raucous, slightly forced laugh.

JD and fit joined in. Fit tapped his heart.

"Thank God! I'm too old for this, General! I'm supposed to be playing golf on Saturday!"

The gathering collectively smiled and relaxed into a comfortable, conspiratorial chumminess.

JD was calculating how many Arabs there were, and how many notes would be required to produce a common currency. He couldn't believe the figures. They were huge. He kept calculating. They couldn't be right.

£$£

Chapter Thirteen

"General, this is a big project. Very big. You're talking of a combined population that must be 110m to 120m people."

"One hundred and twenty-one million to be exact, Mr. Dilworth and remember, we're ultimately aiming for the entire Arab world, that's another seven countries, another 50m-plus population. I'm not counting Egypt. They might join, if they can get the American teeth and claws out of their vital parts." There was contempt on his face momentarily. "But they have their own State Printing Works anyway, so they'd want to do their own. Morocco are the same, but they're mad anyway!" He, Osman and Saif chuckled at that. "So, the plant must be capable of a minimum currency production to satisfy and serve 121m people, and up to 175m to 180m. It must be centred here, and I really mean here." He held his hands out to each side, index fingers pointing. "You will supply all machinery and supplies, paper, ink, raw materials, human expertise. What do you think? I must say, you've been brought into our confidence so much, and witnessed so much even to date that we would take it very hard if you declined at this stage."

There was no doubting the hint of a veiled threat in the statement.

"Oh, and there is one other thing, amongst of course plenty of other things. We must have a line up and running to do our own currency, Libyan I mean, within three months preferably in two." There was a half-amused, half-challenging look in his eyes as he watched their reaction.

Fit raised his eyebrows. JD feigned serious concern, but he was thinking furiously whilst talking to stall for time.

"That's a tall order General, even though your indent is only small. And even for a population of 4m, you'd need the complete line. There are only two viable currency machine manufacturers in the market. They dominate the world. It would be extremely unusual if they had any machinery on the stocks, never mind a complete line. They normally just make to order. That keeps them busy as State Printing Works over-spend on a regular basis - they don't have to make a profit. Not like. . . "

"Mr. Dilworth," there was just a trace of an edge in his voice, "you are the experts. Members of the AIIF. That is why we've turned to you. It is imperative, I assure you, that we are printing our own currency within three months."

There was the briefest of silences, then JD said in a confident, almost jaunty voice, "No worries, General. We can do that. Nearer to two than one. Trust us!"

Fit shot him a glance of almost pure astonishment, but said nothing.

Belazir smiled, his black eyes gleaming. "I knew we could. We do. This is a good deal for all! Now, perhaps you'd like to address the meeting and give some general details of what's required. I know," he said quickly, "you really want time to plan such a plant properly, but you're great experts. You know roughly the population the plant will serve. And one major thing, do not worry about buildings or services. That is already taken care of, as you shall see. Just deal with the machinery configuration, and perhaps a few comments on human resources. Those are important, aren't they? And let my friends ask anything they wish. Anything!"

He was growing expansive now. It was obvious that in his mind, the deal was done, the plant planned, the money manufactured. Like sending a tank division in, thought JD. Conquer or die. Why not? He is a general .

JD already had in front of him the General Presentation.

"Gentlemen. This is a plan for a Libyan State Printing Works." He lied, but no-one would ever know. "This of course, is what we thought the General would require. We didn't, couldn't, know of your great enterprise. This, by the way, sounds eminently sensible and practicable to us given the required political will which you are obviously displaying." He was rather good at these presentations, he thought smugly, even though he mainly made it up as he went along. The result of catholic reading and supreme ego, boosted by ignorance, he was also honest enough to admit to himself. There was no visible response from the gathering. "So this plan will satisfy the General's first requirement, and form the basis for the future. When we return to the UK we will swiftly get our experts working on what's required for the multi-national plant. Now that's not just about populations. It's equally, if not more, affected by the structure of the denominations you use. For instance, and, not knowing we were attending this meeting with you all, we've not brought the relevant statistics so I'm relying on memory, here in Libya one Dinar is worth approximately two UK pounds, in Jordan it's almost one to one, but in the Lebanon there are about a thousand Lebanese pounds to a UK pound. It would obviously be more sensible to base your common currency on something like the Libyan or Jordanian Dinars, so you could avoid all the noughts and don't have to buy Italian calculators!" No one smiled except the Libyans and Osman. They obviously knew and dealt with the Italians. "But levels of currency denominations depend on levels of income, national wealth. I can't remember GNP for many countries, but one comparison does stick in mind, Libyas GNP per head is nearly 20 times that of Jordan. You are probably bankers or economists, General Belazir has not had time to introduce us personally yet, so you know better than me what that means. The lowest denomination of note, and the structure of the currency thereafter, must satisfy and suit your people."

He took a breath. He'd been gabbling a little. He felt he had to impress them.

"But even that's not so simple. Take my own country, the UK, not a poor one, and the richest, America. GNP per head in the UK is about $9000 U.S., it's $15000 in the

U.S.A. But the lowest British currency denomination is the £5 note, worth $8-plus, whilst the Americans have a $1 note, worth 0.62 UK pounds! One's got to be wrong, surely? Well, perhaps, certainly, the British lowest denomination note is inconvenient. It leads to everybody in the country walking round with great pockets full of heavy coins! The U.S. system is better. They even have a much better structure of high value notes, $100, $500 and $1000 notes. The British system finishes at £50. Unsatisfactory at the bottom and the top of the scale and, interestingly, the Americans have found that whilst their various sophisticated electronic, cash-card, charge card and smart-card systems represent 95% of all transactions by value. That percentage is reversed for volume," he stressed the words 'value' and 'volume, "of transactions, 95% are in cash."

He waited for this to sink in. It usually fascinated. It did again. He got the first questions. The ball was rolling. The morning passed swiftly. JD explained the equipment involved in the three distinct printing operations for a banknote, the Litho background printing, followed by Intaglio both sides, then the complex numbering. He went on through the examining and finishing operations, security, packing, storage. He spent a long time on the very specialist artists, designers, engravers, technicians required by a High Security Printing Works, vital to its success. Some, like the engravers, could be numbered on four or five pairs of hands throughout the world. Along with the Tasmanian devil, one of the rarest creatures on earth.

It was nearly 1.30 pm. With no change of temperature and no external view, and with it seeming impolite to look at his watch, JD was surprised when Belazir interrupted and said, "Gentlemen. We're being inhospitable! It is time to have some food and refreshments."

He spoke rapidly in Arabic to the waiters. They were soon drinking ice-cold lemonade and orange, an array of bowls filled with nuts, fruit, figs, dates appeared, which everyone immediately picked at. Some people were standing now, quietly conversing. Belazir and Osman engaged JD and Fit in conversation. Saif listened but hardly spoke.

Hot dishes appeared. Steaming rice, a bowl of couscous, and then a very large platter. Before the waiter placed it in the centre of the table Belazir said, "Gentlemen, in your honour. *One of* our specialities. Did the Turks teach us, or we them? Shish Kebab! Something we know you can eat. No sheep eyes, eh?" He was grinning mischievously. "Or sheep brains!" said Osman, and they both laughed together.

The lunch passed in stilted conversation. JD noticed not much communication went on between the Arabs. As if, he mused, they didn't really know each other well. It was odd.

After coffee came the pleasantries of parting. General Saif would escort all the guests back to Sirte, explained Belazir. He and General Osman had something they wanted to show JD and Fit and to discuss with the Englishmen, which was extremely relevant to the project. They waited until everyone had left. They stepped out into the huge "corridor".

"Please, follow me."

Belazir set off at a brisk pace. Osman was beside him. JD and Fit followed.

"One hell of a corridor" Fit muttered. JD nodded silently. No features manifested themselves. No one else was around. There was no echo. The compound the floor consisted of, which JD suspected was polymer, cushioned any sound like a thick carpet. They'd walked for fully 200 yards. They began to discern an end wall. Not that the lighting was dim, but the metallic walls and ceiling rather merged into one, as the sky does when sunless and grey over a Northern ocean. The end wall became clearer. Same metal, same faintly scored panel, same "key-hole". Belazir went through his unlocking procedure. The door slid open. It was the full width of the corridor. They stepped forward.

JD whistled softly, "General, very impressive. What a hall!"

They were standing at the end of a huge room. The

usual 25ft or so high, it was at least 600ft long and 300ft wide.

As if anticipating their thoughts, Belazir said simply, "It is 20,000 sq. mts. It is completely temperature controlled. It is the largest hall in the nuclear bunker. It is yours. To build our plant."

He turned and waved down the corridor from whence they'd come.

"You can see that you can bring almost any size of equipment into this hall. Before you ask," he raised a finger before his eyes, "you don't have to come through the reception hall. The elevators have sliding, opening ceilings. You just drop machinery in by hydraulic lifting gear. Or crane, as you call it. There is an identical elevator at the other end of this hall. You must have noticed two jets land? They're tucked away in their underground silos now. They travelled down here in that elevator. The Americans think this is just a desert airfield and a meeting place, probably for the Leader! You'll have noticed very few soldiers, guards, on the surface. Deliberate. But beneath ground," he swept his arm around, "we're very very well-guarded! You will learn more. Much more. You will have to, as you will work here with your people."

JD and Fit had no intention of "working here", but they knew what he meant.

They wandered around the perimeter of the huge room, talking animatedly. JD was explaining the rough layout of the three lines of equipment he was envisaging to cope with the volumes required. Belazir and Osman repeatedly asked questions about equipment, the supplies, and the personnel required. They had special offers in mind for the personnel. They were accustomed to accommodating foreign workers because of the oil industry. They had 500,000 such workers in their country now. "Gives the lie to sanctions, doesn't it?" Belazir said with a quizzical smile.

The day wore on. They made their way back to the elevator, back to the reception hall in the desert. They were a little surprised to see General Saif and the Governor of the

Bank waiting for them. They had coffee, and more discussions, and answered more questions. The Englishmen promised to have written briefings faxed to General Saif's office at the base within seven days, and to return for the detailed discussions within a couple of days of that. It would be necessary, then, JD said as tactfully as possible, to discuss finances. That was no problem, said Belazir. "Bring all your financial proposals, contracts. They will be dealt with immediately."

The discussions could not have gone any better. JD was counting the increased profit and imagining the glory he was going to be covered in, the enhancement of his corporate standing. Maybe he'd ask for a Jaguar Sovereign next time. Fit was counting his commission as a 'consultant.' He loved Bermuda for golf.

Late in the evening Belazir stopped the discussions.

"Gentlemen. We have to get you back to Nairobi: you're seeing the Chief tomorrow morning! We've made special arrangements. Your effects are on the plane. Let us go."

They all stood. Two cars awaited them. They drove across the dark airfield. There were lights ahead. They could make out the shape of a plane, a very large plane.

"By George, General, that's some plane!" Fit was laughing, "lllyushin 11-76 M.D. You're not supposed to have those! You're supposed to have Hercules!"

The General cackled.

"The Uzbekis ran out of money and sold us a couple. Fifteen were too many for them! And they build them at the Chlakov Plant in Tashkent! Sorry it's so big. It's all we had available at such short notice, and it's calling at Khartoum on the way back to collect a few things for us. It's not so comfortable, but you've only got about 4500 kms to go. ." He obviously thought that was quite funny.

They didn't. Not after even a short time on the jump seats in the huge empty plane. The crew spoke English, of course, as the international language of the air, but were very businesslike, and JD and Fit were in no mood to talk to anyone else. They'd enough to talk about.

"Fuck me, JD, this is big. Big! Where the hell are you going to get a line in less than three months? You conning them?"

Fit was as near to wide-eyed as you could get at 67 years old.

"No, I'm not, Fit. Think about it, our third line, we're not using it. This is a £60m-plus deal. Cash! At a 15% profit at least. That's more than two year's profit in one hit for us, plus profit on supplies each year which must make us more than a million every time. Talk about a licence to print money. Think about the implications."

They had over six hours to think of the implications and talk as the almost deafening drone of the engines relentlessly bored into their ears and minds. They were almost hoarse, deaf and dog-tired when they landed at Jomo Kenyatta Airport. They shook hands with the crew, trudged through the empty baggage hall and passport control as VIPs, then tumbled wearily into the hotel car sent to pick them up. They'd set off from Sirte just before 9 pm. and got to their rooms about 4 am. They didn't even bother to have the scotch they'd promised themselves as the vibrations of the Illyushin had loosened their teeth through the endless flight. They had to see the Chief in four hours or so.

As JD sank back on his pillow he thought of Vanessa, her back in the lovely white nightdress. He'd phone her as soon as he could tomorrow, no, today he meant. It was today. Then Mary came to see him, he could almost touch her, and then sleep.

£$£

Chapter Fourteen

The thick grey-blue smoke hung from the ceiling. It curled and threatened, with no way out through the locked windows. There was an acrid smell of burning. The chain on the door rattled as Fit knocked hard at exactly 8.20 am.. JD stubbed his almost black cigar out. An Antonio and Cleopatra Dark could make a normal-sized room uninhabitable in 30 minutes. He'd been up for nearly an hour and a half, showered, dressed, had a Seven-Up, a Coke and a block of chocolate from the mini-bar for breakfast, and written out the immediate action plan he was going to phone and fax back to the company to get all the balls rolling after he briefed the Chief about it. He put his jacket on and swept his document case up in one movement and opened the door.

"Bloody hell JD you'll set the smoke detectors off! You haven't even got a window open!"

He knew why. JD hated mosquitoes, and no one would tell him they didn't thrive at 5000ft in Nairobi as well as they did at sea level in Mombassa, and no one would convince him that they couldn't spread the Aids virus. They transferred blood from one person to another didn't they? Fit himself felt uncomfortable about that. It seemed logical to him too. Maybe the medics wouldn't admit it because it would cause panic. There were mosquitoes all over Europe now, too.

"I've neutralised it. Stop worrying. Ready?"

"Ready as I'll ever be."

Reception told them the Chief had set up the meeting in the main cottage. An excellent place for a meeting, they thought. The Cottages at the Norfolk are like fair-sized bungalows in the lovely gardens of the courtyard of the venerable old hotel, opened on Christmas Day, 1904. Very private.

The chauffeur who'd brought the Chief from the airport, and was waiting to take him back, opened the door to them. He was having a coffee in the reception room. He pointed them to the main lounge and, said the Chief was there but he was on the phone. At that moment the Chief saw them down the corridor and waved them in. He finished his conversation as they entered the room. It was obvious he was talking to HQ in London, where it was 11.30 am., because he terminated the conversation abruptly, but as always politely, by saying, "Dennis, I must go. The boys are here - yes I'll pass on your best wishes, and I must have a few minutes with them and be back at the airport by 9.30 am. I'll be in the office by around 10 am. tomorrow. Goodbye."

If he was going down to Malawi JD calculated that meant he'd sleep on the plane again that night in order to be in tomorrow.

He greeted them warmly as usual, as if they were friends as well as employees. He was adept at that. They, JD especially, might be a big fish at Daltons, but that was a very small pond as far as the company as a whole was concerned. Yet still he managed to make them feel as if they were crucial to the success of his operations.

JD opened by stressing they realised how tight for time he was, so he'd launch straight into their report on the Libyan meeting. The Chief made all the usual noises about how, no, his time was theirs, how important this was, how he'd flown specially here that morning for just that reason. Effortless stuff. JD made his briefing even more succinct. He knew that's what the Chief really wanted. JD had watched as many others, some running much bigger companies than his, had so enjoyed the sensation of being in the spotlight with the great man that they'd clung to the experience for as long as possible, slipping in all their favourite foibles, complaints, or evidence of how much they personally, or their companies, were doing for the company as a whole. His courtesy never wavered, but his attention did once he'd registered the essentials.

The Chief was surprised at the scale of the proposals. He'd genuinely thought it was just a plant for Libya. He did know many of those involved. He wasn't sure he agreed with their decision to launch a combined currency first, but that was their business - their money would be most welcome. He understood the need in such a delicate political and economic situation for complete secrecy. They could report directly to him, but as he was away so much he'd brief only Dennis, Director for African Affairs excluding Mining and Hotels to be their contact. No one else at FIQ would know what was happening. They could trust in Dennis' absolute discretion, and his secretary's. They both knew Megan.

JD went through his action plan, as it was composed so far. He'd had little time to finalise it as they'd only got in at 4 am. but all the essentials were detailed. They'd be telephoned and faxed to the company immediately after the meeting. Yes, he'd call the Chief at HQ tomorrow morning and give a more comprehensive up-date. What they would do today, before travelling home overnight, was put the following in train. Engravers would start duplicating the extant Libyan currency, there was no chance the incumbent supplier would supply them with dyes or plates - members of the AIIF did not do that, regardless of what the customer wanted. Wherever possible those materials remained possessions of the company according to contract. They'd destroy them on instruction. They'd never pass them on. Of course, security of origination was always cited as the reason, it would be horrific if they fell into the wrong hands etc.. Estimates for the first tranche of notes would be done, to enable the first contract the Libyans wanted, for their own currency, to be done immediately. Paper would be 'reserved'. JD explained that this was to enable the current suppliers to plan a 'slot' on their huge machines for a few weeks hence, with luck within four or five weeks. No, there was no need to sign a formal contract for that yet, that would be required in about two or three weeks. Ink would probably be in stock for the current supplier, and even if it wasn't, it wasn't a big job to produce the required amount because all the specs and formulations, which took up most time, had already been done. They would use the same supplier. A Board meeting would be called for tomorrow to brief the whole management team (it was a hands-on executive board of course) and from that meeting the planning by the Engineering and Production Directors would lead to the immediate dismantling of the third line which was to provide the initial equipment required for the project. Specific orders for the other equipment required would be prepared, and the suppliers notified tentatively so they could start making their own plans for manufacture or tell Daltons what they already had available on line or even in stock. They didn't like to admit it but they always did have stock available, it just sounded better if they said it was all being "made to order". Complete orders would be formally placed as soon as they got the contracts signed officially. The legal format of the contracts was already extent, drafted for their other "turn-key" operations. All orders would, of course, be placed in Dalton's name as a legitimate High Security Printing company and member of the AIIF, and as the company would do the shipping too, there was no need for even the manufacturers to know the destination of the equipment until commissioning of the new machinery had to be undertaken. In that way secrecy should be maintained for weeks, months. Shipping would be arranged by Daltons, it was another thing which could take place that very day. All machine dimensions and weights were known by the company due to all their own purchases and those they'd done for other State Printing Works. Within forty - eight hours everything would be in place. Forty-eight hours after that they'd be back in Libya with contracts to sign.

The Chief thought it was all, "Wonderful, How could you do so much in such a short time? Well done," etc. The usual bullshit, but still very gratifying to hear. Fit was impressed, though, genuinely. He sometimes forgot how bloody good JD could be. When they were away together he knew JD relaxed from his usual hyperactive state and treated it more or less like a reluctant holiday, even though he didn't like travelling, didn't like being away from "the ranch", didn't like being away from his family, even though when he was at home he hardly saw them! It lulled Fit into a familiar acceptance of "JD the MD." Probably only he ever saw him in that light. He could be a pain in the ass to everybody else with his perennial, draining optimism, drive, refusal to accept that anything couldn't be done, and usually in less time than was humanly possible. There was a limit to how much of that people could stand - certainly not 12 hours a day six days a week! There was sometimes a general feeling that he was better on a plane or in a bar a few thousand miles away from the factory. People could settle down to think their jobs through properly then - or did they just ease off.

They took their leave of the Chief. By the time they'd stopped in reception to ask the manager for the services of a secretary and fax for a couple of hours that morning they could see the car pulling away from the foot of the steps in the warm morning sun heading for the airport with the Chief.

Fit opted to go back to bed for a couple of hours, pouring scorn on the idea that you need less sleep as you get older and moaning that, for all he'd said apart from 'good morning,' there was no need for him to have been at the meeting. He knew, of course, that he had to be there. It was simply company protocol. JD kept an attractive young Kenyan secretary, highly-skilled on her word-processor linked to fax and accurate, but possessed of an accent that sometimes bewildered him, as did the young male switchboard operator he used, busy for the next two hours. He was happy when he was working, the adrenalin was pumping. When he'd finished, he pictured the starburst of activity in the office and he was even happier.

He met Fit at the pool at 11.30 and they had a swim for

half an hour, Fit languorously, JD like a demented ageing relay swimmer, or, as Fit said, "a turtle on Speed." After it, he had to get back in the water for a few minutes to cool down, which Fit thought was hilarious.

"Better than standing there with my stomach pulled in so much that I can't bloody breathe like you, poser," JD said sulkily. Then he insisted they got ready and went to the nearby Nairobi Safari Hotel, where he swore they served the finest chilli-burger in the world (called a 'Fireman's Burger' - "Brilliant marketing!" JD always said) and that's what they could have for breakfast, or 'brunch'.

Fit grumbled protestingly, but he did rather enjoy it there. He didn't rave about chilli burger and French fries for breakfast but when they did go there they always had a laugh. There were Americans in the lobby next to the restaurant in full kit, dressed like Errol Flynn playing a 'white hunter' in a Fortie's movie, waiting for limousines to take them 'on safari' to the National Park, just three miles outside of the city. The Kenyan receptionists and waiters and waitresses looked at them in bemusement. They walked that far home, living not far away from the Jomo Kenyatta Sports Stadium or the Jomo Kenyatta Airport right next to the National Park. (JD and Fit mused over brunch whether President Daniel Arap Moi or the new President ever thought of re-naming any of these things.)

After their long day the day before and their night flight they were both tired. But they were elated. They decided it was time to go 'on the lash' a little. They were on their way home. The job was done. There was nothing else to do until they were back in the land run by the Scots, Irish, Welsh, and Asians, where black people graced the finest football league in the world and enriched the popular culture, and where forty six million Englishmen faded quietly into the background, mowing their lawns, minding their own business, and resolving all the problems of the rest of the world in the local pub every night. The only civilised country left on earth, apart from New Zealand, they were sure. At least that's what they'd decided after a bottle of

Cabernet Sauvignon with brunch and a steady flow of scotch through the afternoon.

They tumbled out of the taxi at Jomo Kenyatta. There was the usual African shambles at the airport. Queues, crowds, officious blacks, arrogant whites, rich and patient Indians, overseen by a man who wore more medals and gold braid than Hero of the Soviet Union Marshall Zhukov in 1945, but who's earlobes had become detached from the rest of his ears through the constant using, since boyhood, of huge ear-rings, in the tradition of his Luo tribe. He dealt with this slight problem by hanging, decorously, the riven strand of flesh over the top of his ears on each side of his head. But this quite spoilt the effect of the grandiose uniform and gold braid when they occasionally fell out from under his peaked cap, modelled on those worn by the German Werhmacht in 1939, designed to terrorise "lesser races", and he had to tuck them back in every so often whilst still trying to look as stern and official as possible. Jesus, thought JD, Africa.

There was an escalator at the airport. In all the years he'd been coming he'd never seen it work. There was also the curious system whereby you had to hand in all your Kenyan currency, but you couldn't get your suitcase through manual baggage handling after that unless you paid the porter a small bribe and you had to conjure up twenty US dollars to buy an airport tax stamp. They wouldn't accept their own currency. Africa, bloody Africa, where the people were sweet, charming, courteous, crafty, cunning, grateful, resentful, vicious, caring, but casual about human life. Like the rest of the world.

JD always felt a strange mixture of guilt, pride, and protectiveness about these people, about all sub-Saharan Africans anyway. What he did know was that Europeans had screwed the continent up. The British were the best colonisers, but they still screwed it up. Mind you, he mused as they climbed the elevator that didn't work, they'd made a bloody mess of it themselves before they were colonised, and an even bigger one after de-colonisation. Poor, suffering, ordinary Africans. They deserved better.

They reached the BA Exec. Lounge on the first floor, towards the end of the Terminal, past all the shops. He remembered the embarrassment and frustration of the number of times he'd had to explain to Americans, especially in America, that, in English, the "first floor" was actually the second floor, the one above the "ground floor". He always did it with propriety pride in his native language, but he really agreed with the Americans. It was logical, wasn't it? Well, it would be. It was the clear-sighted logic of Britons freed from the traditions and constraints of their own society in their islands settled on new shores. And the Constitution. drafted mainly by Freemasons, a lot of them Ulstermen in Orange Lodges, enshrining Masonic free thought and freedom of religious belief and Deism. By the time he was passing the Duty Free shops he was pondering the stupidity of the Tories in deciding to make war on the American colonists. Why couldn't the Whigs have won the day? There could have been "Native Americans" at Westminster, adversarial debates in Washington instead of monologues or prearranged deals, the Queen could be the Non-Executive Secretary General of the United Nations. It was truly amazing the clarity and breadth of thought and vision just a little alcohol could induce.

They made it to the lounge. They were happy now. On their way home. No one could 'get 'em' now.

"Christ, what a result!" JD settled back. Fit got two coffees. Then he thought better of it and poured two Johnny Walkers as well. No point undoing all the good work of the afternoon.

"It's a bit of a coup, isn't it? You know, we've got to shout about it. It'll be great for the company, for the group even. When we get back we'll get on to the trade press. Probably even the Nationals. No, we can't do that. We'll get an Ad. Agency, or a PR company, that'll do it. We've got to make the maximum capital out of this."

"Hang on JD. They can't want any publicity. At least not yet anyway. Surely that will have to come from them?"

"Well, of course. But it's a hell of a deal. If we leave it to them, we'll take a back seat in the publicity. No, this is something that will have to come out eventually, so we should be prepared. It's got to be a professional PR job. We'll swear the agency to secrecy etc., but we'll have it all ready. We're going to get the maximum mileage out of this Fit."

Fit listened as JD rambled on, burbling with enthusiasm. He knew it was a big deal but JD didn't normally react like this. He was normally obsessed with secrecy, discretion. This time he was acting completely differently. He wondered why. JD knew why. He was contriving excuses to see her again. He couldn't lose her, shake her off, whatever he did. She lived with him, continuously and he'd found her again. He couldn't believe it.

£$£

Chapter Fifteen

He remembered it as if it was yesterday, but it was 15 years ago. He could hardly believe that either. He'd walked into the Advertising agency, a stolid old company in Manchester, Barnes and Staples, not far from the Midland Hotel, which he remembered his mother and his grandmother held in such awe because on one of their infrequent shopping expeditions there by train from Leeds they'd made it plain when he'd asked, impressed with the sheer stone Victorian grandeur of the building with a "doorman", that, "we couldn't afford a cup of coffee there". It wasn't far from Piccadilly Square in the old Northern city, rich and glorious during Victoria's reign through the sheer magnitude and success of the Lancashire cotton trade, which served an empire and devoured cotton from Egypt, Sudan and Savannah in the Southern States of America, everything they could grow. Barnes and Staples had been in existence since that time, starting as small printers. They served the Manchester Evening News, their sister paper The Manchester Guardian, and the local evening newspapers in all the towns surrounding their city, some of the largest towns in the country. In fact, the Manchester, or South Lancashire conurbation was the largest area of population outside Greater London in the British Isles, and in 1888 London was not only the capital of the world, it was the biggest city in the world. His own Yorkshire lagged not far behind, with Leeds, Bradford, prosperous through the wool trade, Sheffield that produced the finest steel in the world, Doncaster the heartland of coal.

He was sitting in the small reception area of the PR Agency, feeling smug because he had a half-a-million pound cheque in his briefcase. That was a lot of money then. They'd made the best presentation and they'd got the order, but the didn't know it. He was going to enjoy this. He immediately felt slightly foolish, pretentious, about his air of self-importance. Coming from his very modest working class background he wasn't really much of a bull-shitter.

The four senior executives were all female, all attractive, all intelligent women, all successful. They were arranged in order of seniority. They greeted him with that false cordiality that half a million pounds tends to imbue in a sales team. The bonhomie was tangible. He shook hands with the first three of them, teasing each with a comment half-suggesting they had won the order, joking with each in turn about their particular plans for the launch, unable to suppress his usual discomfort in the presence of women, even though he genuinely preferred their company to men. They were so much more civilised and superior.

Then she stepped forward, hand outstretched. She smiled, and the perfect beauty of her cheekbones and the lustre of her bright blue eyes, dancing with warmth, entranced him with an immediacy which shook him. She was a graceful figure, long dark hair, not quite black, falling over her shoulders and across her forehead. She looked simply superb in an off-white Chanel jacket with an unfussy but elegant blouse and black skirt. And he fell in love (or was it lust?) with her instantly. She was probably 5ft 6in, 5ft. 9in. in her elegant high-heeled court shoes.

"Hi, I'm Mary." He fell in love again, she came from the North-East and he thought that accent was irresistible. And he'd never seen eyes that spoke so lucidly before. God, he thought, it's The Madonna! He'd have given her the cheque there and then for just five minutes in her company alone.

He tried his best to be professional in a business-like way. He squared his shoulders, pulled his stomach in, and disgorged every piece of paper in his briefcase so as to appear as important as possible. But he was mesmerised by her.

The way she walked, her constant knowing humour, her accent, her smile, and her obvious intelligence. She knew her business. Very experienced.

They spent over an hour discussing the plans. He spent an hour thinking desperately how he could involve her personally. He did his best to be friendly and continuingly business-like with the others, but he couldn't keep his eyes, or his mind, off her. Everything she did was resonant with grace and beauty. He'd never met anyone else like her before. He watched her skirt sway against beautiful legs as she showed him her department. He felt guilty immediately when he thought of Vanessa and the kids, but there was something intoxicating about this woman. It had never happened to him before in his life. He had to see her, to meet her, outside of their working environment. As soon as possible. But why should she want to see him? He was no oil painting and knew it. In fact, he couldn't think of any reason why any woman could find him attractive or even "acceptable", certainly not someone like her. She was being friendly because of the contract, and that was about it. End of story.

He called her the next day. He used some spurious excuse to meet. He was embarrassed himself with the crap he came out with, but his pulse raced at the mere sound of her voice.

To his absolute astonishment she agreed to meet. She'd come to his office. When he'd done it, he wondered what the hell he was doing, but inwardly he knew the answer to that. He wanted this woman, this perfect woman who was really "out of his league," but he'd be satisfied, no, drenched with satiation, if he could have just a few more minutes of her time.

She came to see him a week later. She'd deliberately "dressed down" and was wearing a loose, long cardigan over a plain dress. The smart business suits were eschewed. She was happily married and knew what he was after. He didn't fool her, but he interested her. If he'd been her husband she'd have knocked him into shape. She smiled at the thought. Then she wondered why she'd thought it. He didn't need much "adjustment".

He was big, broad, with tousled dark hair that he

obviously took little care of and green-grey eyes. He dressed well. He looked as if his mother had scrubbed him clean before he left home and smelled as if she'd then immersed him in a bath of aftershave and eau de toilette. He had a keen sense of humour, and when he wasn't lusting he was grinning. He was courteous, but she instantly discerned, because she'd spent a career dealing mainly with men in her game, that it was a facade. He liked women. She was going to be extremely wary of him. He was obviously intelligent, but what most impressed her was his drive. She got the distinct impression, and it would apply to business or pleasure, that nothing would stop him getting what he wanted. But she knew he wasn't ruthless, instinctively. If getting what he wanted would hurt anyone or do them any harm she was certain he wouldn't do it. What an odd combination, she thought.

He was so different than her husband, Jonathan (it was funny he was called John as well). Jonathan was younger, better looking, tall and slim, better educated and much more qualified than him (and her, she mused), and therefore should have been in the sort of position he was in, shouldn't he? JD had told her he left school at 15. Jonathan had a degree from Durham University, one of the best. When she'd met him she'd felt somewhat in awe of him. His father was a dentist, her's a miner. He was so middle class and clever. He was a lovely man and she knew how lucky she was to have found and married him. She only half-admitted to herself that from the first moment, from almost their first intimate encounter, she began imperceptibly to take control. It had developed thus every hour, every day, every year, through their life together. He'd wanted to develop his career and become a University lecturer, but various things had conspired against him and he'd remained a primary school teacher. Sometimes she thought that was as well because she'd become so pre-occupied with her own work.

She became a Senior Partner in one of the North's leading PR and Ad. Agencies. He remained slim, good-looking, a loving father and a man deeply interested in the environment. He was a good man and she loved him.

So why on earth was she interested in meeting this man? He could only disrupt her life, and she was sure he would do if he got the chance, without hesitation! But there was something about him. There was a latent threat there, which intrigued and excited her a little. He added just a little more "joi de vivre" to her days, perhaps. She could imagine him laughing if she ever told him any of these thoughts, which she wouldn't of course. She hardly knew him.

She also wondered, only fleetingly, what he'd be like making love.

He kissed her on both cheeks as he greeted her, and gripped the top of both of her arms as he locked her into eye contact, which then never wavered. He told her how lovely her necklace and pendant were, how smart she looked, and how much he appreciated her taking the time to come to meet him. She could sense that innate drive behind the polite facade. Well, JD, what happens next? Not what you think!

She looked just as lovely. She could have worn a boiler suit and looked as good, he thought.

They went to lunch at the most fashionable restaurant he could think of. He wanted to impress her. He drove her there, and tried to sound business-like and professional again. But she had legs to match her eyes. The loose cardigan couldn't disguise the slim firm elegance of her figure, nor the long black skirts those perfect legs. She sat demurely but intelligently in the passenger seat of his Jaguar and they exchanged banal pleasantries, each one selected by him to display his intellectual profundity on a wide range of subjects, desperate to impress her with that too, as they drove to the exclusive impressive country club he'd chosen. She didn't seem impressed at all.

When they were shown into the dining room, she felt a little under-dressed. All the other diners were men in smart business suits or female executives in the sort of suits she normally wore for business herself, or secretaries in attractive cocktail-type dresses who were having lunch with their bosses on the company's account and who had dressed for the occasion for other reasons. She wished she'd put something a little more glamorous on, but the last thing she wanted to do was encourage him. She instinctively knew that he was fascinated by her. 'God knows why,' she thought. She also remembered that she hadn't taken the lamb out of the freezer for tonight's dinner.

She couldn't know that he was watching her and thinking that she would grace any dining room anywhere in the world (and he'd been to most places) regardless of what she was wearing. There weren't many truly beautiful women in the world. She was one of them. What enhanced her beauty was that she seemed completely unaware of it. It had never occurred to her that she could toy with men in the way that a potter could mould his clay (that's Omar Khayam, he thought). She simply didn't realise the power she had. She'd never used it, other than minimally, and innocently, of course, in her business career. She was, in every sense, a "decent" woman, a decent person. It seemed impossible to believe she was unaware of her power, but she obviously was.

She had two children, just a little younger than his own. He was nearly five years older.

They became lovers two weeks later. Never in his life did he think this could happen to him. She felt the same and he could not get out of his mind the pure astonishment of why she'd have an affair with him. With her looks and intelligence, she could have had anyone she wanted.

The first time they met as lovers, in the Queens' Hotel in the old Roman city of Chester, one of the 19th Century North-Western Railway hotels, with it's faded elegance enveloping them, he'd cleaned his teeth three times and had a shower twice after exercising twice to enhance the not-perfect state of his muscles, before meeting her in the bar.

This time she was dressed immaculately, with a short fur coat over a lovely black dress. They'd had one quick drink in the bar, he'd rudely terminated a conversation he'd been having with a nice chap he'd met before she'd arrived, and then they went to "their" room. He gave her a Cinzano and lemonade, her drink, and decided to tell her the truth in a wry tone about how he'd been exercising in a failed attempt to look better. She smiled that smile that lit up her face and any room she was in and told him she'd gone through a "mirror test" before setting out and decided she had "no boobs" so it would be better to tell him before she undressed. It broke the ice between them and they laughed together at themselves as they drank the Cinzano, kissed gently and prepared to make love.

He was 33, she 29, both had been married for a long time and had children, both were accustomed to regularly making love.

But his hand trembled as he slipped it under her arm and reached for the zip at the base of her graceful neck, and he felt her hands around his waist grip a little tighter and her body stiffen slightly as if she was wondering whether this was really what she wanted to do, whether she wanted to take the risks, to her marriage and the husband she genuinely loved and the children she worshipped. Or, he thought, the risk any woman takes when she gives herself to a man, how could she know what his desires, his sex drives, were.

Her gaze, straight into his eyes, remained steady though, and her soul flowed through them softly to his. He kissed her to reassure her as he slipped the dress off her shoulders.

She was wearing white lingerie. He took her under-skirt off, to see the white suspender belt and panties, pale tan stockings. She was breath taking. He felt as if he was in the presence of something that transcended normal experience, as if he was looking at a Rembrandt or a Rosetti. Bloody hell he thought. I'm losing it! But his body was trembling now, ever so slightly, like "butterflies in the stomach" all over him. He sat her down on the bed, and stripped off, un-embarrassed.

She started to take her high-heeled shoes off.

"Don't, please," he said, "you look fabulous in them and I'd like to make love to you with them on."

He said it seriously, with no hint of salaciousness. He meant it, she concluded. She'd never done that before. It was only the first of many other things she'd never done before.

She inclined her head and smiled. She took her hands from the straps of her shoes and reached out for his hands and pulled him gently onto her. They both knew what they were doing, what they were risking, but he wanted her so much, so completely, and he was again astonished that she seemed to want him.

He ranged over every aspect of her body and she objected to nothing. Every part of her tasted as sweet, felt as welcoming. Within one hour they both knew there was absolutely nothing they couldn't do with one another.

Neither of them had ever experienced anything like it before. He took her to the bathroom. They weren't sure what to say to each other. They just knew they had to meet again, very soon.

He kissed her goodnight as she went to her husband and family. They looked at each other, and they both knew that their "affair" was all it would ever be. They'd invested too much in the rest of their lives. They both wondered what life would have held in store for them if they'd met earlier, younger.

It didn't stop her being an erotic dream for him, and for the first time in his life he stopped thinking about women in a predatory way (though strangely, he'd never thought of Vanessa that way).

He totally accepted her as a person. He admired her. He respected her. In a different way to his wife, he realised with a shock, he loved her.

For her, he was her "Seychelles," somewhere to flee to when all else oppressed her, somewhere charming, exotic and erotic, where she was a friend, an object of worship, like a goddess even. She always laughed at the last thought. How many goddesses spent so much time trying to de-scale their kettles every Friday? She loved the immediate warmth and welcome she received from him, the constant threat and thrill of sexual misbehaviour, the solace and support he afforded her and the protective tenderness of his arms as they lay together and sometimes did . . . . nothing.

What she didn't know was how much he loved her. He couldn't believe it. In his business life, his private life, he was quietly confident about everything, he had views about everything, he knew a lot about many things, from philosophy to religion to business to art to Freemasonry. He was putting together, as he grew older, he told himself, the "secrets of the universe" and hoped he'd have worked it all out by the time he died. But he didn't know about her. What made her tick. He loved Vanessa, his wife, but he wanted her. For the first time in his life he wasn't in control, wasn't on the commanding heights.

Once, after they'd made love every week for six months, they told each other they were in love. She lay beside him in black and said simply, "JD. I think I've fallen in love with you". He lay still and satisfied with her head nestled under his chin.

"Yes. I feel the same. But you don't know me. All my faults, short temper, smoke too much, drink too much, eat too much, want too much."

She lifted her leg until it rested across his hips and abdomen and slipped the black silk panties from around her left ankle and over her shoe and put all four of her fingers over his mouth. He kissed them and gently sucked the middle finger.

"Shut up," she said, in that delicious accent, "don't you think I know what your faults are? Hasn't it occurred to you that I might love you in spite of them? Maybe because of them, you goober nickel. I'm not completely stupid."

A wonderful Mary understatement. She was the last person in the world he'd call stupid.

"Darling, you're not stupid at all. I ... I," he always stammered just a little when he was nervous, "I just know what's wrong with me, and I know you don't know what's wrong with me and…"

"JD, that sounded like Groucho Marx, 'the first person

in the first instant is responsible for the second person in the second instant.'" It was an old film they'd lay and laughed at in their hotel room when they'd met for the sixth time. That's not what Groucho had said, but he understood what she was driving at.

He laughed. When he did it came from deep within his soul.

"Oh Lady, Mrs Matthews, Mary, Mother of God," he said, "I know, I know. But you know what the problem is. How could we tell them, and the kids? You're the same. We're in the same boat."

And then they both settled back into their own worlds, gently stroking each other. They never mentioned it to each other again. But they made love regularly every week for two years, and the experience was always tenderly erotic, and what they did together released them from the shackles of ordinary life.

Then he was head hunted and moved to Paris by his new company (15 years now. Christ, he thought) to a small office on the Avenue Hoch just below the Hotel Royal Monceau and not 200 yards from the Arc de Triomph. He tried to phone her. She was always out with clients. The two girls who manned the switchboard, straightforward Manchester girls, were beginning to get very suspicious. They liked her. They knew her husband. She couldn't be having an affair. The caller was obviously a pest, they would do nothing to help him. He had to stop calling. They had never been anything but discreet in their relationship. She called once. His secretary answered in French, which unnerved her then slipped into charming but fractured English. Mary was blushing 300 miles away in Manchester. She had the peculiar feeling that the Secretary knew.

Then she was offered a third more salary to move to the CLW Agency in Leeds. Her husband wasn't doing that well. They needed the money. She took it. He moved to a temporary office in Rennes. The girls on the switchboard were loyally defensive and refused to say anything but "Mrs Mary Matthews has left the company. Sorry," when he called again as soon as he'd settled in. They certainly weren't going to give “the pest” her new number or address. They were sorry she'd gone. She was a lovely person and a good boss and she inspired and amused them in the way she handled men.

She didn't know where the hell he was, the telephone number she had simply didn't exist anymore and she couldn't understand a word of the recorded message from the French PT and T. Anyway, it was probably better if they weren't in touch. They could only hurt other people and each other if they carried on. She didn't want to hurt anyone.

It was a 15-year hiatus. He thought about her every day, a few times a day; with the practicality the female of the species is blessed with she thought about him perhaps once a month. He missed her desperately, she missed him a little, but she had a good husband who she loved and she'd never done anything like that before, and she wouldn't again. She was shocked at her behaviour when she was with him, a little colour rose in her cheeks even when she was alone when she thought of what she'd done, allowed him to do, what they'd done together. At night, sometimes, long after her husband had gone to sleep, she lay back, relaxed and enjoyed it again without embarrassment, the memories washing over her and through her. At these intimate secret moments the desire to call him, find him, became almost palpable. She never did. She never would. Her memories shocked her enough. She couldn't conceive of a reprise of all that. God, she was 43 now.

Then he called her.

£$£

Chapter Sixteen

They were all tired, drained. Governor Celal Dajani spoke first.

"They bought it!"

His voice manifested the exultation, relief, satisfaction they all felt, glowing through their tiredness like St Elmo's fire.

They were all, except Osman, drinking vodka and mineral water. None of their subordinates could smell that. It looked like water, so they looked like Muslims.

Belazir lay back on the chair, tunic unbuttoned like everyone else's. His waist corset didn't hold his extra weight in. It hung over his belt like snow on the edge of the roof of a cottage on a tree Christmas card. He spoke slowly, deliberately.

"They did. Yes. I think they did. That's the crucial first step. The biggest."

Saif looked a little awkward, he said hesitantly, "Are you sure you should have shown them that much of the base'. Everything, you did. Can we not . . .?"

"Mahmoud, they're going to build the bloody plant . . . here," he jabbed his finger groundwards, "they have to know!"

Belazir's tiredness fuelled his exasperation, but Mahmoud's security obsession always irritated him, and sparked him into life. It was the irritation of familiarity. He knew what was coming even before Mahmoud said it. It annoyed him when he did say it, when he stated the obvious, when he was negative, security-obsessed. It annoyed him even more before he said it.

Dajani cut in, he sympathised with the Security Chief.

"Look Youssef, we do have to be careful. And think about what happens now. They'll want a percentage with order. For that first line if it's theirs they'll want more. Then they're bound to go straight to order the machinery for the other lines. That's the longest lead-time. I've got to cover it. It's not a problem really, as Governor, but I need, I must have, the paperwork, and the facts and…"

Belazir was just keeping his temper in check now.

"Celal, don't worry. You were always the worrier! At school, you always thought the Egyptians, the Israelis, the Syrians, were going to interfere in our plans. What plans! We were at the English School in Beirut, for Christ's sake! We were only going out with Christian girls, the easiest lays! Relax. I'll run Libya, well, this bit anyway, or any other bit I choose to concentrate on, you run the economy, and Mahmoud is in charge of all internal security! For the love of God, what can go wrong? We'll pull it off easily. It will work. Believe me. Believe me."

"Yes, yes, I know, I know. But I've got to get the paperwork moving. Soon, now, today." Dajani was serious. Belazir could tell. He'd known him for almost a lifetime. His tone softened, he was persuasive now.

"Celal, you know I've promised you your position as Governor will not, repeat not, be jeopardised. You've got just two months, less probably, where you're faced with the most, the faintest, of risks, and that's covered. Think of it. You've transferred 6m Libyan Dinars to here, our most secure base, from the bank, physically. It's under Mahmoud's protection as Head of Internal Security. It couldn't be safer. It's here because, ostensibly, it's to finance covert operations, which Sadiq is carrying out in Chad for us. It'll be flown to him directly in Khartoum, by Mahmoud's people. But it's covered! It's out of my military budget. Sadiq invoices me. I authorise payment, countersigned by you and Mahmoud. Sadiq gets the money. He, as Head of the Finance Committee of the National Salvation Revolutionary Council, authorises its payment to Daltons in dollars, or pounds, or euros, whatever, it doesn't matter, Good God, the Bank of Sudan are only handling the money for us. Not a cent comes from Sudan's own accounts, and they love Libyan Dinars, a strong currency. Sadiq has all that set up. It's just a paper transaction. They're just a clearing house. That pays for the Dalton's first line, they said it was less than £10m. What we transfer to Sadiq is worth £12m. That's enough to pay for everything else, paper, plates, labour, ink, and the lot. Shipping too. Within two months Daltons have their first line set up and working. You give them the numbering scheme to duplicate the 6mLD. They produce that much "genuine" Libyan currency, and it is genuine! In less than a week! The money is replaced. The paperwork is immediately destroyed. There's no longer a need for it, the money is still physically there! You can send it back to Tarabulus if you want, if it will make you feel better. That's the only period you'd be even faintly exposed, and then only if the Leader ordered a snap audit. That's something he's never, ever done. The covert ops. are authorised anyway, so if he did by some remote chance, and the money had gone, we'd still have the paperwork. We'll keep that 'till it's replaced, so you're completely covered anyway. There's no way anyone can ever know whether Sadiq has actually spent the money that way. He has no intention of doing so of course, eh Sadiq?"

"Of course not. It's for a greater cause." His tone was just bordering on sarcastic.

"We'll just have to trust he doesn't pocket the money and head for Thailand!" Belazir laughed and winked at Osman. "After that, the following payments to Daltons are made as the other notes are printed, to genuine numbering schemes we'll get, and delivered directly to Sadiq again by Mahmoud. You're not even involved. The only paperwork required then is at Sadiq's end. He's already set that up, as I've said. And as it doesn't cost Sudan anything they'll not have any desire to look into it. They'll just pay Daltons on our behalf, take a handling commission to earn themselves a bit of money and if anyone is the least bit curious Sadiq is only helping a fellow Islamic state to circumvent appallingly unfair U.N. sanctions forced through by the Americans. A clearing house. We'll get the next two lines, and raw materials, and pay for the people, the engravers and that crowd in the same way, from Khartoum in dollars or pounds or whatever we print. It's foolproof! It couldn't be easier. They're just smudges of ink on paper, and they're genuine! That's the great secret. You'll have to get over your banker's reverence for scraps of paper Celal! Happy again? No risk, Celal, no risk."

He stared at the Governor intently, with a fixed, expectant smile. Celal Dajani nodded slowly. He brightened up visibly, tension ebbing from his body.

It was left to Osman to remind them.

"To use the phrase which is a reference to the centre of their philosophical and religious life, and which shows how stupid they are, then we'll crucify them."

He smiled sardonically. Belazir grinned. The others smiled warily. There was a heavy silence now.

Only Osman didn't have the look of a thief, a criminal, in his eyes. They were hard with contempt. Disturbing to anyone who cared to look into them.

£$£

Chapter Seventeen

As usual, they enjoyed their overnight journey home. As soon as they got on the BA flight they felt that they were at home, back in civilisation. No-one was begging, no-one was living in the land of the permanently white-eyed bemused, no-one was stamping every bit of paper in sight, no-one stared mutely until money was handed over for services paid for anyway. They'd been upgraded to First Class from Business. They were both long-standing Exec. Club Gold Cardholders. It was full as usual. Full of politicians paid for by poor peasants who couldn't get a seat on a bus. Nobody travels more than African politicians, and their families and "secretaries". In countries where there is a national carrier it's usually the reason the airline goes bust. No-one pays at all in First Class! Strangely, through all such travel, the politicians never seemed to learn anything useful for their countries anyway. But they were very familiar with European banking systems.

By the time they were climbing through the thin Rift Valley air over the clearly visible Wildebeest trails which still skirt the airport, (Wildebeest are unimpressed by temporary human alterations to the landscape) they were both clutching, fondly, two very large Johnny Walker Black Label scotches. They were on first name terms with the steward and stewardess, with whom they'd made arrangements for a regular supply of the wine of the Caledonians while they watched their videos. After their meal they'd switch to Cognac to settle their stomachs, then they'd sleep to Terminal Four. They always stuck to the same pattern. It always worked and they could always sleep. They were surprised when people told them they couldn't sleep on planes. Why, they had no trouble.

Telephone calls to Vanessa and Veronica from the hotel solved their drive from the airport problems. Fit would then take at least two or three days off, "To recuperate at my age." JD would shower, have a couple of hours in bed, with or without Ness, then appear at the plant late morning like Moses from Mount Sinaii.

They were both seasoned travellers. When they stepped out of customs to scan the usual phalanx of eager, worried, disinterested or neurotic faces waiting to meet the home comers, or newcomers, or "we're-here-to-do-you-a-favour-comers", no one would have suspected they'd spent the night mainly "on the lash". Apart from them, of course. They didn't quite feel like jogging to their cars. But they'd washed, shaved, cleaned their teeth with the BA First Class toothpaste, eschewed the BA First Class after-shave in favour of their own, wiped the crumbs from their breakfast rolls from their shirts and trousers and as they strolled, allowing the inexperienced travellers to notice they were strolling, out into the Arrivals Hall, they both automatically assumed the look of jaunty laughing-at-the-world self-mocking disdain they felt it smart to assume.

Fit spotted the girls almost immediately. They'd obviously met and had been chatting animatedly, just occasionally glancing towards Customs to see if "the boys" had actually made it back on the flight (for obvious security reasons, airlines will tell all enquirers what time the flights are expected, but never reveal who is or isn't on board). JD caught Vanessa's eye, grinned and waved. She smiled that smile and the laughter in her eyes seemed to radiate like a wave of energy towards him, good humour laced with mockery and challenge. He waved at Veronica. It struck him again, with the same shock, that she was looking so much like a woman approaching seventy. She was two years older than Fit. She retained the delicate, elegant, classical beauty of her younger years, but now it had taken on the haunt of fragility. He never thought of Fit like that. He seemed, to be forever marooned in his mid-fifties, festooned with Golf Club Captaincies, old flames who met him in Inter-Continentals in odd capitals, and young secretaries who he gave "advice" to.

Vanessa looked gorgeous. She was wearing the long grey coat with the black velvet collar, her hair was casually immaculate, her make-up perfect because it was undetectable, her legs, which he'd wanted photographed and framed for his office wall "like a Rembrandt" (she'd told him to bugger off) were enticing in the "Nearly-black" stockings she favoured. She was (deliberately, he thought) wearing her black 3in. stilettos with small gold butterfly buckles. She looked, as he'd often told her, like every 20-year-old boy's dream of the fabulous mature woman who'd introduce him to 'grown-up sex'. She always responded dryly that that's what she thought she was doing every time she got him to bed fit, fed, sober, showered, and untangled from a telephone.

"Ness, thanks. You look fabulous. How're the kids?" He embraced her warmly. He took Veronicas hand and kissed her on the cheek. "Hi, Ronni, nice to see you. How's the world treating you?"

They walked to the car park together, bade their farewells, arranged to meet for an Indian meal "sometime soon", and then headed home in their own cars. Their friendship transcended business. Over the years they'd become very close. JD's kids thought of Fit and Ronni as relations. No, more like close friends they could turn to at any time. JD and Ness had named them in their wills as surrogate parents for the kids until they reached the age of majority. They were so close.

"I've missed you, Ness. Lovely to see you."

"I always miss you. Do you want breakfast? I can tell you've had Glenmorange for breakfast."

"Johnny Walker, actually, darling. You bugger! I've used half a bottle of breath spray!"

They both laughed and he put his hand on her thigh, and she immediately accommodated him by shifting her left leg sideways to allow the coat to fall from her knee, allowing him to stroke the smooth flesh above her stocking. It was useful driving an automatic with no requirement for left-leg involvement. He was obviously aroused, and he marvelled at how great, how warm she was. So, why was he behaving like such a prat and still thinking about wanting, Mary? He didn't want to think about it. He switched BBC Radio Four News on, he hadn't heard it for two days. She hit the M25 at just over 100 mph.

He always missed milk - cold, fresh milk with his breakfast cereal. That's what he had. She took her coat off and he felt 18 again. She told him he needed a shower and a couple of hours sleep, she'd wake him at 9.30 am. He'd then have an hour or so to "reward" her for the long drive. He immediately said he didn't need sleep.

"Stop being a brave little trooper. Sleep, then be a bravura big trooper, you know it makes sense!"

She was mocking, teasing, but serious, simultaneously.

"If I go to bed I'll make pyramids with the Duvet."

"I'll wake you at 9.30 and I'll loot the pharaoh's tomb. And I want riches beyond my dreams. . ."

He went to sleep loving her, lusting after her, and, unusually after so long a marriage, liking her. Not many men could say they still "liked" their wives, if they ever did. It's not usually a high priority when young people are getting married, and yet it should be the number one. He was thinking deeply about this and was on the very brink of a profound conclusion about it which would help all young couples who were going to get married or live together. He would write it down as soon as he'd had a couple of hour's sleep. Then his body slept, but his mind hovered on the edge of consciousness and sleep, watching him and the room and planning things and feeling the touch of the long dark hair on his face as Mary and her Chanel No. 5 filled his senses . . . .

£$£

Chapter Eighteen

Mary sat for a long time after hearing John Dilworth's voice for the first time in 16 years. Curiously, she felt like she'd done in 1996 after the IRA had blown up the heart of Manchester, the Arndale Shopping Centre. Some old friends she'd worked with there called her in Leeds to tell her it had happened. She'd then spent a morning phoning frantically round to other old friends to make sure they were all right, and still had their legs, arms, hair, ears, eyes, or a spleen.

She'd trembled inside then. Uncontrollably. She was doing so now. She was also breathing quickly, shallowly, her throat was constricted and she was wet, she instinctively stroked herself. Her hand seemed like his, she drew it away quickly, glancing round like a startled gazelle as if someone could be hiding in her office. She told herself how stupid she was being, leaned back in her large comfortable swivel chair, nestled her hands between her legs and closed her eyes.

God, what was it about him? She didn't know. She'd never been attracted to, affected by anyone like that before. She didn't want to be. Perhaps she wouldn't mind if it was just sex. Sexual attraction. Yes, just desire, lust. But was it? It had to be. She wanted him. She became wanton when she thought about him, when she was with him. God knows why. He was OK, but no oil painting; he was affluent, but not rich; he was intelligent, but no intellectual. But it didn't matter what he was. She wanted him and she knew he wanted her, anywhere, anytime, any way and any way was good enough for her. In fact, she wanted him, it, every way.

She was shocked at her thoughts. What was she? What had she become? One phone call. No, no, wait. What she'd become was a decent, affectionate, equal, successful, contributing wife and mother. Sex, OK. But controlled, within the bounds of decency, normality. With him, decency and normality had no place. The more indecent, perhaps even abnormal, the better. No, with him there was no such thing as indecent, abnormal. They were meaningless words. She winced at her own thoughts. Her mind was filled with him. Time didn't matter. She couldn't do anything else. Her office contracted into a world filled with him and her.

She was alone, but she was blushing. She was very wet, and she'd no spare panties. She self-consciously slipped them off to dry, where? She stuffed them under the top of the largest radiator with its wooden surround. She'd do without them all the rest of the afternoon. She had a long, demure dress on, navy blue with white piping, which looked as if she'd also have on something as secure under it, such as a full set of eminently stolid navy underclothes like she wore at school. Or so she hoped and prayed. She was almost angry with herself. This was pathetic. It was stupid. She started thinking about advertising and PR with a furious intensity so she didn't get wetter. She refused to think about anything else. She made phone calls she didn't have to make, talked to people in her brightest, most vivacious voice, arranged meetings she didn't have to have, asked for campaign briefings she didn't need.

And then she started to think. What if the girls came in, as they often did before going home, and they were all having a coffee, and they wouldn't leave and Evelyn insisted on staying while she locked up, and walking to the car with her? How could she retrieve her panties? Lord, why had she taken them off? What was she thinking about? And if she left them there, and she got home, and Jonathan was there and the house was empty and just for once he was amorous and excited by her, how was she going to explain why she had no panties on…? Oh God, It was all happening again. And she'd only spoken to him on a telephone! She couldn't believe it! At her age, with her experience, wouldn't you think she could handle it? She'd get them now. But, no. She couldn't risk it. Anyone might come in. It was mid-afternoon. She operated an "open-door" management policy. They wouldn't even knock. She'd just die with embarrassment. And they were harder to get back on, discreetly, than to get off. Oh God.

But, beneath the slight flush of the cheek, the roller-coaster tummy, in spite of the internal mechanism operating independently on automatic pilot wetting the top of her thighs, the slight tremor of the hands and legs, the artificial brightness of the eyes, beneath it all, there was a desire, a longing, a feminine lust, "unbridled", which "feminines" weren't supposed to have. Except in novels which kept on about it but then left you hanging, waiting for "it" to happen, she thought.

She silently tongue-lashed herself. "Mary, get a bloody grip," She could hear her Da's voice. What would he think? What would her mother think?

She made a mental note to always have a pair of clean black pure cotton or silk panties in her bottom desk drawer, behind the stacks of Dictaphone tapes. She made another mental note to buy boxes of panty-liners, the thicker and more absorbent the better. She'd carry them in her briefcase and handbag. She thought, ruefully, I'm making so many bloody mental notes it's like compiling one of those "Aids" kits for the overseas traveller, but hers was a "JD-kit", no, a "Dil-kit". Why had the bastard phoned? He must have had dozens of women in the past 16 years. Why did he have to phone? She was doing all right. She was doing fine, in fact.

The girls didn't come in. But Evelyn did, to walk to the car with her. She snatched her panties on the way out only after pretending, when they were waiting for the lift, that she'd left her desk unlocked and had to go back. She stuffed them in her handbag, as if she was stealing the office "float", and ran back red-faced to face Evelyn. Guilt flooded through her as it had done when she was 17 and she'd had her first surprising evening with her first boyfriend, who her mother liked, and she was trying to wash her panties in the bathroom before putting them in the wash. It had seemed like a logistical nightmare then, furtively locking the door and secretly drying them, and here she was again, going through the same emotions, twenty-seven years, a marriage, a successful career and two children later. Oh dear, Mary Matthews . . . she could tell she wasn't cut out to be a confidence trickster.

As she drove home, in her smart Rover air-conditioned saloon, after the surprise, after the sexual thrill, after the physical manifestations of pure lust, she thought, and reflected. She was steadying now. She'd stop a few minutes away from home and put her panties back on, she'd perfume herself. Jonathan would suspect nothing, the girls would know nothing, even if they were home. Only she would be left with her thoughts. A successful career woman. Someone with an undeniable record of success in the business behind her. A confident and attractive woman, who wasn't afraid to use her attractiveness to achieve her ends, but only within the bounds of decency. All who knew her knew instinctively that they had to ultimately respect her, be they male or female. She was experienced and confident enough to put all that into context, perspective. She'd been surprised, and naively shocked, by the Lesbian interest, but soon learned how to handle it. Part of the job. Now she wasn't confident. She didn't know herself what she was going to do. She knew what she should do. She hated him for disrupting her life again. No she didn't, he was different. She didn't know why. She certainly wasn't a believer in God-made (whatever that meant) matches, nor was she even capable of stupid besottedness. She almost refused to acknowledge it, but she had to admit, only ever to herself, that the "chemistry" between them meant that a couple of minutes with him inside her were worth a couple of hours of anyone else, even Jonathan. That was an awful thing to think. Anyone else? What was she talking about. There had only been two others, before Jonathan! Just kids, like her. Just growing up, fumbling towards experience. Then him, afterwards.

She pulled into the car park of the Holiday Inn, went to the Ladies room, did her hair, touched up her eyebrows then went into a cubicle to put her panties back on, wrinkling her nose in amusement at the state of them. Outside, back in front of the mirror, she stared at herself. She actually laughed out loud, glad there was no one else in the room. She leaned on the sink and looked into her own eyes. Mary Matthews, you are behaving like a silly adolescent! What on earth do you think you're doing? Get home to your husband, immediately. More important, girl, get a grip!

She drove the rest of the way home with a curious melange of feelings: elated and deflated, aroused and guilty, excited and excuse-ridden, lecturing herself severely on morality, and practicality, on the futility of it. But wanting it to happen. As soon as possible. She had to make it happen. Perhaps just once more.

She hoped Jonathan was engrossed in pollution in the North Sea, or nuclear disposal in the Irish Sea, or the survival of the Scottish Otter, anything. She needed a few more hours to herself. Or did she need Jonathan, as a sort of palliative, a safe substitute? Should she seduce Jonathan? Christ, she'd forgotten how! He'd be astonished! She didn't know. Her mind was full. It was overcrowded, like a Japanese train. She needed an official "pusher" to get everything in.

But most of all, she wanted to see him again. She'd only ever once told him she loved him.

£$£

Chapter Nineteen

It was 10.45 am. He had to get into work. He had to phone the Chief and anyway he was raring to get stuck in and get things moving. His mind was brimming with organisational plans. He wanted everything in place in the next 48 hours. Then back to Belazir.

They showered together and Ness tormented him mercilessly. She kept turning the heat up, she loved a hot, hot shower. He kept leaping out, yelping, and drenching the bathroom floor. She called him a wimp, and laughed at him as he stood there pleading with her to turn the temperature down.

"You look like one of the Three Stooges!" she said as his hair plastered down on his head "Or one of the Beatles in 1964. Yes, an ageing, greying Beatle!"

He wrapped her in a hot thick towel, and told her he had to get going. She told him all his clothes were laid out and pressed. She was wonderful, he said. Then he was off.

She'd loved the morning. She'd waited for him. She knew she always would. She loved to envelope him. She needed that physical closeness. She didn't mind too much if sometimes, when he was tired, it was just like cuddling a hot water bottle.

She watched him pull out of the drive. She was elated because he was elated. He'd told her all he could about the deal as always. She was a "touchstone" for him when it came to important business things, but for most of the time he never bothered her with details of work. He thought it would bore, or worry her. It never did. She wished he would talk to her more about the mundane times. She wanted to help him, but he wasn't like her. She just had to talk everything that bothered her out. It was therapeutic for her. He couldn't, he kept it bottled up. Only when there was exciting good news would he regale her with stories. He admired her intelligence, she'd been the head of a food laboratory for one of the biggest retailers. She was smart. But he didn't think that she or the kids for that matter should ever be burdened with the sort of crap he had to put up with regularly. They didn't need that. Anyway, he could handle it.

She discerned there was something else. Something was troubling him a little. You couldn't live with someone for 27 years and not know. She presumed it was something to do with the deal.

As he drove into work he listened to the news. But he wasn't listening. He was wondering why he still thought of Mary. It was stupid. It was illogical. Ness was great. But Mary. Jesus! Jesus! Was it just about sex? Yes, well.. no, it was.. Oh Christ, he didn't know. How he wished he did. Ness was so… perfect. Well, no human beings were perfect, but she was bloody close, and she'd been a great mother. Prat, he was calling himself again as the car emerged from the shadow of the magnificent beech trees and the large gate and curtain wall appeared. The driveway always looked impressive, and in summer it was glorious with flowering shrubs and tubs of annuals lining it, all the way up to the stately facade of the hundred-years-old house which now served as the office block. Ivy-covered, it looked more like a country hotel than a factory. The original works had once just occupied the house, now it stretched behind it in a series of single-storey smart modern buildings covering eight acres. The buildings were anonymous, there was nothing to hint at the wealth contained inside them in their air-conditioned environment. Even the vaults, which for practical storage purposes were very high-ceilinged to allow maximum storage space for hundreds of millions of banknotes and Travellers' Cheques, were inconspicuous. Their roofline was no higher than the rest of the factory because the height was gained by excavation of their floors to the required depth. The vaults were "boxes" of steel-reinforced concrete accessed by huge silica-filled steel doors impervious to even thermal lances, the whole area blast-proof, served by high-reach fork-lifts moving amongst mobile racking, every move under the scrutiny of 24-hour video surveillance recorded on tape and stored for a minimum of six months. High Security documents had a long gestation period and storage requirement at times. In fact, there were more videos in the factory than there were on a luxury cruise liner operating out of Osaka. Everything in the factory was time and zone access controlled, with colour-coded work-clothes instantly identifying anyone not in their designated area. There were no windows in the building, and only one huge security lock at the rear for deliveries and despatches. It could hold eight of the largest articulated lorries and trailers, and from the moment they entered the lock the outer doors were sealed, providing at all times, with the outer perimeter wall and guardhouse, a double security-ring. From the front, the office block, there was a single pedestrian entrance into the factory. Security, discretion and secrecy were paramount. That's what they sold.

George, the ex-Paratrooper, was on duty at the security check-in. All the security staff were ex-military or ex-police. He greeted JD with something suspiciously like a salute, which caused the Managing Director to look at him, eyebrow raised, with a hint of remonstrating amusement. George grinned.

JD ignored the lift, installed at such expense in the old house, and bounded up the stairs to his office in the Director's suite. The vibrancy of the place was like a shot of Dexedrine to him. He was immediately in the mood to - what did the Yanks say? "Kick ass". Stupid saying. Anyway, he didn't work like that. He'd developed over the years a motivating, enthusing, exciting style of management. Well, that was his opinion. Even he wasn't so sure that all would agree. Didn't matter, he was the boss.

Shirley had obviously been over to the factory, she always put her jacket on when she did, and her good looks still attracted a lot of unwanted attention which she found embarrassing. She was hanging the bright red jacket up as

JD walked into her office. It was the only way to get into his. It suited her, with her streaked blonde hair. She was a nice girl, a genuine girl, and very good at her job. She was young to be an MD's secretary. She was married to a vain self-satisfied "Sales Executive". JD thought he was a pillock, but he was a big pillock, so it was best to say nothing. She sometimes needed help, advice. JD was tempted to give it to her. He would have loved to have taken her out to dinner, sat her down and had a good talk to her. But who'd ever believe such platonic intentions? Her husband? She herself? Ness? Who'd believe he thought of her like a daughter? What was the world coming to, such suspicion?

Christ, you had to be careful how you spoke to kids in the village these days. So sad, even so, she had an attractive figure and legs, and she always smelled like the cosmetics counter at Harrods. He had to admit that, yes, as with all men unless they were liars, he occasionally suffered from a little adolescent lust when he was around her, as was the case wherever good-looking women were concerned. Did men ever grow out of it? He hoped not.

This morning he was preoccupied, he knew he had to talk to the Chief at HQ., but he despised the idea. To get to the Chief he may have to speak to the lackeys, toadies who surrounded him when he was there. They would only want to run to Brandon Spencer with the news, as if in some way it was their doing, as if they were involved. And what for? They wouldn't be able to answer any of the questions, which would arise. Or do anything positive for that matter. They were just stuck, like dead useless wasps in a marmalade jar, there, so you had to deal with them. They were revived, supernaturally, from time to time by injections of news, which would animate the Chief. Surrounding them were even more pathetic creatures, which the Financial Times sometimes honoured with the capitalist appellation of "financial executive". None of them could have survived the first week in a village newsagent's-cum-sweetshop. They'd have had to make decisions, how many Snicker Bars or M and Ms to buy. . ? Too heavy, too heavy.

He slumped back in the big chair. He really wanted to dive straight into the business in hand, not talk to any of that crowd. He looked distastefully at the small mountain of post. He spotted one from the Chief and another from Mary. He had an instant attack of attentiveness.

He opened hers first of course. She'd written on smart blue speckled paper, which matched the envelope. It was very distinctive. Her words were precise. She wanted to see him again, it was important that he knew that she loved her husband, she would never do anything to hurt him or her children, she knew he felt the same, she was going to pay for the next outing, meal, hotel bill, she was in London on three dates, she'd bought a black Basque. For a couple of minutes he couldn't think of anything but the Basque. Life took on new meaning.

It didn't last long. Shirley verbally thumped him in the solar plexus. By the look in her eyes he could tell she'd like to translate that into physical action. She got exasperated with him when he procrastinated, as he was wont to do when it came to bureaucracy, especially if it involved HQ.

"JD, you've got to phone HQ. They've been on twice in the last half an hour. The Chief wants to talk to you. That's what the note from the Chief says, well, it just says he's in and would you give him a ring. But it must be important, he sent it by the morning motorbike courier. I didn't, of course, open the blue one marked personal." Her tone was devoid of any hint of curiosity, but he knew she was intrigued. It was extremely rare for him to get a personal letter, and if he did he trusted her so much he almost instantly told her what it was about, even if only in general terms. He said nothing.

She stood like his mother used to do when he was supposed to be doing his homework. She wasn't going to leave the office till he picked up the phone.

"All right, don't worry, I'm just doing it. Relax, relax. Tell you what to do, do a ring round. Get the Executive Team to meet me, here, at 12.30 pm. I'll be finished by then for sure." She turned and walked back through her door when he picked the phone up.

Switchboard at HQ had obviously been alerted. He got straight through to the Chief's secretary. She was very friendly and pleasant. Of course he could go right through. The Chief was waiting for his call. In seconds, the Chiefs voice came through, suave and friendly. After a welcome back that would have pleased Neil Armstrong he brought the Chief up to date with what had been put in train already, and what he was planning next. The Chief thought it was fantastic, capital, wonderful, worthy of every congratulation. The Chief was so pleased. JD must use the plane anytime for such a huge and important project and so on.

JD by this time was brightening up like a drunkards nose on New Year's Eve. He said he'd call the Chief when he was going back to Libya. The Chief offered the G4 again. UN sanctions meant there were still no regular flights into the country. JD thanked him again. He would use the plane, providing it wasn't in Botswana or Bogotá.

That was over and it wasn't bad at all. In fact, he enjoyed talking to the Chief, but it was so rarely possible without going through the dead wasps.

Now he could get on with proper work properly. He threw his jacket onto a settee in his huge office, which doubled as a Board Room, poured a coffee and reached for his phone. He knew he was going to exasperate Shirley. He was going to phone round and ask the Executive Team to meet him immediately. He didn't want to wait until 12.30. He'd tell her when it was arranged. She could have a moan then. In the meantime she could arrange some sandwiches for lunch. Unless they were with customers, that was the only excuse he'd countenance, no one had time to go out to lunch this day. It was 11.50 am.

Nearly eight and a half hours later he poured a gin and tonic for Bernard Collier, the Financial Director. Bernard was a Lancastrian, from the mill-town of Oldham, sprawling at the foot of the bleak, bare, mist-shrouded sombrely beautiful Pennine moors, across which Lancastrians and Yorkists launched bloody raids to rob, pillage and kidnap as late as four hundred years ago. In fact, they were still doing it if Manchester United played Leeds United. He wore his Northern-ness not just like a badge, but a full-dress uniform. He refused to moderate his accent, and took intense pride in his Northern pragmatic bluntness. He'd come up the hard way, gaining his qualifications in part-time education. He was intensely proud of his FCA. His innate caution caused him to look on JD as a wild gambler at times. They often argued, but their mutual respect and different temperaments made for a good team. JD had the same kind of respect for Ron Law, the Production Director, who opted for a scotch like JD. No one in Europe, probably the world, knew more about the security printing manufacturing process than he did. When JD first got involved with the industry he'd found it hard to come to terms with the fact that the company actually contained experts who could rightly claim they were the "best in the world", or "the only people who can do this". Coming from conventional printing, it seemed to JD that this type of attitude was pretentious or boastful. It took him months to realise it was simply a statement of the actual situation. The limited number of companies in the business were, to his mind, best likened to those Monasteries during the Dark Ages in Europe who kept alive the flame of knowledge. A bit of a lurid analogy, but a good one.

The hours had passed like a video on fast-forward. They'd done everything they could possibly do at this stage on the Libyan project, now code-named "Inshallah" and the only way they would now refer to it. They hadn't stopped until they'd reached this stage.

Engineering were already dismantling their third line, and building the wooden scaffolding to take the plastic sheeting required to contain all dust when they started drilling foundations out. Dust was a nightmare in security printing where tolerances were often plus or minus two or three microns.

Production had briefed and smoothed the alarmed worries of the unionised workforce. The removal of machinery would not lead to any redundancies or loss of earnings opportunities. In fact, it was an exciting development, which should provide them ultimately with more, work and hit the major competitors hard, but it was top secret, something everyone in the factory could appreciate, so no details of the project could be revealed at this stage. Ron Law could be as emollient as an Estate Agent explaining that the dry rot was only in one window. Shipping, which was part of Production, were already lining up land transport from Switzerland, but they hadn't yet a destination. Their job was just to reserve quite a large convoy at this stage. Two full lines would take a minimum of ten articulated low-loaders to move. They'd also earmarked transport for the Dalton's line. Paper and ink "provisions" had been placed by the Production Director himself. He was the only person in the department who knew what the specifications were, and for whom. He and the Prelims Director, who was responsible for Design and Engraving amongst other things, had analysed the Libyan currency as soon as JD had contacted them from Kenya and he'd already been in touch with the suppliers. They were always sworn to secrecy and they'd just think Libya's next indent had been won by Daltons. He'd also collated a short list of "printing trainers", his favourite choice was the ex-Machine Room Manager who'd retired early in a sulk because he hadn't got the Work's Managers job and believed it was "ageism". He now regretted it, because he wasn't married, had no family and now nothing to do. Security Printing had been his life. JD agreed with his choice. Printing training would be a short-term contract, aimed at passing expertise on to printers already working for the Libyan Military Press who Belazir had told him would ultimately be running the lines. They were skilled printers in everything but the Intaglio process and that's what Daltons had to teach them to do in as short a time as possible and banknote finishing and security etc. When it came to engravers Belazir wanted, if possible, young men with young families, who could take them out with them and thus feel more settled, because their involvement was going to be at least six months, probably more, compared to a maximum of three months for the Print Trainer.

JD had spent half an hour with the Sales Director. Nigel Betts had taken over from Fit. There weren't many people JD didn't get on with, or like, but he couldn't warm to Nigel at all. He was so oleaginous he oozed across the room when he came to see him. He was just 40, always immaculately dressed in expensive suits which looked good on his slim average-height frame, in fact, he looked exactly like David Niven in his Hollywood prime, even to the trim moustache and slightly wavy hair, which he had expensively coiffured to remove as much of the wave as possible and JD was sure he slept on a sun bed. He was permanently tanned. Of course, it could be because he always managed to arrange overseas trips to warm and sunny climes during the British winter. Never to the seedier parts of their sales patch, just to tough places like Bermuda or the States or Cyprus. His teeth gleamed so brightly you saw them before him in any situation and JD had a mental picture of the words "Caution, Salesman" stamped on them, in constant view due to the permanent forced smile. But he was, it couldn't be denied, a successful salesman and a good man-manager, protean in ability and the obvious choice. If only JD didn't have to speak to him too much, if only Nigel wasn't so prolix. What he had to get Nigel to do was to prevent his sales team from wasting time and effort on any Arab countries in view of the deal they were now involved in, without making anyone suspicious. Nigel Betts was highly intelligent, and JD knew he could rely on him to achieve what was required. He just wished he could like him more.

He spent a long time with the Financial Director. Bernard was instantly worried and cautious. Were they going to be exposed before contracts were signed and stage-payments arranged? What about UN sanctions? What currency was going to be used in the transactions? What about Exchange Rates? Should they "buy forward"? What about on-going Service and Supply contracts? What about

Training contracts? Bernard looked more and more lugubrious as the meeting went on. He was getting more and more depressed. JD enjoyed the sport of FD-baiting. Bernard gave the impression that he sincerely wished they never sold anything, because it always caused him and his department such trouble. They had so much to do to stop JD and the other wild men in Sales from putting the company in jeopardy. It never seemed to fully dawn on Bernard that there wouldn't be a company, nor his hefty salary paid, or his performance-related bonus and annual share-options unless somebody sold something. FD's were like that. He became positively physically agitated when JD told him casually that, "Oh, by the way, finally, we're giving them our third line, we don't use it." He had to swiftly steady him with a coffee and tell him he was teasing, they were going to sell it to the Libyans for £9.8m, it had cost them £8m, but that was seven years ago, it's Net Book Value was down to £2.4m, so they'd make a small profit of £7.4m immediately and that was cash, in advance. It steadied Bernard's nerves, but then he started rattling on about taking into account the loss of potential future revenue due to not having the line. JD told him to "get real, Bernard". They hadn't used the bloody line for nearly two years, since the installation of the second Super-Intaglio line. It was ideally suited for shorter runs, which they'd been actively avoiding selling because they made such economies of scale on longer runs. It was ideal to do Libyan currency, which it could handle easily on the single-shift system of working which Belazir had stressed was how they wanted to run the whole of the new State Printing Works. Bernard was only partly mollified, and he went off still muttering, but JD knew he could trust him implicitly to get everything moving, with the banks, with the lawyers. He'd just have to put up with him fretting away until all the money was in the bank. Nothing that lots of praise, bits of paper with signatures on and a couple of large gin and tonics couldn't put right.

He spent the longest time with Tony Prince, the Prelims Director. Tony was young to be a director of such a large company, only 32. But he was an excellent artist himself, and his quiet almost diffident manner suited exactly the temperament of the artists, designers and engravers who worked in his department and produced those designs and engravings, using C.A.D., electromechanical and manual methods, which straddled the boundaries of art and craft. They were all undoubtedly fine artists, many of them exhibited in their own right for instance, but they had to be craftsmen of the highest order to transmute their designs into artefacts which printers could use to create plates for security documents. Tall, a natty dresser with, a penchant for pastel colours always carefully matched, which somehow identified him as artistic, he could do almost everything every one of his staff could do and thus commanded great respect. The fact that he was a very nice guy, a "gentle-man", completed the picture, ensured the affection and loyalty of his people, and made for a superbly-run department. It took him no time at all to identify two potential candidates. His department was fully-occupied, but with the gradual switch to longer runs the number of designs and engravings required had been steadily falling, and he'd been able to switch some of his resources to building up the "library" which had always been a long-term objective. This wasn't time-critical, he could see the enormous potential of the project immediately and he had two young good engravers who would fit the bill exactly, if they were both willing to take on the challenge, and he was sure they would for the sort of money on offer, and the other benefits. Double salary, tax-free, luxury villas with personal home staff, all paid for, free schooling if required, free flights home every two months with a 10-day fully-paid holiday. Paul Clay was married with a four-year-old daughter, and his wife Bronya was born in South Africa and had travelled extensively with her job before Laura was born. Simon and Lisa Rogerson had a boy, Daniel, who was nearly four, and loved to travel. They spent as many weeks as they could manage each year touring Europe, even with the child, in their Winebago. She also had given up her career for the time being. Paul was in and they saw him that afternoon. He jumped at the chance. JD and Tony told him to take the afternoon off, go home and talk to Bronya. He was sure she'd be as keen as him. Simon Rogerson was on rota-day off, so they contacted him at home. That was even simpler. His wife Lisa was there and she came on the phone to Tony and said she even had a couple of Arab headdresses her father had brought back from the Gulf when he worked for BP. She was ready for the camels. Tony had been concerned about losing a designer, but was relieved to hear they didn't need one. The first printing would be the extant Libyan design, and the new common Arab currency proposed could be done at Daltons. They had at least two, probably three, months to do that, because it would take that long to ship and install and commission the new machinery.

In the only time JD had to himself that afternoon he called the machine manufacturers. Their response was going to be critical. If they didn't have enough machinery in stock the lead times could be long, probably unsatisfactory to Belazir to judge from his attitude. The call couldn't have been more satisfactory. Yes, they had two almost complete lines of Super-Intaglio and Super-Simultans, and a Cut-Pak 111 banknote finishing line which could handle production from two such lines. They were being built for a customer who'd been half-promising them an order to create a new State Printing Works for years, because they'd been aware for years that their annual indent of notes required provided by a private High Security Printer cost so much that they could build a plant for the equivalent of three years foreign exchange spent on banknotes and passports and the rest. It only hadn't happened because there were one or two groups of people who "benefited" from spending the money annually. The Managing Director of the machinery suppliers told JD he'd be delighted to inform the country that they'd now "buggered around so much" (he was an Irishman working, as he called it, in "the Swiss police State") that they'd have to wait for the next "makings", at least another six months. JD had never heard him so happy since Ireland reached the World Cup Finals in the USA.

So it was all done. There was a tangible air of self-satisfaction about him as JD opened the mahogany drinks cabinet,

"Well done, chaps. I think we're in for our biggest year yet. It's bloody good, isn't it?" Even the FD agreed.

Nearly 2000 miles away Daltons and the deal were also being discussed by an international "forum".

£$£

Chapter Twenty

It occurred to General Youssef Belazir that the 15 men sitting like attendees at a news conference were perhaps the most wanted men in the world, all together, in one room. They were perhaps also the most dangerous men in the world, but not here. Here especially, but really anywhere in this country, they were completely at the mercy of him and the hundreds of troops surrounding them at the base, the tens of thousands of troops surrounding them wherever they went in the desert republic. They were also at the mercy of the cold, unthinking, impersonal defences which made the base a living machine designed to kill, if any person broke its cruel unyielding rules. It amused him to think of the resources one had when you were in charge of the armed forces of even a relatively small country compared to their organisations, so feared in so many places throughout the world. The world never learned any lessons from its history. All this worry about criminals and terrorists, when the greatest criminals and terrorists had always been those who got hold of the reins of power politically: Napoleon, Hitler, Stalin, Pol Pol, Saddam. Such an easy lesson.

It was not quite like a news conference. There were no pens, paper, dictaphones, microphones, cameras. Most were smoking. No one was speaking. At the table on the small podium he was flanked by Osman and Saif. They weren't speaking either, but each of them had one sheet of paper in front of him. It contained the details of each of the delegations.

He knew Wael Murad and Mousa el-Asaad from Hamas, the most militant Palestinian group, he also knew Bachir Riarchi and Nael Goumas from the Lebanese National Salvation Organisation. There had been many dealings with them in the past. He also knew his Italian "friends," Fiorello Malatesta and Giuseppe Massone. He and Saif and Libyan Internal Security had worked with them on certain "projects" before, mainly in Europe. Their two colleagues he'd never met. Introduced as Carlo-Enrico Del Greco and Georgio Beppe Laurentina he greeted them in Italian. He was slightly surprised when Del Greco said in English, with a heavy American accent, "Sorry, we don't speak Italian, General. I'm Charlie Greco and this is my friend George. I'm from New York, and he's from Miami."

Belazir understood immediately. The American side of the worldwide "family". He took it that the Latin Americans, Alberto Espinoza and Juan Barrientos, were close cousins.

Osman introduced "friends from South-east Asia". Belazir knew the Chinese had done a lot of work in Sudan. Even he hadn't realised the Triads had carried the bags for the diplomats, agronomists and engineers. Michael Shiu spoke excellent English. He was Hong Kong Chinese, and a Christian. He was now even happier in his work, because he was helping his Chinese brothers to combat the evil, undemocratic influence of the "anti-Christ", Communism, in his homeland. The Main-landers were totally corrupt, as was their system of Government, and they were easy prey to his organisation, which believed so fervently in the free market. His colleague, Khim Shwe didn't speak English, he was Burmese. Shiu translated into Chinese for him. That suited Shwe. He'd lived as a child in Kunming, Sichuan Province, over the border from Burma, so he was fluent in Chinese. He was the only non-English speaker present.

The two "delegations" remaining were the "other" Americans and the Irish. Saif was wearing his full Libyan Internal Security Service uniform, carrying his silver-mounted baton and sporting the Parabellum pistol he favoured, which he assured Belazir would "penetrate even a light armoured car." Belazir was amused. Mahmoud wouldn't go near an armoured car unless he was in a Chieftain battle tank.

Saif waved his baton towards two men dressed in smart casual western clothes, whose cropped hair and general demeanour suggested they were, or had been, soldiers. Had been, probably, thought Belazir, because they were obviously nearer 50 than 40. In fact, almost all the men in the room seemed to be about that age, apart from the three young men, a little shabbily dressed in worn suits and cheap ties who sat impassively at the back of the room. They were in their late twenties. They looked nondescript, shifty, surly, threatening; they could have been all these things, and they probably were.

"Gentlemen," said Saif in English, "Mr. Calvin Oxenbould and Mr. Harry Durham are here as representatives of the North American League of Militias. They have over quarter of a million members." The two men nodded round the room. Nobody nodded back. Saif pointed the baton now, precisely, like the conductor of an orchestra, at the three young men. "And Mr. Michael Donegan, Eamon O'Brien and Willy Fitzwilton have joined us from Eire," he paused, "Ireland. They are each Commanders of Brigades in the IRA Continuity Command."

Only the Americans turned to look at them. As if taking an oath all three Irishmen raised their right hands loosely in acknowledgement. Belazir idly wondered why the gesture was familiar. He remembered. It was Adolf Hitler returning the Nazi salute. When he did he always looked as if he was hiding his armpit.

He stopped idly wondering, and decided to stand to add effect.

"I welcome you, I hope you're comfortable here." They'd decided in advance that English would be used. "I won't waste any of your time. I will get immediately to the business in hand, the reason you're here. The proposals, the project we have in mind, which will be of great benefit to all of us, and our organisations."

He'd automatically adopted the universal officer briefing voice, tinged with a touch of Hollywood. All that was missing was a little dramatic background music and cameras panning the faces of the audience, then back to the speaker.

"You are all here because you are fighting oppression. You're fighting for justice, for freedom, for self-determination, against tyranny, for your country, for your fellow-man."

He was an accomplished speaker, and he'd thought about this for a long, long time, as the plans had evolved in his quiet moments, in his car, in aeroplanes, in his study, his office, in the awe-inspiring but peaceful still of the desert where the stars were nearer to the earth and you could reach out and touch them where they met the sand and rock on the horizon just a few kilometres away. This day had been over four years in the planning, starting in the second Christian millennium.

Charlie Greco pulled his lips back as he drew on his newly lit Cuban cigar and raised an eyebrow at George Laurentina. Belazir was pleased at the impact his deliberately selected opening words had obviously made.

"I can see you, my friends, from North and South America and South-East Asia, are surprised by these words. Don't be. Think about it. Yes, I can see some of us here, Hamas, the IRA, the US Militiamen, are more obviously "freedom fighters", but you are too. Most definitely so. You work in societies which are rotten." Belazir spat out the last words. He was actually saying something he really believed. It was unusual for him. He was warming to his theme. "Children cannot be left alone for fear of being sexually molested, old people aren't respected, they should be revered. They live in fear of physical violence, even in their own homes. They're trapped in their homes! Often the violence comes from children, spoilt out-of-control kids. Your women can't walk their own streets, they'll be raped. Violence and sexual depravity is everywhere. The Governments are helpless, or useless, at doing something, anything, about it. Really, they don't care. Yet those same Governments, these same Governments. . ." He was sweating a little now, his body was charged, stomach quivering, his hands were trembling with excitement and indignation as he gesticulated, "Condemn you as criminals! You, who are only providing the people with what they want! They condemn you for supplying drugs, for organising prostitution, for being involved in gambling. Hypocrites! Bloody hypocrites! All these Governments countenance the worst drug in the world, alcohol. It sloshes around your societies. You're drowning in it! It robs men and women of their minds, it induces violence, it makes pigs out of men, sluts out of women. But it's everywhere! There probably isn't a decision, however profound, which hasn't been influenced by it for hundreds of years in your societies. Prostitution, prostitution: it's healthy, normal. It's as old as our race. It's in the nature of men, and of women. It's a contract between men and women. They both retain their dignity. But your Governments, in many cases, say it's wrong. They, who allow more vile, licentious sex onto your prime-time TV, into your newspapers, your literature, than would be witnessed in an Ottoman harem, boudoir. All of it degrading, women treated like things, sex objects. Homosexuality, promiscuity, adultery, and other perversions, all tolerated, displayed, encouraged, and they call you criminals! They! They are the criminals! Gambling, again, they condemn you. But they run the biggest gambling rackets of all, National Lotteries, Lotto. Poor people can't feed their children, but your governments blatantly, wickedly encourage them to spend their pittances on National gambling schemes! What bloody hypocrites! How can they condemn you? The drugs you supply, they're largely harmless. Much less so than alcohol. Cannabis, hashish, a mild peaceful drug, - you're condemned by societies which drug their people into passive torpidity, from 19 to 90, with Prozac! Cocaine, happiness and mental alertness, clarity, in a simple white, harmless powder, Opium, God-given for the relief of pain, Heroin, Queen Victoria took it every day! So did Gladstone! A balm for the soul. None, none, are as bad, as evil, as alcohol. Yet you're condemned, criminalized. Outrageous hypocrisy!"

Belazir felt young again. Like that 28-year-old

revolutionary idealist who'd helped sweep away the last vestiges of colonialism when King Idris was removed; not only colonialism, the rotting flesh of the Ottoman empire was excised as well. The years slipped from his shoulders like a lead cloak being removed, his mind cleared of the blanketing fog that had formed through thirty years of disappointment, disillusion, cynicism, the years when dreams coagulated like blood on the sand after a goat is killed for a feast. He was feeling good about himself. He was in that world of inspiring self-delusion where the fact that his motives were base meant little when set against the greater good that would result from his, their, actions, their plans. There was still a chance they would change the river of history, re-direct its course. His dark eyes were intense and piercing, burning with enthusiasm.

It impressed Osman. Charlie Greco felt like Thomas Jefferson. He was serving his people. He'd never thought of it like that before. A glance at George and the Latinos revealed the same little swell of pride. Even he was amused. You couldn't tell what the Orientals thought.

Belazir tugged at the bottom of his tunic to smooth its lines. He did the same with the reveres. He leaned forward, tips of his fingers on the table, gold Heuer-Tag heavy and glistening on his left wrist. He spoke slowly, deliberately, with a kind of suppressed power, voice pregnant with a mixture of promise and, somehow, threat.

"Now, gentlemen, we want to provide you with the opportunity to change all this. To change the world, to empower you, to borrow a word from the feminists. We are going to provide you with money beyond your wildest expectations, dreams. This money will be free. Change your societies. Change your organisations. Change the world. It doesn't matter to us. Do whatever you want. We only want you to take the money. In doing so you will fulfil our aims. You will help our cause. You will benefit the world. You may even want to use it to go, as the Americans say, "legit". That's up to you. We don't care. All we want you to do is use the money we give you."

Still nobody spoke. Belazir straightened, relaxed, put one hand in his pocket and waited. After a couple of seconds he brought out a gold cigarette case, took out a black Sobranie and lit the Turkish tobacco with a gold Dunhill. The silence was broken by one of the Irishmen, Michael Donegan. His rich Southern Irish accent, spoken softly, had an edge to it.

"What do you mean, General, give us money? What kind of money? How much? And why would you be doing this?"

Belazir put the slim cigarette case on the table. He was still holding the lighter in the hand that drew the Sobranie from his lips. He stared intently at the Irishman, then very slowly and deliberately around the other "delegates", like a politician pausing to make a profound point at a crucial stage during an after-dinner speech. His face was set.

"We have special and genuine reasons for doing this. Believe me, us. Your only job is to take the money, and use it."

Again, the silence. Michael Shiu spoke.

"What kind of money?"

"U.S. Dollars, Euros, Libyan Dinars. All hard, strong currencies."

Shiu translated, in a low voice to Khin Shwe. There was no response.

Another few seconds' silence.

"You mean, you're just going to give us millions of dollars for nothing?" Charlie Greco's thick black eyebrows were knitting together as he frowned.

"Not quite for nothing, Mr. Greco. You, all," Belazir swept his hand around the room vaguely, "all you have to do is obtain from your Central Banks legitimate schemes of serial numbers for banknote, current, or preferably future, issues."

Belazir knew that this would be the critical moment. There would be, there had to be, a reaction, probably violent. Comprehension would begin to seep into these minds. These men weren't stupid. In fact, these men were clever, intelligent. They were also experienced. He stared hard at them. He was ready.

It was Charlie Greco who exploded.

"C'mon, General. What is this shit? You bring us out here into the fucking desert, into this asshole place to tell us you want us to distribute fucking forgeries! You're fucking mad!"

His features were contorted. His lips were drawn thin, teeth clenched. The muscles in his cheeks were flexing agitatedly like a hamster feeding. He kept exploding.

"This is shit! You know who you're talkin' to? We're not fucking low-lifers, fucking two-bit schlock's. What'dya think you're trying to fucking pull? You must be fucking mad! I'm outa here! C'mon George. You guys do what you want. I'm outa here."

Greco was on his feet, thick hairy arms pulling his trousers up by the broad belt, the frown turned into a contemptuous sneer. George Laurentina pushed his chair back. He was making to stand up.

"Sit down!"

The voice hit Greco like a pan-full of scalding water. He looked startled. He stopped moving. The sneer froze on his face, Laurentina sat still. They stared at Belazir. Everybody stared at Belazir. The old, short, overweight man in the tight uniform had turned into a dark brown, powerful, menacing bear, ready to rip a throat out.

The bear snarled, in English.

"You're going nowhere! No one is going anywhere. You'd be dead before you'd moved one step in the corridor. Try it."

The bear's snarl mutated into a threatening growl.

"There is only one way out of here. If the humans in the corridor don't kill you the building will. The "elevator" you used is a gas chamber. You noticed the indentations in the walls? Unless otherwise instructed some of them will release that gas. Not something as humane as Zyclon-B. Something else we got from the Germans. You've heard of Tabun, Sarin? They've been developed since the Master race invented them 60-odd years ago and, we now have VX. Our friends in Iraq supplied it to us. One spot on your skin and you die vomiting and shitting yourself to death in intense pain for about forty minutes. You're also, by the way, choking whilst you go through that. The other indentations are mainly light machine guns, also awaiting instructions not to activate. Your only choice is to choke to death or to be cut into at least four by soft-nosed bullets. Soft-nosed because we don't want to mark our walls."

Greco had eased himself back into his chair. His small eyes were flickering and he licked his bottom lip. Fear was mixed with surprised bemusement. He understood the situation now. The other 14 also understood. They weren't unfamiliar with this scenario. But usually, they were in the General's position. Everyone in the room began to pay real attention.

The General's voice had become pleasant again, almost silky.

"They're very expensive walls."

Belazir flashed a smile. He'd stopped being a bear. He was the little General again. Osman and Saif remained impassive.

"Now, gentlemen. Listen very carefully. Open your minds. I trust I will never have to say this again. You are not, repeat not, being asked to distribute forgeries, counterfeits. Such operations are always doomed to ultimate failure. There is always a flaw, or series of flaws, in such documents. The paper is not genuine, or the ink, no intaglio printing is used, the U.V. fluoresces in the wrong spectrum, the engravings are usually just photographic copies, flat, lifeless, the notes have little tactile feel, if notes have a "reading" feature counterfeits won't go through their reading and verification machines. They're short-lived. They're produced by fraudulent methods. They're always produced for short-term gains, usually petty profits for petty criminals. You who deal in drugs usually end up circulating them amongst yourselves anyway, as your "foot-soldiers" try to make a little more for themselves "on the side" as you say. Quite pathetic stuff really." Belazir's face registered his contempt.

Behind Michael Shiu's inscrutable oriental expression his Middle-Kingdom mathematical brain was retrieving, analysing the number of times he and his colleagues had done just that, in Burma, Laos, Cambodia, Vietnam, Malaysia, Indonesia. It didn't seem so petty or pathetic to him. Quite a few million dollars had been used, and made, in that way.

"We are not producing forgeries. That is the difference. Remember this, it is of crucial importance. All paper money, all genuine paper money, is a giant confidence trick, bits of paper for goods, for gold even. Just as long as people believe the bits of paper are genuine. And we are producing genuine notes. We are building a plant here, to do so. Genuine U.S. Dollars, Euros, Libyan dinars, most of you are not involved in the latter. We will deal with those, with help from Hamas and the NSLO, the Lebanese. We want your help in Europe, Russia, South East Asia, South America and North America to deal with the rest. The plant is costing us £50 m, $75 million in U.S. Dollars. It will produce genuine notes. You have two roles. One minor, one major. The minor role is to obtain as quickly as possible, the current or future numbering schemes from your Central Bank or State Printing works in Europe and North America. These are always passed to the printers, whoever they are, by the Bank, for every new run. A few hundred thousand well-placed dollars or Euros, or any other European currency, should suffice to elicit this info. Your organisations are in ideal positions to get this. It will be a tiny advanced investment when you set it against what you will receive, believe me. Two of the world's newest and best currency printing lines will be operating 24 hours a day, seven days a week to supply you. Let me give you a very rough approximation of what these lines will produce for you. One line, on $100 bills, can produce over 1.6 billion dollars per week. The machines run at 3000 sheets per hour, there are 32 banknotes on every sheet, that's $9,600,000 per hour, over $230 million per day. That's the $1.6 billion per week. From one line! A 100 Euro note is worth $112, so that means over $250 million per day, $1.75 billion per week. In one week then, the two lines will produce $3.35 billion-worth of notes. To save you working it out, that's about $44 billion in three months. This does not include the Dinars we will produce. They'll be done on a smaller line, which will be in operation first, within 6 to 8 weeks we hope. These machines only produce 1500 sheets per hour with, again, 32 notes per sheet. That's 48,000 notes per hour. A Libyan Dinar is worth £2 Sterling, $3.20. That would be $153,000 per hour if we printed single Dinars. We won't, of course. They'll be at least 20s. Again, to save you laboriously calculating, that's $3,072,000 per hour, $73,728,000 per day, $516 million per week, over $6 billion in three months. So, gentlemen, there will be over $50 billion in genuine notes for you to use in the first three months. If we, the Arabs," Belazir used the American pronunciation, A-rabs, with a heavy hint of sarcasm, "deal with the $6 billion worth of Dinars your organisations, four of them, will have $11 billion each to do with as you wish. In just the first three months. That, and the numbering sequences, is all we ask of you."

Belazir reached for the cigarette case and took out and lit another Sobranie. He snapped the case shut, looked at Osman and Saif, and with theatrical finality, sat down, pushed his chair back, leaned back drawing heavily on the cigarette. Through the cloud of aromatic smoke he said, softly and with innocent geniality.

"It really is as simple as that. Do you have any questions, gentlemen?"

The silence was heavy, like the air before a tropical storm. The size of the figures was obviously almost incomprehensible. Men accustomed to dealing in millions were lurched into another dimension, their astute criminal brains wrestling with another facet of relativity. Like children in a junior class no-one wanted to ask a question which wasn't appropriate, worthy of, the enormity of it all.

Shiu's voice sounded small.

"Why?"

The eyes switched to him, with a kind of relief.

"Why? What do you get out of it?"

His "perfect" English sounded accented now.

An answer came, not from the podium, but from an Irishman.

"It's de-stabilisation, isn't it? That's the aim at the end of it all, isn't it General?"

Michael Donegan's question was a statement. From beneath the shock of black hair the blue eyes locked onto Belazir.

"That's a sum bigger than the National Debt of the British."

"Mr. Donegan, we'll leave the British to you and remember, that's only the first three months." Belazir smiled. A strange smile, part smirk, part sneer, part challenge, part condescending.

Behind the smile though he was impressed that the young Irishman had so swiftly cut to the core of the matter. He was not to know, because the brief biog. in his notes didn't tell him, that Michael Donegan had a First from Trinity and if he hadn't been fighting to right the wrongs of 600 years of English/Irish history and to re-establish a united homeland he would have probably been teaching history in a Grammar school somewhere in County Cork, or working for the European Union like so many of his highly-educated compatriots from the small sad island where there weren't enough jobs for the graduates pouring from the Universities like ants from a nest during summer. The Irish had become the new Jews of Europe.

"De-stabilisation? What the hell is that when your Mama's at home?" Greco looked resentfully puzzled. The room was humming now with whispered muttered exchanges.

"Ah so!" Michael Shiu had a sense of humour. He was being exaggeratedly Chinese. "You massively artificially increase the Money Supply of the US and the EU, undermine and de-stabilise their currencies. Their stock markets and economies take a battering and they're weakened, more than they would be in a war. If they were in a war."

Calvin Oxenbould interrupted. He spoke quietly but with authority. He had a pleasant Mid Western accent. He hailed from near Moline in Iowa where the real "Wild West" started. Where fur trappers traded with Indians on the banks of the Mississippi long before the land-rush to the West across the river. St Louis, the great ford on the great river was to the South. The river was the main artery for trade and exploration. You could canoe, if you were crazy enough, from Moline to the Gulf of Mexico. The people in the area were proud of their antecedents. They had a great sense of humour. A life-size stuffed Grizzly greeted visitors to their small airport. In winter they froze. In summer they baked. Magnificent electric storms played about their skies over the vast plains, and the weir on the mighty river still yielded salmon and trout to anyone sitting with a line at the riverside restaurants. English, Irish, Scots, Welshmen, Scandinavians, Germans and Frenchmen had carved out a decent stable community there, threatened only by slimy politicians in Washington D.C. That's why he was so interested, so committed to the Militias. They were only upholding the decent, genuine American way of life. They would do, by force if necessary. There were millions of them, strangers now in their own land. Blacks, Jews, Hispanics were taking over their lives. They weren't intolerant or prejudiced. They just wanted to live the lives their predecessors had bequeathed to them, and they'd pass on to their kids.

"I'm an accountant by profession. I don't think that's what would happen, sir." He addressed his remarks to Shiu. "I think the money would just be absorbed, if it was genuine, and we take the General's word for that. I'm sure he's right. It would just be absorbed. My guess is that it would take months, years, for anyone to even notice there was something affecting the Money Supply, and….."

Belazir cut in.

"Gentlemen, gentlemen. Please."

His voice was authoritative. He wasn't quite the vicious bear again, but he wasn't the family pet.

"This discussion is interesting. It could go on for a long time. But I have to tell you, it's pointless. It is none of your business. We do indeed have our plans, our aims. If you discerned or guessed them in their complex entirety we would not confirm, deny, or enlighten you. You are here as representatives of your important organisations because we believe you can help us achieve what we want, whilst at the same time acquiring riches beyond your normal dreams. You have only one decision to make. You're with us, or against us. I will put it in terms you will even better understand - do you want the money or not? Now is the time to decide."

The threat in the General's words was crystal clear. Every mind in the room fully understood death to be the ultimate persuader. They didn't know whether the "gas chamber" really existed, but they suspected it probably did. This was not an unfamiliar situation in their lives. They knew that the General, and the other two, knew that. There wasn't much chance of walking out. That was one train of thought. The other was the astonishing anticipation of what to do when they got home and casually mentioned they'd soon have 11 billion dollars each to spend for, on, their organisations. Even drugs, the second largest "commodity" in the world after oil, didn't hold such immediate promise and they were beset with dangers. It seemed ideal, too good to be true. But they could see it was true. These men were serious. What their ultimate aim was didn't have too much relevancy. They'd have money almost beyond imagining.

"Mr. Oxenbould is right. You'll be well into your second 11 billion before anything is even noticed. By that time, gentlemen, it will be too late much too late. You'll understand what I mean by that in time. And then you'll have cash, genuine cash, to do with as you please, to do all you've ever wanted to do."

The bear's face was serious. The black eyes scanned the room.

"Are you with us or against us?"

Michael Donegan spoke for them all.

"We can't lose. We're with you and may God, our God and yours, be with us."

"He is the same God, my friend."

The tension cracked like ice on a pond. One by one they committed.

Belazir was smiling again. Osman nodded and smiled. Saif merely observed. He'd actually been thinking that the bodies would be easily disposed of over the Gulf of Sirte by his men. Every single person on the base was hand-picked by him and waiting to be rich men.

"Right gentlemen. Thank you gentlemen. You have made the right decision. We are already set up. This is what happens next. Remember, gentlemen, we need those numbering schemes. That's up to you. We require them within the month. General Saif will give you all secure fax numbers. Do not, please, do not, use E-mail or the Internet. Not secure. Use the fax lines."

The discussion that followed was sharp and businesslike, almost curt. It centred on secure communications, shipment and reception. Any attempt to discuss distribution thereafter was met with refusal, swept away. That was their problem. The Generals neither wanted nor needed to know.

No one in the room could tell that darkness had fallen outside, and that the desert was cold and still. Their watches displayed a time, but they were outside of it. Food was served and cigarettes and cigars brought in. They were staying at the base that night anyway. They were staying 'til everything was done.

£$£

Chapter Twenty One

The snake had crawled onto the rock to catch the first rays of the sun. It was cold, torpid, and immobile. It needed the heat to quicken it, to hunt and feed and live. Osman's first bullet blew its body in two, both parts writhing on the rock. The second bullet blew its head apart and the grey rock stood out from the rest, decorated with crimson motifs like an Afghan rug. The bits still writhed.

The two men were cold too, but icily awake mentally at least. The amphetamines had worked well. But, whilst their minds were blade-sharp their bodies were weary. The desert dawn chill was bracing. They were a few hundred metres from the "monolith". The rectangular outline of the "other elevator" lay camouflaged with grey-brown netting, with its out-door swimming pool winding mechanism clearly visible at ground level though it was covered in sand and rock sunk into its polymer coating. This was the "Fox-bat's" elevator, where they disappeared into the desert like Gerbils.

"I hate snakes." Osman's voice was thick.

"I do. Except in Taiwan, for lunch," Belazir observed wanly. He noticed how careless of killing his friend was.

Both men were tired. It had been a long but fruitful night. The "visitors" were packed off now to the Guesthouse. Only the Speed was keeping them going. Amphetamine had that quality, where the mind was active though the body was almost finished. The two separated. The mind operated alone, in isolation.

"Sadiq. Do we have to go through all this? It's so … big. It's bloody huge! What was wrong with my, our, original concept?"

Belazir sounded as tired as he looked. There was a pleading note in his voice. There was a slight irritation in Osman's.

"Youssef, for the love of God, we've been through all

this too many times. From the moment you said yes to the Hanifs this was decreed. This was ordained. Neither you nor I can change or stop this now. You know that."

"But the original idea was so simple, just the Dinars. You and I, Mahmoud and Celal, everybody involved, would be multi-millionaires. We could live wherever we wanted, do whatever we wanted. No one would have known 'til we were well out of it. And you'd have still got your money, enough to finance your own bloody civil war, keep things boiling in Chad, money enough to finance those savages in Northern Uganda. They could have been shooting people with expensive automatic weapons instead of hacking them to death with machetes, or cutting their feet and lips and noses off."

"Youssef, the Acholis are good Muslims. They're the only ones who fought Musaveni. They're still the only ones still fighting Kirikulu. They're the only bulwarks against Christianity in that God-forsaken country."

"They're savages, Sadiq. You know it as well as I."

"Youssef, it matters little. Calm down. This is bigger than that now. The Hanifs see it as a chance to redress the imbalance between the West and East, or North and South, or rich and poor, whichever you choose. We can't stop it now. We have to go the whole way. We'll still end up rich. You'll still get away. So will Celal and Mahmoud if they want to. I don't want to. I want to see it through. I want us to do everything we've said we'll do. Teach the infidel bastards a lesson, change the world, Youssef, change the world and remember, we need the Hanifs' help now. It's the only way it will work. How else can we get all the Arabs, Mali, Niger, Burkino Faso, Mauritania, Senegal, Iraq, Iran, Syria, Turkmenistan, Tadjikistan, Uzbekistan, Kazakhstan, Pakistan, Afghanistan to help us?" He recited the countries names like a creed. He'd obviously done it many times before.

"But do we need their help? Why does it need to be so big?"

"To stop us looking like common criminals, and to fulfil

our destiny. Come on, you know that. This is a "crusade", their own word, the Christians. Anyway, you know, Youssef, it's too late now. We're committed. We are but servants now, as always. Remember, Youssef "Islam" means "submission", "Moslem" means "the submissive." We are all but slaves. It is out of our earthly hands. What does the Qur'an say? "Allah leads astray whom he pleases, and guides whom he pleases, and no one knows the hosts of the Lord save Himself and every man's destiny have we fastened on his neck." Further, Youssef, and perhaps even more apposite, what did the Prophet himself say? "The best and most beautiful of my creations is a compassionate man who gives alms. If he does so with his right hand and hides it from his left, he is more powerful than all things." That's us, Youssef. That's what we're doing. Come on. Youssef, we're here to pray. Qibla is that way." Osman indicated the direction of prayer with his arm. "Two rak'a is my endurance this morning. I'm very tired."

The rak'a consisted of eight separate sets of devotion. They were too tired to worry about the dust on their uniform trousers. They had no prayer mats.

They walked back towards the monolith to wash. Belazir was a little breathless. Bending did that to him now, and Osman's pace was brisk, militaristic. Belazir couldn't get it out of his mind.

"Sadiq are they as powerful, as ubiquitous, as you think?"

Osman knew he was referring to the Hanifs.

"Youssef, no Islamic Government is untouched by them. It has been so since the Prophet. They've never stopped growing. The Arab League 1945, and the Islamic Conference 1971, are but babies. Just babies, even yet in the womb. For more than 1,400 years they've been the only constant in every Islamic state, whether Caliphate, Sheikdom in the past, or Baa'thist, militaristic or secular in this century. They're the only true voice of Islam now."

Osman was sounding Messianic, a bit fanatical. It was disturbing. Belazir tried to sound interested.

"A bit like Freemasons in the West?"

Osman reverted to 21st Century speech mode.

"Youssef, wash your mouth out!" Osman had a number of American expressions he loved to use, remembered fondly from his college days. "Freemasonry was only important in Colonial times because it accepted freedom of thought. That's why the Christian Churches hated it. It accepted any race, creed or colour, so long as the man believed in a Supreme Deity. That's why Hitler and the Communists hated it. We were grateful to be thought of and treated as equals, even if it was only in the Lodge. But those days are past. Who wants to worship with, be locked in with, Christians, Jews, and Hindus? A nice idea, but look what it's led to in the West. Decadence, drift, no firm belief. And Hinduism and India is a shambles. They still burn wives if the family doesn't "cough up the dough". Barbarians. Nobody has a firmer belief than the Hanifs. There is only one way to God. That's through the Prophet, not bloody Caliphs or Ayatollahs."

"I hear you, Sadiq, but, are you a Hanif? Why do they call themselves that? I've not heard the word since school. Why aren't they called "Ansars," they are disciples, students, aren't they?"

"Yes, they are. But the Hanifs are not. They're Searchers, after the truth. Remember what the Meccans called the Prophet before he saw the Archangel Gabriel and received Sura I? "Our Mohammed has joined the Hanifs", they said. They understood. Only now, we don't need to search too much. The Prophet has shown us the way, we only have to follow him. You remember almost his last words, Youssef. "One God, One Faith, for all the world," that's what we, believe."

Belizir noted his use of "us" and "we". It was the first time Osman had ever acknowledged his association or membership of the organisation not even suspected by the West, obsessed with military or secular rulers posturing in their little countries, not representing the great mass of Islamic adherents. Only a Moslem could understand. If they'd known, they wouldn't have been so surprised at the fall of the Shah, the support for Nasser, Saddam. He was quiet for the rest of the walk back. He knew Osman had said all he was going to say. Anyway, he was part of it now. It didn't matter. He'd go through with it. Then he'd go to live in Malaysia. It was an Islamic country, but it enjoyed all the trappings and luxury of Europe if you lived in K.L or George Town on the coast. He would live the life of a very rich man, the women would join him, and he'd give alms to the poor on a grand scale. Just a few months to get through.

Osman needed Belazir, and all his operations, for the next three months, minimum. He knew the older man was tired, disillusioned. He hoped he had the balls to go through with it. He had to. This was the biggest, the most important operation yet. Only the toppling of the Saudi, Kuwaiti and UAE monarchies would release so much money for the cause. That was planned, but it would be messy. It would take years to settle down. This was the opportunity. The Libyan's plan, crude and greedy and self-serving was the perfect vehicle. The next Hanif Council was in less than a month's time, in Alma Ata. It was the greatest gathering yet. All Islamic countries would be represented there. He would have so much to tell them. Then he would go skiing in the Alatau Shan, which ringed the city in a beautiful horseshoe, Kazakhstan on one side, China on the other. He'd played horseshoes in America. They thought they were symbols of luck. Perhaps it was an omen, but he didn't believe in omens. He was a Moslem. Allah alone would guide his steps.

£$£

Chapter Twenty Two

Daniel was fed-up with Laura. She was pretty in the bright white dress, but she was a typical girl, no fun. She couldn't even think of a game to play with Eddie, his pocket-sized tattered blue Panda that he carried everywhere with him. In fact, she didn't want to play at anything. She was stupid. She wasn't like his friend Johnnie Fox. Johnnie knew everything. He was five. He always had games to play. He was really fed-up with her so he stuffed his ice cream down the top of her dress. It wasn't a great sacrifice. He couldn't eat it, they'd been there for hundreds of hours and he'd had crisps and biscuits and Coke and lemonade and he couldn't eat any more. Anyway, he could beat her up. She was soft. All girls were soft. Johnnie Fox was right. Typically, she started crying and her mother got involved. Worse, his mother got involved. He knew he was wrong, but he denied it. It wasn't his ice cream he said, so it couldn't be him. Grown-ups were stupid too.

Her mother, Bronya Clay, laughed falsely and cleaned her up, with tissues, as best she could. His mother grabbed him by the arm and yanked him to her side on the Spartan terminal seats.

"Daniel! What are you thinking about! Come here and stand still!" He was still for about five seconds.

Bronya laughed and said. "Lisa. Don't worry. He's just fed-up with her. He doesn't realise he's got six months of this to come!" She gathered her daughter up and comforted her by stroking her long honey-blonde hair. She soon stopped crying.

The two fathers were having a pint. They could see there was a little altercation. They were glad they were in the bar.

"Your son's just attacked my daughter," Paul said.

"The girls will sort it out. Leave it to them," Simon

retorted, hardly looking.

"Typical Rogerson." Paul drained his drink.

"Another pint?" Simon was searching for his English money. The rest were Dinars.

"Yes please. None where we're going. What about the girls?"

It was like a holiday. But better. They'd been driven to the airport. Separate cars. They couldn't get their entire luggage into one car each. The firm had been good about it. They felt like VIPs, they were VIPs. It was an adventure. Paul Clay and Simon Rogerson were old friends. They'd been to the London College of Printing together, they were both fine artists. Printing had been furthest from their minds when they'd left school. Both had exhibited locally and were keen on watercolours and oils. By different routes, Paul through glass engraving, hey'd ended up at Daltons as banknote engravers. They were the younger members of the Prelims team. They were good and they knew it. "MD/JD" as he was affectionately and sometimes cynically known had asked Tony Prince whether they were available personally. You couldn't turn it down. Good pay, super bonuses, free housing, schooling when the kids were ready, they loved it. The full colonial life! Servants! Gin and Tonics on the veranda! No, it was a Muslim country. They mustn't forget that.

Their wives were old friends too. It was going to be a great experience. They'd be living in close proximity. The kids would be playmates. What was the odd ice cream attack?

They'd already got a rough of the Pan-Arab design. General Belazir had been very helpful. So had the Governor of the Central Bank, Dajani. They'd passed useful comments about the initial designs. No Arab country could object to the main design element they'd chosen, surely, a scroll, containing the last words, or at least the last speech, of the Prophet: "Ye people! Hearken to my speech and comprehend the same. Know that every Moslem is the brother of every other Moslem. All of you are of the same equality." In classical Arabic on one side of the note, in the indigenous language on the other. It was perfect. Common meaning. European numbering, called an "Arab Dinar", based on the Libyan exchange rate, with a built-in "comfort", one to two US Dollars, instead of Sterling. They were excited. It would be a completely new world currency, and they'd designed and engraved it.

As they drank their second pint, the girls didn't want any more Coke, they laughed about "MD/JD" tearing around the place like a demented wasp. He was in his element. Everything was humming. Engineering and Production were working flat-out. About time they did something apart from find every reason known to humankind why something couldn't be done. Anyway, they were out of it now. They were looking forward to working with the Libyans and the Sudanese. They were impressed with the new Sudanese Dinar produced in the new State Printing Works built with "Italian help" in 1994. They were doing all right, these "fuzzy-wuzzies".

The two men were artistically very alike. They were both good at portraiture and lettering. They knew they were amongst only thirty or forty people in the world who could do what they could do. They were proud of that, and it was paying off. Neither of them had travelled Business Class before, their wives were impressed (as women tend to be), and the idea of an air-conditioned pair of chauffeur-driven limousines to take them from Tunisia to their villas in Libya was a real thrill. Certainly Bronya and Lisa thought so. Daniel and Laura couldn't care less.

Both men kept that distance from their children that men tend to do, but both adored them. Neither could imagine having anything but a son and a daughter respectively, Daniel with the dark eyes that were redolent with ancient wisdom and Laura with her long blonde hair and pert mouth. Proud was an inadequate word. Treasured was probably better. They wished they could express it better. But the girls were better at that.

The kids were "grizzling" on the way out, and again on

the long car journey to Sirte, but the pleasure of their parents when they finally arrived at their spacious new homes obviously transmitted itself to the children and they all settled in without demur and with every manifestation of approval. Belazir and Dajani had met them at the end of their journey, and quickly pointed out they were only about an hour's commuting distance from the Base where they would work. With the girls settled in, and the kids happy, who could want for more?

Stanley, the Print manager, had come out on the previous flight. He was hard at work when they met him. He only had three months, and he was staying at the base. On the morning that they got together he already seemed like a fixture. He was determined this installation was going to work, efficiently, superbly. Daltons was going to make it happen. One of the best installations in the world. He loved it. They were impressed.

His crew were not English speakers. It mattered little. They were all professional printers. They were mastering the art. In fact, the first line was not unlike their own line in Khartoum. The Libyans in the crews were familiar with everything but the intaglio printing. But in many ways that was simpler than the complex Litho printing they were accustomed to. Stanley was already like a cross between a martinet and a father figure. He was in his element. No one could have given him a more perfect environment. Air-conditioning, temperature-controlled, hermetically sealed print hall, and the latest equipment. A dream come true, late in life, where the real stuff could be produced, created and they were all so keen. They wanted to go immediately on to three-shift working, to run the plant for 24 hours a day. Such enthusiasm, so different from the Union-raddled business he was used to.

£$£

Chapter Twenty Three

JD didn't get the G4. He knew he wouldn't. The Chief was back in South-East Africa. The plane was in Maputo. He made the trip by car from Tunisia; he was alone. Fit was genuinely worried about Veronica. The Specialist was undramatic, but there was something wrong. He wanted to stay with her. In the end they were all they had, each other. Anyway, JD was only "reviewing the troops" and getting the final contracts signed. The money for the first line was already in the bank in Switzerland. The Sudanese were very efficient. Fit didn't have to be around for that.

Belazir and Saif met him at the Guest House, and took him out to the "Monolith". There was an exaggerated formality about presenting him with a "key". The guards knew him now and joked with him in Arabic as they saluted. Saif briefed him as Belazir and Anan looked on. He would always, obviously, be accompanied by the driver and security guard they'd assigned to him for his "own protection", but whenever he arrived at the Base he was his "own man", the superior. The others didn't have a "key". The "key" worked simply, but, with Arabic logic that he had to remember, it was used in the opposite way to a "Western" key, a European key. It turned from left to right, the way Europeans would lock a door, then a half turn to the left, then back. Saif stressed the need for the simple combination turn, anything less would activate the defences. That's why the "keys" were so sparingly distributed. Only the most senior men had them. He was greatly honoured by being issued with one. Improperly used and the defences were automatic. Machine guns, anti-tank missiles, activated if the sensors detected metal in bulk, enfilading every cubic metre of the elevator space. Finally, and most importantly, the most deadly of all gas, VX gas. Just a couple of particles on the skin would cause a horrible death in minutes.

Supplied by the Iraqis, who manufactured tonnes of it. Enough to kill everybody on earth! And that, Saif said, would kill the whole base. It was a suicide, a doomsday scenario. Designed to be activated if the key was wrongly used. Or if any other penetration took place, such as bombs, or an attempt to dig into the base by any means. When JD questioned the logic of the doomsday scenario Saif's reply was beautifully simple. It was designed to counter-act a situation in which someone had got hold of a key and was going to use it without knowledge of the combination, thus breaching the base security with obvious malicious intent. If the surface or perimeter guards hadn't stopped such people the worst must be happening, and every man on the base knew when they took up their duties that this was the ultimate deterrent for intruders. The work of the base was of the utmost national security importance and all were willing to make the ultimate sacrifice. To JD, It seemed preposterous, like a bloody James Bond movie. But it was real. These people were serious. JD felt like a child given the front door key to the home for the first time by his parents. It was a privilege, and gave him power. He put the long slim "key" into his wallet and passport-holder. He was taking it very seriously. The "elevator" was obviously a very, very dangerous place.

He met Stanley and enthused over what he'd already done, achieved. Stanley loved it. But it was impressive. They were already in a position to print Libyan Dinars. Outside the constrictions of the U.K. the older man had worked a minor miracle. The General was very gracious. He followed him round the developing plant in the great metal-lined hall, but he was obviously bored. Saif had left them. JD was satisfied, more than satisfied, with what had been achieved in such a short time. His request to see Paul and Simon was natural. Belazir's response struck him as a little odd. It might be better to meet them next time, next week, with their wives. They weren't at the base at that moment, they were at the compound. They were very tired. They'd been working 16 hours per day. Let it wait 'til next time.

Was that all right?

JD agreed. He didn't want to put them under more pressure, and, yes, he would see them next week. But he felt uneasy, though he couldn't put his finger on why. But he now had the contracts signed, Bernard would be happy, and the project was really a “go-er”. Head Office would be pleased. He contacted the Chief by satellite phone from Belazir's office. The Chief was as delighted as he was.

£$£

Chapter Twenty Four

"I'm not doing that!" Paul Clay said it fiercely. He looked at Simon Rogerson. They were in Belazir's office. Saif sat in the large black Parker-Knoll chair. Osman stood just to the right of Belazir.

"You are." The words came from Osman, his gaze was impassive, inflexible.

Simon Rogerson cut in, pre-empting his friend.

"But, that's bent, you can't do that, we're not here for that, you didn't say."

"Mr. Rogerson, that is what you will do."

Osman was matter-or-fact. If anything, he sounded slightly weary, bored.

The two men looked, and were, bemused. Neither responded.m Belazir broke the uneasy silence.

"Gentlemen, that is what we want you to do. Please do it."

"You can stuff it! I'm not." Paul Clay was angry. His friend joined him. "You must be bloody mad!"

Osman spoke again, very quietly, with that faint trace of an American accent, "No gentlemen. This is what we want you to do, what we insist you do. Please do it."

The silence was even more awkward.

Belazir said, in his most avuncular fashion, "Come on. Gentlemen. You're being paid a lot of money for...."

"General, we're not being, paid for this and we won't do it!" There was a lot of emotion in the office.

The General looked at Osman, who almost imperceptibly nodded at Saif. The latter left the office.

"Gentlemen. Let's take coffee, and consider the options. Please, be seated."

Clay and Rogerson hesitated, and then took the chairs offered by Osman. They weren't sure what to do. They were out of their depth. They were both just sure of what they would not do.

"What are you trying to do, General?"

"My friends let us wait for coffee. Then we can talk."

They sat there, helpless, with a growing sense that something was wrong, very wrong. Nobody spoke. The coffee was served. Thick, black, Arabic.

"You like it?" Belazir's question was superfluous.

"General, we're not here to do this. You know that. I think we should see the MD." The voice was tense.

"Of course," said Belazir, soothingly, "he's coming back in a week's time. Please, enjoy your coffee. What is your estimate of the time you'll finish?"

"Finish what?" Clay couldn't contain his anger.

"I'm sorry you feel this way. Please excuse us, gentlemen. We'll return in about 90 minutes time. You need time to yourselves. Think about this proposition, please."

They were left alone.

Paul said to Simon, "I'm not doing it."

"Neither am I. The Boss needs to know about this."

"Yeah. What the hell are we into?"

They sat alone. There was nothing much else to say. Both men felt helpless. They were helpless.

Nothing happened. The excellent air-conditioning made the office a little cold. There were no external sounds. The time passed like a jet liner out of earshot.

Osman and Belazir came in first, followed by Saif. The latter was, incongruously, carrying a green Marks and Spencer's bag. He gave it to Osman.

Osman, without a word, turned it upside down on the desk. It was hard to see at first. Then it became obvious. There was a large handful of honey-blonde hair, baby-soft, still tied with a pretty white silk ribbon, and a bedraggled blue panda toy.

The two men felt colder.

Osman said, in a pleasant, business-like voice, "We've talked to your wives, and your families. They want you to stay, and help us."

£$£

Chapter Twenty Five

Apart from the absence of any natural daylight, and especially North light which all hand-engravers in the Northern hemisphere prefer, the facilities the Base provided were ideal. No noise, no vibration, no distraction, perfect temperature and humidity. They had, of course, their own graving tools, but everything else had been planned and built with them in mind as individuals, based on information and dimensions provided by Daltons. They were using the same Japanese binocular microscopes they had at home, but new, sitting on the same high swivel chairs manufactured by the same company in the U.K., at the identical engravers benches, shaped to accommodate their bodies, copied to perfection. The steel they were using for dies was if anything even better finished than they were accustomed to. They guessed, correctly, that it came from India. Their non-English-speaking "servants" treated them well, with great courtesy. The food was good. Their rooms were very comfortable, with excellent shower facilities, TVs and a raft of games. They talked to their wives by telephone every day. They knew they were OK. And so were the kids. But that's all they knew. Everybody was just .... frightened. Living in luxury prisons with good money flowing into their bank accounts every week (they were given copies of the bank transfers) just no longer seemed so attractive.

It took them just over eight weeks, working around 14 hours per day, six days per week (the Sabbath rest day was agonisingly long) to engrave the four dies. Fronts and backs for the $100 U.S. notes and the Euro 100s. They were perfect. Every cut, every etch, every dimension. Line for line. They faithfully and perfectly executed the processes the original engravers had created, learning much about the men who'd put such care into the originals. At the end of three weeks they knew exactly how those men thought about shade and light and how deep they would cut an individual line in a particular place. They became those men, suppressing their own creative tendencies to do so. There was that much at stake. They became the world's most expert copyists. If the same men had done other notes they could have reproduced them without copying, like a student of Leonardo's could have "knocked out" a few Mona Lisas leaving the Louvre eating whatever the French is for humble pie.

They proofed the dies on the small intaglio and litho machines provided for their Studio. They were identical. All that was now needed was for all the rest of the raw materials, processes and devices needed to turn them into "genuine" notes. Paper, inks, chemicals, and holograms, numbering sequences and they were ready. All faithfully duplicated to match samples provided by Daltons for "test" purposes to the plant at the Base by paper mills in Iran and Pakistan, ink and chemicals acquired from Italy, holograms from the U.S.A., numbering boxes from Germany.

They left the Studio for the first time to oversee the plate making. Their "servants" accompanied them. Superb machinery was being used and no expense spared. First the plastic pressing and welding of the original dies to form the single images into a 32-set "page", then the "growing" of copper plates electrolytically, finally the "chroming" of those plates to guarantee extended wear. From these plates, endless copies could be made to run long into the future.

They worked on the final plates, correcting any small blemishes. Again, the plate makers spoke no English. Within three hours they were back in the studio. In over eight weeks they spoke only to each other, made the telephone calls that became the most important few minutes of their days, and to Belazir, Osman, Saif and Dajani, who visited them every couple of days to observe their progress, always singly. They were always polite, but the pretence was gone. Ended now. They were there to do a job. They did it without demur because these men had complete control over what they both held dearest in life, their wives and children. They didn't even know where their families actually where. And they could get no information out of the four men. Belazir smiled a lot, reassured them, and told them “not to worry - just hurry”. Saif was always surly and uncommunicative, Dajani fussed a lot and would only talk about engravings, the work in hand, Osman introduced an air of cold impersonal malice and threat every time he stepped into their Studio. They couldn't know that he was the principal architect of the infamous “ghost houses” in Sudan. They could simply tell he had no feelings towards them at all. They weren't people. It was in his eyes. He always left them by asking how their wives and children were, pointedly, with affected courtesy and concern.

Once, in the first few days before they'd become inured to the inevitability of their situation, when their hands still trembled with such suppressed rage and stark fear that it was hard to work, Paul had snapped and snarled back at him when he'd asked. “You should know, General. You've got them, not us!” Osman's answer had chilled them both.

“Yes, gentlemen,” pause, “we have.” He hadn't even stopped examining the newly commenced dies to look at them as he said it. Then he walked out with that feline grace and power which characterised his every move and the door locked behind him leaving the air tense and still like the aftermath of a terrorist bomb before the shock releases its awful grip and people start screaming.

Now they'd done their job. There was nothing left to do. They waited and now no one came to see them who spoke any English - and the phones weren't there.

£$£

Chapter Twenty Six

"Fit, are you sure there's nothing we can do to help?"

JD asked the question with that feeling of pathetic inadequacy, which inflicts everyone when faced by serious illness of those near, dear or enmeshed in friendship with them. The question was hopeless, but expressed genuinely. It sounded lame even as he said it. Corporate aid to combat cancer? Unlikely.

Fit, always urbane, cynically enthusiastic, disguising every hardship and unpleasantness with his easy manner, until now. Now he sounded flat, weary, worried, and older.

"Thanks JD, but there really is nothing you can do. She starts radiotherapy this week. I don't know how long it goes on. What I do know is that I've got to make it my number one priority from now on."

"Of course you have, Fit. No question."

"Look," there was a pause, "I can't be any use to you for at least the next few weeks. If it'll make things any easier for you, please terminate the Consultancy Agreement. Don't worry about it. I fully understand that."

Once again, for the umpteenth time, JD was impressed and affected and marvelled at how those with real problems, worried about those without them. He would have loved to do something, anything, to help. But he could only mouth the empty words.

"No, no, Fit, don't even think about it. We need you."

He was trying desperately to say all the right things. "Get Ronni right. Ness wants to come down and see her. She'll call. Then we've things to do. I'm going back to Libya, it's a cracking plant, Fit. The Base is up and running, almost full-blast. It's a bloody marvellous installation. I want to see it. You should and I've still got to do that Gulf sales sweep we planned. I'll take Nigel. He's a poor stand-in. Better you. But we'll do it again soon as you're back.

One thing's for certain. I'm not staying anywhere with him where they have illuminated magnifying shaving mirrors in the bathrooms!" JD said it in a deliberately petulant voice. At least it made Fit laugh. They had a standing joke between them that Nigel Betts was too vain to look into a shaving mirror, unless it was on the magnifying side. That's how he saw himself.

"You won't change him," Fit retorted with a little chuckle.

"No, but I'll bloody-well make sure he knows what I think of him! God, he is such a prat!"

"Good luck, anyway. He's not so bad. You'll find he knows his stuff. I'll see you as soon as I can."

"Cheers, Fit. Give Ronni my love."

That was it. That was all JD could do. He felt guilty asking Shirley to get him the Gulf file. As if getting on with normal life was a betrayal of an old friend. What in God's name would he do if someone told him Ness had a life-threatening illness? Ness, who did everything at home, looked after everything, leaving him to get on with his job? Ronni had never recovered from the death. Who would? he thought. What could be worse? You should die before your children. So her refuge was to smoke. Who could tell her that 40 or 50 a day weren't much good for you? People who hadn't been through what she'd been through?

He had to go to Libya. Everything was going so well. But where were the engravers? Every time he wanted to see them they were "out", with their families, or visiting museums or historic sites for "reference material". What was going on? Were they performing, or was Belazir just being polite? If they weren't, if they were "swanning", he had to see them to put them right. This was the biggest contract Daltons had won. They were crucial to it. The Libyan Dinars were easy, engravings delivered from Daltons, the new currency was another thing. It had to be right and on time. Time was running out. So, had they performed? Only seeing them and their work and talking to them would reassure him. This time, he would. Whatever Belazir said.

Nigel Betts, teeth gleaming, came to see him. They planned the Gulf trip. JD made sure that he understood that he alone would go on to Libya. Nigel would fly home. Nigel was disappointed with that, but he welcomed a few flights with JD. Perhaps he could convince him to trust him, and to recognise his expertise if they had some time alone together. Nigel may as well have tried to convince JD that behind his salesman's smile lay a warm-hearted human being totally dedicated to the company. Like convincing a tiger that killing was unnecessary in order to eat....

JD and Nigel Betts landed in Shazah, at the under-used international airport the old Sheikh had built out of sheer competitiveness to match his relations in Dubai. They took the 10-minute taxi drive across what used to be desert to where they'd be ensconced for the whole trip. The Sheraton Hotel, on the Creek. Their own Business Travel Agency hadn't known it was an alternative to over-crowded Dubai Airport. JD only knew because Fit had told him, but he still criticised the kids who now ran the Agency. They could operate PCs but they probably hadn't a clue where the bloody Persian Gulf was.

There were a number of meetings planned before he and Nigel parted company. Betts did well. He knew his business. He didn't like Fit's shadow falling across what was now his domain like Attila the Hun didn't like the shadow of the Cross-before-Rome, but he tried hard. JD tried hard to empathise with him. Compared to Fit, with his deliberately laid-back manner, Nigel was a surprising revelation. In some ways he was polished and on the ball. In others it was like having a young and thrusting (he loved that word) PR Consultant running your major Sales Department. Perhaps that was the future.

They wanted to go to Abu Dhabi. JD objected to flying and all the delays it entailed. So they got a taxi, driven by a Pakistani who swore he spoke English, but didn't, and didn't understand their requests and kept the air-conditioning on "cold" even though the desert was cold and it was raining. They were freezing. They may as well have been in Manchester, Minneapolis or Malmo in autumn. Poor people of the UAE, where oil was discovered last, offshore, in the peninsular, wandered along the road in a desultory fashion, going...... where? Dead camels and auto-wrecks littered the side of the road, even though there was a camel-fence all the way from Dubai to Abu Dhabi. Nobody cleared them up. Grey deserts and grey skies merged to make it a boring and trying journey. The Pakistani driver had his prayer beads hung over his interior mirror and recited the 99 names of God. JD and Nigel didn't even have a sandwich and prayed to God that he'd turn the air-conditioning off.

JD relented half way back to Dubai, after they'd done the business in Abu Dhabi which was a Manhattan in the desert. Nigel wasn't so bad. There could be worse. It was he who was wrong. Prejudiced. They'd take a break. It had stopped raining and the sun was burnishing the desert.

The driver had waited for them everywhere. They were going to be his best customers for weeks. He'd look after them, he'd become their aide-de-camp, he'd take them anywhere.

"Let's go for lunch and a bloody rest," said JD. Nigel was surprised, but gratified.

"Driver, take us into Jebel Ali." JD stabbed his shoulder with his finger. The driver laughed uncomprehendingly. "Jebel Ali. There, Jebel Ali." JD was pointing across the desert, to an outline on the horizon. One of the only lateral roads they had come across led straight to it. "Now."

He cottoned on. They drove along the new road to it. An oasis in the barren, boring desert. It was a beautiful seaside resort hotel. It had shark nets, and even more important, poisonous sea-snake fine-mesh nets to keep the Gulf's most repulsive predator at bay. JD would rather be attacked by a Great White Shark than swim with a snake.

The Maitre-d was an Indian. The Test match was on radio. They spent a lunchtime living "cricket", as the Maitre-d, and everyone else serving their table, told them the latest scores.

It was incongruous. What made it more so, in the midst of a desert, was that Germans peopled it. It was a Lufthansa "watering hole". The stewardesses were Teutonic and beautiful. The guests were Teutonic. Nobody, but JD and Nigel, and the Maitre-d and the Indian and Pakistani waiters were interested in cricket scores. They didn't even know, obviously, what a "Test match" was. They finished a good lunch and went out onto the terrace. They could watch, ogle, everyone from there.

Nigel said suddenly, "Christ, JD. There's Vernon Forshaw!"

He was their biggest rival's Mid-East Sales Director. In some ways they were old friends as well as competitors. They often bumped into each other. It was curious to see him there.

"Let's go across, he's not seen us!" As far as JD was concerned he'd have talked to Martin Bormann rather than go through another hour trapped with Nigel. He sure as hell didn't want to hear anything more about Nigel's re-structuring of their Overseas Sales Department "post-Fit". He'd now formed a new opinion of Betts. He talked his potential customers into orders. They gave them to him to stop him talking. . ! Good plan, as far as the company was concerned. JD's conclusion was a kind of respect.

Vemon's white, slug-shaped body lounged in a white recliner thonged with green and blue striped cushions. He was drinking what looked like a large Coke with lots of ice (it turned out to be full of Bacardi, tinged with Coke). He was surprised to see them obviously, but he recovered quickly. He sat up and greeted them warmly.

His body crumpled into fleshy tyres around his mid-riff, a pale flesh-coloured life belt, like those kids use while swimming. His saggy pectorals were like water wings.

"How nice to see you," he lied brightly. "What'll you have to drink? Are you staying here? How long have you been here?"

He didn't look it at that moment, but he was a

consummate Sales Operator. Very successful. This had been his territory for years and years.

JD didn't answer any of his questions.

"No, we'll get it. God forbid you should ever buy us anything! What would you put on your expenses?"

"Helping the under-privileged," Vernon shot back.

"Touché, Vernon," said JD. "Right, now that's over, you fat bugger, what do you want?" He sat down on the uncushioned li-lo next to Vernon.

Nigel pulled a chair into the sun at the round table, making sure the parasol didn't shield the sun from his tan. He hitched his powder-blue trousers with the razor-sharp creases up to prevent "knee-bulge", showing his gleaming white stockings over the white buckskin shoes. JD noticed all the whites, socks shoes and teeth, were all different shades. He couldn't help thinking what Fit would have made of the encounter. A challenge, no doubt. JD played Fit.

"We're on holiday, I've discovered a new sexual orientation. I love him in powder blue."

Nigel coloured up under the tan. Vernon's body quivered with laughter. His torso behaved like a concertina. No, more like a pair of bellows. His breasts beat a gentle strum on his abdomen rolls.

"I'll spread that round, immediately. I'll have a Bacardi and Coke. Large one. I've never had anything from Daltons!"

"Not what Fit's expenses say, Forshaw!"

The waiter brought the drinks. Nigel had a "French very dry" white wine, "preferably Sancerre" and soda. JD knew it. They watched the air-stewardesses and male cabin crew leaping in and out of the lagoon. They were immediately identifiable. The rest of the German guests were white, red, old and overweight.

"C'mon Forshaw," JD said in his best mock aggressive gruff unfriendly voice, "Cut the crap. What're you doing here? You can't have sold anything. We've got this God-forsaken place wrapped up, from Kuwait to Oman. You're out of it. You should never have stayed loyal to supplying

Iraq! You did do the lraqui currency before the Gulf War didn't you?" JD knew how touchy they were about that.

"You know damned-well we did. But we've never broken sanctions, as you also know JD and it's not affected our business in this area in any way. I'm glad to say."

Vemon Forshaw was emphatic. Defiantly aggressive. JD knew he'd got him a bit irritated, so he went on.

"Well, you've not sold so bloody much in the last couple of years, Vernon, my old China!"

Vernon's small blue eyes almost gleamed from beneath the white blonde eyelashes. His soft mouth metaphorphosised into two entangled bloodworms.

"You're not in Fit's league at goading, JD," he openly grinned now, "but I will tell you, because it's all been legally tendered for openly, and it'll soon be released. I was surprised you lot weren't tendering. I've just had my most successful 14 days in this region. Five re-prints, 16 denominations."

JD couldn't help it. His sickly smile must have betrayed, his feelings. Nigel stared fixedly at him. He was professional enough not to look at Forshaw. He could see it had stopped JD like a knee in the groin. They'd spent all their time on this trip not selling banknotes. There soon weren't going to be any local currencies. They were providing all that was needed with the common Arab currency soon to come. Why should anyone re-order?

JD recovered quickly.

"Congrats, Vernon. You've stuffed us again!"

Vernon now looked like the Buddha imitating the Mona Lisa. The three men settled down to an hour of banter and Bacardi and Sancerre. But Nigel could see the spark had gone out of JD. He was obviously perplexed, anxious to get away now. They needed to talk about it, analyse the implications, immediately they had the chance. The orders were obviously "covers", but how many were ordered? Would it delay the Pan-Arab Currency launch? They needed to talk. Vernon wouldn't reveal any more details. He'd said enough to enable him to enjoy the glow of satisfaction that warmed him more than the sun.

As soon as it seemed reasonable, JD summoned Matin, the Bangladeshi waiter. He was in top form. The Sri Lankans were thrashing India! Anybody who thrashed India had a supporter in him. JD asked for the bill, told Matin to add another triple Bacardi and Coke for Vernon, plus bowls of nuts and crackers and crisps. Vernon protested but JD insisted, "The nuts will keep your skin over those powerful stomach muscles taut and healthy-looking. For the girls. Providing you're dressed." Vernon was giggling again. The slug in spasm.

They got back to the cab. The driver was somewhere around the 80th name of Allah, and listening to the BBC World Service, for cricket news. After the heat on the terrace the cold car was a relief.

"What the bloody hell was all that about? Why are they ordering more currency?"

"It's a smoke screen JD," Nigel said confidently. "It must be."

"It doesn't make sense. It's bloody odd, Nigel. If they've ordered those now they'll not get them for at least six, possibly nine, months. The way Belazir's pushing the plant they'll be ready to issue the common currency in a month. Well, they could start now but they'll probably wait 'til they've got supplies in every country so they can do a simultaneous launch with all the PR hoopla and all that crap. It's bloody odd."

"It's got to be a cover JD, anyway, you'll be there tomorrow. You can check it all out then."

"Yeah, yeah, I can and I've got to see Paul and Simon. If they're delaying things by arty-fartying around, trying to create "the world's most beautiful currency", I'll kill the little buggers."

They didn't say much on the rest of the journey back to Dubai. JD was preoccupied. He was worried about the engravers. They could be holding things up, but there was something else not quite right. Something gnawed at the back of his brain. He wouldn't feel happy 'til he'd seen and talked to them. He supposed it was because Belazir always seemed evasive about them, and he'd noticed Osman and Saif never got involved in any conversations about them. His innermost worry was that Belazir was putting immense pressure on them to finish the new designs in totally unreasonable time. He didn't like the idea of anyone putting pressure on his people. They were only young. They were good lads, nice families. He felt completely responsible for them.

They got back to the hotel late afternoon. The driver was delighted with the tip. He swore he'd sleep in his cab and be waiting to take JD to the airport next morning. He probably would. They were friends now, too. He gave JD his cousin's address in Bolton where he'd settled with his family after going to Bolton Technical College. He owned a taxi business. JD should go and see him. He'd be made very welcome. Two hundred miles from Daltons to Bolton meant absolutely nothing to the driver. England was so small he was obviously convinced everybody must know each other.

JD told Nigel he was going to have a shower and change, then go for a walk into town to buy Ness a watch, so he'd meet up with him for dinner in three hours, at about eight. He wanted some time to himself to think. When you travelled together you became like Siamese twins. You had to plan and explain separation.

He did want to buy Ness a watch. Dubai had some wonderful jewellery shops. There was a fantastic Gold Market, built by the Sultan for the traders. It was a hall of glistening metal, and it was all gold. There were gold belts, and buckles, and brooches, and rings, even complete ladies evening shawls like fine chain mail. All gold. All of it run by people from the four corners of the great sub-Continent who, with the Chinese, must be the greatest traders in the world. He walked down the steps from the palatial reception and looked back again at the hotel. The architect, whoever he was, had captured the spirit of the place perfectly. It was built in the shape of an Arab Dhow. It sat like a fort on the banks of the Creek where modern ships were in the minority and where you felt as if you'd slipped back a thousand years in time as you walked along the quays and watched ancient, and new, sea-going Dhows being loaded and unloaded by characters straight from a Hollywood "Sinbad the Pirate" movie. Men with daggers, and bandanas and eye-patches. He loved it. If you spoke to them they grinned exposing teeth the colour of Demerara sugar and called back, in Urdu, and Gujurati, Arabic and Farsi. The evening drew in rapidly as usual. The Creek was aglow on both sides with ship's lights and lanterns, then above them the harsher brighter lights of the modern city that had erupted like acne onto the age-old landscape in only forty years. JD didn't see the lights. His mind was flooded with images of what this place was like in 650 B.C. when the Phoenicians controlled the trade of the Persian Gulf, and long before that the Hittites, Sumerians, Assyrians and Babylonians had traded, through the Chaldeans, and the records of that trade was found in the Palace of Nebuchradezzar and referred to by Ezekiel. This place was living history; much more evocative than Venice or Rome or Athens. Those places were "Johnny-cum-latelies".

As he walked, and enjoyed, and thought of the engravers, there was something else puzzling him. Old Stanley Mortinsen, the Print Manager, had told him they were hell-bent on working three shifts at the Base, round the clock. Even seven days a week. What the hell for? There was enough machinery there now to produce everything they said they needed on one shift, perhaps with the odd few extra worked every week in the initial stages to satisfy the first-launch requirements. Why were they going so O.T.T.?

He bought the watch, and thought he'd sort it all out tomorrow.

£$£

Chapter Twenty Seven

The ancient River Medjerda made its way steadily down to the sea which was created when the sombre and ominous Atlantic pitilessly smashed its way through the Pillars of Hercules to flood the Mediterranean basin. An event just a remote, barely remembered memory for mankind, enshrined in only myths. On the shores around that sea there developed the original thinkers, the philosophers, the religious visionaries, the warriors, the seafarers, the traders, the empires that have influenced, permeated, controlled, the minds of mankind for the last 5,000 years. The river still ran into the Gulf where the mysterious city had stood which held sway over the greatest trading empire the world had seen. Carthage. Founded in 800 BC by those seafarers held in awe by the ancient Egyptians and spoken of many times in the Old Testament Books of Kings, Isaiah, Jeremiah and Ezekiel, the Phoenicians. Tyre and Sidon, their original home ports, were too Easterly in the Mediterranean. They needed another great port in the West to protect their trade with the Tartessians of Gades for the gold and silver of Spain and the tin of Brittany and Cornwall. They'd controlled the Pillars of Hercules since 1200BC. Now they had more to protect. For they'd created an "empire" which spanned the known world, a trading empire. Carthage was to be its Capital. And so it remained for 654 years, until their inability to appease the new and greedily violent and militaristic power of Rome led ultimately to their destruction. Rome wasn't satisfied 'til all Carthaginian power was destroyed, however hard the ancient and worldly-wise city tried to appease the bullying brutish newcomers. A lesson in history Winston Churchill preached in vain during the desolate third decade of the 20th Century under the gathering clouds of the Nazi storm.

From this cradle of history, from the shores of mighty

Carthage, Himilco in 500 BC sailed through the Pillars into the dread Atlantic and bore North, to Brittany and the Tin Islands, His contemporary Hanno left the same shores, breached the Pillars and sailed South to within eight degrees of the equator, to Sierra Leone. No one reached this Latitude again until Henry the Navigator nearly 2000 years later. In their two voyages these Carthaginians trebled the size of the known world. After 146BC Carthage was no more. Destroyed by the Romans. But 2000 years later, during the greatest of World Wars, the armies of five powerful industrialised nations fought the last decisive strategic battle in Africa across the Carthaginian River and one of them was Roman, the Italians, with their allies, the Germans and the French, confronted the British and the Americans on the historic plains on the banks of the Medjerda. This time justice prevailed and the greedy and the violent and militaristic left the shores of Carthage and sailed home defeated.

Now it was a bloody airport. That's all JD could see. A great, flat, ugly, concrete, glass, lights, noise, sand, cars, trucks, buses, people-full airport. Tunis Airport, for all Tunisia. As far as he could see, Tunisia was overflowing into the sea with tourists. He imagined it happening at the other end, all the tourists spilling over into the desert, like locusts at the edge of a plague.

All that concrete, just a few inches/centimetres thick, covering all that history. Hannibal's Dad was under there, that's why Hannibal crossed the Alps to stuff the Romans and avenge him, then there were tens of thousands of Roman and Carthginian soldiers, women, kids, all sorts. Horses, donkeys, and loads of dead elephants. The Romans were terrified of Hannibal. He terrorised them for over thirty years. They chased him all over their Empire and he finally utterly defeated them by killing himself on the borders of Turkey and Tajikistan before they could get to him. They never did set hands on him. History just below the surface, the surface just keeping the lid on time, a crust on the simmering broth of history active all around all of us anywhere, everywhere, but here the difference was it had all been recorded. We knew all about it, if we chose to read the historical newspapers.

This was Carthage. Extreme emphasis on "was".

JD stopped meandering and stared out of the window of the Merc. "His" driver and Security guard had met him as usual. They'd looked after him, he was a VIP. He was grateful. They were almost friends now. But they had an 11-hour-plus drive ahead of them to Sirte. The air-conditioning and the delightful snacks provided to obviate "victualling" stops couldn't relieve the boredom. It was like flying to Tokyo or LA from London, so many hours in a metal tube. But this was a metal cube. JD almost prayed for the hold-ups at the Tunis/Libya border posts, as sanctions were busted as frequently as a black teenager driving a black BMW 5-Series in Brixton or Harlem, to relieve the tedium, but they were never held up. Diplomatic plates, and elaborate preparations sped them through the desert like sand-dolphins. Still, it was an 11-hour journey, minimum. JD kept staring; he couldn't sleep. Anyway, oddly, it somehow seemed impolite.

In that 11 hours, as they crossed the desert, banknotes, perfect, flawless, worth $257,642,000, were produced in the glorified air-raid shelter under the desert outside Sirte, a round-the-clock shuttle of huge Hercules C-130 transports flew from there to Sudan. In those 11 hours banks in Khartoum transferred, ceaselessly, millions to banks in Iran, Iraq, the Yemen. And through and from the Lebanon millions flowed to Sicily, to Italy, then onwards to Switzerland and all parts of Europe. From Iran and Iraq money flowed into Afghanistan and Central Asia, Tajikistan, Turkmenistan, Uzbekistan, Kazakhstan, from Italy and Spain and Portugal and Switzerland to the USA and Latin America. The Libyan Central Bank was able to provide the same service for Africa and the Gulf. All supplies were electronic transfers, backed up by physical transfer immediately thereafter. All transfers were honoured. Southeast Asia took the notes directly on privately owned Tupelovs, ex-bombers, with the markings of the Vietnamese Air force. They didn't land in Vietnam. That regional superpower was too well organised. The Chinese preferred chaos in which to do business. Laos, Cambodia, Burma, Thailand, provided sufficient chaos, for any organisation, and from there it was easy to deal with Indonesia, Malaysia, Hong Kong, Macao, Taiwan, North Korea, South Korea. Perhaps it would aid re-unification and then, the drugged giant itself, the Middle Kingdom, China. What opportunities!

The distribution flow seemed seamless, flawless. Every hour, by truck, by plane, by ship, it didn't stop. It was quietly relentless. It was beyond Belazir's most optimistic expectations, Saif had no expectations, Dajani was impressed, better by far than he'd expected. Osrnan kept in constant touch with the Hanifs. They kept in constant touch with the main aim of the grand strategy. The money was distributed, used, to buy assets, shareholdings, commodities, arms, people. They organised the absorption of the murky tidal wave for the good of the faith.

Gold, platinum and rhodium bought in huge quantities, costing nothing, just scraps of paper. Prices rose. Oil bought at prevailing prices, sold to the African South and East for knockdown prices, all to help fellow Moslems. With just scraps of paper. After the IMF had been paid, with the exorbitant interest rates the developed world laughingly called "aid" the main item on all the poorer countries' bill was oil. When Osman and the organisation created by the Hanifs which had penetrated all Moslem and many non-Moslem countries, supplied it at such a low price they would be able to raise the prices of their raw materials, and the West could pay for them or do without them. Copper, cobalt, uranium, gold, bauxite, platinum, rhodium, diamonds, amethysts, tobacco, wood, cotton, sugar. Normally, they were all so strapped for cash that they'd charge anything the world would pay for their raw materials. With oil at a reasonable price they'd have a surplus and they could charge more meaningfully, more sensibly, more to their advantage. The West wouldn't like it. But the West needed the raw materials. They'd never had to pay the proper price for them before, though. It was all so simple. It was the will of God.

Osman launched a "Hadj" fund. The Hanifs helped. Publicity in the poorest Moslem countries was easily and swiftly organised, by TV, by newspapers, by radio, through the Mullahs and the Immams and the local Mosques. It was for the faith. Hundreds of millions of Moslems wanted to undertake the "Hadj", the pilgrimage to Mecca. Their problem, as always, was money. The Prophet had decreed that the poor didn't have to make the pilgrimage. Allah the Merciful would understand. But the poor, more than anyone, wanted to. The General's fund could provide the money. Loans, with no interest as befits Islamic laws on usury. Lifetimes to repay. Cash loans, crisp new $100 notes, Euros. Tens of millions of pilgrims needing $500, $1,000 each. An ideal way to distribute money, and help less fortunate brothers in faith.

In the Americas, North and South, another organisation was at work, a "family" business. Property deals of major proportions noticeably increased, there was a flurry of activity in takeovers and acquisitions in hi-tech industries on the US West coast, Research and Development funding, in return for minority shareholdings, became suddenly more freely available in a healthy smattering of small but exciting high-risk bio-tech companies. Luxury hotel chains, of limited size, changed hands in Mexico, Brazil and Venezuela. Two small oil companies with modest but lucrative fields were sold at extremely good prices in Texas. New casino developments, European-funded, were announced in Vegas, Tahoe and Atlantic City. One or two sharp-eyed investors on Wall Street noticed the growing interest and activity shown by Arab and Swiss banks acting for European and Middle Eastern investors, and there were some German and Italian banks doing the same thing. Obviously the Old World wanted more of a share of the action in the New World. The conclusion was drawn in more than one quarter that money was quietly moving out of Europe until the stresses caused by monetary union had worked themselves out. The Southern European economies especially were struggling. Only Germany and the Benelux countries seemed to be prospering. The way it looked from Manhattan the crafty British had called it right, they were OK. There was no discernible increase in British investment in the US, no extra activity by UK banks. Still, considering they already owned more of America than any other nation in the world, they hardly needed more. But the others, well, it was a safe haven for their money in these uncertain times. Reflation in Japan at the end of the Second Millennium hadn't worked. Southeast Asia was a mess. Europe was still in mild recession and throughout the EU the financial markets were all "bear" markets. Yes, obviously the USA was the right market.

The picture in Europe though, began to follow the American pattern, but on a slightly smaller scale of course. Welcome new investment, through certain Italian and Portuguese banks lightened the gloom of the recession. The financial world noted with approval how well the Euro worked in the cross-border deals. Some Belgian banks got in on the act, and US dollars flowed quietly but steadily from Switzerland. Things were perhaps picking up.

Central Asia, Kazakhstan, Uzbekistan, Turkmenistan, Tajikistan and Azerbaijan all witnessed an in-flow of dollars for mining and raw materials investment and development from the Lebanese, Palestinian, Pakistani, Iraqi and Iranian banks. It was all a welcome boost for the privatisation of the state-owned industries. Foreign investment was very welcome, in return for minority stakes. Islamic influence spread quietly riding on the magic carpet of US dollars.

A couple of thousand miles away Michael Donegan's organisation helped the French, Israeli and Russian arms industries in a small but useful way, using the Euro and the dollar through the usual Dublin and Cork banks. The leadership were able to tell their American cousins and supporters in New York and Boston that they were eternally grateful for all the help given in the past, but now it wasn't so desperate. The political settlement and ceasefire had to be given every chance to work. At long last the gun could be taken out of Irish politics. Give peace a chance. It was deeply appreciated in the US. It was proof of the sincerity of the patriots, wasn't it just? Of course, the leadership and the boys were preparing for the collapse of the political settlement, which was inevitable. Ireland was still not united. But money was now no object. After the arms purchases, the Euros were plentiful enough to fund and expand greatly the community work they'd been long involved in, helping poor Republicans, and the Garda, and local politicians and their political machines and the Army and the Navy. There was enough for all.

And the scraps of paper smudged with ink kept flowing, gushing from that underground money-well in the desert, creeping steadily over the face of Europe and Asia, Africa and the Americas like blood on the shirt of a man executed by firing squad.

In the silence of the limousine cruising in the black night watching the brilliant white lines rush towards him in the headlights as they sped along the superb coastal highway, with only the ghostly green of the dashboard and the bright cold moon to gaze at, JD wasn't thinking of any of this. He didn't know any of this. He didn't even know where his engravers were. Or where they were up to. One thing he did know though. He was going to see Simon and Paul next morning. Whatever Belazir said. He had to make sure the lads were all right. Just as important, well, almost, he had to make sure the great project was on schedule. It was getting towards financial year-end. It could make a few million pounds difference to the bottom line.

£$£

Chapter Twenty Eight

She was asleep now. He gently withdrew his hand from hers and stood up to inch the bed cover over her slim neck. He gazed down at her for a few seconds. Her face was like porcelain. He experienced a frisson of fear, of panic, when it seemed to change, when she didn't look like Veronica. Then she was Veronica again, and he started to breathe. He stepped back and slumped into the armchair, never taking his eyes off her face. He didn't want her to change again.

Beneath the perennial golf-tan his own face changed. No longer the mask he was wearing for Ronni. No longer the persona of Fit the urbane, sardonic, slightly cynical, deeply experienced, always slightly amused veteran traveller and Senior Sales Director moving in elevated political stratum, no longer the easy, friendly, ever-welcoming golf club President and former Captain playing off 8 and scratch on the 19th. He was an older man, approaching 67 and he looked it. His eyes and his flesh were suddenly tired and revealed so to the world that had never brushed away the fine coating of persona-lacquer before. The hands, which rested on his knees, were like his father's hands. His body folded into the chair as only an older person's can.

He was alone in the small private ward. There was only silence to keep them company. The light above her head was the only illumination. Twelve weeks, it was only twelve weeks since she'd picked him up from the airport after Libya. She was OK. Then now she was here. He studied her face intently. He wanted, he willed her, to wake up, to say something, anything, to him. To tell him to stop worrying, to stop flapping. To get up and tell him she was going to make a coffee. But there was only the silence, and the face in the light.

His mind wouldn't stop. He wasn't in control of it. It

insisted on playing newsreels, going back 51 years, then scrolling forwards, and then back again. There was a 17-year-old boy with jet-black hair, and a girl of 19 with the beautiful delicate face in the light in the bed, half-sitting, half-lying next to their bicycles on Ealing Common on a warm sunny summer afternoon making a feast out of potted meat sandwiches and drinking water out of a lemonade bottle and laughing together for hours. In his mind that operated separately next to the newsreels he knew with solid certainty that it was one of the finest meals he'd ever had. No restaurant, or banquet, or Presidential dining room could ever match it. It was captured forever on the film in his mind. He could hear the traffic on the Uxbridge Road, smell the grass and her lavender water perfume, taste the water warmed by the sun in her saddlebag. It couldn't be 51 years ago. That was a …. lifetime. Where had their lives gone? Their first small house, with the front door that opened straight onto the street, with the bus stop three doors down where they caught the No.27 every day together to work until she stopped to have lain. Then they were in Iain's room and he was five and they were doing OK and he looked smart in his first school uniform and she walked him to school and came home and cried a little and couldn't wait 'til lunch time only three hours later to collect him. She never let him stay for school dinners. She pretended there wasn't enough nourishment in them.

The newsreel flashed forward and it was Christmas and Iain was 15, standing for the photograph on the little rear patio in the frost with his new Armstrong Moth Super Light-weight racing bike with the drop handlebars and eight gears and he was as tall as she was. And that was the last Christmas photograph. It was the photograph on the display cabinet in front of which she silently placed a posy of violets on the anniversary of his death and on his birthday for 22 years. They were the flowers he brought home from Sunday school every Mothering Sunday until he stopped going when he was 11, but which he remembered and bought until the year he died. After the first few months, when talking about him was the only palliative for the awful pain which ached in the pit of the stomach and blocked the throat and for the hollow emptiness inside and in everything she never spoke of him until the 15th anniversary of his death, when she quietly said over dinner, "Iain would have been 30. We'd probably have been grandparents Frederick." And they'd stopped eating and cried together for the first time in all those years, and after that they'd never stopped talking about him. He still lived with them, and he shared their big and little triumphs and their holidays when they went back to Cornwall and threw stones on the beach at Porth and wondered if Ian's dam had changed the course of the little river and laughed like they had done next to their bicycles.

The newsreel was still running when she took her arm out of the bed cover and Fit got up quickly and slipped the mask on and his hand into hers. Her face changed, because there was a faint smile playing on her lips, her eyes opened, and she whispered, so faintly he had to bend close to hear anything, kissing her forehead softly as he did so. He could barely make it out, but he was convinced later, and forever, that she had said, "Don't worry Frederick. Stop fussing. I'm just going to see lain. It's OK."

He put his finger to her lips. "Don't talk. I love you. Rest." She closed her eyes, but the smile remained.

He stood for a while, and then sat down, never taking his eyes off her. The silence cloaked them again, and they never spoke to each other again for the rest of their lives.

£$£

Chapter Twenty Nine

Not meeting him wasn't discourteous, but not leaving or sending a message was, he decided. A case of familiarity breeding contempt, he supposed. He'd been so many times in the past three months. Before, though, one, or a pair, of the "oily trinity", as he and Fit called the three Generals, had always met him at the Guest House when he'd arrived, no matter how late. This time, after his driver and "guide" had gone - immediately he walked into Reception, as they always did, relieved to be rid of him he had no doubt, - all that met him was a bowl of fruit in his room

He'd had a shower and felt fresh, but he was tired, weary. Too tired to lie down to sleep. Tired like he used to get sometimes as a kid when you didn't know what to do with yourself and it made you feel like crying. What he really needed was a large scotch or two. He'd sleep then. No chance of that here. He attacked an orange from the bowl with the ferocity of a tortoise, and took papers out of his pilot's case. He wasn't going to read them. He was looking for blank paper or a pad. He was going to plan his every thought and move for tomorrow. He'd be ready for anything, he thought. Then he wondered why he'd thought it. He was only reviewing the plant progress, discussing further raw materials supplies contracts and seeing Paul and Simon for Christ's sake. What did he think he had to be ready for? Well, he thought, it's best to plan in case they still don't let me see the lads. Plan what? Well, his reply. A reply that would force them to spare time out of the lads' programme. Yes, that's what he'd plan. A stunning reply to any "No," or "Next time," or "In two or three days". Even if it was a, "They've gone away for a break for a few days."

He wrote "Reply Stratagems" on top of the blank word processor paper. He left fingerprints all over the paper and his pen stuck to his fingers. Orange juice was an adhesive!

Amazing. He stared at the blank paper. His eyes were heavy and pricking as if they were filled with fine dust. He wrote the four side-headings down. "Straightforward No", "Next Time" etc., leaving a space below each for his clever and withering reply. Then he stared some more at the paper. If he'd had a scotch it would have flowed, he thought petulantly. The minutes ticked by on his travelling alarm clock. He watched them go. He felt even more tired. He leaned back on the low-backed bedroom chair. He looked at himself in the dressing table mirror through half-closed eyes, and then he closed them. Sleep stole over him from out of the silence. His head lolled back and his body was twisted and arched. He knew where he was, that he was asleep, but conscious of being asleep. He knew he was dreaming, and so many images filled his mind, constantly renewing themselves. He was with Fit and Veronica at Tunis Airport, then Ness came and they set off into the desert on the straight road, but it was the desert between Dubai and Abu Dhabi, so he knew that wasn't right and they couldn't get to where they were going. There was only the one road but they didn't know how far along it they had to go so they kept stopping to ask, but nobody spoke English. It was frustrating. Even asleep and dreaming he could feel the intense irritation. They were running out of time for a meeting. The meeting was at the base. They got to the base but the gates outside were shut. He was told to get out of the car and the guard grabbed him from behind, with an arm round his neck and a knee in the small of his back and he was choking and his neck was being bent backwards, so was his spine. It was hurting, and he was only saved because the base security alarms all started ringing and the guard let him go. He lurched forward and put his hand behind his neck to pull it back onto its socket on the top of his spine. He always pictured a head and a neck with a ball-knuckle to slot into the spine socket. He put his other arm out to steady himself . . . .

He woke up when he knocked his alarm over. It hit the dressing table with a sound like the first strike of a judge's gavel. He stared, disorientated, into the dressing table mirror. His neck and his back were sore and stiff. He leaned forwards slowly, un-creaking himself and lowered his head, rubbing his neck with some pressure. God, he'd been asleep five hours. It was 6.30 am. He could still taste oranges. He wanted to clean his teeth and have another long hot shower and put clean clothes on. And he had to pack what little he'd bothered to un-pack. They were coming for him at eight and he was taking everything to the base with him and going home tonight. They'd promised him a flight back to Tunis in time for the early-evening plane home. He'd time for all that. His head was clear now. He didn't want breakfast. He'd have coffee and orange juice and the Snicker Bar out of the fridge; they weren't, of course, called mini-bars where he was.

He was ready long before eight, and sat in Reception chatting to the friendly young Libyan in the brown blazer who was eager to speak English. They were a charming crew, he thought, always polite and eager to please. Child-like, innocent, almost feminine in their gentleness. If only people from the US, the UK, or the "rest of the West" could meet them. Not at all like the mindless, noisy, rabid extremists demonised by the media. All over the Arab world he'd been treated in the same way.

He was thinking his way through the politeness and friendliness of the Islamic world when the doors almost burst open and the "Lone Ranger" and "Tonto", his driver and his guide, strode in. It was precisely eight. There was no one with them. He did a double- take, and glanced through the glass doors at the car. No one in there.

There was something different.

Not with his men in the car. They tried chatting to him in English. He wished he could speak as much Arabic. Not with the guards on the incongruous gate. They saluted, then smiled and waved. Not with the young stewards who opened the huge door of the Monolith for him. They looked so young compared to the old soldiers all around them. Not even with General Belazir, who greeted him warmly at the door of the anteroom outside the vast reception hall, and then led him into the hall.

"Let us sit here for a change, Mr. Dilworth, my friend," he said motioning JD to a glass-topped coffee table framed with gold-coloured metal fittings, flanked by two exquisitely ugly white leather couches, "It will make a change for us."

The stewards were already beside them with Arabic coffee and glasses of cordial.

"I'm sorry we couldn't meet you. Pressing business." Belazir said it in such a way as to invite not even a polite response. "General Osman is hurrying to meet you."

JD weighed the emptiness of the comment. Osman wouldn't hurry to meet anyone, except perhaps Allah.

"It's good to be back in your country again General. But I must say I'm delighted you're flying me back to Tunis. That journey by car is certainly a long one."

"It is the least we can do after all you've done for us. The plane will be ready when you are. But yes, you're right. It is time these ridiculous sanctions were lifted. They achieve nothing. And they've been on for years now. What really upsets us you know is that everybody involved knows that our Security Forces played only a minor part in the unfortunate incident. We were little more than bag-carriers. Even the "Economist", six months after Locherbie, argued our case. Of course it was the Iranians, in understandable revenge for the Americans shooting down their helpless innocent civil airliner over the Gulf who carried it out, helped mainly by the Syrians. But they were vital to the Americans and your Government during the Gulf War so their role is now ignored. Politics is a dirty business, I'm glad I'm just a military man. It's stupid anyway, everyone knows we get all we want, and export all we want. In fact, the West wants our exports! They're produced by their companies! Such hypocrisy! The ban on civil aviation is so petty."

JD had heard it all before. It was one of Belazir's favourite themes, and he had a great deal of sympathy for him. Libya was being singled out. They made such easy "baddies" in simplistic American minds and propaganda. That wasn't really an excuse though for the cynical sophisticates of the State Department to perpetuate the injustice. He was going to voice his opinions in sympathetic support when Belazir carried on.

"Anyway, you know, if you were going, as most businessmen do, to Tarabulus, it's not even too long a journey from Tunis. I'm afraid, unfortunately, that to date, we've had to meet here. But this should be your last visit. There's nothing more for you to do here. We can meet in Tarabulus if we ever have to in the future."

There was finality in Belazir's tone, in the bald statement. His smile was fixed, and his small black eyes gleamed, not in an unfriendly way, more a combination of sardonic challenge, anticipation and wariness. He could tell JD had registered every word and inference. Now he waited for his reaction.

If Belazir had lunged with a razor-sharp knife and slit his scrotum from back to front he couldn't have been more shocked. He hoped it didn't show, but he was sure it must have done. Belazir never took his eyes off his face. His mind was frantically processing implications, questions, meanings, hidden meanings, the future of the supplies contracts, and the position of the engravers and what about the launch, and the publicity for Daltons? Surely they'd want a big splash, this was history in the making. He recovered in a split second. He had to guide this conversation, protect the company's interests. But he suddenly became starkly aware of how little ammunition he had. He hadn't thought of it before. Before, it had all seemed so friendly, such plain sailing. He used his friendliest, most familiar voice.

"Well, General. I hear what you say, but I think there is much we still have to do here together for our mutual benefit. You know, raw materials supplies, the international launch of the Pan Arab currency. We also…"

Belazir cut in smoothly, "Mr. Dilworth. I don't think so.

We have decided to delay the launch until we have first, enough currency to change everything at once, and secondly until we've convinced one or two "ditherers" to come in with us in the first wave."

It was the first time JD had heard anything like that. It didn't ring true anyway. After three months they must have millions printed, worth billions, and the "ditherers" were politically highly unlikely to join the "Club" until it was launched and proved itself conclusively. It was a perfect parallel with the UK's stance on EMU.

"Of course, General, I didn't know anything about that and, of course, it's none of my business. I didn't, however, think there was much chance of the others getting involved until it was all working smoothly, which I'm sure it will."

He was being emollient whilst he thought of what to say next. He had to lead the conversation around to the materials supplies contracts. He needn't have bothered. Belazir went on. "As for supplies, Mr. Dilworth. We've sourced what we need from Islamic countries. I hope you don't think we're being ungrateful for all you've done for us, but we believe it's vital that we Arabs work steadily towards self-sufficiency in industrial goods. Oil revenues flowing in so freely have largely caused us to ignore this until the last 20 years or so. Now it is our top priority. The common currency should play a part in this. I'm sure you understand."

For the second time in a matter of minutes JD was shaken. Where the hell were they sourcing currency paper, security inks and chemicals? Only Iran, Turkey and Egypt had the facilities, surely? No, His mind was racing. There was Pakistan and Uzbekistan. They could even get them from Russia or India or Indonesia. Christ! This must have been going on under their noses, and they'd not spotted it. But why? Relations had been so good, so friendly. They weren't even over-charging them, ripping them off, which he had to admit was a pretty standard practice in High Security Printing when you got the fish on the hook. His recovery rate was getting better. He said, with as much sincerity as he could muster.

"I couldn't agree with you more. If you've managed to do that and all the technical specifications can be met it's exactly what you should do. We'll still be here to help you of course should you require it, rest assured."

"We appreciate that. We will always be grateful to you for setting up our plant, which is superb."

"It's one of the best, most modern in the world, General."

He was going to enlarge on that, and edge the conversation back to the supplies when the door opened abruptly and Osman strode in, erect, purposeful, as graceful and immaculate as always. He greeted Belazir in Arabic briefly, Belazir replied a little more lengthily. JD guessed Belazir was briefing him as to where the discussion had got. Osman swung towards him, hand outstretched, with a smile not reflected in his eyes.

"Mr. Dilworth, good to see you again, as always. Good trip?"

He didn't give JD a chance to reply. He obviously wasn't interested in the answer.

"I believe the General has filled you in on our latest plans and developments? Thanks to you, we feel we can go it alone now. We're very grateful."

JD was tired of hearing how grateful they were. He had the distinct impression he was being rail-roaded. He missed Fit. They could have digressed onto some unrelated topic together to give themselves time to think. That was the problem with travelling alone. On big deals, pairs, or more, were better.

"Yes, General. I must say it's something of a surprise and a disappointment, of course. I came believing we'd be able to sign materials supply contracts today. Still, it's not to be. That's the way of the world, the capitalist world anyway! I'm really surprised about your decision to delay the launch. Are you sure that's the right thing to do?"

Osman raised his hands like a Moslem at the beginning of prayer. His reply was short and decisive, almost curt.

"Of course we are, Mr. Dilworth." He left the words stamped in the air, like the final, sealing, granite block in the passageway to the king's chamber in the Great Pyramid.

JD noted again that whenever Osman came into a room, or joined a conversation, he changed the atmosphere, if he wanted to. He exuded confidence, he could be direct to the point of discourtesy, he could be cold enough to chill any gathering, even if it was in the noonday temperature of the desert. JD had no doubt he could be frightening if he wanted to be. He wouldn't like to be his subordinate, or to cross him.

The two Generals watched him, not speaking. It was obviously his turn to do so. He sat on the white sofa and looked down the vast room to the huge black throne under the eagle. He wasn't sure what to say. Two of the main reasons for his visit had just been dismissed, as no more than chaff in the wind. He was alone. He felt alone. He swiftly appraised his options. He didn't have any. He was in charge of a modest business, they were in charge of security and military forces in their countries. No contest. There were still two things left to do. To inspect the plant and make sure it was all in order and still working efficiently even though there were now no Daltons technicians at the base (they didn't want blaming for faulty operations in the future) and to see the engravers and satisfy himself that they were OK and on target. Even the latter now wasn't so important if they really were delaying the launch. It took him a second longer to reply than it should have done, betraying, to his annoyance, that he had been thrown by what had taken place. He tried to make light of it, and sound matter-of-fact friendly.

"No, no, of course. You obviously know best. What I would like to do, if it's all right with you, is take a final tour of inspection to make sure the plant we supplied is running satisfactorily. I've left my "key" in the UK for obvious security reasons because I've just been, as you know, on a pretty lengthy sales sweep, so I'll have to rely on you to let me into the base. I don't want gassing! And also, as you know, I'd appreciate some time with the engravers to make certain they're on time and providing you with everything you need. Is that OK?"

Belazir started to speak. He sounded friendly as usual, if anything somewhat relieved that what had been said had been said.

"Mr. Dilworth, I don't think you need to bother…"

Osman cut in sharply, "That will not be necessary. We are perfectly satisfied with the performance of the machinery and have every confidence in the Libyan and Sudanese technicians."

There was no friendliness or relief in his voice.

"Of course. I'm sure they're doing a fine job. But general, we selected that machinery, installed it and planned how it was to run. I'm sure you understand. We feel responsible for it."

"You are not, Mr. Dilworth. We have paid for the machinery, have we not? It is our responsibility. Do not trouble yourself." Osman had adopted a distant, clipped, militaristic tone. It left no room for doubt. JD looked at Belazir. He was obviously just a little uncomfortable with the way the discussion was being conducted. JD addressed his next comments to him.

"Well, yes, of course it's your machinery. I just thought . . . . ."

"As I said, Mr. Dilworth, don't trouble yourself any more about it." Osman's tone had softened slightly, but he still stared at JD with the eyes of a panther. JD spoke to Belazir again.

"Surely you don't mind me having a final look at the plant General."

Belazir opened his hands and tilted his head to one side in a gesture of apology. "We don't really have a lot of time Mr. Dilworth. As I said, pressing business even prevented us meeting you, and…."

"It is not necessary." Osman's voice was at its coldest.

JD knew he wasn't going to get anywhere. His mind was racing. What the hell was going on? There must be something they didn't want him to see. It would have only taken half an hour to go down into the base and do a quick tour of the Press Hall. Was the alternative raw materials supply already being used? If it wasn't up to scratch, would they start blaming Daltons for whatever went wrong? No, it had to be more than that. He didn't have time to think about it now. He had one task to complete which he wouldn't be bloody deterred from, to see Paul and Simon. He started, "The engravers, Paul and Simon . . . "

"They are not here." Osman coldly dismissed the attempted inquiry with almost a flick of the wrist. JD's embarrassment was mutating to discomfort, but he persisted.

"Well, I think it's important that I at least see them. I'm responsible for them, and . . . . "

"It is not important." There was no mistaking the irritation in Osman's tone. "There is no need. We have finished with them. They have completed their task. They will be coming home in a week's time. I'm sure you can discuss all you want with them then, Mr. Dilworth and, as I've said, they are not here."

"May I ask where . . .?" he knew he sounded irresolute, whimpish. He didn't like himself for it.

"They're taking a break at the coast." Osman held his hand up. "Before you even ask, it is too far to drive you today. They are fine. Being well looked after, I assure you. In any case we, General Belazir and I, have to leave in a matter of minutes. We have pressing business of state that can wait no longer. Your guide will see you onto the plane. I'm afraid you're going to be back in Tunis early. Perhaps there are earlier flights, I hope so. Thank you again, Mr. Dilworth."

Osman was already stood up and making for the door. He made no attempt to shake hands with JD, who thought Belazir looked uncomfortable, and was going to say something else, but Osman's fixed look at him seemed to change his mind. He too stood, smiled and he did shake hands with JD, and left with more words of thanks following in Osman's wake, like a panther cub after its mother.

JD sat for a couple of minutes in the great room. His sense of resentment at being so coldly brushed off was extremely short-lived, to be replaced by an over-crowding of worries, images, puzzlement, concern, especially for the two lads, and their families. What the hell was going on? He couldn't think what. He needed time to think. He suddenly felt, with a genuine impact, the vulnerability of his position. He was alone, at a secret military base, engaged on a secret project, entirely at the mercy of the people he was dealing with, who weren't exactly normal people. He couldn't just order a taxi and ask it to take him to the airport. He couldn't even get out of the country without their help. He didn't like feeling vulnerable. These people didn't play games, and he was no hero. He wasn't in a position to push things, and he had a healthy respect for erring on the side of caution when it came to looking after his own neck. He was very sensitive to fear. He didn't like it. He needed time to think.

He didn't get it. His guide came in, he wasn't unfriendly, but he was unsmiling. He simply said, “The plane, it is ready to go. Your bags are on the plane. I drive you.”

He walked out into the heat. He saw Belazir's Mercedes speeding off from the outer gate with the two generals sat in the back. His sense of helplessness and smallness was emphasised by the vastness of the featureless desert that surrounded him. Shelley's “Ozymandias” flickered into his mind for a nanosecond. But it was replaced immediately by his old geometry teacher's biblical quote (usually with regard to “misplaced” homework.) from I Kings 10.7. “Behold, the half was not told me.”

£$£

Chapter Thirty

Death blankets a house like a cold, dank fog. Every brick and pane and board is coated with it. The air is thick with it on the drive, beside the front lawn, in the porch. The house is segregated from its neighbours by invisible mausoleum walls of morbidity.

It was the same house to look at. But it wasn't the same small detached warm friendly place just outside Tring which JD had turned up to so many times, and had a cup of tea and a whisky, and took the piss out of Fit and pretended to seduce Ronni. Because she was dead. Gone. It was impossible. Unthinkable. Not real. Veronica, slim, vivacious, bright-eyed, always laughing, with a chuckle which came from deep within her throat, more like seventeen than nearly seventy. (Nearly 70! She can't have been nearly seventy), a lovely person. A lovely girl, he wouldn't, ever, call her anything else. If he hadn't married Ness he'd have loved to marry someone like Ronni. Now she was dead. What was he going to say to Fit? What could you say to someone who'd suffered what he had? Whatever it was it would be inadequate. Inappropriate. He'd lost a son and now a wife, a partner, a lover, a friend. What the bloody hell do you say to someone in that situation? He sat in the Jaguar round the corner and thought and thought about it, as he had done for the whole of the journey. None of his thinking did any good. He climbed out heavily, still not knowing what to say.

Fit said, "Christ, JD, you look as bad as I've ever seen you look. You look like 5 am. in Mombassa!"

"Fit, I'm awfully sorry. Ness is coming down. She was at the hospital on that handicapped thing when I called her. What happened? I thought everything was OK. I thought the treatment was working. I thought it was just a matter of time, and perhaps a lung." He winced inwardly even as he said it. But Fit knew what he meant. He hurried on, “They just take a lung away, and the other carries on.” He wasn't babbling, but he knew he was close to it. Fit was considerate, as usual, even in this situation he marvelled.

“JD, sit down. Calm down. You look bloody terrible. Tea, coffee or a large one?”

Fit was controlled, under control. JD couldn't even think, imagine, how he felt. What would life be like without Ness? He knew he'd never faced the really big problems in life. Mothers, Fathers, Grandparents dying, you were crushed, but you expected it. It was part of the normal pattern of things. Sons, Daughters, Wives, Husbands, they weren't. You couldn't imagine your children dying before you. That wasn’t the way the world was ordered, or at least it shouldn't be and everyone who feels deeply about their partner must secretly wish they'd die first.

“She knew and she didn't fight it. She thought her life was over when Iain died. I suppose in one way it was.”

JD didn't know what to say. He had all sorts of clever things to say that he'd thought of on the way to Tring, but sitting in his car round the corner they had one by one revealed themselves to be puerile, insensitive or just empty. He wished there wasn't the unwritten rule amongst men which constrained them from expressing their feelings too emotionally. Of all his friends in life Ronni was someone who he treasured, whose company he enjoyed, who meant something to him. How do you explain that to your wife . ? It didn't matter. Ness understood. Good God, she was twenty years older than him! Well, now she wasn't. She was dead. How could she be? Veronica, who'd sat and listened to his nonsensical meanderings, which even Ness wouldn't “wear”, who's counsel JD equated to his Grandma's, who knew everything until he was thirteen. He couldn't believe she was dead. She couldn't be dead, not Veronica. But she was. Why? He didn't know why, just as he didn't know what to say. In the whole of his adult life, Veronica was often the only person he felt he could frankly talk to. She had this marvellous quality; she wasn't judgemental. She just accepted you for what you were, warts and all. Ness was good, but she was his wife, and there were many things he couldn't say to her, tell her, as much because he didn't want to cause her any concern or hurt as because he was ashamed or embarrassed about them. But Ronni, that was different. It didn't seem possible. She was still young.

They sat in the cosy lounge with Veronica's handiwork quietly exuding her personality all around them, and the fire glowing, it's warm reflection caught in all Fit's golf trophies, and the photograph of lain which she'd placed a little bunch of flowers in front of before she went into hospital. JD's throat was closed. It made it hard to swallow as he fought back his tears. He mustn't, for Fit's sake. Fit had obviously got past tears. He did the talking.

"Mercifully, it was very quick. It was too far-gone. She was conscious and talking and not in pain until the last 24 hours. Even then I think they kept her free from pain. It seemed so. They were great, couldn't have done more. I'm not having flowers. I've said donations to three children's charities. That's what she would have wanted."

It seemed to help him, letting him talk. It certainly helped JD. After a few minutes he gained control again. He said all the right things, conscious that nothing could be the right thing to say in a situation like this. He slowly realised too that Fit and he had nothing in common, even though they'd been friends for all these years, except work. Even on their numberless nights out socially the girls had left them to it because that was all they talked about. They'd always gone off and done their own thing. So he could only really talk about work. Thankfully, Fit obviously felt the same, because after relating in great detail all that had happened in the past few weeks, which he seemed to recall with absolute clarity, even to the precise timings of sending for doctors and entering hospital, and what she wore and what she said to him and the instructions she left him with about food and bills and what to do about the old lady down the road who she always shopped for, he brought the subject up. JD realised almost guiltily that Fit had been sensitive to his emotional state and had given him time to compose himself but he could also tell now that Fit wanted to talk about something else, anything else. Even work. It all seemed so trivial now in the house with only half its soul, but he plunged in. He did have a lot to tell him.

He started at the beginning of the trip. He praised Betts, and Fit murmured how pleased he was and hadn't he told him so, he told him of their successes and how the social side of their trip had gone. He remembered all the old friends to him and brought all their messages of greetings to him, leaving out all the concerns and messages of goodwill about Veronica other than to say they were all thinking about him. He related the story of the trip across the desert with the mad Pakistani and the story of Jebel Ali and the chance meeting with "Fatty Vernon". Fit was seemingly enjoying it all, but JD couldn't really tell whether he was just being the superb professional Sales Director listener as he'd had to be so many other times in his life. From Vernon and Jebel Ali, and what he'd learned there, he began to relate the strange and serious side of the trip. The unexpected revelation of the continuing normal ordering of currency from their competitors when the countries in question should have been winding down such tenders in preparation for the Pan-Arab currency, the strange discourtesy of the Libyan meeting which unfolded into the uncomfortable, tense and embarrassing meeting with Belazir and Osman and what looked like their premature and arbitrary dismissal from the great project. He unloaded all his worries and the theories he'd developed, on the plane home, at home and at work for the few hours he'd had before Fit had contacted him with the awful news, to try to make sense of it all. He talked about the engravers and about his failure to even talk to them and his worries about them.

Fit listened intently. JD thought for the first time that he'd managed to get him to exercise his mind about something outside the hospital, this house, the past and the future, which was obviously only discernible to him as far as the day of the funeral.

"You're right, JD. There's something bloody odd going on. You're right, too, there must be something they don't want you to see down there. I don't agree that it could be something as simple as shielding their alternative suppliers. Why should they? They've already told you that's what they're doing. What can you do about it? Nothing. It's their right, of course and, JD, those two especially, Belazir and Osman, have been blunt about tougher things than that, like telling people to kill people, or torture them, or help them to 'disappear'. Don't forget what we found out about Osman. He virtually invented the "Ghost Houses" in Western Sudan. A lot of people disappeared into those. God knows what happened to them in those houses. I think your theory of them printing something they shouldn't be doing is probably most likely the truth. I can't think of any other serious reason why they wouldn't let you down into the plant. It can only be what you say. They couldn't hide millions of banknotes. Remember the problems we've had with visitors when we've been printing something we didn't want them to see."

"Yeah, and printing for Iraq makes most sense, doesn't it Fit. Nobody has done any for them since the Gulf War. It drives them mad with frustration because of the inconvenience and because it's such a tangible proof to the population that there is still something seriously wrong. There's nothing more obvious to even the poorest peasant. They all need paper money. The regime has tried umpteen times to order paper and other materials through Jordan and Egypt and Syria. They've never succeeded. They've always been reported to the UN sanctions office, and one-way or another it's been kyboshed. But what about my idea of printing for Hamas? Or the other extremist groups? Israeli Shekels do you think? Or extra Libyan or Sudanese Dinars for them to use? Or even printing dollars for the madmen in Tajikistan, or the Taleban in Afghanistan? For arms."

"JD, I think it could be any of those, except the dollar

idea. C'mon JD, they wouldn't do that. They are very senior State officials. Both of them are probably de facto number two or three in their respective countries, and Dajani is Governor of the Central Bank for God's sake! They just wouldn't risk it and no Government would countenance, authorise that. It's like bloody poison gas, it can just as easily flow back your way. Remember what happened in the Second World War when first the Germans tried it, dropping fivers into Britain, and then we did it back and the Japs and the Yanks tried it too. They all soon realised the errors of their ways! It quickly dawned on all the dopey buggers that they were all in the sticky brown stuff if their own people didn't believe in the bits of paper! I don't count Saif. He's a nonentity. He'll do whatever Belazir tells him. They just need him for his particular position at this precise moment, Internal Security. That alone tells you something, doesn't it?"

"It does. It does. And you're probably right about the dollars, even though they're the easiest bloody notes to copy! Whatever it is, though, the question is, what do we do about it? Whichever way I look at it, I keep coming back to the main point. Whatever they're doing we're involved, implicated. We built the bloody place! We've trained them. We provided the engravings for their first run of Libyan Dinars! And we've had our engravers there for months, Christ knows what they've been producing!"

"There's only one thing you can do about it at the moment. The first thing to do is get hold of the Chief and tell him everything. It started with him, remember, and he knows the big cheeses. He can probably get to the bottom of it faster and better than anybody. Seeing him will cover your ass as well. It's your next step, JD. Take my advice. Do it now, today."

"I know. You're right, but he's probably in bloody Venezuela or Venice! But yeah, you're right. I'll start as soon as I get back to the office."

"JD, don't go back. You'll only get enmeshed in all the usual crap. If I were you, I'd go home and do it from your study. Just phone in from here and tell Shirley you're on urgent business and can't be contacted. You'll contact her regularly to check in. And turn that bloody mobile off!"

JD knew he was right. Fit had all those years of experience behind him. He'd worked for half a dozen different MDs who reported to a succession of three different parent companies. Theirs had been the longest working partnership. That's why they'd become such friends. That's why he was here. That's why his thoughts returned to Veronica and his intense concerns about what was going on in a distant country with shady and sinister individuals in thousand dollar uniforms and their effect on his little company suddenly jarred into perspective. What did it really matter, compared to a precious and irreplaceable life, extinguished now, lost forever. No way to call it back, no way to put things right, to rectify the situation. There was no one to call to sort things out.

When JD had gone and the adrenaline had long gone, Fit sat alone in the same chair he'd always sat in by the fire, drinking Glenmorangie from the same Stuart crystal tumbler he always used, in the same cosy room. It was all the same, but it would never be the same again, ever.

£$£

Chapter Thirty One

For a boy born in Grand Rapids, Minnesota, who grew up and went to college in Minneapolis, San Diego was paradise. The temperature never dropped below 65 degrees and it hardly ever went above 85; it never rained, well, hardly ever; there was the beautiful Pacific to the West, fringed with white sand, the desert to roam in and wonder at in the East, Mexico to the South, L. A and Frisco to the North. From his window he could see the smoked glass of the Arco building and the sleek high-rise buildings of the banking and business district, but he could also see the 'We Are Sailing' bar with the white and red sign highlighted in neon 'Bottomless Waitresses - 24 hour service.' And lots of other clubs and bars and 'New and Used Mag.' shops. It was a wonderful city. Perfect climate, superb offices, great shops, elegant housing - and all the porn, perversity, pulchritude and pestilence that only a great port can produce and this wasn't just a port, it was a Naval Base too! Christ, half the US Fleet was moth-balled here and there were always lots of operational ships in the harbour which Admiral San Diego, when he sailed into it 500 years ago, had called "the greatest natural haven for ships" in the world. He loved it. Something to do each evening before he went home to Sandra. She'd kill him if she knew! Still, no kids yet, and he did truthfully work late very often. In Minneapolis it was too damned cold for any of that! If you put tables outside a bar in Minneapolis there were months in the year when you'd need St Bernard's to find the customers. What did his English cousin say? "Cold enough to freeze the balls off a brass monkey!" He liked that.

He was feeling chilly now. Why did they always have the air conditioning on? It was set at 72 degrees as usual. All they needed to do was open the damned windows. It was never even humid in this paradise. Bit of smog under the inversion layer, that's all. But the windows wouldn't open. Anyway, they were alarmed and bulletproof. He was just thinking of putting his jacket back on when his PC ordered him to key in his password, and gave him only 30 seconds to do it. 'These machines run our Goddamn lives,' his mind muttered. He obeyed rebelliously, sullenly. "Welmerp" he typed. It was derived from his name. Elmer Westerdorp. Jeez! Where had his father got 'Elmer'? Why couldn't he have chosen a good, masculine-sounding German name like Karl, or Hans? He should have done. His grandfather was German. That would have been a proud name. Or why didn't his mother, who came across on the Goddamn "Mayflower", or at least on the next trip or something, insist on giving him a straightforward English name, like Joe or Bill or Tom? 'Elmer' sounded like a schlock or a nerd. As soon as he could after meeting anybody he got them to call him 'El'.

"Mornin' El," Chick Jiminez burst in like water in a holed sub. as usual. "How'd your week-end go? See your old college friend? Do anything special? Did he take you hunting?"

The small dark good-looking Angelino was a perfect ringer for a Hollywood Central Casting Mexican bandit in the Robin Hood mode and wherever he was he stole the peace and tranquillity of an office and handed it to the insouciant. Most of the time, though, he was a great guy. He always livened things up.

"Yeah, we went hunting, but not before he took me on a world tour. You'll never believe where we've been."

"How come?"

"Would you believe me if I tell you we've been to Rome, Utica, Carthage, Troy, Syracuse, Alexandria? Then we went to Copenhagen and Amsterdam, then on to Oxford and Norwich."

"You're shittin' me!"

"No, I'm not. He's got a helicopter!"

"Come on, man! He'd need a fucking space-shuttle to do that in a week-end!"

"Hombre, I tell you ze troot! On the grave of the Blessed Virgin!"

"The Virgin hasn't got a grave, atheist Gringo She was "assumed" into heaven from Ephesus. Il Papa has been to the house and confirmed it. He musta seen the burn marks or something. Anyway, she wasn't buried anywhere! C'mon, cut the crap and tell me about your weekend, or you can get your own coffee and I'm not giving you a Doughnut and that's final. In fact, I might just log your racist remarks. How am I supposed to work with a neo-Nazi?"

"Shut up Zapata. And I'm not a damned atheist. What I say is Church of the Assembly of God true. No, Y'know Chick, he got me too. He had me going too. But he really did take us to all those places. In his helicopter. They're all towns within range of his place in Albany, in Northern New York State. Would you believe it! He gave us the grand tour to please Sandra, I think, before we left the girls in Albany and went to his lodge at St Regis Falls, then on to Great Sacandaga Lake. He's got a boat there, a real smart one."

"Man. He's doing well out of auditing!"

"You better believe it! His house is beautiful. You can imagine what Sandra thought. It's time I went private!"

"She's right." Chick was enveloped in the arms of his office chair, which seemed too big for him.

"Probably. But he's a senior partner now. He made the right decision to stay out of New York. He's a big fish in a small pond. Good thing to be. Still, he's a nice guy. Hasn't changed at all since college. We re-lived our decadent disgraceful youth over a couple of bottles of Old Crow Sourmash. Remember Marjorie, the girl I told you we both went out with, the nympho? He's got her damned knickers nailed up in the lodge john, signed by her! Jesus! His wife's cut a newspaper headline out and stuck it across 'em with super-glue that says "Untouched By Human Hand"! Sandra would super-glue my prepuce if I tried anything like that!"

"Prepuce?"

"Foreskin."

"Jeez ,I thought you was Jewish! Anyway, I've told you amigo, you got to get a grip on that girl. She isn't grateful enough."

"She loves you, Chick. She revels in your unreconstructed chauvinism."

"Don't talk French to me, I keep telling you. Anyway, why the hell are you in so early? I'm nearly an hour before my time. I got a lot to do. What's it with you?"

"The two families. I've not been able to get them out of my mind since Friday afternoon. I'm baffled. Where the hell they getting the money from?"

He sat back in his chair, and put his gold pen in his teeth. There was a look of puzzled concentration on his face. He stared at his PC screen and was absorbed back into his own world.

Elmer Westemdorp was an auditor too, an excellent auditor. That's why he'd been recruited into the FBI. His buddy had gone to Albany and got rich, he'd gone to Washington and got trained. In the year Judge William Sessions took over as Director of the Bureau, 1987. The crazy Hoover days were over. The Bureau had put its house in order. It was again a force for the good, a force for the good guys. He wasn't making much money, but he had a nice house in a nice city and he drove a nice new Mercury, and, for all his carapace of cynicism, he felt he was doing a worthwhile job. His remit was organised crime. He carried a Browning GP 35, but his real weapons were his mind, his training and his PC. Organised crime was what brought him to San Diego, one of the 60 Field Offices the Bureau had across the States. It was from here that they monitored "questionable" activities in Las Vegas, Tahoe and Reno. They had their people in those places but it was better doing it at a short air-trip's distance. Less obvious, safer too.

What was now going on in Vegas troubled him. And what was going on in the Dominican Republic. He'd got the information just before the weekend. If he hadn't faithfully promised Sandra he'd have probably worked through it, not that there was much he could have done in that time. He needed to speak to a few people.

Chick interrupted his thoughts.

"What are the 'I-ties' up to now?"

"They're rolling in money, seemingly legitimate money, and they're investing like crazy."

"Hey, great! Good for the economy!"

"Yeah, Congress'll be delighted. But they haven't got that money, so where are they getting it from? You can bet your ass it's not legit."

For nearly four years now he'd been investigating and monitoring the Cavalieri and Mazzini families, headed by Mario and Aldo respectively. A charming, warm-hearted lot. Citizens of New York, big in clothing, meat and ice cream, benefactors to their local church, boa-constrictors to their local community, and anything else they touched. He knew everything about them, and even more about their financial affairs. He knew how much the women of the families spent on clothes and cosmetics, what the men spent on hookers, which ones were gay, how much their houses cost, where their off-shore money was, how much spending money they gave their kids and the colour of their pyjamas. He hated the evil bastards and he thought he was close to nailing them, at least financially. Then came Friday's news. They publicly announced that: "The two family business organizations have pooled their resources and are working together to build a completely new hotel, casino and leisure, complex on the new strip in Las Vegas. One that will be bigger than the Hilton or the MGM, glitzier than Caesar's Palace. Initial estimates of the investment are in the order of $200 million."

That shook him a little. What came next rattled him.

"A sister complex, an identical complex, is going to be created in the Dominican Republic, at the delightful beach resort of Boca Chica, just 20 miles from Santo Domingo and close to the Las Americas International Airport. We don't have Cuba any more - we don't need it!"

They always used their smart and smarmy Investment

Brokers, Stobart, Kravitz and Lord for their PR, and they'd made it sound good, as usual. But $400 million? What the hell was going on?

"El, if the Dom. Rep.'s involved that's out of our territory. That's for the Agency. You'd better get onto the Dep."

Chick was right. This had moved into CIA-land. He had to speak to the Deputy Director of the Bureau in D.C., but first he wanted to know the source of the money. They wouldn't have made any announcement unless they had some of the funds at least.

Before, he'd just been rattled. By the end of the morning, before he rang Washington, he was as baffled as he was whenever he tried to envisage that mathematical singularity with which astro-physicists contended the universe had started. The money was in the Chase Manhattan Bank, it had come through the impeccable channels of Credit Lyonnaise in Paris and Deutschebank in London, from UBS in Switzerland.

It was . . . . legitimate.

In the cloying noon-time heat of the Dominican Republic security guards with sweat staining the back of their shirts opened the back gate and David Page drove out of the huge US Embassy in Santo Domingo. The Marine guards were smart and on show at the front. He knew the locals called the Embassy either "The Presidential Palace" or "The Government Compound". They'd never really forgiven the US for "saving" them in the 1960s. They were fiercely independently minded people, who else would have kept electing an octogenarian blind president who wouldn't suck up to the USA? He loved the locals. They had a wicked sense of humour, proud people. Wasn't this where Columbus landed? Where he was buried? They'd built a huge statue on the harbour to commemorate it. This was the birthplace of all the Americas. There was a touch of the Wild West about the place, the frontier. It was the only place he knew where the police or security guards got wary if you didn't hand a gun in at the door of any official building! As he drove through the narrow streets of terraced houses with iron gratings at their windows, girls and older women sat on their doorsteps within inches of his tyres, scrawny dogs playing chicken with the car, stocky dark moustachioed men were climbing onto dusty battered pick-up trucks with rifles slung across their backs, and they were only carrying fruit! There was a decaying beauty about the old streets, but he'd never come to terms with the street children in their rags, with their plastic bags, or tattered ruck sacks if they were lucky. He'd seen it all before all over Latin America, but it was different here. The place was small. You actually got to know them, to recognise them. They became people. That was dangerous. Their dark imploring eyes followed you. What was most disturbing was that they weren't aggressive, so they didn't furnish the easy excuse to shoo them away. The quiet, polite knock on the car window and the solemn gaze always brought the picture of his two daughters when they were six or seven sitting on their bunks as he said goodbye to them for the umpteenth time after a couple of weeks leave when they'd all been a family again. They recognised you, too. Implicit in their gaze was an understanding, an acceptance, of the fact that what you'd just had for lunch probably cost as much as they could live on for a month. The people here were fervent about their politics, not a place to venture on to the streets on election night, he'd learned! When you saw the poverty you understood why they were fervent. Something had to be done. He often wondered what America was doing, what he was doing, there. He hoped tourism was going to do for them what it had done for Florida, or Spain and Greece in Europe. Massive inward investment, careers as waiters, bartenders, hotel cleaners. Jobs at least.

That's why he was heading for the Hotel Juaragua to meet Antonio. Antonio de Los Santos knew all about tourism, and who was involved in it, locally, politically and who were the "inward investors". In fact, there weren't many businesses on the island of Hispaniola that he didn't know about. His "friends" in Haiti were as numerous as those in this third of the island. Antonio had been his "main man" since his posting. He'd "inherited" him, but they'd got on superbly from the first day. Page had done many years in many places in Latin America and he considered Antonio the best he'd had. He trusted him, and the fact that he knew the Agency were his main source of income made him trust him more. He admired that about Antonio. He wasn't too greedy. He survived very nicely and lived very well off his US dollar retainer, and he made sure he never stuck his nose in or neck out in any other business but small deals, mainly in the local amber for jewellery market, which kept him in circulation in the "business community" but not in the front line, and certainly never in danger. Antonio had a long-term plan. To exceed the normal life expectancy of 61 years in his country by at least 30 years.

The sea was calm and indigo on his left, looking as if it came right up to the road, as he turned into the front gates of the hotel, past security, into the lush gardens. Langley HQ had used the word "urgent", not one the CIA ever used lightly and it had come from the Assistant Director, responsible for Domestic Liaison. The FBI prompted it. He'd contacted Antonio directly, not something he usually did, because of the tone of the message. He saw him almost immediately at the bar in the 'Nightclub', which doubled as the Lobby Bar during the day, and headed straight for him. Antonio made a great fuss of greeting him and buying him a drink, obviously as ostentatiously as possible, but then said he couldn't stay, he'd see him at some other time and they'd have to have dinner together, "Perhaps here, yes, and we'll take in the show." He left, and half an hour later, after another Seven Up on ice, Page did the same thing. He knew where to meet him. There must be something going on for Antonio to be so wary, and want to use the stand-by arrangements.

He made his way to the Parque Colon Plaza. Antonio wasn't sitting by the statue of the Genovese Admiral so he must be at the tomb. He really did want to be discreet. He crossed the plaza, already sweating slightly because of the heat and humidity now that he'd left the air-conditioned car, and entered the quiet and cool shade of the Basilica Cathedral of Our Lady of Incarnation. Antonio was on the wooden bench in front of the tomb of Columbus. The only other people in the 500-year-old beautiful ornate building were a small group of tourists who looked Scandinavian from their blonde hair, casual but expensive dress and from the sound of the lilt of the hushed tones they were using. He hoped so. It would put Antonio at ease. He could tell from his demeanour that he was in ultra-cautious mode.

The CIA man sat down and wiped the faint film of perspiration from his forehead and nose with his folded silk pocket handkerchief. Antonio de Los Santos looked, as always, cool and immaculate, in his lightweight well-tailored suit, crisp white shirt and sober tie. His spotless white Panama sat beside him on the bench. Medium height, slim, looking much younger than his 54 years but still effortlessly distinguished, he radiated class in the Iberian sense. After dinner, after enough Bermudez Rum from Santiago de los Caballeros, he would sometimes become garrulous in his genteel way and relate the history of his family, a tale which began in the court of Diego Colon, son of the great explorer, first Spanish Viceroy of the Americas, which was held in the Alcazar de Colon, still standing in Santo Domingo. His father's fathers, and so on, were a personal friend of the Viceroy's wife, Maria de Toledo, he would say. No Indian blood had ever flowed in his family's veins, not that he was prepared to admit anyway. His manner and manners were as stylish as his looks, sometimes to the point of seeming exaggerated, but if it was an act no one had ever seen him out of his greasepaint. He addressed Page as he always did.

"Mr Page, how good of you to meet me. I do apologise for the clandestine theatricals." He spoke English with a cultured English accent, flawless, the result of an education in England from the age of seven to sixteen, after which he went to University in Madrid, and then home to the oldest University in the Americas. The family had been rich until the Trujillos envied their land and their businesses. They'd left them with only their elegant house in the capital. He'd "worked" since then.

"No problem, Antonio." Page knew it was no use telling him once again to call him Dave. He didn't belong to that generation, and had studiously avoided assimilating American culture. He never even watched American films.

"Your message spoke of certain investments. I am aware of these."

"How come you didn't say anything in the usual way, Antonio?" Page made sure he didn't sound censorious.

"Because, Mr. Page, it has all only manifested itself in the last week. I have never known anything so sudden. Or anything dealt with so swiftly at so high a level. And the transaction you're referring to is only one of three which are to take place and which involve the same parties."

Page looked at him in surprise.

"You mean there's more on the cards?" His voice conveyed his genuine surprise.

"There are indeed. I was waiting to garner the full facts before contacting you. As yet, my information is incomplete, I'm afraid."

"Don't be afraid, Antonio, just tell me what you know already! I'm all ears."

"First, your information is correct. The two families you mention are indeed building a complex at Boca Chico. Stobart, Kravitz and Lord are the lead as usual. They're also planning one in the tourist zone in the North of a similar size between Gaspar Hemandez and Rio San Juan, and, they've bought into the amber mines. The people involved are quite unsavoury, as you know, hence the caution and they have influence at the highest level of the administration, and with the police and the army. All of these will benefit from the swift approval and aid to build. That is even more reason for caution. You understand."

"I certainly do. That's one hell of a lot of money coming

in."

"Mr. Page, it is already 'in'. In the new bank - the, Banco de Hispaniola. It is said to be over $300 million. Give me a few more days and I will have details of where it came from for you. You'll want documentary evidence of course."

"Thanks, Antonio, yes. Please do that. I think we may already know, but it will be good to get independent corroboration, on the spot as it were."

"I'll call you for our "dinner date". You know our phones are bugged, even yours in the Embassy, as far as local calls are concerned. I'll pass on all I glean over a good bottle of the Juaragua's Chateau Smith Haute Lafite. I will leave by the West door. I'll call you as soon as possible. Be careful in this sun. I do wish you'd let me buy you a hat."

Page smiled at their standing joke, and remained on the bench for a good ten minutes after Antonio had left. He was thinking hard anyway. Then he went back to the Embassy and used the secure lines to contact Langley. For once he thought he might be passing something to them that they didn't already know. It would surprise them.

When it went back through Langley to the Bureau and the Deputy Director passed it on it surprised Elmer Westerndorp in San Diego even more.

If there was one thing Muscovites couldn't stand it was mild weather in winter. If the temperature did what it should do it dropped below freezing in early November and stayed that way until March. The snow was dry and soon packed and it was easy to walk and drive on with the right shoes and tyres. If it thawed the city was a carpet of slush and mini-lakes, everything was wet and filthy and it felt colder with the dampness exacerbated by the omnipresent winds. There was much muttering about Global Warming. The fact that Canada and the Northern United States were experiencing their coldest winter and worst blizzards for years only made the natives more miserable and sullen. It had to be Russia that bore the brunt of the changing weather. Beneath the surface of every Russian there was a romantic paranoiac manic-depressive. The weather was yet more proof that everything conspired against them. Warren Bannister was thinking all this as he looked out of his double-glazed window on the fifth floor of the Kempinsky Hotel, next to the bridge, drinking a glass of Bourbon on the rocks in his luxurious suite as he watched the small dark figures below him slosh and slide around in the gathering battleship-grey gloom of the mid afternoon. He turned when the phone rang with the call he'd been expecting.

"Giorgi, thanks for calling back. What have you got?"

He listened intently, put his glass down and picked up the pen tucked into the spiral of the phone pad.

"Restaurant Libanon? Yeah, I know it. Upstairs, first floor, Lebanese and Arab food, yeah? I'll be there. What about the plane? Yak? Christ, Giorgi, not one of those old Presidential Flight crates? Hell, they've only got a range of about 2000 miles. That means re-fuelling at least once, probably Omsk. OK, don't worry, remember, when they stop to refuel the bloody heating goes off! Bring something warm for in the cabin! How much do they want? $25,000! Hell, it gets more expensive every time. I suppose they want cash? No problem. And it's still on? Definitely? And they've published, officially? Then we've no other choice. We have to be there. I'll see you in the restaurant at seven-o-clock. We'll have an early one my friend if we have to be at the domestic airport at 5 am.! I hate that airport. It's a shambles, makes Shemtaevo look like Schippol! All right, see you there Giorgi, and thanks."

Bannister looked at the phone pad. Giorgi Medveshvili was good. He'd sorted it all in less than 24 hours. So the Uzbekis really were inviting tenders for the new gold mine. Well, well, that should bring the bad guys out. Every "organisation" in Moscow would want to get some of their "dirty" money invested in that! Well, so would Mississippi Mining Inc., and he'd be there at the tendering meeting as their Executive Vice President Overseas with his Senior Assistant and interpreter Giorgi Medveshvill. Not that he needed an interpreter. He spoke Russian with a better accent than Giorgi with his heavy Georgian inflections! It always paid to play the gullible ignorant foreigner though. If the 15 Republics which had evolved from the former Soviet Union had an iota of common sense and weren't driven by stupid nationalism they'd make sure that Russian continued to be taught in schools from Latvia to Tajikistan, he thought. It had certainly made his job easier as a businessman and investor in the old Soviet empire in the last four years.

He almost grinned. He really was beginning to think of himself as a businessman! It was the right way to do it. The CIA had for once taken careful note of British Intelligence and he knew it was working. He'd been at the original briefings by MI6 senior officers. Their point was simple, obvious but sweetly apposite. They'd learned, especially in Africa, that when political influence waned with the end of Empire there was no need to lose influence. Just invest in the strategic industries in the countries and the intelligence flowed as well as the influence could be exerted whenever it was needed. The Agency had taken it fully on board. He was one of the first batches of agents who didn't come on a posting as a "Commercial Attaché" or some such, attached to the Embassy. If you were there, you were inside the Moscow Ring Road, inside a virtually separate country from the rest of Russia or the new Republics. Not so different from being inside the Washington Beltway in D.C. That was a different country from the rest of the States! He'd made his home the suite at the Kempinsky. He was high profile there. If he'd got an apartment in the city, or a dacha outside, the FSB wouldn't have felt so comfortable about him. Here, they could monitor everything he did. And they could see that everything he did, to advance the interests of M.M. Inc., was legitimate. He even paid a little "protection" money to the locals, and complained about it to his FSB friends. They shrugged wearily and always said they'd look into it. As they were sharing it he thought it was decent of them not to have put it up in the last couple of years.

What was interesting the Agency greatly now, and what he spent most of his time on, was where the "Mafia" money was going. They didn't care a damn where it went in the old Soviet Union, unless it gravitated towards strategic arms companies; nor where they too bothered by money flowing into Europe, the Europeans were well aware of that danger and on the job there; what they were intensely interested in was money flowing into the States, into drugs, or into Islamic fundamentalist regimes with the capacity to affect the stability of the West.

That was his job. That's why he was going to Uzbekistan to buy into a goldmine - and to see who else had the same idea.

In London it was a mild but grey day, spotting with rain. It added to JD's sombre mood. His windscreen wipers wouldn't clear it properly, they just streaked his screen; it was the sort of weather which made it necessary to carry a raincoat around but it was really too warm to want to wear it; he really should buy an umbrella but he felt like a poser carrying one. He couldn't get Veronica off his mind, and the message he had to give to the Chief wasn't exactly a happy one. He drove up The Mall and turned into Trafalgar Square, then into the car park under the British Council building. He was driving himself because he'd taken Fit's advice and not gone back into work, but contacted the Chief and arranged an urgent meeting. For him to do so was so unusual the Chief knew something important was in the air and he'd agreed to see him immediately even though he was engaged with "important foreign visitors", and was at the Private Apartments. The car park had never let him down in 15 years and he found a space way down on Level 8.

His mood was still grey like the day as he walked up the Haymarket to Piccadilly Underground Station and caught the Piccadilly Line to Knightsbridge. It was only a couple of stops away. He quite liked the Tube, outside rush hour. He hardly ever got the chance to travel on it these days. He gazed at the cosmopolitan crowd in his carriage and wondered what they were individually doing in London. What did it matter? They enriched London life, and ensured a proliferation of the most interesting restaurants. He wondered if thinking that was racist or patronising. He didn't think he was racist. They probably all lived here anyway, second or third generation Londoners!

He was a bit brighter as he left Knightsbridge Station and walked down the side of Harrods into Pont Street. Even the message for the Chief slipped into a sort of perspective.

It had to be passed on, and it could be time-critical. Best to get on with it as soon as possible.

The company had a luxurious and elegant three-storey apartment just off Pont Street that was used extensively for entertaining overseas visitors. They could stay there if they wished, and a permanent staff would look after their every need and all the shops around could look after the every need of their wives or girlfriends. It was often used, though, as merely a meeting place, or for business lunches or dinners. The Chief preferred it to corporate headquarters and he often stayed on there after such meetings. JD knew the Chief was meeting the Malaysian Minister of Finance and his team for lunch. He'd just squeezed JD in for half an hour before they were due to arrive at 12.15 pm. JD rang the security intercom at precisely 11.40 am.

They sat in the very large beautifully furnished lounge, which took up most of the first floor. Ornaments from all over the InmTraCon empire decorated the room, flooded with warm light by the elegant wall mounted mini-chandeliers and the circle of smaller chandeliers which surrounded the magnificent central crystal and silver main light which wasn't lit. The warmth of the reflected gold was counter-balanced by the cool of silver and the delicate blue and white porcelain which blended with the deep blue carpet and armchairs and couches piped with silver grey amongst which were arranged dark-wood occasional and coffee tables, all inset with the most exquisite parquetry. Crystal water sets were conveniently at hand around the room, and a smart-suited waiter stood by the large matching, bureau which contained gleaming shelves of bottles, silver ice buckets, pure white linen napkins and bowls of olives and sliced lemon, lime and orange.

There was no time for the niceties of even a soft drink, JD decided as he politely declined the Chief's offer. He told the Chief he had too much to tell him. The Chief nodded to the waiter and he left the room.

"Thank you, JD. You know I've only got 30 minutes. Fire away. Please, dispense with any superfluous details. Cut to the chase. Let's talk as if we're on the plane, just you and I, with no one else around and I'm au fait with the background. I don't need that. I've followed this business with real interest. You and I started it, remember."

JD remembered. Though it seemed like a year since Entebbe State House, not just the four months. He launched into the story. As had often been the case when he'd had to face a real crisis his doubts and anxieties and nervousness fell away. He was here now, he was determined to tell it like it was. Daltons had done nothing wrong, anyway. They'd just responded swiftly, professionally, and expertly to the opportunity. They'd done a fantastic job in an incredible time. What was happening now was out of their hands. The story had to be told. He told it. The Chief sat back, fingertips touching and held to his lips, like a child at prayer. He didn't say a word. It took twenty minutes. The silence that followed seemed like minutes to JD, but it was only a few seconds. The Chief leaned forward and put his outstretched fingertips on the table.

"First, we must get the boys and their families home."

JD was impressed. It wouldn't have been the first thing he'd have thought the Chief would have concentrated on. He didn't get a chance to respond, the Chief carried on: "You really do think it's Iraq?"

"It's the only thing that makes sense, Chief. I think my wilder fantasies are just that, fantasies."

"Don't be too sure, JD. I've seen some very strange things in my time. Remember the Zairean banknote problems and their diamonds and the Lebanese, and the

Angolan diamonds. And what about the Kenyan gold export affair in the Nineties: there isn't even any gold in Kenya! There isn't much that politicians do, or won't do, which should surprise any of us any more. Don't forget, many people say we've built a business that way!" He smiled and grimaced at the same time.

"JD, I'm awfully sorry I can't invite you to lunch. The guest list is fixed by security and protocol, of course. The Malaysians are ruled by protocol, you know. Could you possibly come back to see me at 3.30 pm.? They're scheduled to leave at three. I'll put some calls in to my friends in Libya. I'll try before they arrive, and if I can't locate them then I certainly will do so by 3.30. Will this inconvenience you?" JD said of course not. He was just relieved the story telling was over, "Are you sure? Good. Thank you so much. Eric will see you out. I'll look forward to seeing you at 3.30."

He rang the bell and JD walked out into the light but now steady rain.

He decided to have lunch at the Institute of Directors, so he headed back to the underground and Piccadilly, his mind full of the meeting. Had he told the story coherently? Had he over-clubbed his worries? Was he not just being too sensitive, over-reacting? Back home now, out of the uneasy atmosphere, he could think of a number of other possible reasons for Belazir and Osman not wanting him in the base, playing things close to their chest - but the boys? No, that didn't add up, why would they want to keep him from them? Why get rid of all other help, the technicians, so quickly? Why run the damned plant 24 hours a day, seven days a week? Why not launch the Pan-Arab currency? Where were they sourcing their raw materials? It wasn't normal. Something had to be going on.

He sat at the bar in The Bistro downstairs at the I.O.D and savoured a long vodka and tonic. An excellent place for lunch. Affluent surroundings, swift service, good food, reasonable prices, great atmosphere, and upstairs he could work in the library after lunch and do some telephoning. He quite enjoyed the quiet and freedom of being alone. Planes, cars, lone lunches and the corner of a bar were where he'd done some of his best thinking, until he'd had his fourth drink!

He phoned Vanessa as soon as he settled in the library. He just wanted to hear her voice. What had happened to Fit had suddenly made her precious. No, not suddenly, he thought. He always thought of her as precious, and the kids. As he thought it he knew he was dissembling, even to himself. Of course he thought she, they, were precious, but usually, normally, only in the way he sometimes became conscious of background music and thought it was beautiful. If only it wasn't like that. If only it was possible to appreciate, to treasure those people who should really mean something in life, all the time, for their full worth. As a child can treasure a mother, the centre of its life. A purely selfish treasuring, but genuine, without guile. But it wasn't like that was it? You couldn't go through life treating those you loved as if they were going to be snatched away from you within the next breath. Nothing would work, you wouldn't go to work, or let the kids go to school or play out on their own or let your wife go shopping on her own. The family would narcotise

Vanessa was fine, the kids were fine, the dog was fine. She'd called the AA in; the car wouldn't start and Julia had taken the Honda. Paul and Alexandra were definitely coming home at weekend. Her mother was ill again (she'd been ill for 80 years, he thought. But Ness had to be sincere. It was her daughterly duty). What time would he be home? Did he need food? Everything was exactly as normal, except Ronni was dead and everything was different. He told Ness he loved her and that he'd be home as soon as possible. Did she want to go out for a meal? If so he'd leave it to her to book wherever she wanted. She said she thought she'd do stuffed trumpet mushrooms, and they'd open one of the twin bottles of Valpolicella they'd brought back from Florence and spend the night in. He said it sounded great.

Then he called Mary, they arranged to meet. The

conversation was brief. She was with customers. But she obviously wanted to. She pretended he was another client and they were arranging to meet in London. He'd pretended, even to himself, that in the new mood of reflective appreciation engendered by Ronni, he wouldn't be doing it. Yet again his gonads got the better of his cerebral cortex.

When he got back to the Private Apartment the Chief was sitting in the same chair. He was courteous as always, but tight-lipped.

"JD, I spoke with two Ministers. They didn't know what I was talking about. The base at Sirte is merely a little-used military airstrip. There is no large underground base."

"But, Chief, you know, you've seen. . ."

"JD, I do not think you've transported £30 million worth of machinery into the desert and dumped it. I know there's a military base there. I can understand them not wanting to confirm such over a telephone. They know the Americans and GCHQ monitor everything. But that doesn't explain why they were both so genuinely adamant that we're not involved with them in any joint venture. I know, you don't need to say anything. I've got a copy of the contract. I didn't press them JD or enlarge on my comments. There is something distinctly unsettling about this."

JD was nodding and about to speak when the Chief went on.

"We're going to the Foreign Office. I'm sorry, JD, but can you be back here by 8 am. tomorrow morning. I know it's a long journey for you, especially at peak time, but I believe it's necessary. Bring your papers with you, including the original contract, will you? Now, I'm so sorry, I have to go. As you know, until yesterday I didn't know we were going to meet today. I've got a diary full of engagements that I can't change. Do you mind?"

Of course he didn't. He felt so relieved that it was out in the open now, and it was no longer just his worry. It was off just his shoulders. This one was too big for him to follow his usual instincts and handle it himself and then tell HQ. Now he felt that they might get somewhere. He was fitting in at the right level now. He could actively and constructively think about it and work on putting together the relevant papers and not just waft around in a cloud of suppressed anxiety. The Foreign Office - Christ! The Chief was obviously as worried as he was. He always did grasp things quickly.

As he drove home from Trafalgar Square in the drizzle with the darkness made day by man's own hand he thought about Vanessa and his home and the evening. He'd only have to venture out into the night to walk the dog. It was as if Mary and the sex at the Savoy they'd just planned were happening to someone else. For the time being everything would be OK. His family and the 27 years or so he'd invested in his home and his relationships were safe. After an hour's driving, as the six-o-clock news was starting with the chimes of Big Ben, each time it struck seemed like a marker on his personal path to the edge of the abyss of his own making. Why the bloody hell was he putting it all at risk? Jesus, still a prat at 48!

£$£

Chapter Thirty Two

The silence was as deafening as anything he'd ever heard. If it had metamorphosised into liquid concrete it would have permeated every square centimetre of his office. Belazir abruptly got up and walked stiffly towards his filing cabinet with the PC on top of it, watching his image reflected in the blank screen. A man captive to his own churning thoughts. He didn't reach it. He stopped in front of his internal Base communications board, turned to look at Osman, then returned and just as abruptly sat down again. He didn't take his eyes off the Sudanese General. Osman returned his look coolly, leaning back relaxed in the chair opposite Belazir's, hands folded together across his diaphragm. Saif sat, impassive, on the chair beside Belazir's desk, his back to the wall.

"Sadiq, this is crazy. We can't go on. We don't need to go on. We've got all the Dinars we could ever use, we've done $I0 billion worth of Euros, we've done $40 billion worth of U.S. For the love of God it's time to stop! What do we need to do more for? We've penetrated as far North as Moscow, as far West as L.A., in the East to Malaysia, Singapore, Australia even! We're as far South as South Africa, Chile. It's been successful beyond our wildest dreams, beyond any of our estimates. Why? Why go on? With all the risks, it's bound to come out soon. We'd be crucified!"

"I don't think the Christians use that form of execution any more Youssef." Osman's drawl was patronising.

"I'm serious Sadiq. We can't go on." He jabbed his finger downwards towards his desk at nothing in particular, just an attempt to emphasise his point.

"Why not?"

Osman's attitude grated on Belazir even more. It was a combination of disdain, cynicism and amusement. He was supercilious, scornful. Belazir was tense, his stomach was in a twisted knot, his teeth were sensitive through grinding them, and his jaw muscles ached through damn well clenching them. He felt the weariness of frustrated anger and anxiety sapping him. He heard himself speak, but they weren't the words he really wanted to use. He didn't want to bluster, but he sounded to himself as if that was just what he was doing. He couldn't voice his anger and frustration properly. So it sounded like a "bluster", and that frustrated him more.

"Why not? Are you serious, Sadiq? Why not! Because we've printed enough! It's all over the bloody world! Nothing can stop it now. We've done our job. It will soon be discovered. They'll soon realise what's happening! There'll be the most violent reaction! We should get out! We said we'd do it for just three months and our time is up. We can retire in luxury, well earned. We can get out now, before our dice roll off the crap table. That's as good a reason as any, isn't it?"

"I'm much too young to retire, Youssef." Osman was smiling.

"Sadiq, be serious! This is too big to be treated with your sarcastic bloody levity. We've got to stop, or we'll be stopped!"

"My friend, you're worrying far too much. It will take them ages to figure out what is actually going on, where it's going on and then, what can they do about it? They're not likely to attack Libya. They'd be crucified by the U.N., attacking a foreign sovereign state, an Arab Islamic state, unthinkable. Imagine the outrage in the whole Islamic world. Imagine the oil prices! Now that really would hurt them, in their pockets. And how could they attack this base? It is impregnable. You have done a wonderful job on it, I congratulate you. It must be the best in the world. Anyway, remember, both our Governments would deny any and all knowledge of any of this going on. So, what else is there they can do? Change all their currency? Hardly. If all the lousy counterfeits already swilling round the world were dredged in, that alone would be enough to sink the mighty dollar and its mighty issuer overnight, never mind our little contribution! How can they exchange so many duds for good? Hey Youssef, that's not a bad blurb, "dud for good". We should suggest it to them. Sell it to them!"

Anger and frustration were coalescing in Belazir's mind now to something more akin to cold, calculated, self-interested fury laced with a survivalist's cunning. He was in control of his voice now and his thought patterns had returned to what they were best suited for, looking after himself, protecting himself.

"Our little contribution, Sadiq, just happens to be, after only a few week's operation, worth something over $50 billion U.S. I don't know whether you've thought of it this way but that is the equivalent of the actual cash in use in any one year in the combined economies of Sweden, Norway, Denmark, Finland, Belgium, Portugal, Greece, and Ireland! Or Britain and Spain combined! We've already added 35% to the U.S. budget deficit! We can't go on. The international outcry will be appalling. The Western nations will stop at nothing to stop it. Don't underestimate them Sadiq, remember Iraq in 1991. They crushed it like a cockroach! We've done enough damage. We've achieved everything we set out to do. It is time to get out. In military terms, which we both understand my friend, we've accomplished a Blitzkrieg, we're not equipped to fight a war of attrition."

"Look, Youssef, you've planned this superbly." Osman's tone was smooth now, Belazir resented the insult of bullshit layered thick. "Let's say the intelligence forces in the West are picking up on what's going on round about now. They'll be disjointed analyses, it'll take them a couple of weeks at least to start putting two and two together, and then they'll have another couple of weeks before they can get senior people in the Executives to listen to them, then another couple of weeks will go by before decisions on any action are taken. You know how weakened by their facades of democracy they are. They can't act decisively on anything unless their tabloid newspapers or TV tell them something should be done, in any case. They're not likely to be releasing anything, regarding this. How can they? Do you think they want all their people looking at their bits of paper, doubting them all the time? There'd be panic. They've got to play this close to their chests. It'll be six to eight weeks at the soonest before they get round to doing anything. Believe me, friend. So why don't we just carry on 'til something starts happening. Think how much good we can do for the poorer countries of the world with eight or so more weeks of production. Another $34 billion at least. Think of the poorest members of our brothers who'll fulfil the dream of a lifetime by making the Hadj, from Indonesia, Malaysia, all over Africa. Just let things roll on Youssef, let it roll on."

He was leaning forward now, eyes fixed intently on Belazir, animated. Saif remained absolutely impassive. But Belazir was coldly resolute now. He returned Osman's gaze icily.

"No Sadiq. I hear what you say. But I don't agree. It is time to stop while we're ahead, while we can get out as planned. We finish as planned. That's my final word. We're running on the Cut-Pak finishing machines three days behind the printing machines. We'll not bother examining the last printings, we'll just go straight to Cut-Pak. We will therefore stop printing in seven days. That will be it. It will be over."

There was a few seconds silence. Osman continued to stare at him. Then he spoke, very softly this time and very carefully."That's not what the Hanifs want, Youssef. They want us to. . . ."

Belazir cut him off. As he raised his voice he motioned with his hands as if he was delivering two horizontal karate chops to each side of his chest.

"Sadiq, I don't care a fuck what the Hanifs want! It's my neck that's on the line and my country's and yours, I'll remind you, all of our necks! I started this, Sadiq. I'm ending it. I'm grateful for the help and support you've given me in the last few months. But that's it. Finito!"

Osman sat back in his chair and this time Belazir could see he was gripping its arms. "My country is also involved, you remember. Without us you could not have got any of this out, at least not in any quantity. My neck, I'll look after. But we cannot ignore the Hanifs, Youssef. They. . ." he hesitated, then went on, "they were the reason I got involved in the first place. They've been behind this, supporting it all the way."

Belazir blinked. He was surprised, but he shouldn't have been. Of course! That's why it had been so easy to use Government facilities in Sudan, Lebanon, Palestine, Syria, and Iran. But it didn't matter. It didn't alter the facts, nor his resolve, now was the time to bring the operation to an end. Now.

"This is our plant, Sadiq. . ," he started. Osman cut in, "The main technicians have been ours since the British and that lot left. Our printers are running the main machines. You can't just. ."

"We can. It's our plant, our base, our transport, our country." He swung his chair round to face Saif.

"Mahmoud. How many men do we have here?"

Saif's impassive expression didn't alter. He simply intoned, "Just over a thousand, one hundred surface troops, the rest underground."

"And they'll do as we say, without question?" Belazir was asking Saif but now looking directly at Osman.

"Without question. They will do exactly as I order them. I handpicked them. They've either got records, or we're "looking after" members of their families."

"We close down as planned, as per the timetable Sadiq."

Osman's face had hardened, skin tight, mask-like, but his voice was steady and normal.

"Youssef, I can only ask you again to reconsider. The Hanifs are most anxious that we carry on for as long as possible. They consider it vital."

"I consider it vital to terminate. That's what we are doing. Gentlemen, can I ask you to leave me alone now. I have much to organise. Thanks for your views."

He swivelled his chair and reached for the internal phone. For a moment he thought Osman was going to continue arguing. The two other Generals stared at each other for a second, and then Saif rose quickly followed by Osman. Neither spoke. They just left together.

He dialled Internal Control.

"Ask Colonel Anan to come to my office, immediately."

He leant back in his chair and twisted his gold pen between his fingers. He thought of Anan. He was his oldest friend. They'd been together since the late Sixties. In many ways Anan had foregone many good career moves in order to stay with him. Still, they hadn't done so badly together. They'd both benefited rather well. It was their original plan to guarantee themselves a very substantial "pension" by printing their "own"! How he wished now that they'd simply carried that out. Osman, and the bloody Hanifs, whoever those bastards were, had created a bloody monster! Well, there were certain things he could do to ensure he, and Anan, got out of it all as they'd planned, rich, unscathed, and free.

Anan knocked and came straight in without waiting for a reply.

"Sit down, Achmed. Well, I've told him. We terminate to schedule. Seven days, the machines stop."

"General," Anan, old friend that he was, never wavered from official military address, even when they were alone, "that's excellent. What was the reaction?"

"Just as we suspected. He wanted to carry on. The Hanifs, you know."

Belazir said this with heavy sarcasm.

"Of course, of course. It would be, but . . ."

Belazir interrupted.

"My friend, I've not got much time. I've got to get back to Tarabulus. The plane's ready. Sorry for interrupting, but listen, there's one very important thing, and I may not get much chance to talk to you in the next few days, depends how things turn out with the Leader, so we must sort it out.

You know what Osman and Saif think we should do with the engravers. That is not in our interests. Everyone will be suspicious about such an "accident", and when the full facts come out as to what's been going on they won't just be suspicious - they'll be sure. That's murder. That's what even the flabby West won't tolerate. They'd hunt us down wherever we went. It would be a populist cause. You know how they love those. Their people would support them wholeheartedly. They'd go to the ends of the earth to get what they call justice. Even for nonentities. That's not what we need. For just a "scam", as they call it, they'll not bother all that much. They've got tax-dodgers and corporate thieves littering the globe and they do damn all about them and they won't want publicity about this anyway. They'll do anything to maintain trust in their little bits of paper. So, we've got to get the engravers out and home. I have a plan to do just that. I want you to make sure it's carried out, especially if I'm not here for any reason. Osman and Saif cannot know of it or suspect it."

"Of course and I agree entirely with you, General. What do you want me to do?"

"It's not much Achmed, until the day of termination. Then I want you to see that they get to the right place at the right time personally. It's simple really. I'm going to phone Daltons before I set off now. I'm going to tell Dilworth to come to meet the engravers on the day of termination, but only if he can get the company plane. I'll say there is no way we can do the Tunis trip again, I'll think of a reason, so will he land at such and such a time on the day. They'll do it. I told you how worried Dilworth was about them after our last meeting. Osman played that all wrong. He excited suspicion. Anyway, when he does land, I want you to have them available at the surface without anyone knowing and I want you to take them to the plane and explain that we've had a last minute change of plan, they can go home immediately and we'll send their belongings on to them. Tell them the families are already on their way home. I can rely on you to make it sound plausible on the day. The difficult part is getting them to the plane without anyone wondering what's going on and alerting Osman or Saif, even if they just do so innocently. I'll make sure their departure time coincides with ours, of course!"

They both smiled.

"I understand completely, General. Leave it to me, just give me the departure time."

Belazir reached for the phone.

"I'll phone the U.K. now. I'll confirm departure time with you from Tarabulus. Just a time, by phone. No other comment. OK Achmed?" The Colonel nodded.

He was asking for Dalton's number as Anan left.

JD took the call in the sitting room at home just as he was starting to eat a sandwich and waiting for the Nine-o-Clock News to start. Switchboard had by-passed the standing instructions never to give out home numbers (for obvious security reasons in the light of the business they were in) because General Belazir's name was at the top of the very short list of exceptions, which JD had left them with when he told his people he was working from home for a few days after Ronni's funeral. When he left the list he had little reason for optimism that Belazir would phone. He was amazed and delighted that not only did he phone - but also he did so with the message JD was hoping against hope he would get, but which every day had seemed least likely to happen. Now it had. He could go to meet the engravers! JD told Belazir how grateful he was, but the General obviously didn't want to talk much. The conversation lasted only a minute. The time and date were set. JD immediately went to his study for his diary and telephone list and called the Chief at the apartment where he'd left him just a few hours ago. He knew there would be no trouble with the plane. The Chief was as anxious as him about the boys.

One more thing he knew for sure. If he was seeing them, he was bringing them home. He wasn't too proud of the way he'd so quickly caved in to the two Generals when he was last there. He wasn't too proud of being such a coward. Well, they wouldn't dare try to prevent it if the

Chief was with him. They could come on the plane. The families would surely follow. No-one would try to keep women and children against their will. More importantly, they were of little use to the Generals if his suspicions were correct, and they were obviously no threat to them. They knew nothing.

He hadn't felt so good for days. It was the first good news since Ronni. It gave him a positive boost in time for his meeting with the Chief and the Foreign Office the next day. Something would now be done, surely.

£$£

Chapter Thirty Three

Uzbeki champagne really was good, thought Bannister. Probably a little too sweet, somewhere between Cave, Asti Spumante and a Lansing Black Label. They'd soon re-established their vineyards after old Gorbachev had made them tear them all up in the I980's! They'd probably not torn them all up anyway. The Uzbeks had an interesting track record of holding on to what they wanted in regard to their ancient society whilst at the same time learning and benefiting from their Russian masters. Not that an Uzbek would ever accept that the Russians had ever been their "masters". They'd accepted Czarist rule in the Nineteenth century, becoming a "Protectorate", as a positive way of modernising their country, and had done the same with the Bolsheviks. All thinking Uzbeks were glad that the latter had crushed the Basmaji Islamic Insurrection and set up the Republic in I924. Their secular society worked and they hadn't been over-run with Russians to the extent of their Northern neighbours, the Kazakhs, who were now very much a minority in their vast country. That was now seventy per cent Russian. The Great Patriotic War and Stalin's "re-locations" hadn't helped there. Inclusion in the Soviet Union had helped them in their hour of greatest need, too. When Tashkent had been destroyed, obliterated almost, by the I966 earthquake, the true value of the old system proved itself in the Soviet response. Brehznev had used the structure created in the late Fifties by Khrushchev and the All-Soviet Sovnarkhoz and Supreme Economic Council in Moscow had rallied support from every other Republic and Tashkent was re-built, in an astounding feat of reconstruction, in record time. Gosstroy, the All-Soviet Construction Organisation, worked miracles. Timber flowed in from Novosibirsk and Krasnoyarsk in Siberia, builders from Volgograd and Rostov-on-Don. It all came as "fraternal aid". No Uzbeki ever forgot it. But time moved on. They'd been independent for over ten years. They were a potentially rich country, gold, oil, cotton, gas, heavy machinery, and aircraft production. Sizeable population, a country for the future.

That's why Bannister was there. He liked the Uzbeks. Behind the Mongol features which always looked cruelly impassive to Western eyes lay, he knew, some of the warmest-hearted, but most emotionally volatile people in the world. They worshipped their children, especially if they were boys, and treasured their friends. Their hospitality knew no bounds, you just had to get used to their quaint belief that it was important that they "bested" you in any deal! To succeed by a "trick" was a triumph. It came as no surprise to learn that it was in this Central Asian region that the original "Arabian Nights" stories were really set.

One thing Bannister didn't like was the way they'd rebuilt the city. It was a monument to old-style Stalinist "Giganticism". Apart from the fact that being the centre of the most earthquake-prone zone in the world prevented building above four storeys, everything was on a grand scale, from their boulevards, to the war memorial, to the vast square around which the most important Government buildings were set, and where they held their huge Independence Day celebrations now. Before, it was May Day.

That's where he was now. In the inner courtyard of the Executive Buildings which backed on to the Main Block of the Central Bank of Uzbekistan. It was a hot, dry Central Asian day. The tomatoes and cheeses, cold mutton and horsemeat were all looking a little worse for wear. They'd been set out at 11 am., it was 1 pm. as the meeting broke up and they made their way into the courtyard. Still, it was good to get outside. He made a mental note that there was a potentially lucrative market for portable air-conditioning systems in this part of the world, and drank his champagne.

That was a little too warm, too, but enjoyable. That was another thing. If they'd bottle it properly, instead of in those dreary dark brown bottles with the thin metal caps, they could export it. The Turks and the Greeks would love it. He made another mental note.

Mindibar Sulemeinov and Kharrulah Khamanov stopped speaking Uzbeki, and slipped back into Russian. They'd obviously finished with the confidential bit. Giorgi immediately commenced the charade of translation. Sulemeinov was Deputy First Minister and Khamanov was Governor of the Central Bank. They were wearing the self-satisfied look of men who were pleased with the way life was treating them, specifically today, and in general. Both men wore suits and shoes that wouldn't have been out of place in Washington or Paris. So different from the old Soviet days. Then, even if the suit was OK the shoes were always a give-away.

"You didn't put a Tender in my friend!" Mindibar said in mock surprise. His Ghengis Khan moustache did callisthenics when he spoke and smiled. Bannister always had to remind himself to wait for Giorgi to translate before he replied.

"C'mon, Mindibar," there was no formality between the three of them. They'd become friends over the years. Giorgi, as "translator" was a different thing. He kept his place and addressed them as "Minister" and "Governor". Seventy years of Communism had taught people their place. "Where in God's name is a modest company like mine going to get $500 million? I've got to tell you, I was astonished when you announced the bidding terms and said that was going to be the minimum. Why did you decide to sell off in 25% traunches?"

"Why complicate things for ourselves? It's a superb opportunity. Probably the greatest since the early South African or Australian days. It's worth it. Surely you agree?"

"Oh I agree, Mindibar, but that sort of minimum rules out all but the really big boys. You know, the Minorcas, Anglo-Americans, Rio Tinto or….," Bannister said this slowly and deliberately, "organised crime."

The two Uzbeks looked at each other, and smiled, a

private joke.

"Ah, Warren, you couldn't be more wrong. That's exactly why we set the traunches so high, to keep out the bad guys!" Mindibar was positively grinning. Kharrulah was nodding like a Jew at the Wailing Wall.

The reply took Bannister aback. He was thinking about it when the Deputy Minister went on.

"Think about it, my friend. Yes, I know the last ten years have seen the spawning of so many vicious, rich "mafias", the Russians, especially, blame the Uzbekis second only to the Chechens for their problems. I don't know. Perhaps those Uzbeks who did so well in the old KGB have turned bad, they didn't have far to turn!" He laughed most at his own joke. "But we have thought about this very carefully. We have done a lot of research. You know and we know that there are at least 10,000 criminal groups operating in the former Soviet Union, over a thousand outside. We know over half the banks in Moscow are in their hands. We know of the three-stage "placing" then "layering" and "integration" which these banks do for the gangsters. Some estimates say that half the Russian economy is in their hands or influenced by them. Who knows, but one thing we do know, they hate each other! They will not do business with each other. They fight bitterly for "territory". They kill each other more than they kill legitimate citizens! The police and the FSB are delighted. It saves them some trouble! So, what does this mean? Think about it Warren. It means that they can't, as you would say, get their acts together and co-operate on really big projects! They've got the money, they have neither the will nor the organisation to pool it and go 'big-big' in a legitimate way." He paused for effect.

"That," he said almost triumphantly, "is behind our decision to offer only $500 million traunches. They can't get that kind of money together quickly! And this Tender has been prepared very carefully over a longish period of time, but, as you know, it is only in the last couple of days that it has been made public."

Bannister had to admit it was a sound approach. It did rob him though of what he thought was going to be a good story to tell HQ.

"That's good thinking, Mindibar. I can't fault that. But it leaves me out in the cold, I'm afraid," he smiled ruefully to show he wasn't sore, "it's down to the big boys then."

It was Kharrulah who disabused him.

"That is not so. Yes, you're right. All the big American and British companies have come in. We invited them, like you. But we've had a couple of outfits that we've never even heard of, who we were suspicious about initially, but who've already put their money where their mouths are."

"How do you mean, Kharrulah?" Bannister was genuinely puzzled.

"They've both deposited 50% of the $500 million in the Central Bank to validate their seriousness! Very nice for us, too!"

Bannister's mind was racing. Maybe this hadn't been a wasted trip after all.

"May I ask, if you don't mind, who these bids are from?"

"There is no secret, Warren. It is an open tender. This afternoon the full list will be published. I'll tell you now, the submissions are from the Lebanese Salvation Bank and the Bank of Hebron. Good, eh? New players."

Bannister knew his trip hadn't been wasted. But things weren't what he thought they'd be.

He paid the usual price to go through the VIP lounge at Tashkent Airport, and walked across the tarmac to the Yak. He was surrounded by a sea of Uzbek Air airliners with their green livery. They'd had a large number of Aeroflot's planes on the ground when they suddenly achieved their independence in 1991, so they'd kept them and quickly, before anyone else could do it, formed their own airline. It was successful. Lufthansa looked after the passenger service side, they were already a major engineering service centre under the old regime. They were now one of the main carriers from the Indian Sub-Continent to Britain and

Western Europe. The Yak looked incongruously small in the midst of the Illyushins and the Tupelovs, but it would get him back to Moscow by this evening, and, once he got back to the Kempinsky he had a lot to tell Langley.

"I prefer Chateau Margaux anyway Mr. Page," Antonio de Los Santos said with a faint smile. He was delighted the Juaragua had no Smith Haute-Lafite left.

"Antonio, are you sure about this?" Page was serious.

"Of course. I enjoy my wine."

Page laughed.

"OK Antonio, good one. But seriously, are you sure?"

"Mr. Page, I'm as surprised as you. I did not think it would be possible for me to glean the necessary information in less than four or five days, and I thought it would be quite costly. This is simply not the case. I have never known anything be so transparent. The Bank was proud of their transaction. The papers were shown to me without demurrence. It cost only a few dollars for the favour of a copy by the secretary, and a promise of lunch. An attractive girl, intelligent too. No, it is all above board. The money is definitely there. It is definitely at the sole disposal of Stobart, Kravitz and Lord. It did come through Deutschebank and Credit Lyonnais. They did receive it from UBS. A Lebanese bank placed it there. There, I'm afraid, the information runs out. I do not think anyone is hiding anything. The chain from Europe is legitimate enough provenance for anyone, seems to be the extant opinion."

Page often wished he spoke his own language with the precise clarity with which Antonio spoke his second. He'd been surprised at Antonio coming back to him within 24 hours. At first he thought there must be a problem. Far from it. He now had all the information he needed for the Deputy Director, in double-quick time. Well, that would make him look good. As long as they didn't think everything could be done so quickly! Still, it was a puzzle.

He finished his Steak Bearnaise and ordered two cases

of Chateau Margaux, one for Antonio and one for delivery to the Ambassador. He knew the latter only stocked and drank Californian wine all the time in the line of duty to US exports. He'd enjoy a little French, and Page always cultivated his Ambassadors. They came in useful sometimes.

Elmer Westerndorp was drinking coffee that turned into super-glue when it dried and eating another of Chick's doughnuts when he got the call from D.C. He couldn't believe it. The money was legit. Well, as far back as could be traced. The D.D. passed the message on personally. They were obviously concerned over there as well.

Why the hell would Arab money be lent to those Italian bastards? He left nearly half of his doughnut and his coffee and pulled his PC into place. The D.D. wanted a briefing paper, not more than one side. It was going "up". He started it right away.

First, brief summary of who they were and what they were into, then where their money was, on-shore and offshore, their previous contacts, their relations with other families. He decided it would be prudent to refer to the Group of Eight Economic Powers 1996 report (the latest published, it needed up-dating) on organised crime monies held offshore. They calculated there was $2.4 billion held in various offshore havens such as the Seychelles, the Cayman's. The two families couldn't have got hold of nearly a quarter of that! He'd attach the full report as an appendix. He summarised the estimates of the British SIS, the Germans and the Swiss as to how much Russian "mafia" money had swilled into Europe. These ranged from $26 billion according to the Germans in a 1997 study, to $40 billion estimated by the British and the Swiss. He was inclined to believe the latter figures. The British still had one of the best intelligence services in the world, and the Swiss probably had the bloody money! Jeez! It was so corrupt. Between 1991 and 1998 $46 billion worth of aid and loans had flowed into Russia. Most of it had flowed back out again. It hadn't aided ordinary Russians much. Most of it had ended up in criminal hands. The old KGB had turned into expert criminals! They'd achieved in a couple of years what it had taken the Sicilians and Italians 70 years! Maybe it was the colder climate. But this money was totally disparately held. There was no love at all lost between the rival factions in Russia, less so than between the creeps in the U.S. He could not believe they could co-operate to organise major funding on single projects and he said so. He was coming to the end of his single page. He wrapped up with a short paragraph, ending in a question.

"I predicate there is a new source of illegal finance, capable of being targeted on major projects. Otherwise, why would legal finance be integrated through dubious channels?"

He wanted to know the answer to that question himself.

£$£

Chapter Thirty Four

The car phone rang as soon as they got into the back of the dark grey Jaguar XJR and the Chief only finished the conversation as they passed the Queen's Gallery and were nosing down Birdcage Walk on their way to Whitehall.

"They do it on purpose you know, JD." The Chief had that wry half-smile on his face that he often adopted when he was being sarcastic or cynical.

"Sorry?"

"They do it on purpose. If these Government wallahs ask you to come to a meeting at 9 am. they're taking the you-know-what. They just want you to spend ages in traffic. Puts you in your place, y'know."

JD knew what he meant. It had taken them I5 minutes to cover about a mile, down Sloane Street and through Eaton Square.

"I could cycle faster."

The Chief was leaning back relaxed, and only familiarity with his minute-counting normal schedule would intimate the frustration the wasted time was causing him. As usual, he displayed none of this. He'd long-since mastered the Zen-like ability to accept most situations and drain each minute of its full usefulness. As he grew older he became ever more adept at it. He had much to do and time was melting away. He shifted in his seat to talk to JD.

"We're going to see Sir Julian Urqhart, the Permanent Secretary. I know him. Have done for a long time. He's OK. I didn't have much time to make the arrangements yesterday, as you know. Anyway, the Foreign Secretary is busy with the Americans - the Secretary of State is over of course, and Jimmy Sutton is in China."

JD knew that Secretary of State Teitelberg was in Britain, and he knew that James Sutton was Junior Minister at the Foreign Office. He didn't know the latter was in

China and he'd never heard of Sir Julian Urqhart.

"The Permanent Secretary is closest to the Foreign Secretary anyway. Jimmy and Ken aren't that close. Ken thinks the PM. appointed him as a counter-balance." The Chief chuckled. He had a tolerantly amused but cynical view of politicians. He didn't think many would get far in "real life". They'd be drowned in the swamp of their own egos.

It was apparent that the Chief knew these people quite well. JD knew he regularly briefed the Foreign Office about his multi-national activities. It was a valuable source of very high-level intelligence. All major exporters and multi-nationals did it. He also understood the comment about "counter-balance". Kenneth Beswick, the Foreign Secretary, was an old-style party politician with a patrician style, "bit of a Bevin" in JD's eyes, James Sutton was one of the PM.'s close circle of "whiz kids". He and Beswick had had differences of opinion in Opposition. There was no reason to suspect anything had changed in Government.

"Do we tell Sir Julian everything?" JD wasn't sure how the Chief wanted to play it. They'd had no time for discussion.

"Yes, of course. We've behaved honourably in all ways. We've supplied a sovereign government. If they're doing something dodgy, that's their affair. Our affair is to inform our Government. That's what we're engaged on. Leave it to me, JD. I'll do the talking. I'll bring you in when, if, we get down to details, I'm sure that's the way to play it, don't you?"

JD didn't think he even needed to answer that. They were in Whitehall now anyway. He'd driven and walked down there so many times, but before had always only noticed Downing Street and the Cenotaph. When he was a boy he'd stood outside the famous old door, and since then had enjoyed a couple of good lunches and quite stimulating conversation inside Number 10 when he'd been a guest, with Ness, to honour a visiting President, both times from African countries Daltons dealt with.

He'd been pleasantly surprised to find representatives of the Opposition at the lunches, as well as a clutch of businessmen like himself, a nice touch. He was re-running these memories as he stepped out of the car, and also wondering how he'd managed to overlook the small fact that Downing Street is virtually a charming little Mews sandwiched between the imposing piles of the Cabinet Office and the Foreign Office. Still, it was a pity about the railings and gates which were now an unwanted feature of the place. It was always a matter of a kind of pride that, prior to the railings, anyone could walk up the street and almost knock on the door of the First Minister in the land. A bit like still having unarmed police.

He followed the Chief across the broad Whitehall pavement to the main entrance in King Charles Street. He was glad to be playing a secondary role. The Foreign Office was majestically impressive. If Number 10 reflected the charming, comfortable, elegant luxury of an upper-class but bourgeois British home of the late-Nineteenth century, the Foreign Office spoke grandly, and unashamedly, of Empire, of power and glory. In this place Disraeli, Palmerston, Curzon, Lloyd George, Balfour, Churchill weren't ghosts. They were the Old Masters who still gave tutorials. They didn't just hang on the walls.

They were expected. They were shown up the magnificent staircase that JD had a recollection was built by somebody famous. Imagine being remembered for a flight of stairs, the thought stole idly into his mind.

He didn't get much more time for idle thinking. They were shown into a plain and efficient Reception Room-cum-office, not much bigger than a vestibule, in which a plain and efficient Secretary rose to greet them, and immediately usher them into a quite large, well-furnished office. All the furnishings seemed to be of wood, including the filing cabinets, and the lighting wasn't particularly adequate, creating an air of solidity but inertness. It reminded JD of his first venture into a Building Society as a young boy clutching his Savings Book.

A slim, etiolated man of about fifty rose to greet them. He was wearing a suit and a striped shirt that would both have been fashionable 15 years before. His hen-like features, hollowed cheeks and almost no chin running into his neck, weren't softened by gold-rimmed half-glasses.

"Mr. Spencer, Mr. Dilworth, thank you for coming. Do sit down, I am the Permanent Under-Secretary (Economic). Sebastian Beaumont. I represent the FCO on the Joint Export Control Directorate. Please, sit down."

His accent and his hairstyle registered "Eton" on the class scale. His Honourable Artillery Company tie, dark red and dark blue, registered "zero" on the taste scale. His shirt was green and white striped.

The Chief didn't sit, so JD didn't. Neither did Sebastian Beaumont. There was a few seconds silence.

"Mr. Beaumont, I'm sorry, I was expecting to meet Sir Julian. Is he tied up?" After a couple more seconds, the Chief did sit down on the faded straight-backed chair in front of the desk so JD followed suit. The Under-Secretary then sat down, rested his left hand on the arm of his large comfortable chair and spread the fingers of his right out on the leather-inlaid desktop.

"The Permanent Secretary is with the Foreign Secretary on important business."

JD wondered if he meant it to sound insultingly patronising. It did. The Chief's expression didn't change.

"I believe you will find our business to be of great importance, Under-Secretary. I trust, when you have heard what we have to say, that you will pass it on to Sir Julian, and the Foreign Secretary, with expedition."

The hen-like face twitched in a sniff.

"I can only judge that when you have passed on your information, Mr. Spencer. Rest assured, of course, that anything of importance would be relayed to Sir Julian, when that is possible. At the moment he and the Foreign Secretary are waiting for the American Secretary of State and his party, and cannot be disturbed. But please go on. Your message to Sir Julian referred to Iraq, always of importance to us." He raised his arm and looked at his watch. "I have no more appointments until 9.30 am. Please continue."

JD thought he detected a slight hesitation on the Chief's part, but then the moment passed and he began to speak. In succinct and measured tones, without any hint of sensationalism, he told the story JD had told him the day before. He structured it differently than JD had done, but it was a precise exposition of what had happened, why it had happened, and what they were worried about, what their fears were. He ended pointedly.

"It could therefore be Mr. Beaumont, that even as we sit here thousands of banknotes are being printed for Iraq, perhaps passports and other security documents. They could be doing anything. It is of great concern.

The Under-Secretary leaned forward and pulled a ruled pad towards him, picking up a pencil. He looked at the Chief.

"You say this plant is at a military base at a place called Sirte?"

"That is correct, Mr. Beaumont."

"And that it has possibly been operational for many weeks, possibly three months?"

"Yes."

Beaumont stared at the Chief. He didn't even glance at JD. He tapped all his fingers at once on the leather. He spoke very slowly.

"It wouldn't appear to me, Mr. Spencer, that too much could have been done in that amount of time, even supposing your suspicions are well-founded."

The Chief retorted, a little sharply JD thought.

"That is not the case Under-Secretary. JD, how much do you think could be done with the plant we've built for them?"

"One hundred and eighty thousand sheets of banknotes per day." JD knew the statistics by heart. He'd been thinking about them every waking hour lately, and some of the time when he was asleep.

"Y-e-s." Beaumont managed to make the single word

sound like a considered pronouncement. "That's not an awful lot, is it"?

"Depends on the denomination printed. If it was a British £50 note, for instance, that would be £288 million per day."

"Are you sure?" The face looked like a hen, which had picked up a pebble instead of a pea. It simultaneously managed to register displeasure and disbelief in equal measure.

"Mr. Beaumont," JD's voice was steady, "I'm absolutely sure. They have, as Mr. Spencer told you, three full lines. They are capable of 7500 sheets per hour, 180,000 per day. Each sheet will contain, probably, at least 32 banknotes. Work it out for yourself. In £50 notes that's £288 million per day."

Beaumont did just that. They waited while he did the calculation himself on a desk calculator, there was silence, then he spoke again.

"They are not of' course doing £50 notes, and there is no actual evidence that the Libyans are doing anything of the sort you're imagining, is there?"

The Chief replied, in measured tones this time.

"No, there isn't Mr. Beaumont. But Mr. Dilworth is an expert in these matters and you've heard why it is that we are worried that something… unusual is going on. Our great concern is that it is carrying on going on every minute of the day. As we sit here, the machines are still rolling. That's why we believe this to be a matter of the utmost urgency. It is why I tried yesterday to contact the Foreign Secretary."

If the hen-head had possessed a crest JD was sure it would have risen.

"I'm sure this is not something the Foreign Secretary should be bothered with." Beaumont's voice was laced with dismissive smoothness. It was a mistake.

The Chief slowly sat upright and folded his fingers together in front of his chest, forefingers pointing to the ceiling in the familiar pose.

"You are wrong Mr. Beaumont. The Foreign Secretary

should, and would, be very bothered with it." There was a touch of ice in his tone.

Beaumont didn't discern the danger signs. He almost snapped back, "That is something for the Permanent. Secretary to decide, after I have briefed him. I will do so on Monday morning, at our regular meeting. He cannot be disturbed before that."

JD admired the Chief. He had one more try.

"Do you not think, if the Foreign Secretary is meeting the Secretary of State this very day, that this is something, which just might be of great interest to them?" He spoke very quietly.

"Certainly not. They have an over-full agenda as it is. Please, leave it with me, and…."

He got no further. The Chief simply lifted his right hand, palm towards Beaumont, reaching into his pocket with his left hand. Beaumont stared as he took out a small mobile phone. Without consulting any list the Chief dialled a number, looking directly at Beaumont. The hen-face took on an astonished look.

"Excuse me, Mr. Spencer. May I ask you what on earth you are doing?"

"I'm calling the Foreign Secretary at Carlton Gardens. As you know, that is where the meeting with the Secretary of State is taking place."

It was amazing, thought JD, that a hen's face could register astonishment, mortification and panic simultaneously. He had a momentary mental picture of Beaumont starting to flap his arms like wings and squawk…

Within two minutes it was all over. They were rising from their seats, Beaumont sat transfixed.

The Chief said, with great courtesy, as they reached the door, "Thank you so much for your time Under-Secretary. We'll see ourselves out."

At the top of the staircase the Chief paused and called the driver. The car was waiting for them as they stepped into Whitehall.

"Take us to the back of Pall Mall, Fred. We'll have to

walk from there. It's only a couple of minutes JD."

"He wasn't very helpful..." JD didn't get any further. The Chief interrupted.

"He was only doing his job. I shouldn't have stayed and wasted that time. I should have realised we'd have to get to Sir Julian and Ken to get anything done. I didn't think quickly enough. No matter. It was only half an hour. I'm only bothered by the time because if they get into plenary session we really can't interrupt them. That will start at 10 am. I'm counting on the Americans having arrived last night and stayed at the Embassy. I think they did. That means we can snatch a few minutes with Sir Julian and/or the Foreign Secretary before they start. They both know I wouldn't have said what I did unless there was a real urgency about a meeting."

JD understood now the rather peculiar form of words the Chief had used with the PPS he first spoke to, then with Sir Julian. It was obviously a prearranged "code" for want of a better description. He ventured that thought to the Chief, who chuckled and said.

"Well, hardly, JD. No, I suppose you could call it that. Really, it's just that they know I deal almost exclusively with heads of state and their ministers and other henchmen and the meeting this morning is particularly concerned with the part of the world we're talking about, the Middle East, Iraq. That's what got the response. Look, we're going to Carlton Gardens. It's the official London "home" of the Foreign Secretary. They're holding all their talks there today, and then there's a banquet being held in the ballroom there. They have the most magnificent ballroom. Sir Julian won't have had much time to organise security clearance for us, so be prepared for a few delays when we get there. Leave all the talking to me again."

Willingly, thought JD.

In the event, there was no difficulty. Sir Julian had even ensured that the ever-vigilant, smartly dressed CIA men, waiting as inconspicuously as Beefeaters for their Secretary of State, didn't leap into heavy-handed action.

As they waited in the small ground-floor office just off the main hallway for Sir Julian the Chief just had time to tell JD how much he'd done for the Foreign Office and for Kenneth Beswick in particular. JD was surprised to hear that InTraCon were major contributors to Beswick's party. He was going to ask the Chief more when Sir Julian came in. To his surprise he was followed by the man he recognised from his newspaper and television viewing as the Foreign Secretary.

Although the three of them used formal modes of address, they called the Chief, 'Mr. Spencer,' there was a brief out-break of smiling and greetings. Then the Chief introduced him. The Foreign Secretary said they'd be better sitting down and that he had about eight minutes.

"That's enough," the Chief said, and launched into a précis of what he'd told Under-Secretary Beaumont. Sir Julian started to apologise for Beaumont but the Chief said he understood. He hadn't realised though that Sir Julian hadn't received his message of yesterday, and that Beaumont had at least seen the potential importance of the meeting and undertaken it himself. JD hadn't said a word, then the Chief asked him to run through the statistics which haunted him. They sounded even more threatening when he was relating them to the number three in the Government. All the time the awful thought kept crossing his mind that he might be wrong, that nothing was going on, other than in his imagination. Oh God! He thought, what a complete prat I'd look then! He had the good grace to remind himself that he was a prat for certain other things he was doing.

The Foreign Secretary stood up, looking concerned. He turned to the Chief.

"My God, Brandon. That's some story. If it's true, the implications are enormous. Imagine what the Americans will think about Libya giving such material support to Iraq! Imagine what we think! I'm glad you came across. Glad you took the trouble not to be put off. I wish I had more time to talk about this with you. I wish I could bring some of our people in to listen to the story with us again. But I'm running out of time now and … Hell! Wait a minute. We've got to pass this on right away to the Americans. The Secretary of State is on his way to the Middle East after our talks. He needs to know this now. Have you met him?" He addressed his question to the Chief.

"Yes, I have. Over the Aleutian oil deal. He got involved as well as the Secretary for the Environment because of the Russian problem up there and, remember, he's stayed in our hotel in Venezuela. I met him very briefly then. Good chap."

"I'm going to ask him to spare us five minutes before the talks begin. No Julian," Sir Julian was obviously going to intervene, "I know all about protocol. You know all about my attitude to protocol if something needs to be sorted out."

"Of course, Foreign Secretary and I do agree. It is essential we alert the Americans as soon as possible. Perhaps we can hold protocol in abeyance for just a smidgeon of time on this occasion. But we will, Foreign Secretary, only have a couple of minutes, at most." There was a shadow of a smile on Sir Julian's Senatorial countenance.

What happened in the next few minutes seemed to JD like nothing so much as some great controller fast-forwarding the video of life. The Foreign Secretary and Sir Julian went out, they came back in again, they had the U.S. Secretary of State with them, he had someone JD took to be his Assistant and a security man with him, the Secretary and the Chief exchanged greetings as if they were old friends, the Secretary joked about the Chief "running a much bigger business" than he did "before he was put in chains by President Sunderland". The Chief joked that the Secretary was running a much bigger business now, the Foreign Secretary told the story of the plant in Libya in no more than three sentences, the Chief introduced JD. Sir Julian suggested that the working sessions planned with "officials and the Intelligence people" the following morning would be "the ideal forum for more detailed discussions", everyone agreed. Everyone left except Sir Julian and the

Chief and JD.

It was surreal. It had all taken place in a matter of three or four minutes. No one had sat down. They'd all seven of them been crowded into an office designed for one. The very large American security man alone would have filled it in JD's opinion.

"My apologies, I must go," Sir Julian was speaking as he wrote something on a slim leather-cased note-pad he'd taken from his pocket. "Please ring this number when you get back to the office. They will brief you accordingly. I'll set it in train before I join the session. Thank you so much for coming. The security man who brought you in will show you out. Good-bye." With that, he was gone and the video returned to normal speed.

"Excellent, JD. We did the right thing. You did well. Let's get back to the Apartment. We can talk there. And we'll see what's on the cards for us for tomorrow."

The smart young member of the Diplomatic Protection Unit waiting for them in the elegant hall politely offered to call for their car for them, but the Chief demurred and said. "No need, but thank you. Just walk us out so the CIA won't shoot us, will you. That would be most kind."

The young man smiled and did just that. Fred picked them up on the corner of Waterloo Place and Pall Mall. The traffic was much lighter and they were back in the Apartment in twenty minutes.

By 11.30 am. it was all arranged. JD was to be at the Chancellor of the Exchequer's country residence, Dorneywood, in Burnham Beeches, near Beaconsfield in South Buckinghamshire by 9.30 am. the following morning. The Foreign Secretary was "borrowing" it for the weekend because it was very close to Cliveden, the exclusive luxury hotel, formerly the home of Lady Astor, which the Americans had taken over completely for security reasons for the duration of their stay. They'd only used the Embassy for the night of their arrival. Chevening, the Foreign Secretary's own country residence in Kent, was too far away. JD's car registration was recorded, he was to come alone, he was to carry his passport and his Dalton's I.D. card as identification. The Chief was to meet him there. He was to carry all the relevant documents such as contracts and details of the plant with him. He was quite shocked when he was told, in a very matter-of-fact way, that he was already "security-screened and OK." The Chief laughed at his indignant reaction.

"Remember, JD, they've got files on more than a quarter of a million people stored at Thames House in Central London. The Head of MI5 F Section told me mine was particularly thick! They do all businessmen more or less, especially if you travel abroad and deal with Government officials there. You'll fall into that category perfectly. Half the I.O.D and C.B.I. are in there anyway. Watch it JD, they'll be asking you to do something for them now you're up on their screens! There's one other thing, JD. Do you know Dorneywood? No? Well, I've been a couple of times, and I've got to tell you, Burnham Beeches is a bugger! It's very easy to get lost around the place. It all looks the same! Set off early!"

Fred had moved a car to allow JD to use one of the Apartment's allocated parking spaces so he stepped right into his car and was on his way home before noon. Ness would be glad to see him back early. He ran through a mental checklist and decided he had everything he needed in his study. He'd collated it all for the meeting with the Chief, so he didn't need to call into the office. He phoned Ness whilst he was queuing in traffic outside the Natural History Museum and told her to get ready. He was going to take her to her favourite haunt for afternoon tea, Hartwell House, and then on to Le Manoir for dinner if she could book a table for early evening. He wanted to take her out. There was a worm of guilt gnawing at his soul, and he had a strong feeling that he might be going away again soon.

As he headed for the M4 he wouldn't have believed how right he was.

£$£

Chapter Thirty Five

He was shown into what looked like a drawing room, comfortably furnished with a large suite of muted but warm green chairs and couches, with tall Georgian windows which allowed light to flood in and wash over walls and carpets. Marble and alabaster ornaments added charm, two large gilt-framed well-lit paintings style, to the room, and the centrepiece was an elegant Adams fireplace, the grate shielded by a beautiful Chinese-lacquered screen. His "guide" was an athletic-looking young man wearing a small-check waistcoat, as part of a "uniform" which seemed familiar. He remembered: It was the same, or similar, to that worn by the "doorman" at No. 10 Downing Street.

The Chief was already sitting relaxed in an armchair, using his mobile phone. He raised his hand in acknowledgement as JD entered. The "waistcoat" asked him whether he'd like tea or coffee, but he declined and sat down waiting for the Chief to finish his conversation. He did so within seconds.

"Morning, Chief. You were right about Burnham Beeches. It's like a damned maze!"

The Chief chuckled.

"I told you so JD. I'm familiar with it now, but my driver got lost when first I visited. Did you bring everything?"

"Yes, I had it all at home because I'd collated it for my visit to you."

"What on earth for? You know I never read anything !"

It was an "in" joke. The Chief was well aware that the army of sycophants who surrounded him at HQ constantly complained that he didn't read their "position papers", by which they justified their existence and generous salaries with regular submission, on everything from the share price of InTraCon to the political situation in Thailand and the progress of exploratory surveys for gold in the Falklands. JD wondered again why he let it go on. His own best guess had always been that the Chief felt that he needed them to preserve a facade of conventionality for the institutional shareholders and the media, and that he tolerated them so long as they didn't try to do anything that remotely resembled trying to run the business.

"They were for me to check my facts, Chief." JD smiled.

"Come, come, JD. You've got a memory like an elephant, otherwise we'd have caught you out years ago!"

The Chief was in fine form. He'd obviously decided that he had to dedicate this time to this meeting, so he was in a mode of comfortable acceptance.

They didn't have time for any further conversation. Sir Julian Urqhart entered without announcement and greeted them courteously.

"Good morning, good to see you again. Thank you for making the trip into the forbidden forest."

Hell, thought JD, it's a comedy sketch-writer's conference. He didn't like to admit it, even to himself, but he was feeling a bit nervous. This was high-level stuff, he and his company were in the middle of it, and they wouldn't be overjoyed at the story he had to tell. He was glad the Chief was with him.

"Let me tell you who you're going to meet in a matter of just a few minutes. They're meeting in the Library. They began at eight."

Sir Julian sat down and placed his papers on an occasional table in front of him, as if he needed to check from them whom he was about to introduce them to. It was, of course, just an elaborate little ritual. He was as familiar with them as his own Foreign Office team.

"As you know, the Secretary of State flies on to the Middle East tonight, so that troubled region has been the focus of attention."

JD was fascinated by his perfectly-modulated tones. He sounded for all the world like an excellent British actor playing the part of the most senior Civil Servant in the Foreign Office in a big-budget movie about international power-play. JD realised quickly he was meandering in thought again and re-concentrated.

"Secretary of State Teitelberg is accompanied by the Head of the CIA, Director Wendell C. Grey, and the Head of State Department Intelligence, Graham L. MacParland, I do love their propensity for initials, don't you? Do you know them at all, Brandon?"

"No, Sir Julian. I'm very familiar with Fred Greenbaum, the Deputy Director of the CIA, and I know their Deputy Director, Operations, Sol Juanito; I've met, but I don't know well, the Deputy Director, Intelligence, Gad Isaacs. I've had few dealings with State Department Intelligence."

JD didn't even know there was State Department Intelligence.

"Few have met MacParland. He's a good man, but to continue. Our people are Sir Richard Webster, Sir Norman Swaffham and David Crichton. You're familiar with them, of course, Brandon." He turned to JD. "They are senior Government officials, Mr. Dilworth, who will be most interested in the information you have to proffer. They're breaking for coffee at 10 a.m and would be most grateful if you could join them then. I must join the Foreign Secretary for a few moments now, but a member of staff will come in shortly and take you to the Library. I'll join you there, will you excuse me for now."

His manners were as exquisite as his accent.

"Let me quickly tell you who he's talking about JD. Neither he, nor anyone else, will tell you more, that's the way they work. But Sir Richard is Director-General of the Secret Intelligence Service, the top dog, Sir Norman is Director of MI6 and David Crichton is Deputy Head of MI6. They're OK. I've known the two Knights of the Realm for a long time, Crichton I'm not so familiar with."

JD wondered again just how much the Chief had to do with the Intelligence community, and about the inter-lacing of British business in general with that community. It all made eminent sense, of course, but it didn't explain the pretty lousy service, as he saw it, provided by the Embassies to business abroad. That seemed contradictory. Perhaps it really was as simple a problem as most of the Diplomatic Service never having had anything to do with the sordid affairs of business. They were usually recruited from Oxbridge, as the brightest members of their years, before they'd ever done anything useful in life except pass exams in Oriental Languages or Classics. He was just admitting to himself that his working-class background didn't lend itself to his being an altogether unprejudiced critic when they were collected to be taken to the Library.

They didn't reach it. Just before their guide opened the tall highly polished wooden doors leading into the Library a voice interrupted them. The staff member turned abruptly and stood formally against the doors. They turned to see the Foreign Secretary and the Secretary of State walking towards them. They were both dressed casually, the former with a sports jacket and open-necked shirt, the latter a dark brown blazer, pale fawn shirt and dark brown silk cravat. It gave the American a Noel Coward look. They all shook hands. JD judged Ken Beswick and Bruce Teitelberg to be about the same age, around 60. Both were quite tall and in good trim for their ages. The Foreign Secretary had those eyes which always looked as if they were laughing and thick dark hair heavily tinged with grey, the Secretary of State, silver-grey but with a smart modem style, looked just like what he had been before the President asked him to join the administration, the President of one of the largest international law firms in the world. The Foreign Secretary spoke, animatedly:

"Just going in? We're going out for a walk for half an hour or so. Get some fresh air, at least, as we chat. It's a lovely morning. We'll come in with you first, though. We can effect the introductions personally, and set the scene for you. It'll save time and get you off on the right foot. They're all very serious men in there."

His laughing eyes were genuinely laughing.

"Foreign Secretary, I think that's a splendid idea. After you, Mr. Secretary." The Chief held his arm out, gesturing to the Secretary of State, who followed Ken Beswick through the doors held open by the staff-man. They followed and Sir Julian materialised suddenly behind them, like Burn's Tam O' Shanter.

The five men inside the Library all rose swiftly to their feet. They'd been sitting in a semi-circle in easy chairs at the near end of the book-lined, long room drinking tea and coffee. They were all in their shirt-sleeves, jackets hung over the backs of chairs which sat at various angles around the heavy conference table running down the centre of more than half the large and elegant room. Their papers remained on the table.

The Foreign Secretary ensured he made the first introductions. He wanted to save the Secretary of State any embarrassment in case he'd forgotten the details regarding Brandon Spencer and John Dilworth. He'd personally done a little homework that morning to make sure he was familiar with InTraCon. He had a gut feeling that what the entrepreneur and his colleague had to say would turn out to be of great importance to the transatlantic team. The British intelligence men were all in their late fifties and deeply experienced. They were adept at making anyone feel at ease, and in any case he knew Brandon Spencer was already on friendly terms with them. It was Dilworth he wanted to put at ease.

The Secretary of State made his introductions. In doing so he made sure he casually informed everyone that his two men were not only professional colleagues but genuinely old friends. They'd spent a year together in their younger days studying at the National War College at Fort MacNair, Washington D.C and had struck up an enduring friendship there. As usual with Bruce Teitelberg there was nothing casual about his introduction. He particularly wanted the British team to know how close they were. No one should imagine they could insert as much as a hair between State and the CIA.

After the usual pleasantries, with everyone still standing, the Foreign Secretary suddenly became serious.

"Gentlemen, allow me to just say a few words. I think it's important that I explain that. Brandon Spencer runs one of the biggest companies in the U.K., InTraCon Plc. You already know that, of course, but let me add two things: First, his company is very close to the Government and has rendered us great service in many parts of the world, so I want you to feel confident that you can speak freely with him. Secondly, Mr. Dilworth runs a company within InTraCon which treats secrecy and security in a way which may make even you all a little envious!"

The Chief waved the words away with a false sheepish grin, JD felt sheepish. The Foreign Secretary's words were obviously designed to make the Americans feel more relaxed. They seemed rather obvious.

"Now, Mr. Secretary, let's leave these chaps to do some real work. They can brief us afterwards. We'll go out and get some sunshine! It's like California out there!" The laughter was back in the Foreign Secretary's eyes.

As soon as they'd left Sir Richard said, "Please, come and join us." Motioning the Chief and JD to seats in the cluster of armchairs around the large coffee table, he asked, "Would you like some tea or coffee?"

They both declined. The Chief spoke immediately he sat down. "Gentlemen. I know how busy you are and how little time you have left. I believe your party is leaving this afternoon?" He was addressing Wendell Grey.

"That's right Mr. Spencer, but we've done well with our agenda this morning, thanks to the careful preparation of Sir Richard and his team, and in any case we're genuinely interested in the story you bring. We know a bit about it, but I for one would appreciate a run-down from the top."

"That's what you're going to get Director. Let JD tell the story. He came to see me two days ago. It was immediately apparent that it was a tale to be told to the Foreign Office as expeditiously as possible. You, and the Secretary of State being in London were fortuitous. JD do the honours, and if you would, tell our friends all of your theories and suspicions, please." He stressed "all". JD knew what he meant.

JD had thought about it so much, and told the story in his head and in actuality now so many times, that he'd honed it to the sort of perfection a Masonic Master would aspire to in ritual, or a Shakespearian actor with "the" soliloquy and now his nervousness had dissipated. It was a story that had to be told.

He told it. But he didn't mention anything but his suspicion of printing for Iraq. He was saving his other thoughts for later in the discussion he was sure would ensue. For a moment he thought the Chief would interject and ask him to voice all his suspicions, but he didn't. He was sitting back, relaxed now, obviously willing to leave the floor entirely to JD.

There was a silence at first when he finished speaking, then the CIA Chief and Sir Richard both started to speak at once. The CIA man deferred to the Briton.

"That's quite a story. It's impossible not to draw the conclusion that something is indeed going on. Otherwise, why keep the engravers, why seal the base, why is there no sign of a Pan-Arab currency launch, why the denials that there is indeed a base of that size there? No, I believe you're right to assume there's something going on. But, I have to tell you . . . Iraq? I'm not sure of that. Our information is that, yes, they're short of banknotes, but they're getting through with new coinage, which they can do themselves, very old and worn notes (no worse than India's are normally!), and the sort of low-level notes which places like the Ukraine and Uzbekistan issued when they were first independent in the early nineties, vouchers, really, which they seem capable of printing themselves."

JD was pleasantly surprised that the S.I.S. head knew so much about the subject. Sir Richard went on, You will, of course, understand that we are, er, quite well "represented" in that country, the regime has many enemies, they won't act, but they will talk! And as far as we can tell there has been no bulk shipments of any suspicious nature into the country in the last two or three months, the period you're referring to. We know this from Basra, their main port, and from Jordan. We're quite confident relations aren't good enough with Iran to create the possibility of supply through that long frontier, in spite of the so-called rapprochement. Wendell, what's your opinion?"

The CIA Director was quick to respond. JD was impressed with his brevity.

"I concur."

"What about air transport, Mr. Dilworth?" It was Sir Norman Swaffham, Director of MI6 who spoke.

"Not likely, Sir Norman. You'd need a lot of aircraft, or many trips, all attracting your sort of attention I would think. Banknotes are normally packed in metallic foil-lined waterproof boxes of 50,000 notes, about 3ft by 2ft by 2ft; a demonetisation, that's a completely new issue of all denominations of paper currency, for a country the size of Iraq, with a population of about 18 million, would require between 250 and 300 million banknotes. It varies depending on the denominations selected, of course. In the States you still have one-dollar notes, in this country our lowest denomination is worth around eight U.S. dollars. The pre-Gulf War value of the Iraqi was one Dinar to something like three dollars. The 300 million notes I referred to is based on a similar structure to that they've always used, that's 6,000 boxes. Sea or land freight, in containers is really the only practical way to ship that many. You're talking about 15 to 20 containers, accompanied by very special security measures. For instance, the containers would be welded shut from the outside, immediately noticeable. Accompanied at all times. The usual. Eminently noticeable by your people I would guess."

"One would hope so, Mr. Dilworth," Sir Norman said dryly.

"Yes, we couldn't fail to pick something of that order up, Mr. Dilworth." Sir Richard looked at the Americans, who both nodded. The CIA chief gave a wry smile and said to the Chief and JD:

"We know if the Iraqis order a pizza from outside. It's when it gets into the damned country that it disappears sometimes!"

The intelligence men all obviously appreciated that. It sparked a discussion amongst them about what were seemingly routes into the country and their surveillance of those routes. From the conversation JD got the clear impression that they were happy with what they had in place and certainly didn't think they'd miss shipments such as he described. They were quite careful in their discussions, which was understandable, but JD had the feeling that they'd taken the Foreign Secretary at his word.

The Chief interrupted the discussion.

"You do know that I've spoken to two senior ministers in Libya and that they deny there is a major base at Sirte? Or that they have done a deal with JD's company?" JD sensed the Chief wanted to move things on.

"Yes, we're aware of those two facts. The latter isn't so strange, is it? If they're doing something nefarious they're not likely to acknowledge it and if the base is what you say it is, it must be one of their main facilities. We weren't fully aware of that."

Wendell Grey interrupted Sir Richard.

"We look at every inch of that benighted country every day, satellite and manned surveillance, and we've got it down as a small air base. Doesn't seem to be more than a refuelling facility. Of course," he said quickly, "we're going to look a lot closer now. That's already in hand."

Sir Norman had been looking steadily at JD, who was conscious of it. He suddenly spoke.

"Mr. Dilworth. It's obvious by your account that you're rather worried about your chaps, the engravers, and the families they have there. You're going to see the chaps next Thursday. I think we might just know where the families are."

It was so unexpected that JD didn't answer immediately. the Chief did it for him.

"My goodness! That is good news! How? Where, may I ask?"

"As you know there are many foreign workers in the country. They are able to supply us with very useful background information in a steady flow. We never ask anyone to do anything which would be in breach of the law of the land, but it is amazing how much can be discerned by piecing together all the disparate threads of quite innocent information. Many of these families like to live by the Mediterranean. The climate is most clement, and as all ex-pats do they tend to want to live close to each other in their own communities. The Libyans are very good to their foreign workers, good housing, and even schooling up to a point. These communities are close to the coastal highway that runs from Tripoli to Benghazi. Between Sirte and Benghazi the highway passes through Bin Jawwad and As Sidrah, close to which are many pleasant villas. A little inland, and closer to Sirte, is An Nawfaliva. There are consistent reports that, near there, in two smart houses side by side, there are two young British women living alone, or should I say with just one child each. No husbands have been seen. Indeed, the women are not seen outside of their own "compounds." They don't mix, their children don't go to any nursery, and no one has their telephone numbers. They don't even seem to go shopping. Perhaps most significantly, their properties are protected by what look like Military Police. It's not ostentatious protection. It is simply that there is someone there with them at all times. We were becoming mildly puzzled by these two young ladies. We think you have provided us with an explanation of who they are."

"That must be it." JD was quite excited. "Are the children a boy and a girl of about three or four?"

"Mr. Dilworth, to be honest I can't recall that information. I will check that out as soon as we've finished our business here."

Apart from the good news about the families, JD had the feeling that the discussion was slowing down. He could tell the Chief felt the same, and he was conscious of what the Chief had said in introducing him, voice the suspicions. He decided the time had come to toss the grenade into the tent.

"Look. Please forgive me, but I feel I must say something..."

"Mr. Dilworth, that's what you're here for. Fire away, we're listening!" Wendell Grey had that easy familiarity of tone that comes naturally to Americans, but not always to the British, especially not to such senior figures as the two Knights. David Crichton simply maintained a silent vigil.

JD glanced at the Chief. He nodded encouragingly. He continued, "Well, look, I know you gentlemen know infinitely more than I do about what's going on in Libya and Iraq etc., but I do know a lot about security printing and I know everything about what's gone into the Sirte base. All I don't know is exactly what they've done with it! But I know they've done something! They've been running the damned place 24 hours a day for nearly three months, maybe more. They're printing something, in vast quantities! What it is, I don't know. What I'm pretty certain about now from what we've found out ourselves from travelling in the Arab world, and from their re-order patterns, is that they're not printing what they said they wanted to, a Pan-Arab currency. I gather from your lack of comment on that subject that you've heard nothing about such a project." He could see no one disagreed. "What bothers me is that it could be anything. Anything. They've got the most up-to-date equipment in the world, they've got the full range of it, they've been trained to use it, they've got experienced people from Sudan, they've even got two of the best engravers in the world to create whatever they want. And, from what General Belazir said when I was last there, they've got independent sources of all raw materials. They could, literally, do anything they wanted to which is done by the Security Printing world, anything." He paused for effect, then he said softly, "And no-one, absolutely no-one, would be able to tell the difference from the genuine article.

In fact, gentlemen, it would be the genuine article."

He stopped to let it all sink in. Wendell Grey spoke first.

"But …surely ... not .., everything?" It was a question, not a statement.

"Gentlemen - everything. There are 15 privately-owned High Security Printers in the world, there are 51 State Printing Works, such as the Bureau of Engraving and Printing in Washington and Fort Worth and the Bank of England Printing Works in the U.K. Certainly the 15 private printers could produce anything that any of the others could do. The State Printers could do, in most cases, but they'd all probably need more training and some more equipment. They're all geared solely to printing their own government's stuff of course. But it wouldn't take long for them to expand their repertoires. The private printers already have the kit. That's why I know your organisations, and the FBI and Interpol and the FSB keep such a close eye on members of the AIIF, to which all the private printers belong. We know and as you know, we co-operate fully. The big worry has always been the criminal element getting hold of the machinery and the people. I don't think any of us envisaged a state doing it. I didn't. We didn't. You can tell by our actions in setting up the Sirte plant that, to us, it was genuinely a case of a country wanting to be in control of it's own requirements. That, and the Pan-Arab project, of course."

There was another silence. Sir Richard spoke.

"What do you think they're doing, Mr. Dilworth?"

"Well, I'm sure they've printed a raft of Libyan Dinars. That's self-evident. We supplied them with plates to do so, if you'll remember! After that, you can run through a list. The Sudanese are involved, so they could be doing Sudanese Dinars, they could be printing Dinars for the various organisations supported by Libya and Sudan. You'll know more about those than I do, but I know they're a pretty unsavoury bunch. They could be printing Shekels for their Arab brothers in Palestine, or Euros or dollars for any of their "friends", or for themselves. The possibilities are frightening. It's the volume that troubles me. So many of whatever they're doing must have already been printed. I used an example when we were at the Foreign Office yesterday. They have the facilities to produce a steady 7000 sheets per hour. There are probably 32 notes per sheet. They're running 24 hours a day. If they were printing British £50 notes, that would be £288 million per day. If they were printing U.S. dollars, 100s, that's $538 million per day! My calculator won't count the noughts if they're printing $1000 dollar notes!"

"Jesus H. Christ!" Wendell Grey said slowly. It was the first slip into strictly non-diplomatic language of the day.

To JD's surprise the Chief came in, and he made a point that JD hadn't thought of.

"There is one thing for sure, gentlemen. This is not a criminal act. Not only has it been perpetrated by a State, We have dealt with no less an organisation than the Central Bank of Libya in this affair but if it was for personal gain, the people involved would have had all they could ever use in a lifetime in a matter of a couple of days. It runs into billions in a week."

The silence was heavy now. It had the almost physical aspect of a sea fog.

The Head of State Department Intelligence Graham MacParland spoke for the first time since the exchange of greetings pleasantries.

"Wendell, didn't you say that our friends in the FBI were getting a little exercised by "new money" suddenly appearing in some weird places?" It was the soft lifting drawl of a Southerner, Probably Kentucky or Tennessee JD thought. Somehow, it was more effective for its gentleness. It was obviously a "prod". The CIA man shot him a worried glance, then took a deep breath and leaned forward, elbows on his knees.

"Yes. Well, what it is, what's been happening, only in this last two or three weeks, is that FBI monitoring stations, tracking illegal money being handled by criminal or suspect organisations, have reported some very large inexplicable tranches of cash, I stress, cash, suddenly being made available to those organisations. Our own operatives, mainly in Latin America, have followed these up when the trail has led their way, and they have also had the same experience in the territories they cover. The thing is, the provenance of the monies seems legitimate. It originates in Swiss, Belgian, Italian, Lebanese banks, often comes through London, or Paris or Germany and often has links with Sudan or other as yet unspecified Arab sources. Perhaps Islamic is a better description." He paused, and then addressed Sir Richard directly. "It's so recent we haven't gotten around to even passing it on to you, or anyone else for that matter yet. We are truly still in the process of evaluation."

"And then there's the hi-tech investment." MacParland was prodding again.

"Yes, I should explain. Some of this money is being ploughed from the most unlikely sources, criminal I mean, into hi-tech industries. Small, very advanced computer and biotech companies, deep into research, long payback type businesses. Why is beyond us at the moment. It is not the usual route for these guys."

JD and the Chief had become just observers now. There was obviously a serious discussion going on between the intelligence communities.

Sir Richard looked at Sir Norman and said, "I think we should throw our two-penneth in here. It's highly speculative, but it just could be relevant."

All eyes turned towards Sir Norman. The collation and ordering of facts in his mind became for a second or two almost an external exercise JD thought. He spoke precisely.

"We too have witnessed a sudden burgeoning of the availability of money. Our Irish friends have recently placed large orders for weaponry on the Continent and in the former Soviet Union, all of them backed up by cash deposits, in dollars. Strangely, though, they have simultaneously asked their North American friends to hold fund-raising in abeyance, making a great play on doing so, supposedly to further the peace process. It has made a great impression in Boston, New York and Chicago. As that was the main source of their funding it has been a mystery of great interest to us. Why do it? And, having done it, where has, and where will, the money come from? But the most peculiar development has been the planes."

"The planes?" Wendell Grey looked as puzzled as he sounded.

"The planes. There aren't enough. Let me explain. It must sound as if I'm talking in riddles. Sorry. You're familiar with the Moslem's obligation to make the pilgrimage to Mecca at least once in a lifetime, with only poverty or sickness accepted by Allah as an excuse for not doing so? Well, of course, millions do so every year, but the vast majority of the billion or so Moslems are too poor to undertake the Hadj as it's called. God knows what would happen to Saudi Arabia if they all did. They'd run out of water or sink! However, in this last few weeks, something most peculiar has transpired. The volume of pilgrim traffic has rocketed. The Saudis are extremely worried. The pilgrims are emanating from the most unlikely sources. We, as you know, have vast commercial interests in Africa and we keep a close eye on almost all the continent. It's not too difficult. We don't need many members of "the Firm" there. We get much of our information from genuine commercial and trade attaches in our Embassies and High Commissions, from publications now that the majority of the continent has at least some freedom of the press, and from normal commercial companies operating there. There has suddenly been a dramatic increase in bookings for the Hadj. So dramatic that it is being picked up by such disparate sources as cigarette importing companies in Ouagadougou, Burkino Faso, brewers in Dar-es-Salaam and tour operators in Mombassa. The way they've all come across the phenomenon is that they've not been able to get flights or planes. Islamic groups for pilgrimages are chartering them all! It's not just the usual Ukrainian or Russian or Uzbeki planes that are being chartered because they're cheap, it's the normal civil airlines. Companies like Ethiopian Airways, Ghana Airways, Kenyan and South African, you name them, they've all been approached. Scheduled flights by Saudi and Gulf Air are packed. Travel operators have approached all the European charter companies, including British Airways. There is an acute shortage of planes, and it is stretching out in actual bookings for months ahead. Not just the immediate future. Our initial inquiries have yielded immediate results. None of this is clandestine. It is a service for poor Moslems being offered by Mosques throughout the Islamic world as far as we know, though the effects are being felt first in Africa. The money to finance this is from a charitable fund set up by "a group of Moslem countries", so we are told. Our attempts to trace the money source has so far only led us to Sudan and the Lebanon and two Banks in Palestine. In each case they are adamant, and there is nothing to prove otherwise, that they are simply acting as conduits. We believe, but our information is scarce because we don't have the infrastructure of informants in the area - yet, that a similar operation is extant in Central Asia, Turkmenistan, Tajikistan, Kirghizstan, Uzbekistan and Kazakhstan. We have no hard information yet about Afghanistan or Pakistan and so far there has been no whisper in Indonesia. Just as well, perhaps. It's the world's most populous Moslem state. There are over 200 million of them. Dispensing with religious fanaticism and/or altruism we can see no possible way so far that this money can in any way bring any returns. It simply goes into the pockets of the airlines and operators. Most strange."

Silence joined them again as the main spokesman for a little while. MacParland interrupted it. "Friends, have any of you heard of an Islamic organisation called the Hanifs?"

The silence grew a little uncomfortable.

"Director I think we all have, but that seems to be the sum total of our knowledge. Reputed to be a powerful secret organisation, behind so many things in the Islamic world it fits into anyone's and everyone's conspiracy theory. Why do you ask?" Sir Richard looked at the Director of State

Intelligence intently.

"Because one of our guys, working out of Lagos but visiting Kaduna in Northern Nigeria to organise some articles for the Department as part of a "heart and minds" campaign, was talking to New Nigerian Newspapers who're based there. He was told by a prominent Immam that there was to be a great pilgrimage from Islamic West Africa, from Nigeria, Niger, Mali, Senegal, Burkino Faso, Chad, and more, organised and paid for by "the Hanifs". That's all we got, apart from our Arabic department translating the word for us. What I've just heard brought it immediately to mind. It should have done. It was part of one of the last briefings I read before we left Washington. The information was fresh."

Everyone was quiet. JD couldn't tell whether the intelligence men had nothing to say, or wouldn't say anything. To his surprise it was the Chief, who spoke next, in his usual languid tones that cloaked intent.

"I'm sure they do exist, very much so. Many years ago King Saud told me, - I'd known him for years. We were young together, - that his most constant worry was the Hanifs. In 1963 he indicated to me that they'd finally overwhelmed him. Those were his words. He abdicated the following year. Ten years later, his brother Feisal told me he was having trouble with the same people as Saud. It was obvious who he was talking about. He was dead within less than two years and I know Sir Muda Omar, the grand old man of Brunei, felt that his many years advising his son as ruler were not made easy, but rendered vital, by the organisation. These men were not gullible conspiracy theorists. They were troubled men of great responsibility."

Quite clearly no one knew what to say. Equally clearly, it seemed to JD, everyone present wanted to question the Chief further, but preferred to do so discreetly - preferably alone. It seemed to JD that the gathering was in danger of "losing the plot" but Sir Richard brought immediacy back into the proceedings.

"Gentlemen. We seem to be in danger of making some

rather vaulting connections from the disparate threads of tenuous evidence we have before us. Where..."

Wendell Grey interrupted him gently.

"Sir Richard, if I may. I agree, we may be in danger of jumping to dangerous conclusions here. But one thing we can all agree about without any jumping is that something strange is going on. Something that may be doing a great deal of harm. In Washington this Tuesday coming we have set up a meeting between the CIA, FBI and State. Graham, the Director, and I are flying back from the Middle East on Monday but we hadn't planned to attend the meeting. Our deputies were handling it. What we have heard here today underlines for me the importance of that meeting. I think now that it's important we do attend." Graham MacParland nodded assent, the CIA man went on:

"I would like to take this opportunity to extend an invitation to you Sir Richard, and any of your team you care to bring to join us. I would also like to ask you, Mr. Spencer and you Mr. Dilworth, to do the same. I believe we may very well need your expertise on the spot. My gut feel for this is that time may be running out on us. We may only have time for one meeting. The figures Mr. Dilworth quoted are frightening. If what I think we might all be thinking turns out to be true we may have to act - and fast."

"Director, you can count on our support. Whilst you're away for the next 48 hours we'll liase with the Deputy Director in Washington. I know you'll prepare the ground for us before you leave today. Sir Norman?"

The Head of MI6 merely nodded agreement.

"Of course. I'll speak to the Deputy Director immediately after this meeting and before we go on to the other topics. Are you prepared to join us Mr. Spencer?" Grey looked at the Chief.

"Certainly, Director. But can I point out that my presence is rather superfluous. The person you really need is JD, Mr. Dilworth."

"You're right, Mr. Spencer, agreed. But please, join us if you wish."

"Thank you Director, but I doubt I can be of much use compared to JD."

"No, you're right Mr. Spencer. Mr. Dilworth should join us. My department will make all the arrangements and be in touch with both you and Mr. Dilworth later today or tomorrow. Thank you so much." Sir Richard sounded eminently sincere, but JD got the impression that perhaps an opportunity to talk to the Chief about the "Hanifs" before the Americans did might just have influenced his attitude.

JD also got the impression, with a sinking feeling, that his meeting with Mary at the Savoy Hotel on Monday, their first for 16 years, might just not take place, and he couldn't contact her to say that he couldn't make it. She was at home, he couldn't call her there, and he knew she was travelling down to London straight from home Monday morning, so he couldn't even do so by phoning her at the office. Jesus! They'd arranged it all so carefully. As he drove home through the cool shade of the Beech trees with the dappling sun occasionally signalling to him like a boy scout with a mirror he couldn't decide whether he was glad he might not have to go through with putting his marriage in possible jeopardy, or miserable because after all the longing and lust he wouldn't see her. What was a few thousand million dollars going astray and an international crisis compared with that. The bloody CIA, FBI, SIS, MI6, Hanifs, Libya, Sudan, dollars, dinars, they'd all be there when he and Ness and Mary were all dead. Like Ronni.

£$£

Chapter Thirty-Six

Lust laced with fear served with apprehension and seasoned by guilt is a heavy and barely digestible dish, and JD spent thirty hours that week-end gorging on it, wishing he was bulimic.

He'd arrived home from the meeting at Dorneywood early afternoon in the bright crisp winter sunshine to Ness at her most interested, concerned and warmest. He felt guilty immediately. She'd prepared a small table laden with a delicious-looking cold buffet in the TV room. Spiced meats, sliced breast of chicken, a large bowl of Italian salad tossed with balsamic vinaigrette dressing, fresh baguettes and salted butter, a cheese board decorated with apples and grapes and a scattering of walnuts and she'd decanted a bottle of Perequito they'd brought back from Portugal to let it breathe. She thought he might feel a bit stressed after what she knew had been a tough three days walking on eggshells with the Chief, and mixing with Ministers, foreign politicians and chief spies. He felt even guiltier. Rather than put the sports programme on which she offered to do he took refuge in his tried and tested defensive strategy. He told her how important everything was that he was involved in. Like a veteran method actor he adopted his most solemn mien and declaimed with gravitas whilst he ground black pepper on everything and related the events of the morning. She ate slowly and listened with absorbed interest, just as she'd listened when little more than a teenager, to his plans for their future before they were married. He wondered at the fact that she still believed in him, he watched her as he played his part so well and knew that he loved her and felt even more guilty.

But it might never happen. The arrangements being made even as he peppered his Polish sliced sausage might prevent him from seeing Mary on Monday. The decision would be made for him then. Great matters of State could preclude his priapic predilections. Everything would be OK again. Until the next time lust flash-bombed his brain. He refused to acknowledge anything but lust. To un-cage anything more was too terrifying.

"So we'll be getting a call, or some calls, from either the Chief or someone who'll probably say they're speaking on behalf of the Foreign Office. Just get me to the phone wherever I am. I don't intend to go out anyway, so I should be able to take them."

"Oh, that's good. We're having a family dinner tonight. The kids are all coming. I've spoken to them all this morning. I suspected you might be going away again soon so I thought it would be nice if we could get together. I thought, of course, that you'd be going back to North Africa. I'd no idea you'd be going to see the President of the United States!"

She was teasing, using her voice of mocking wide-eyed awe.

"I'm not going to see the President, smart-alec. I'm going, if I have to go, to a meeting to tell an even bigger bunch of people what I've already spent the last three days telling increasingly larger gatherings! I don't know why they want me there. They can tell the story themselves, surely."

His actor's voice indicated subtly but perfectly that he didn't really want to go, that he thought it was a waste of time and that he would rather spend the time getting on with his normal work, and with her and he thought it was especially unnecessary that they wanted him to catch so early a flight on Monday for a Tuesday morning meeting. They were five hours behind the UK anyway, weren't they?

She laughed lightly as she told him to stop being sulky and eat more salad and a civilised trip on a plane, with time to prepare for the meeting in Washington was surely better than going straight into a meeting after an over-night, wasn't it?

He kept on acting and growled a bit and kept on eating.

But in his mind the battleground between deserving faithfulness and selfish lust was a killing zone littered with writhing corpses. Mainly his, and their past and their future.

They watched the Rugby together, and he held her hand. She rested her head on his shoulder and filled his glass when it was empty. He kept on pretending to be solemn. He put his arm around her and she nodded off. He immediately started enjoying the rugby and stopped being solemn.

The arrangements changed a few times, but by 9 pm. on Sunday he knew exactly what he was to do. The Chief had decided he couldn't go to Washington, it was in JD's "expert hands". He was collecting tickets, First Class, from the British Airways desk on Monday. A room had been booked for him at L'Enfant Plaza Hotel. The meeting was scheduled for 8 am. Tuesday. Would he take all relevant papers? He was booked on a flight back over-night Tuesday night, which would arrive back 10 am. U.K. time Wednesday.

So it was decided. Fate had taken a hand. He could see Mary. They'd have six or seven hours together. It had been almost 16 years. He had to do it now, didn't he?

Vanessa packed his lightweight suit-bag, toiletries, one complete outfit for Tuesday, and laid out Monday's clothes for him. She didn't always do it, but she'd been so good this weekend. She was proud of him. He didn't always seem to realise the importance of the things he got involved in. She loved him for that. Sometimes he was as foolish as only men can be, but he wasn't pretentious or false. They were the same two people who'd bought their first flat together when they were so young, where if anyone stayed with them they had to give up their bed and sleep on the living room floor, the same two people who'd grown more affluent together, then spent most of it on their kids. She was looking forward to the rest of their lives together. She wondered how many of her friends could honestly say that.

He felt the same, and it made him feel awful when he waited for her to step into the shower then slipped a spare shirt, underpants and socks into the bag. But he did it. He thought he might need them after Monday afternoon.

It was 9 pm. when Mary Matthews put the last La Perla lingerie in her case. She was wearing Valentino to travel in. She'd already selected the Armani suit and body she'd go down in. There was a purpose to the choice, and she calculated she might not have time to change fully before she met him. Just underwear, replace her tights with stockings and her stylish but business-like Bally shoes with her favourite pair of elegant Seragomo which she knew were glamorous. He liked glamorous shoes as much as she did. There should be time to check in and do that much. She checked her toiletries. All her Decleor was there. Her Chanel perfume was in her Prada purse, it was a "neat" handbag. She was really pleased with it. She was glad she'd bought it for Christmas for Jonathan to give to her. If she'd left it to him she'd have ended up with something like the bag Indiana Jones carried in all those movies! God, he was hopeless when it came to presents, or taste for that matter! No, that wasn't fair. She only had to look round the bedroom of their converted farmhouse to see his handiwork and his taste. He'd done a great job, it had taken years, but the house was superb. Its value was so many times that which they'd paid for it when it was barely habitable. Even now, they wouldn't be able to afford to buy it as it was! It was a third "pension", not that she could bear the idea of selling it. It was a home, and they'd been, by all the yardsticks that could be applied in this day and age, happy here. That's where his job was ideal. All those school holidays. He'd never stopped! The girls had grown up in a building site! She often wondered whether his building projects and his environmental and conservationist involvements compensated for his disappointment in not getting further with his career. She hoped so. He deserved it to be so because he was such a good man, a good husband and great father and he was so wrong about how important teaching such young ones was. He'd probably influenced more young lives for the good than most men in their lifetimes. She was sensitive to his feelings on the subject of her earning twice as much as he did. It truly didn't matter to her. Her earnings had simply ensured them of the worry-free affluence that they'd enjoyed for years now. His contribution had been as great in creating this lovely home, always being there when she needed him - not just in the "American" sense of emotional support, but in far more practical ways such as seeing to the kids when they were young especially. She'd been busy ice-picking her way up the frozen rock-face of corporate life, he'd collected the kids from school and taken them to ballet and Brownies. All her salary went into their joint account. Her only unspoken stipulation, and sole extravagance, was her love of beautiful clothes, and she justified that to herself, (he'd never ever questioned it) by believing that her tasteful and sophisticated elegance had played its part in her career success. Just occasionally, in moments of introspection, she slapped her own wrist mentally when she noticed that she'd just spent more on a pair of knickers than she'd paid as a young woman for a suit! What would her Da' say if he were still around?

She went through the case again. She had everything. She'd better lock it. She'd put a couple of things in there she'd die with embarrassment about if Jonathan saw them. It might just make even him doubt that it was one of her normal London trips! In fact, she thought with a start, he might think that's what she'd been doing on every one of her trips! How unjust! She'd only ever been unfaithful with one man, and this was the same one! She laughed with embarrassment at herself when she thought of the absurdity of that self-justification.

She felt wonderful. She'd lounged in a very hot bath, fragrant with oils, for ages, thinking about the next day and those days now so long ago, then she'd had a leisurely shower, and taken a lot of care over her long hair. It didn't look at all bad for a 44 year old. That's what she told herself anyway. Even after the time taken packing she was still glowingly warm inside her thick soft towelling bathrobe. She caught sight of herself in the full-length mirrored doors of the walk-in wardrobe. With the white robe and large white bath towel wrapped round her head she looked like a damned attendant at the Golden Temple of Amritsar! She laid the locked case on the armchair and stood in front of the mirrors, opening her robe. Not bad. She was lucky, she thought. She really hadn't changed so much. She'd had the kids when she met him anyway, so the worst damage had already been done. A bit thicker, she thought, round the waist, likewise the thighs, but no cellulite! She did keep fit, anyway, she'd never thought of herself as much of a glam-puss. It was only JD who enthused so much! She wondered if it would be the same ... and him? Well, in her experience, men had so much of an easier time of it than women. They aged so much better. The legs! Oh God! She hadn't done her legs, or her bikini line. Damn it. She hated that job, even with the epilator. Still, much better than waxing! She'd already been ages, but it didn't matter. Once Jonathan settled down with the Sunday Times after dinner he was incommunicado for five or six hours. She could have had an affair every Sunday night if she'd wanted and he'd never have noticed!

But she'd never wanted to have an affair, ever. She still didn't know why she had done. God knows she'd asked herself the question enough times. The answers were never satisfying. Over and over again she'd told herself that it was an aberration, some one-off wild act of irresponsibility, totally out of character. Driven by simple, beautiful, animal lust, something she'd had to do just once in her lifetime. Wasn't he the same? It hadn't interfered with her 'marriage, or his, had it? Over and over again she'd had to admit to herself that it wasn't that simple, and now the fact that she was going to do it again rendered that self-justification spurious.

She stood and stared at the mirror, and the woman with the open bathrobe. With a slight toss of her head she whipped the towel-turban off her head, enclosed herself in the robe and reached for the epilator.

The taxi pulled off The Strand and stopped at the main entrance of the Savoy. He was bang on time, unusual for him. He slung the suit-holder over his shoulder and picked his pilot's case up after he'd paid the driver and walked into the foyer. JD was curiously conscious of operating on two levels, mentally. On the first, he was excited, confident, and even arrogant. He was sure that lust and a lack of principle would see him through an afternoon of pleasure-sating, he'd bask in and never want to forget. On the other level there was something else. Something he'd kept imprisoned in his mind for many years, eighteen to be precise. It was something that was powerful and restless and struggling to escape. It had already chiselled its way out of its high-security cell, it was now almost over the prison wall. He wasn't sure anything could stop it. Not when he saw her, he thought. Even he had to admit that a feeling that had lain not dormant but central to his being for sixteen years, through so much, couldn't be shrugged off as just lust, desire, and infatuation. But it mustn't be anything else. That was too disruptive. That would change his life. It would change her life. What was he thinking about, change her life? That was a typically arrogant presumption! She couldn't think like that about him. She'd not thought about him for sixteen years, she'd not tried endlessly to contact him, had she? She'd got on with her life. She was only seeing him because she was independent, intelligent, confident, and curious, and she could be sexually driven. Christ! He knew that! He'd never known anyone like her, and he'd been no saint in his life. That's why she'd agreed to meet him and looking like she did, if she hadn't changed much, and somehow he couldn't see how she could, she must have had many offers, perhaps a few she'd taken up. She moved in some sophisticated, some smart circles in her business. Even as lhe was thinking it he knew he didn't believe it. Perhaps it would be so much better if it were true, so much easier. He suddenly realised he was nervous. There was a little tremor in his stomach in harmony with his hands. It was like their first meeting as lovers. He hoped nobody noticed he was a middle-aged man behaving like a teenager.

Well, she'd been right in her calculations. That was the first time she'd known that train to be late. There was no time to change completely. She threw the case on the bed and unlocked the large toilet bag. Take it out, take the small one out of it and put it in the bedside drawer. Rest in the bathroom. What a lovely bathroom. Marbled vanity units and smoked mirrors. Most important rooms in any hotel, restaurant, bar, pub. Come on Mary Matthews, you're wandering! She took the suspender belt out and the shoes and put them on. She'd have to leave the body on. In the mirror she watched herself take her tights off. They really are asexual, she thought. No, worse than that. They're like a damned body-condom, be honest. She didn't look too bad. She was glad she'd put this suit on. She looked OK. Well, she looked 44, but OK for 44. She was going to move the case, but she hadn't time. She wanted to be in the restaurant when he arrived. She didn't want to make an entrance. Anyway it could stay on the bed. She still wasn't absolutely sure she was going to invite him to her bedroom. That's just what he expected was going to happen. As she was closing the door she mocked herself for keeping up the pretence.

He saw her as soon as he walked into the Grill Room. It hadn't happened to him before in life, but it stopped him short. It took his breath. Any director of an amateur dramatics production would have derided him for theatricality. But she hadn't changed. She hadn't bloody changed one iota! He almost forgot to grin. She was wearing an off-white suit which for all the world made her look just as she'd done that day eighteen years ago. Oh God! The prisoner was over the wall and well on the run now.

She'd just had time to order and take a large drink from a glass of Chablis. She'd composed herself, and assumed her most relaxed and confident air. She tried not to stare at the open entrance, but she couldn't stop herself She tried to rehearse all the pleasant opening lines she'd thought about all the way down on the train, but she couldn't think. She told herself to breathe slowly and deeply. Then he sauntered in and she caught her last breath somewhere in her throat. It certainly didn't reach her lungs. He was taller and broader than she remembered. No he wasn't. He was exactly as she remembered. God, he hadn't changed one bit. Not one bit.

She stood up and held her hand out. Even as she did it she felt foolish about it. But he took it and for a second they stood frozen in formal introduction. Then they both started to laugh out loud and speak at the same time. He took her shoulders and kissed her on both cheeks. She held her other hand out, he took it and she kissed him gently on the lips. For him, the rest of the Savoy Grill dissolved into nothingness, just a background mural, and there was only her and her eyes and her perfume and her beauty and her elegance, and for her he filled her world again with his grin and the same after-shave she always remembered when she thought of him.

They kept trying to speak at the same time. It was as if they'd last met only a week ago. Like it used to be. When they did meet almost every week. They had so much to tell each other. But he couldn't tell her much for telling her how fabulous she looked. She told him not to be ridiculous, but to keep on saying it because she loved it! They sat like teenagers holding hands on the table. She didn't believe him when he said she looked still in her twenties, but she felt twenty-eight again. What struck her forcibly, physically almost, was the overwhelming feeling that the intervening years had simply not happened. He felt exactly the same. They kept trying to tell each other that was the case. For two articulate people they didn't think they were doing such a good job of it. She offered him a sip of her wine. He drank it all and said it felt better. It was calming him down! He told her how nervous he'd been, still was. She told him she'd been nervous since they'd arranged it. She told him some of the things she'd practised saying on the train and they laughed again. She told him the knickers on the radiator story and he was doubled up. She had a way with words and the most wonderful self-deprecating humour. They didn't do anything but talk and laugh and hold hands tightly as if one of them was going to run off. He ordered a bottle of Chablis, and told the waiter to leave them for half an hour before they were going to order lunch. She blushed because he told the waiter they were old lovers having a reunion. She thumped him on the shoulder when the waiter left and they kept talking and laughing.

He'd never in his life felt so immediately comfortable with anyone, he was almost sure she felt the same. If he'd read her mind, which she was sure he could do, he would have found she was thinking exactly the same. If they could have occupied each other's minds they'd have immediately learned that it was so perfectly true that at mind's core it frightened them both.

"Shall we have some lunch, Mrs Matthews?"

"Of course, Mr. Dilworth. I said I'd buy you lunch."

"No. You can't buy me. Just because you want my body!"

"Who said that, I didn't!"

They ordered, then they burst out laughing again. They'd done what they did when they first went out to lunch together. They'd ordered the plainest food on the menu so they wouldn't be breathing garlic or onion or anything else on each other.

"And I had no nefarious intentions at all when I first took you out."

"You liar, Dilworth! You had every nefarious intention known to the male sex from the moment we met! I could tell instantly that I couldn't trust you!"

"You were in bed with me in two weeks! You seduced me! You were a loose woman!"

"You .... What! I was young and inexperienced and you took advantage of me. It was obvious you'd been at it for years."

"Inexperienced? You'd had two children!"

"They were very young and anyway, that was it for me

as far as sex was concerned. It just caused a lot of work. What a price for ten minutes pleasure!"

"Ten minutes! Mrs Matthews, You've never made love in less than an hour! You're insatiable!"

She hit him again. She loved that habit of calling her by her married name. He did that when he made love to her. Her face was burning with the pleasure of blushing. She couldn't stop smiling, grinning. She felt completely alive. For both of them there was no one else in the restaurant, even though it had now filled with its usual lunchtime clientele. They didn't wonder whether anyone could hear them. Or see them. They didn't care, as only lovers can't care.

It was difficult to eat because they talked so much. It was difficult for him to eat because desire was eating him and it had reached his throat. He couldn't know it but she felt exactly the same. She also remembered, so clearly, that when they first became lovers it was she who'd suggested it. She remembered her words, every word, "You know, JD, women want to jump in bed sometimes as much as men." Pause. "I do with you." She'd been appalled at her own effrontery after knowing him for such a short time. She was now. They were waiting for the coffee.

"JD, don't you want to make love to me?"

He looked at her and stopped smiling for the first time since they'd met. He said slowly.

"Bugger the coffee! I've thought about it every day for sixteen years Mrs Matthews."

"So have I."

"I don't believe you."

"Well, not every day. Not all the time. But, sometimes. When I've thought about sex. About once every two months that for a mother and a manager…" She was teasing now.

She drank her coffee in one gulp.

"Let's go!" She jumped up.

He was laughing again. She grabbed his hand and pulled him round the table so he had to get out at her side. He protested that he had to get his bags, and she picked his pilot's case up in mock urgency. She walked to the Maitre'd's desk and flashed her room key asking them to charge lunch to the room. They were both giggling like teenagers as well now.

"I can't wait for the lift, come on!" She headed for the stairs.

"Hey, I'm too old to climb stairs and then make love to a siren like you!"

"Come on, John Dilworth. Let's get you to bed!"

They were walking down the corridor to her room. She suddenly said.

"Where does Vanessa think you are?"

"She thinks I'm on a plane to Washington. I'm due there for a meeting tomorrow."

"JD, that's awful! How could you tell such lies, to your wife."

"Wait a minute! Where does Jonathan think you are, little Miss Truthful?"

"He thinks I'm here, in the Savoy on normal business."

"Why, do you do this regularly?"

"Oh, you ... you smart-alec!" She pretended to try and hit him again.

She put the, "Do not disturb", sign on the doorknob, and the chain on the inside. He took the pilot's case from her and put his bags down on the suitcase stand immediately behind the door. He turned to her and they embraced each other and kissed for the first time in sixteen years. It felt as if they had never happened, never come between them. It felt as if nothing could ever come between them, ever again.

She'd imagined what it would be like, this moment, many times. It was as she'd thought. There was no awkwardness about if, none at all.

"Let's clean our teeth." He was startled by her first words in the room, but then they both burst out laughing, and went into the bathroom with their arms round each other. He was going to unpack his toilet bag but she produced a travelling-pack toothbrush and they stood side-by-side scrubbing their teeth and watching each other in the smoked mirrors running the whole length of the bathroom wall. They couldn't stop laughing at the incongruity of the situation.

"We're supposed to be here for wild sex Mrs Matthews. Not a bloody dental hygiene course!"

"Oh shut up, and get on that bed!"

"Your cases are all over it!"

"I've only got one, and it's full of lingerie! For you!"

He lifted the case off the bed and put it onto the armchair. It was a spacious room, and there was a sofa and another armchair making up a little sitting-room area at one end. He thought of all the other rooms they'd been in. They'd only ever made love in hotel bedrooms. She started to undress. He stopped her.

"No, that's my job, remember?"

She smiled and let him do it. She stopped him once, and said she'd take the body off and put something she'd brought for him on. He said she wouldn't. He couldn't wait. He simply unbuttoned her body and they started making love.

He hadn't forgotten how she felt and tasted and she hadn't forgotten how tender he could be, even when he was doing all those things that Jonathan didn't do. After they'd been making love for about half an hour, and she was sitting across him and in control, she slipped him out of her and told him to wait a minute. She had a promise to keep. She went to her case and took the black Basque out. She took the pale satin suspender belt off and the light tan stockings and the body. She put the Basque on and sheer black stockings, and her heels back on.

"I told you I'd got this for you."

He made her stop so he could look at her for a long time.

"Mary, I don't think you've ever looked as beautiful as you do now."

She was moist with pleasure. She felt beautiful. She'd never felt like this with anyone else. She felt sexually attractive. She was suffused, vibrant, with sexual desire. He suddenly slid off the bed and she thought he was coming over to her, but he went to his case, and took out a small gift-wrapped box. He gave it to her. When she opened it a thrill of appreciation ran through her body. It was a lovely pendant, gold with a small diamond. It wasn't the gift that thrilled her, which brought almost a tearful feeling. It was the fact that in the midst of what could have been, what was, a torrid and passionate sex "session", he should be thoughtful enough to present her with it. It lifted everything they were doing, everything they were going to do, onto a different, tender level somehow. He said to her, as he stood behind her fastening it, with his flesh pressing against her buttocks.

"It's a very small present. It's an even smaller diamond. But diamonds are the only things tough enough to survive a nuclear war, Mrs Matthews, to last forever. That's what I feel for you." He pressed her to him.

She couldn't have loved him and wanted him more than she did then. There was nothing they couldn't do together, wouldn't do together. There was nothing she didn't want to do with him. They realised if they moved the bed a little to the side that they could see each other in the mirror while they were making love. They played the game they used to play of making love on every chair and sofa in the room. She wanted to try the small coffee table, so she knelt on it, and loved every moment as he brushed her hair as he made love to her like he always used to do. She said wouldn't it be a laugh if they made love at the window, watching everybody, and no one would know what they were doing, so they did it, watching the boats on the Thames and the traffic on the Embankment. She changed twice to show him what she'd bought for him, and he loved them all, but wanted her every time to put the Basque back on. He never changed. They had a time like no time they'd ever had before. Then they had a shower together and did what was best done in the shower, and he dried her and massaged her with moisturising cream, massaging her internally at the same time, she loved that. She got dressed in black again and they lay on the bed. She wanted to make love again. He protested.

"Mrs Matthews! Give me a minute. Give me a break! I'm getting older! I keep telling you!"

She teased him and played with him with her hands and her mouth.

"Get off! Stop it! You're a sex-maniac!" He was wrestling with her. "Stop. I'll do it to you."

So she let him and enjoyed it. Then she said, and she loved saying it, she'd planned saying it, "JD, just go in the drawer next to the bed. There's something for you and for me."

He looked a little puzzled, but he reached into the drawer and took out her toilet bag. He held it up by its corner.

"Go on, open it. It won't bite you."

He did. His face was a picture of surprise and pleasure. Shock. He took out the two vibrators and looked at her. She wasn't embarrassed. She looked amused and sexily defiant.

"Jonathan went through a bad patch, JD. I got them for him to help him through. I've come to quite... enjoy them. Especially when I think of you, on my own. With him they might be a necessity. With you I want you to use them with me for... fun, for pleasure. Will you?"

He thought she'd never looked as sexually attractive. He was so stimulated that he immediately didn't need them. But the invitation was so perfectly tempting that nothing would have stopped him using them, even though he'd never done so before. She instructed him. They had a great time, a lot of writhing, panting and laughing. She enjoyed them but she soon wanted him again. He certainly wanted her.

Neither of them could believe that four hours, a little more, had passed. Only the natural light completely fading outside indicated the time. He switched on all the lights. The bedroom overlooked the river and was on the sixth floor so there was no problem of being overlooked.

They ordered a bottle of champagne and room service sandwiches. They didn't mention it but they both realised that their time together that day was running out. He put his shirt and pants on to wait for room service. She slipped a silk robe on over the Basque and stockings. They opened the mini-bar and poured themselves long gin and tonics whilst they were waiting. They both admitted to each other that they couldn't make love any more. They needed a break! And they talked.

"Mr. Dilworth. I don't know how you make me do what you make me do, so many times!"

"Mrs Matthews, you're exactly the same with me. Honestly. Only you have this effect, can stimulate me, as much as you do. Have you honestly not had a string of lovers since we last met? Where did you learn all that?"

"No I've not, JD! Promise. I'd never had a lover before you, and I've never had a lover since you. You, well, you just bring it out in me!"

"You've been watching naughty videos!"

"No I've not!" She grabbed a pillow off the bed and threw it at him. He jumped up and grabbed her by the arms pretending to fight her and kiss her at the same time and she pretended to struggle. They were giggling as they struggled when room service arrived.

They sat side by side on the couch eating their sandwiches off the small coffee table, and drinking champagne. When they'd finished eating, she asked for the black and gold sex toy and she enjoyed it while they drank champagne. She congratulated him on learning so fast. He told her she was driving him wild and he had to make love to her again. So they did, for another hour.

She didn't want it to end. He didn't. But they both knew he had to leave at 7.30 to get to the airport. They had another shower together, and then they lay, warm and naked, on the bed and he asked the question which she knew was coming and which he'd been thinking about all afternoon.

"Mary, when can I see you again?"

She waited a long time before she answered.

"JD, do you think it's a good idea if we do?"

"It's the best bloody idea I've ever had!"

He said it in a voice that made her laugh aloud.

"No, seriously."

"Seriously. Very Seriously, darling."

There was another long pause. She said quietly.

"John. Do you love me?"

She never called him John. He answered with all the truth he could project with his voice alone.

"Yes Mary, I do. I've always loved you. You should know that after eighteen years."

"I think I do, JD. That's the problem. Because I know I love you. I told you once, a long time ago. I meant it then. I've done everything I could to forget it since. We could hurt so many people."

It was his turn to be quiet now. He knew she was right. He didn't want her to be right. And why couldn't they just meet and love each other sometimes. Like they'd done this unbelievable afternoon.

"I don't want to hurt anybody, Mary. But I can't wish loving you away, as if it was only a sad thought. You, even though we've not met for so long, have been central to my life, to my existence, to me being me. I can't explain it better than that. But it's true."

She sat up, turned and she looked into his eyes. Her long hair fell softly over one side of her face. He was shocked to see there were tears in her eyes.

She said, "I've never heard a better explanation, JD. Maybe it's because I understand it anyway. Don't you think I've felt exactly the same?"

She lay down beside him again, and wrapped her arms and legs around him and held him very tightly. He pressed her to him and buried his face in her hair. He hoped desperately she wouldn't cry. She didn't. They lay without speaking for a few minutes.

She looked up eyes steady as she gazed at him. She grinned, then unwrapped herself from him and jumped off the bed taking him by the hand.

"Come on, Mr. Dilworth. You've a plane to catch!"

They didn't talk about it again until he kissed her

goodbye at the door as he was going. A long kiss, and a refusal to use the word goodbye. She carried his pilot's case outside into the corridor for him. She stopped him for another kiss before he headed for the elevator, and she whispered to him as she let go, “JD let me think about it. Promise me that you will too. I promise I'll be in touch with you next week. Promise.”

He turned to look at her as he reached the elevator. She was brushing her hair back and she blew him a kiss. She stepped back inside and closed the door.

£$£

Chapter Thirty-Seven

He took Mary and he laid her in the lead-lined vault with the foot-thick stainless steel walls. He closed the huge lid that sealed itself heavily. It was a perfect seal, like a Giza Pyramid foundation stone. There was no extraneous handle or indent. No way to re-open the vault. Then he did the same with Vanessa in a separate vault. He kept his eyes closed and pictured nothing but the two vaults. It was a psychological exercise he'd used before. It had to work. His brain was hurting with thinking, and he'd a lot more to think about in the next few hours.

Then he remembered. He had to take Ness out again. He had to speak to her. Bugger.

He checked the time. Better do it now. He reached for the phone and dialled home.

"Hi darling. Just on my way out so I can't talk, but I thought I'd give you a ring and let you know I've arrived and all's OK. I'm in the lobby. You OK? Look, I'll call you again tomorrow as soon as we take a break. That should be mid to late afternoon your time. I'll let you know whether I'm going to be on the evening flight. I should know how things are going by then. Really, must go. We've got a meeting then dinner. Speak to you tomorrow. You know where I am. Love you." She told him she loved him too, and that she was going to bed early.

He sank back and closed his eyes again. The reception desk in the Terminal Four BA First Class Lounge announced boarding for the 9.30 pm. flight to Toronto. He'd timed speaking to her just right. The announcement would have been an embarrassing give-away, but he had to call her. He always did so as soon as he could wherever he was to put her mind at rest. God knows what she'd do to him if she knew where he was. She'd put him to rest forever.

He sealed Vanessa back in her vault again and went to

the bar and poured himself a very large vodka, picked up a little plate and filled it with crisps, Twiglets and salted peanuts, took a slim-line tonic from the cool cabinet and settled back in the comfortable armchair. He'd got at least half an hour now and he wasn't going to think about either of them. They were sealed up again. He was just going to think about lining his explanatory ducks up in a row so that his bit tomorrow would run smoothly and swiftly and he could make certain he was on that return flight. He was a little tired of telling the story. And anyway, it was up to them now. He'd, the company had, done its "duty". He drank the vodka in one single draught, and went for the same again. He needed three good shots before he got on the plane. Always vodka. Stewardesses got sniffy if they thought a passenger had been drinking too much. Bloody rich, that, when First Class cost twice as much as Economy for a free newspaper, a glass, metal fork, a plate to eat off and beef carved on a trolley. Curious how airlines thought people in Economy could only be trusted with plastic.

He settled into the luxurious seat on the 747. It had so many controls in the arms now that the videos had been added that he always played at being Captain Kirk on the Starship Enterprise when he sat down. He really did wonder when he'd grow up. But he soon resumed the persona of "international important business traveller" and asked for the "Herald Tribune" when the stewardess asked. At least he'd have some informed casual American conversation when he got over there. He had his plan. He was travelling at an awkward time, which meant he'd be arriving at the hotel around mid-night. So he intended to have a couple more large ones, then sleep. When he got there, he'd sort his room out then go to the bar and get into conversation for a couple of hours, then have three or four more hours sleep and be fresh for the meeting. He'd never failed to make a connection in bars all over the world. The coincidences were amazing, there was always some common thread, somewhere, somehow, sometime. It reminded him of that book on coincidence which Arthur Koestler had written back in the Sixties. He enjoyed those kinds of conversations

He read the stewardess's name badge again.

"Miriam, look, will you just bring me a couple of large scotches, blended, not malt, I drown them with water. That's sacrilege with malt!, Then leave me alone. I don't want any food, or coffee, or tea or anything else. I'm going to sleep to America! So you can bring me a blanket as well if you would, then forget about me! I'll wake up before we arrive, then I'd love a coffee and a juice, but I'll give you a call then. That OK?"

It was obvious that it was more than OK with Miriam. She brought him two glass jugs, one with whisky and the other water, and a glass.

"Black Label, Mr. Dilworth. Goodnight!"

He slept for more than five hours, then went through his usual routine of wash, shave, teeth cleaning, dousing with aftershave, and a coffee and fresh orange juice. His Circadian rhythms told him it was nearly 5 am. He knew he had a long night to get through yet, though.

Getting through Washington International was the usual pain, the Americans obviously recruited their Customs people from descendants of the Waffen SS, and getting a taxi driver who spoke English was even more painful. His man looked and spoke as if he'd just swum the Rio Grande and it took a long time to convince him that he didn't want "Loew's Plaza" but "L'Enfant Plaza". Perhaps it was his French.

He knew the hotel. He'd stayed there before. It was virtually opposite the Headquarters of the U.S. Postal Service and within easy walking distance, so long as it was daytime, of the Bureau of Printing and Engraving. Daltons had long connections with both. As the taxi drove into the brilliantly lit Plaza, with its little gardens and surrounding shops, it all looked so familiar. He couldn't really believe it had been five years since he'd stayed there, an excellent hotel. He walked through the capacious lobby, checked in, unpacked in five minutes, and headed downstairs for the bar. As he walked back through the lobby he noticed the information-board sign announcing their meeting. “Universal Software Solutions Inc.” Nice touch that. “USS Inc.” Somebody in the CIA who'd been in Naval Intelligence perhaps.

Americans are experts at friendly informality. He’d once worked for a giant U.S. concern whose President had said to him when they first met, and he was so far down the Organisation chart as to be almost subterranean, “Call me Bill. I'll call you John - even when I'm firing you!” It was what the Americans would perhaps call an “insightful” comment he thought. When he walked into the meeting room, after showing his passport for identification to the girl on the ‘reception desk’ at the door to the suite, the Director of the CIA and the Director of State Intelligence greeted him like an old golfing partner. It had a significant effect on the others present, and was undoubtedly meant to do so. It saved a lot of subsequent explanation and introduction. He was an “insider”.

Sir Richard Webster smilingly motioned for him to sit between him and Sir Norman on the far side of the horse-shoe shaped table, which was covered with thick green baize and jugs of water and glasses. There were no name-cards or badges. The meeting commenced at precisely 8 am. The CIA chief introduced him, and then asked everyone to tell him who he or she was. He gave JD a verbal build-up which was almost refulgently embarrassing, “one of the world's leading experts in this field, senior member of the management team of one of the largest companies in the UK, even Europe, working closely with the British Government” etc.. JD was going to give them all “a thorough briefing on one of the most fascinating and potentially dangerous situations that the Islamic world had posed to the Free World.” JD wondered whether he was using the terminology and rhetoric of the old “Cold War” purposely, and concluded he was. Probably apposite.

The introductions were made. Charles P. Fortas, Director of the FBI; Peter Kostesky, his deputy; Fred

Greenbaum, Deputy Director of the CIA (the one the Chief knows well, thought JD); Deputy Director, Operations, CIA, Sol Juanito; Deputy Director, Intelligence, CIA, Gad Isaacs, then a face he knew well, Theodore DeCicco, Director of the Bureau of Engraving and Printing. They grinned at each other.

"Please, Mr. Dilworth, tell the meeting, just as you told us in London (JD smiled to himself. Anything south of Birmingham was London to most Americans) exactly what has happened, what's been done by Daltons, quite legitimately I hasten to add - and what your thoughts are as to what is being done now, even as we speak. Please, fire away. "

JD did just that. He was word-perfect. He spoke without referring to any notes and he remained seated. By 8.30 am. he'd finished. He'd even swamped them with all his statistics and worried them with all his suspicions. No one interrupted. Everyone made notes.

As soon as he'd finished Wendell Grey spoke again, "You guys know why this meeting was convened in the first place. Listen to something else from our friends across the pond before we continue. Sir Richard, or Sir Norman, will you brief us as you did on Saturday."

It was Sir Norman who spoke. They obviously knew what his role was, and why he was doing the talking. He told them of the reports emanating from Africa. Sol Juanito, in charge of CIA overseas operations, asked him a few questions. Sir Norman and Sir Richard responded at length.

The CIA Director then asked the FBI chief to "throw his hat into the ring". He responded by giving his deputy, Peter Kostesky, the floor. He started talking about organised crime. The CIA and State Department chiefs joined in what had now developed into a discussion. To JD, as an outsider, there seemed to be definite leanings towards two preconceived ideas. The FBI thought the monies swilling into the system were probably organised crime funds, and the CIA favoured the idea that they were Russian "mafia" funds. JD was feeling frustrated. None of this seemed to be taking into account what he knew was happening, and what he thought he was here to explain to them. It was left to Sir Richard to re-focus the discussion on what JD believed was the crucial, central, pivotal fact.

"May I say, gentlemen, that the broad options you are discussing don't seem to be addressing the two most important points, as far as I can see it. First, there is a plant, in a secret base in Libya, which is doing something." He stressed the last word. "And, why would the criminals, or the Russian mafia, pour money into financing tens of thousands of pilgrimages, or long-term high-risk investments? It doesn't seem to make sense, does it?"

There was a pause, and then Sir Richard went on.

"What does make some sense, and I hate to be the one to bring this up but, as you said last week Director, this could be a deliberate attempt to destabilise the dollar, or at least an exploitation of the dollar's role as the one international universally acceptable currency. The U.S. accounts for only 27% of global production and 18% of world trade, but the dollar represents nearly 60% of world finance and this is being perpetrated we suspect, God help us, by a sovereign state. An Islamic state at that!"

The words stilled the discussion. It was a little while before Wendell Grey spoke again.

"You are adamant, are you not, Mr. Dilworth, that such a plant as you have built could produce any currency in the world? I don't think you'll think me sceptical if I ask our own expert, Mr. DeCicco, what he thinks of this scenario."

Theodore DeCicco, a large, powerfully-built African-American, who'd entertained JD a number of times in Washington in the past, and shared JD's taste for blues and jazz in the happy steamy summer atmosphere of Georgetown, who JD and Ness had welcomed into their home when he'd been across in Europe for various reasons, almost echoed JD's own words on the subject.

"Mr. Director, a plant like that, built and equipped by Daltons, who're one of the world's leading experts in the field, could print anything for anyone. If the raw materials spec was right, no country would be able to tell, without weeks, perhaps months, of investigation, whether the product was genuine or not. Any kind of investigation would have to go back to determining where the cotton was grown from which the paper was made, details such as that. It would take months, as I've said - and that's assuming you could get hold of notes you knew definitely were printed at the Libyan plant. How you do that I don't know. It seems to me, we have a problem." For such a big man, his soft Louisville accent added, if anything, more emphasis to his words.

A lively general discussion broke out. JD was beginning to feel decidedly uncomfortable. This was U.S. national security policy stuff. In reply to Graham MacParland, Director of State Department Intelligence, he could only reply honestly. In his opinion he thought the plant was being used to print "legal currency", probably U.S. dollars.

The ensuing outburst of discussion was only quieted when a tall young man came into the room and addressed Graham MacParland.

"Director, The Secretary of State is on the line. He's with the President."

A hush fell over the meeting as MacParland got up and went to take the call. The Director of the CIA broke the silence quickly.

"Mr. Dilworth. Your presence has been of the greatest help to us. You'll realise that we have one hell of a lot to discuss. I would be most grateful if Sir Richard and Sir Norman would give us some more of their valuable time, but I don't think we should keep you any longer. I know Director MacParland will feel the same. We sure are grateful to you for coming all the way across here at such short notice, and for being so expert in your exposition. It would be wasting your time to ask you to give any more of your time. I'm sure you have a heavy workload back home."

It was all JD needed. If he got away now, 9.30 am., he could catch a plane by noon and be home by not far past midnight U.K. time.

"Director, my time is yours. But if you feel I've told you all I can, I'd be delighted to get away and get home. As you say, I've certainly got a lot I can be doing back in the U.K.!"

Before he left the room everyone shook him by the hand and wished him a safe journey home. They all thanked him. The CIA Director and Sir Richard both wished him well "for Thursday". He caught a few curious looks, and then he was out of it. One phone call to BA and he was on the noonday flight. It would be one of the last ones to land at Heathrow that day, before the airport closed.

He'd already left the room when Graham MacParland returned, looking serious. What the Director of State Intelligence had to say made everyone look serious.

"The President has called us to a meeting in the Oval Office at I pm." He was addressing Wendell Grey and Charles Fortas. "He wants us, CIA, FBI, the Chairman of the NSC, the Head of the Federal Reserve, the Secretary of the Treasury and the Chairman of the Joint Chiefs of Staff. He also wants, before the meeting, a single-page brief detailing what we believe is possibly happening and options for action. We can do that here. Virginia," he indicated the young woman at the door, "has her lap-top and printer. She'll act as secretary."

There was no discussion. The CIA Director simply turned to the two Britons and said, "Will you help us in the preparatory stage, Sir Richard? Then, if you don't mind, you can leave it to us to write the brief and if you'd retire to the Embassy we can have immediate secure communication with you from the White House this afternoon."

The British Intelligence men understood the score and readily concurred. Sir Norman suggested he contact his deputy David Crichton to get the very latest up-date on the "Pilgrim position". The Americans agreed and asked the CIA and FBI Deputies to do the same with their people. The three men rose and went to the end of the suite where half a dozen phones were scattered on a single large table. It was 5 am. in the U.K. so Sir Norman went through GCHQ in Cheltenham. There was urgency now about everything each man in the room was doing.

£$£

Chapter Thirty-Eight

Jim Sunderland sat in the small office with his jacket off. He liked to work in here. When he went through that door he became President, the most powerful man in the world, or so everyone told him. That's what he constantly read. Laughable really. It was only when a man became President that he fully realised that the President was only a man. In the little office he felt more like the man he knew he was. Even the Secret Service had to leave him alone. There wasn't enough room to stick to him like a shadow. His man had to wait outside and let people in. Poor bastard! Whoever was on duty could stand there all day, with his only bit of excitement being to press the under-carpet button to unlock the door. When he walked through that door into the Oval Office he felt, without fail, like a Sixteenth-century Monarch ascending the Throne of State to utter some pronouncement, or maybe the Pope occupying the Throne of St Peter. He wondered if the Pope ever doubted, even sitting there, that he was more than just a man.

The President heard the faint warning buzz signalling that the door was being opened and the Secretary of State came in. He spoke immediately but quietly. The White House Chief of Staff, Ray Lanfemann, was standing almost beside the President, speaking, or rather, waiting on the green phone.

"They'll be here at 1 pm. Mr. President, brief by 12 noon."

"Thanks Bruce. Let's wait for Ray. He's still trying to get Howard." Teitelberg knew he was referring to the Head of the Federal Reserve, Howard Cunningham. "He's in Philadelphia. We'll send a 'copter. He finishes his speech just before 12."

He'd hardly finished speaking when Lanfemann uttered a couple of words of obvious confirmation and put the phone down without any of the normal conversation-terminating pleasantries. The Chief of Staff didn't waste time on such things. No one liked him much, but everybody agreed he was extremely efficient.

"Confirmed. 1 pm. He needs the copter. I'll organise that."

Lanfemann never wasted words or effort. The President always thought he spoke like a high-speed computer printout. Staccato sentences. No emotion. If there were sexual relations at the Lanfemann household Jim Sunderland was certain they'd be time-tabled three months in advance. He'd selected him as his Chief of Staff because he was extremely efficient but he didn't like him much.

The President smiled to himself picturing tall, lean, ascetic, independent Howard Cunningham interrupting his programme. He'd only do it for the President of the United States. He took his position as Chairman of the Board of the Federal Reserve very seriously and why not. He could be credited as the main architect of the unparalleled success story of the economy, and therefore, probably, of the unprecedented approval ratings the President enjoyed even a year into his second term. Jim Sunderland counted him as an equal, and everybody listened when Howard Cunningham spoke. Providentially, he was meaner with words than Ray Lanfemann.

"Sit down, please." The President motioned towards the only two chairs in the small office. "Take your jackets off if you feel like it."

Neither Teitelberg nor Lanfemann did so, but they sat on the two straight-backed chairs.

"You know," the President went on, "I've been thinking about this since you called me Sunday from Syria, Bruce. It seems to me that the most obvious thing I could do would be to call the "Leader", or whatever he's calling himself these days, and ask him directly what the hell is going on. I'd get some sort of response, at least, rather than us just thrashing about in the dark as we are. Opinions?" he was leaning back and looking at them questioningly.

"Not possible, Mr. President. We have no direct line, nor even a secure line."

As usual, Lanfemann's response was purely practical, pragmatic and direct.

The Secretary of State replied more diplomatically.

"Mr. President, that's probably not a wise move just yet. We haven't consulted any of our allies, except the British. They're involved in any case, of course, and this will almost inevitably have to come out at some stage in the near future. When it does, we want to be in a whiter-than-white situation, with no-one being in a position to accuse us of any clandestine negotiations or contacts, especially our Arab allies and the Israeli's."

The look on Lanfemann's face spelled, "disdain, slight," in physiognomic semaphore. All he said was, "It could be a normal praxis on our part."

"Not when we've been using the Swiss for so long for all communications. As you say, Ray, we have no means of direct communication." The Secretary of State was conscious that his reply perhaps sounded a little too "diplomatic" for the President so he expanded on it a little. "We could talk to the South Africans about acting for us. They're far less neutral than the Swiss, and Mandela when he was President established excellent relations with the Libyans starting with that visit in 1997, when he argued their case for the removal of all international sanctions and for the beginning of a real dialogue. They've had "favoured nation" status with the Libyans since then, but they're also desperate for our help with their economy now they're in such bad shape."

"Can contact be made before our one-o-clock meeting? I like the idea of the South Africans, by the way, Bruce." The President addressed the first sentence to Lanfemann, and his second to Teitelberg, but it was the latter who replied.

"I can get that moving immediately. But what exactly is the question or questions you want posing?" Teitelberg was conscious that only the President could determine such a matter. He certainly wasn't going to formulate the question.

"Quite simple, Bruce. We just say we've got strong evidence to suggest that they've set up a major security printing plant at Sirte and that it's turning out hundreds of millions of notes per day and we're concerned about the effect of such printings on Money Supply in the whole Mid-East region. We can't mention printing anybody else's money, of course. But just saying that should elicit a response, even if it's to go boil our heads!"

"Leave that to me Mr. President. Will you excuse me while I start that ball rolling?" The Secretary was keen to get on with it, using his Department. The last thing he wanted was Lanfemann and his staff diving in like the diplomatic equivalent of Special Forces.

"Carry on, Bruce. Come back as soon as you can on it, will you." The President used the words as an instruction rather than a question. The Secretary said he would, and left the office.

"Ray, shall I ask the British to come to the meeting this afternoon. After all, they did instigate this. If that company, Daltons isn't it, hadn't gone to the Foreign Office it might have been weeks before we started piecing this together, and I'm not criticising any department when I say that. We wouldn't have picked up so quickly on the pilgrims. It's not really our territory. My God, Ray, think of it. Weeks more at - what did they say? $588 million per day, if they're not producing $1000 bills! My God! We've got to do something fast, Ray."

"I agree Mr. President. But we can't ask the Brits to attend. State and the CIA would scream, and the NSC wouldn't be too happy. It would look a little too much like they were involved in U.S. policy-making."

"No, you're right, Ray. They're at the Embassy, anyway. We can be in direct contact at any time."

"What I think we should do now, Mr. President, is think about your diary plans for today and tomorrow."

"Yes, yes, of course. I was supposed to be going to Camp David today, wasn't I?"

"So was the NSC, Mr. President, meeting you tomorrow? The Russians arrive the next day, late Thursday afternoon. We meet formally on Friday morning, but you have invited them to an informal evening on Thursday. Tomorrow was supposed to be our briefing and planning meeting, with the NSC and the back-up teams. You can still do that if you set off tomorrow morning. That will give you time this afternoon and tonight for whatever comes out of the one-o-clock meeting."

Lanfemann was a gem, thought the President. He just wished he'd smile sometimes.

"OK Ray. We'll definitely not go up this afternoon, and we'll wait 'til after the meeting to finalise tomorrow's arrangements. Will you see to that?"

"If I may use your phone, I'll do it immediately." The President waved his agreement.

For the next hour the President and the Chief of Staff used the time to deal with more routine matters, Lanfemann never allowed a minute to pass its use-by date. But Jim Sunderland was finding it difficult to concentrate. He kept imagining billions of dollars gushing out of the desert like oil after a strike. More sombrely, he kept thinking that this may be the situation where he may have to consider something that he was proud to have avoided so far in his Presidency - the use of force. He hated the thought. He was the first President who'd fought in a war since George Bush and he hadn't been on the winning side in his war. From the poverty and backwardness he'd seen when he went back to Vietnam on his South East Asian tour he didn't think anybody was on the winning side. He never wanted to see a handful of nametags without owners, or a line of body bags with owners, ever again.

His door was buzzing again. The Secretary of State came in. He didn't look as if he felt he'd secured his place in American history just yet. He spoke without sitting down.

"Mr. President, the South Africans did a great job for us. They got right on the case. But the outcome is more or less what you predicted. We should at this moment be boiling our heads…! Let me cut a long story short. There is no such base, only a Libyan Air force re-fuelling and emergency landing strip at Sirte, they are outraged, this is a feeble attempt to discredit them yet again internationally, no such plant exists, it is not possible for it to do so, they. . . ”

“OK, OK Bruce. Even I get the picture. Goddamn! It's what I expected, but it's not what I wanted to hear. But thanks for getting it done so quickly. It was necessary, even though it gives them forewarning that we know something's going on.”

There was a pause, and then the President went on.

“Look, it's 12.25, the guys will be here in half an hour. You may as well join me for lunch, I'll treat you to a sandwich from the White House Mess! It'll be a first for you, Bruce!”

There was almost a smile on Lanfemann's face. The Secretary of State was legendary for his love of haute cuisine, and his careful arrangements to ensure he constantly enjoyed it. He'd never let accepting high office interfere with the style to which he'd become accustomed. But his equally legendary diplomacy was up to the challenge.

“That will be a treat, Mr. President. I pass the Mess every time I go to the Situations Room and it always smells so delicious.”

They ate a light lunch in the Oval Office, where the heavy glass green bulletproof windows cast a slightly unnatural light. The doors onto the Rose Garden terrace were firmly shut. Washington in winter was a city paying homage to central heating. They received the briefing paper the President had asked for before they'd taken their first bite. Everyone else attending the meeting would receive it at the same time, except the Head of the Federal Reserve. He would have to read it when he arrived from Philadelphia.

Howard Cunningham was landing on the heli-pad on the lawn next to Interstate 395 when the President put his jacket on and said he thought they'd be better in the Large

Conference Room a few steps away from the Oval Office. They concurred, and stepped out into the small Reception Room with its wall of French windows overlooking the Rose Garden, to find the Chairman of the Joint Chiefs of Staff Clayton H. Holyoake and Chairman of the National Security Council Arthur Littlejohn already in there. They were just greeting them when the CIA and State Intelligence chiefs walked in.

"Let's go into the Conference Room, gentlemen. My secretary will send Howard and Charles in." The President spoke as he walked out of the room.

"The Secretary of the Treasury is joining us as well, Mr. President."

"Yes, I know Ray. He'll find us."

In fact they walked into Gregory Krager on their way out and within seconds of entering the Conference Room, under the gaze of the large portraits of Franklin and Theodore Roosevelt, and FBI Director Charles Fortas joined them.

"He's not late yet. He'll be jogging across the lawn just now." There was a ripple of laughter at the President's comment. Howard Cunningham jogged for no man, and there was a serious doubt that he'd have jogged for the Almighty unless the afore-mentioned could prove that the return was worthwhile.

The President was as precise as the Head of the Federal Reserve when it came to meetings, and he commenced at spot-on 1 pm., at exactly the moment Howard Cunningham entered the room. The President included his cordial greeting to him with his opening comments.

"Thanks, and welcome Howard, for coming gentlemen. You all know why we're here. I make no apologies for interrupting your schedules. Whatever you were previously doing I consider what we now have to consider being a higher priority. Bruce, you've been closest to this for longest, even though that's only four days now. Will you deal with the opening remarks please? One thing, before you do. Gentlemen, the taping system has been extended from the Oval Office to this room, so we need no secretary. We'll get it all transcribed later, copies for all. Bruce. Over to you."

The President slid Howard Cunningham's copy of the briefing paper along the table to him as Bruce Teitelberg started to speak.

The Secretary of State was a masterful speaker, and a master of summation. Within a few minutes he'd given the meeting a comprehensive run-down on his meeting in the beechwoods in Burnham and the fears of the British. He led the story adroitly to their own intelligence agencies and asked the FBI and CIA to brief the gathering. They did.

The FBI Director ended his comments by simply stating.

"The flow of investments continues. Reports are still flowing in. There is not enough organised crime money, held anywhere, to account for what seems to be going on."

Wendell Grey added to that.

"At the CIA we remained until almost this lunch-time convinced that Russian "mafia" money was involved. Almost all the $40 billion we've seen flow into Russia has come back out again, illegally of course, but it simply doesn't make sense. There is no earthly reason why these criminals should use this money for the uses we're seeing it used for. Especially the pilgrims. There is just no return. The British are right."

The President was watching the Chairman of the Federal Reserve. He'd finished reading the briefing paper for the third or fourth time. Maybe now he'd understand why he'd been summoned to a meeting of "politicos", almost unprecedented. Jim Sunderland knew that Howard Cunningham was not only the finest choice of mind to comment on the implications of what seemed to be going on. He was also the voice of expertise which everyone in that room would listen to. He treated him with respect, the rest of the Administration treated him with reverence. He switched the focus of attention to the Secretary of the Treasury.

"Gregory. Could this plant do what the British think it's doing? In the volumes cited?"

Gregory Krager was a political appointee. He'd only ever been to the Bureau of Engraving and Printing once, to open a new press hall at the old premises in Washington. He'd never visited the new plant at Fort Worth at all. But he had complete faith in Theo DeCicco and he'd just had half an hour on the phone with him, so he knew the score and he had to tell the truth. This was too serious to obfuscate.

"Undoubtedly. The volumes are practicable, the value depends only on what denominations they're printing. I have to tell you, Mr.President, that it's made all the easier because our currency remains one of the easiest in the world to produce."

He wasn't belittling his department, and he wasn't scoring political points. They had discussed on two occasions, in cabinet, the "physical" vulnerability of the dollar. They'd reluctantly come to the conclusion that other administrations before them had reached. It was virtually impossible to dramatically up-grade the notes, without a massive domestic backlash, and, just as importantly, without having to face the immense problem of counterfeit notes in circulation throughout the world. To tackle the latter would run the grave risk of undermining public confidence at home and abroad in the currency, not to mention outraged reaction in many parts of the world where they knew the counterfeits were being held by legitimate businesses and individuals. It would be a nightmare politically and fiscally. The Treasury couldn't stand the strain of exchanging such notes without risking the inflationary dangers of simply "printing money", in the Weimar Republic sense of that description. So he knew he was speaking to the initiated.

The President nodded grimly. He spoke, almost to himself.

"Jee-sus, the most technologically advanced nation on earth, with one of the easiest currencies to copy. Would you believe it? But... I thought there were machines, you know, in banks and the like, which could verify whether a note was genuine?" He spoke the last words almost plaintively, as if wanting someone to give him some hope. Gregory Krager knew he couldn't. He replied.

"There are, Mr. President. But think about it. They're in use in major banks in the U.S., and the advanced countries, but even here every note is not read through them. It couldn't be. It would be a massive, an impossible, task. And there are more banks etc. without such machines in the world than there are those with them. More importantly, if we tried to insist that all our notes were read in such a way we'd immediately create a huge wave of doubt and mistrust in any of our currency. Anyway, it is seriously not possible to do it. In the present circumstances, to address the problem we are here to discuss, it isn't even a runner. There is too little time for it."

He could almost feel the President's disappointment. The President spoke again.

"Howard, I'll come to you in a minute." He'd watched the Federal Reserve chief grow as close to agitated as he'd ever seen him. "First, Wendell, what the hell are these Hanifs, or whatever you call them?"

It was the question the Director of the CIA had been expecting. Since that meeting at Dorneywood on Saturday, only four days ago! It seemed like weeks. He'd instigated an intense programme of research on that very subject. The British had been helpful. He studied the meeting, took a deep breath, then started, slowly articulating every word.

"I'm afraid, Mr. President, that I will have to bore you with a little history. I promise I'll keep it brief."

Almost everyone smiled, including the President. Jim Sunderland was haunted by, and constantly reminded of, a remark he'd blurted out in exasperation at a Presidential news conference early in his first term, irritated by persistent questioners comparing his Administration with previous ones, he'd said: "If we were dictated to by history we'd still be fighting on the 38th Parallel, de-foliating trees in Cambodia and singing Heartbreak Hotel." He'd had to put up with being tagged as, "The Man Without a Past," since then. He accepted it ruefully, with good humour. His team often referred to it to lighten the mood when things got heavy. He liked that.

"Carry on, Wendell."

"It is, of course, an Islamic movement. Its history is shrouded in secrecy, but it's a venerable history. The founder of Islam, Mohammed, was a remarkable man. He was born 570 A.D. as a member of the Quaraish tribe, which was entrusted with guardianship of the National Sanctuary at Mecca. He was brought up by his Uncle, Abu Talib, and lived a perfectly normal life at Mecca till he was 40. He married a widow, Khadija, and had six children. Tragically, two of them died very young, and the effect of this on him was profound. He became, and this is the first time the name assumes any significance in this story, a 'Hanif'. He stopped eating, his clothes became ragged, and he wandered alone a lot, seeking after some truth or other. Such people weren't so unusual in that region at that time, or indeed before it. The nearest Judeo/Christian parallel is probably Ezekiel, who did more or less the same thing. During these wanderings, on the night now known as "El Qadr" he had a vision in a cave during what we would probably call a "seizure" brought on by religious hysteria of some kind. He heard a voice calling "lqra", recite. Like the verse in the Bible, Isaiah xl.6, "cry". In fact, the same verb is used. Then came the vision of Sura 1, written in fiery letters on a cloth. As well as the voice and the vision Mohammed believed he saw the two great eyes of the Archangel Gabriel. He fled in terror back to Khadija and she calmed him, within her embrace. It is from that moment that his teachings began in earnest, and his attacks upon the cults of Mecca and it's Megalithic idols. He began to draw converts, friends and relations at first, but his word was spreading. I won't go into more details of his exile with his closest followers, the "Muhajirun", or the new young converts he attracted called the "Ansars", nor into the problems he had with what he called the "Munafiqun", who he considered to be those who only paid lip-service to Islam, hypocrites without real conviction. But there is one name I will specifically mention. It is that of Warqa. He was renowned as a 'Hanif', he was blind, he was respected as a holy man, and he was the first such to believe in the veridical character of Mohammed's experience. He. . ."

"Sorry, Wendell, I have to interrupt you." The President felt he probably spoke for all, but they wouldn't say anything. "Can you tell me what veridical means, please? Forgive my ignorance."

"No, sorry, Mr. President. I've only been familiar with it since I read my briefing papers. It's a well-used word in theological studies, it means truthful spiritual vision. To continue: This crucial endorsement, for want of a better word, seems to have had profound consequences. There commenced, almost from the very beginnings of Islam, an organisation of, well, devout and devoted mystics who from that day have kept alight the flame of purity of Mohammed's original message. We, in the non-Islamic world, through the prejudice and ignorance of anti-Islamic bigotry over the centuries, have had next to no knowledge of this movement. We seem to have picked up Sufism, another mystical movement that developed about a hundred years after the Prophet's death. Sufis are people who believe that a kind of deep initiation is the only real guide to knowledge. They're contemptuous of material things, extremely ascetic. Their name, for instance, derives from 'suf', a rough woollen robe worn to display such a disregard for temporal wealth. There are a number of brotherhoods of Sufis, each with their own particular methods of seeking truth etc. We know quite a bit about these, for instance, the Dervishes, of the "Whirling" kind, who the British fought in the Sudan in the 19th century, but what we don't seem to know is that the Hanifs preceded the Sufis by nearly a hundred years, and that they have coexisted for the whole 1,400 years of Islam. More important, in the context of our current deliberations is this. The Sufis have always remained a mystical religious sect, seeking religious truth, knowledge and purity. The Hanifs have done the same, but they have, for centuries, also donned the true mantle of militancy worn by Mohammed. You don't need me to tell you that he preached the religious concept of "Jihad" when it came to spreading and defending the faith. The Hanifs have adhered rigidly to those teachings for centuries. They have mixed mysticism and devotion with political and military reality. There hasn't been a major political or military event in Islamic history that hasn't been influenced, touched, to a greater or lesser degree, by them. None."

The CIA Director let the words sink in, watching the fixed stares of the most powerful men in what could be called the Christian world struggle with registering his message.

"The trouble is, we didn't realise any of this. We are literally only now, because of this crisis, beginning to piece together wildly disparate pieces of information from all over the world, from across the centuries. It's only in this age of computers and the educational Internet that we have the capabilities to do so. It must be one of the greatest oversights of history."

The President spoke first.

"What about the British? They're usually on the ball about these kinds of things."

"No joy. They are in exactly the same position and, anticipating your next question if I may, so are the Israelis. As far as we can tell, so is the whole Arab academic world. They have references and records that indicate to them that the movement is just a sort of Sufism, a "background noise" in Islam. There is only one Islamic academic establishment which doesn't treat the matter as such, and they are our main source of information and insight at the moment." He paused.

"Wendell, stop being mysterious. Who the hell is that?"

"I'm not being mysterious, Mr. President, I was just taking a breath!"

"OK. Sorry, Wendell. Carry on, please. Intrigue us or worry us more."

"The Turks, Mr. President. There appear to be two main reasons why the Turks have gleaned so much information on the Hanifs, and why they've been so concerned about them. The first is that the Hanifs have always displayed, it seems, a strong and enduring rejection, on religious grounds, to Turkish domination, especially of Arab countries or, should I say, populations. The Seljuks, and then the Ottomans, had reason to fear them. That's centuries of clandestine opposition. And the second is that Turkey, under Mustapha Kemal Attaturk, was for a lengthy period in the first half of the Twentieth Century, quite virulently anti-Islamic, no, that's not the right description, it was anti-clerical, like the French Republic after the Revolution. Attaturk was fiercely opposed to religious interference in Government, he believed Islam retarded the growth of the modem secular state he wanted to create. He wanted Turkey to belong, wholeheartedly, to Europe. Sadly, we know that hasn't happened yet, the Europeans aren't at all sure they want the Turks, and Islam gaining ground in that country all the time. Attaturk, then, had good reason to keep a close eye on the Hanifs. Well, as close an eye as anyone can on so secret an organisation. How can any Government dictate how men secretly think? We all know an idea is more powerful than any bomb." Wendell Grey paused again, then he said quietly.

"After all that, Mr. President, I have to report that, whilst we're now sure they exist, we haven't got a clue as to who they are or what they're doing, if anything, or how to contact them, or even whether they have any kind of central organisation. There is just one possible link with the situation we are faced with now. The Turks point out that there was a revival of fundamentalist Islam in the early part of the last century. It was centred in North Africa. The Senussi movement. Two of its main centres were in Libya, around the Gulf of Sirte and Benghazi, and in Sudan, around Khartoum/Omdurman. They are sure it was a Hanif-inspired movement. Our British friends tell us that the two main protagonists the company, Daltons, dealt with are a

Libyan General and a Sudanese General. We know these men. Their ranks mask their true importance. They are both amongst the three most influential men in their respective countries. Neither of them has a reputation which would win them a Nobel Prize, unless it was for extirpating opposition."

The meeting was quiet for a few seconds, Bruce Teitelberg just beating Howard Cunningham so speak.

"So, if I understand you correctly Director, and this is not a criticism I assure you - we all appreciate how much you've been able to do in such a short time - we are still not sure, in the sense that we have any concrete proof, that this organisation even exists?"

Before the CIA man could respond the President cut in. He spoke sharply, but not with annoyance, just the tone of a man in a hurry.

"We don't have any proof, gentlemen, in a concrete sense, that black holes exist in the universe, but everyone believes they do. We should think of this organisation like a black hole. We can be sure it's there because of what happens to everything around it."

When it was required Jim Sunderland had the ability to cut to the heart of any matter more surely even than any of his team, and they were all good. It was at times like this that they realised how good he was. He went on.

"So, let me get this straight. You now suspect, and the British suspect, that this strange secret organisation might be behind what's going on? It can't be Libya acting alone, or with Sudan? Or the Arab League or the Islamic Conference?"

Wendell Grey realised that the CIA, as things stood, was the only source of information for the assembled meeting, but he was acutely aware of how little they really knew. He wished he could ask for more time for reports and analyses, but he knew time was a luxury they didn't have. All eyes focused on him.

"Mr. President, the Arab League ceased to be very relevant in the 1980s. It was spawned by Arab nationalism in 1945 in a very different world, in the aftermath of the Second World War, when Arabs felt they'd been trampled on by everyone - because they had, of course. The Organisation of the Islamic Conference made some sense when it was formed in 1971, but it now has 55 members and their internecine arguments, differences and divisions are greater than any they have with non-Islamic countries! We consider it wildly improbable that they would have the cohesion to mount some sort of attack upon the U.S. currency, or Western currencies in general. In any case, many of the members of the Conference are not only close allies of ours, they depend on us to maintain the status quo and in some cases to shore up their regimes, which I don't need to remind anyone here are often anachronistic and undemocratic. Not to mention the little point that most of their money is invested in the West! As for Libya and/or Sudan going-it-alone, highly unlikely. How would they organise the widespread distribution of monies that we're apparently seeing? And why would they take the risk of acting alone? This is almost certainly a Pan-Islamic phenomenon. It's touching countries as widely disparate as the Central Asian republics and sub-Saharan Third World states. We can only postulate that a Pan-Islamic movement is involved. The only one which seems to fit the bill is, unfortunately, one we know precious little about, The Hanifs. We could be dealing with something very deep here, very profound. A concerted Islamic-world effort to change the world-order, the balance of influence. There would be no better way to do that than to cause chaos, or collapse, in the economies of the Western world, especially America. In the eves of a fundamentalist Islamic movement such levelling-down would be of no consequence. The vast majority of Moslems live in Third World countries at more or less subsistence levels. Collapse of Western affluence would only mean to them less money to spend on armaments to keep them in check, as they see it. It could also help them to spread the faith. People have been known to turn to God and religion when things aren't going well. If all this is the case, they have hit upon a method of distributing, of laundering the monies, which is brilliant in it's simplicity, impossible to track. We can do the latter with the organised crime outlets, terrorism and political organisations and investments, we can do precious little to stop the funding of tens of millions of pilgrims all over the world, through their own religious organisations. It would be the greatest distribution network in human history. Worse, imagine the outcry in the Islamic world if we even tried to stop it. I've mentioned the Crusades, they'd treat it as another one of those!"

It was obvious to the President that everyone at the meeting wanted to say something, but he decided the time had come to break out of the geo-political-historical loop. There was no better man to do that than Howard Cunningham. Anyway, the President wanted to ensure the Chairman of the Federal Reserve didn't suffer a cardiac arrest. He looked as if he was on the brink.

"Howard. You've sat quietly through this so far. I know it's highly unusual to ask you to come in to something like this, but I think you'll understand why I did so from what you've heard. Any comments?"

Cunningham took off his steel-rimmed reading glasses and leaned forward. When he spoke it was in the modulated tones of East-coast Establishment America, old power, old money. As usual, he chose each word like a sniper choosing a target.

"Thank you, Mr. President. Implicit in my words is an acceptance that U.S. dollars are being produced. The President has used an astronomical analogy. I will use another. Einstein's General Theory of Relativity was proved by his prediction for the orbit of the planet Mercury, Newton's Theory of Gravity was disproved as a result. The exception proved the rule. You have, I contend, identified enough "exceptions" to prove the rule. Dollars are being manufactured."

As usual, Howard Cunningham's tone was unemotional, precisely matter-of-fact.

"I speak as a trained economist and banker, the nation's banker. After reading the briefing paper, and for the first hour as I listened to your concise and erudite comments, I was focusing on the obvious economic fall-out from a flood of new money manifesting itself in the world economy, on the effect of illegal, worthless, (in the true sense) money buying goods and services on a huge scale. Such monies might initially increase the volume of output, lead to fuller employment, then inevitably lead to rising prices and inflation and thus falling output and ultimately unemployment. I know it is unnecessary for me to give you a lecture on classic Kenyesian economics. But then, as you continued to speak, and as I had more time to reflect, the real, the awful, full implications of what is presumably happening thrust itself into even my dull mind. What is happening frightens me more than nuclear proliferation, more than illicit stockpiles of germ or chemical weapons. If it is happening it could very rapidly lead to economic chaos and collapse which would make the effects of the irresponsible use of such weapons seem a paltry problem. Unless this is tackled and stopped, immediately, this could lead to the collapse of confidence world wide in paper money and paper money, gentlemen, is what makes the world turn. If nobody believes in it any more, political chaos, hunger, famine, disease, a total breakdown in communications, a disintegration of society as we know it, will follow as surely as the next eclipse of the sun."

His voice did not alter, which somehow lent even more gravity to his words. "Because, gentlemen, to almost quote from one of the standard economic textbooks which I'm sure almost all of you have studied, paper money is a gigantic confidence trick. It can be defined accurately only as "a generally acceptable means of Payment for goods and services". There isn't enough bullion in the world to honour the commitments of just the Bundesbank, or the Bank of England, never mind the dollar. Twelve hundred Frenchmen trying to invade England in 1797 caused the near bankruptcy of the Bank of England! We've seen similar panics in the last century many times. But we have never seen the results of a loss of confidence in the U.S. dollar, which accounts for 60% of world finance. If the dollar fails, all Paper currency fails. I've already briefly alluded to the consequences. I will not repeat myself. This must be stopped."

Jim Sunderland had been deeply worried before the meeting had started. What the Chairman of the Federal Reserve said simply reinforced his feelings. This was a crisis.

"Gentlemen. What I haven't had time to tell you yet is that I have been in touch with the Libyan Government through the good offices of the South Africans, who are close to them. I did it before this meeting. They deny everything. Totally."

No one spoke. The President didn't really expect them to. By a subtle change of tone he transformed the meeting from information analysis and consultation mode to a Presidential briefing.

"Gentlemen, I want us to meet again tomorrow morning at 10 am. That is the maximum time I can give you, Clayton, as Chairman of the Joint Chiefs of Staff, to formulate a plan to deal with this base, Sirte, and close it down. Ray, I want you to rearrange the Camp David meetings to tomorrow night. I need tomorrow morning and as much of the afternoon as possible to deal with this. Bruce, I want you to stay with me now. We are going to talk to the British, at both the Embassy and in London. I'll speak directly to the Prime Minister. Wendell, Charles, and Graham, I want the very latest CIA, FBI and State Intelligence up-dates for the 10 am. meeting. Everyone clear?"

There was murmured assent.

"Right, gentleman, this meeting is terminated. Thank you. I'll see you all tomorrow."

He looked directly at the Chairman of the Federal Reserve.

"Not you, of course, Howard. There is no necessity to

occupy any more of your time. I will call you personally with an up-date before I leave for Camp David. OK?"

"Of course, Mr. President. I'd appreciate that."

"It's the least I can do, Howard, now you've put the fear of God up us!"

Jim Sunderland was an expert at leavening even the most sombre occasion with a little humour. At this crucial moment he wanted everyone leaving the meeting with the warm glow of belonging to his team. He knew he might need every single one of them before the sun had set a couple more times.

£$£

Chapter Thirty-Nine

There was nothing particularly different about 9 pm. G.M.T. that Tuesday, but for everybody who knew about the hole in the ground in the desert in Tripolitania it seemed in retrospect like a pivotal moment.

Twenty-four thousand feet above the North Atlantic JD changed his Heuer watch from 4 pm. Eastern Seaboard Time to 9 pm. U.K. time. He was a bit bored now sitting in First Class on the B.A. 747. He'd read the Financial Times for that very morning, watched the ITN news, eaten an excellent three-course lunch, enjoyed aperitifs, wine with the meal, Heine XO Cognac after it, and was on his second whisky and soda. He knew he didn't have to drive at the end of the flight, and that he was in for a tough day on Wednesday so he was relaxing and treating himself. That's what he told himself anyway. He was also remembering, forgetting, fretting and steeling himself all at the same time. He'd asked for an old film from the video stock, "A Touch of Class", with Segal and Jackson, something he'd enjoyed so many times before. But he'd switched it off. It was too close to home. He'd had tears in his eyes as he watched the love story unfold, involving a happily married man and a woman he'd "inadvertently" fallen in love with on a skiing holiday and the way their romance had affected both their lives. Fluffy nonsense really, but not to him. He kept viciously reminding himself that it was only alcohol that was making him so pathetically maudlin, but the sober side of his mind also kept reminding him that he was living in exactly the same scenario and it wasn't a movie. He was stimulated by the sexual passion of Monday, exhilarated by the ego-trip, but it was all negated by the counter-balancing guilt, and the sobering fact that he was being picked up by Vanessa, anxious about his well-being, concerned about the stress he was under, glad to have him back in the country and in their home. Worrying, probably, about the fact that he was flying away again on Thursday, without a proper rest, without re-charging his batteries. Friend and partner, mother of his children. Jesus! He was getting bloody maudlin about that now. He must be pissed. There wasn't much of a sober side left now. But, seriously, how could he face her? Lie, like you usually do, the tiny smug voice sneered in his mind. And tell her how vital all this is to the world. Through the window he could see they were flying from daylight into darkness. It was dramatic. Was it symbolic? If he'd not had quite so much to drink he could have thought of something really cleverly symbolic, apposite, to say or write about it. In his diary, yeah, in his diary. He signalled to Andrew, not a Steward, but Cabin Director. He'd like another drink. He'd phone Fit tomorrow, see how he was. Maybe he'd like to come along on Thursday for the ride? The Chief wouldn't mind. In fact, the Chief would probably not even go along. What he'd better do is have a sleep before he got off the plane and met her. Sleep some of it off. Yes. Would he be able to act completely normally? How would he explain the extra shirt? It was time for another drink. Oh, he'd ordered one.

The President took the Secretary of State by the arm as they crossed the corridor.

"Bruce, come into the office. It's four-o-clock. Sir Richard said they were catching the night flight, so we'll talk to them at the Embassy. They'll still be there."

They entered the Oval Office and the President headed straight for his desk. The Secretary of State sat down without being asked. He knew he'd be spending some considerable time with the President.

"Rose, get me Sir Richard Webster at the British Embassy please." He flicked the intercom switch down and settled back in his chair.

"I'll put it on squawk box Bruce, and we can talk to them together." He picked the briefing paper up and stared at it without reading. He voiced what was obviously uppermost in his mind. “Howard came on strong, didn't he?”

“I got the feeling, Mr. President, that he'd just witnessed his worst fears possibly coming true and if it is the case, I share them.”

“So do I Bruce, so do I. The real problem is, I think we can only act as if they are true! There's no easy way out, no middle course. If that's what's going on, and nobody will admit it and stop it, we have only one course of action. We stop it. If it's our currency, and we have to presume that it is, we stop it alone. The danger is to us. One of the biggest dangers, as Howard said, is that it gets out, becomes public knowledge! We can't allow that. I don't care what the “International Community” says. The only people who would help us anyway are the dear old Brits, God bless 'em. The other bastards won't, and they won't do anything whatever we do.”

The Secretary of State was glad the President sounded, and looked, resolute. He meant what he said. That was important. To his mind, history clearly demonstrated that belief in an action made it successful, even against the odds, a lack of belief, whatever the power wielded, always led to failure or fudge. Vietnam was the perfect proof of that. For an instant an image of when he first met the President flashed through his mind. Hue, during the Tet offensive. A young, fit man, a lieutenant, standing sweating, back pressed to a corner wall, waiting to fire back. What had impressed him was the young officer having the confidence and time to glance at him and explain why he was using an AK-47. “They're better. Their Goddamn guns are better!” Jim Sunderland just couldn't help communicating. In any situation, the Secretary said what he knew the President wanted to hear.

“I agree with you totally, Mr. President and I'm sure every single other person in that Conference Room would tell you exactly the same thing.”

Rose came through and told him the Embassy was on the line. He put the box on audio. After the minimum courtesies the President came straight to the point. He told

Sir Richard, who'd explained that the Ambassador and Sir Norman were with him, that the Pentagon would be contacting them again within the hour. Sir Norman said they'd be delighted to help further if they could but that they thought they'd passed every item of information on already that they could, but one. They had a lay-out of the Press Hall at the Sirte base, and the Managing Director of Daltons had done his best to draw a rough plan of the size and lay-out of the rest of the base as far as he knew it or could guess at it. He wasn't a military man but he was reasonably intelligent and he'd had a lot of building experience. They thought the lay out might be fairly accurate and they would fax it over to Chairman of the Joint Chiefs of Staff Holyoake (Jim Sunderland and Bruce Teitelberg smiled at each other at the Brit's careful use of proper titles whatever the circumstances). The President told them of his instructions to the Chairman of the JCS, and the 10 am. meeting. Glancing at the Secretary of State, but without hesitation, he also told them of his attempts to talk directly to the Libyans and the denials and 'brush-off'. He stated categorically that the U.S. was going to stop what was going on, whatever it was. His tone left no room for misunderstanding or demurence. There obviously was none from the other end. He asked the Ambassador to arrange a call with the PM to take place after the Wednesday morning meeting, probably around 12 noon Washington time. Could that be done? The Ambassador said he'd get right on to that through the Foreign Secretary and wherever the PM was in the UK at the time they'd ensure that call could take place. Wednesday at 3 pm. U.K. time was Prime Minister's Question Time in the House of Commons, it would obviously be better if the call could be taken at No. 10. Jim Sunderland laughed and said he was glad he didn't have to go and answer questions every Wednesday in Congress. Most of them didn't agree with a damned thing he was doing! Sir Richard came back on the line. There was just a hint of hesitancy in his usual precise tone.

"Mr. President. You know that Daltons are flying in on

Thursday morning to pick up two of their men who they believe may have been held at the base against their will. This is scheduled for noon Libyan time, 11 am. G.M.T., 6 am. your time. We are thinking of, we're planning, an operation to lift their families out at exactly the same time, as a precaution. We don't expect any trouble, but we want to make sure that these young people are simultaneously re-united. We, er, were going to do it clandestinely with a very small group of Special Forces, and we've been casting around for the fastest, surest way of getting this small unit in and out. Our people in Nato tell us that the aircraft carrier USS Columbia, with her task force, is in the Med. just outside the Gulf of Sirte, and we were contemplating approaching you to ask for your assistance in getting the team in and out by using the carrier. Two helicopters. Are you prepared to sanction such action?"

"Sir Richard, I'll give the PM my formal approval when I call him tomorrow, but consider it done. Go ahead with whatever arrangements you need to make. I'll give instructions when we've finished this call to give you every assistance."

"Thank you Mr. President. That is much appreciated. Can we take it that, whatever you decide to do, you will give us time to get these families out? If all goes well, the operation will be over with by 12.30 pm. Libyan time, at the very latest."

This time the President hesitated just for a moment, and then he said, "Sir Richard, of course. Whatever we plan to do will not take place until after 12.30."

Between the men gathered at each end of the telephone system there were many words unspoken. They were all experienced. They were reading between the words as well as the lines. No more was said.

At the British Embassy, the Ambassador looked at Sir Richard enquiringly.

"Two helicopters?"

"Ambassador, we're sending one to the base, too. Just in

case there is any slight problem for Daltons or the InTraCon plane. We consider it prudent. We could "lose" a few technicians in the desert without the story blowing up. We'd have a little more difficulty explaining the disappearance of the £30 million jet owned by one of the highest-profile company's in the world. One of Britain's biggest. Especially if Mr. Brandon Spencer is on board. Our American cousins might get quite cross."

"Quite ... Would either of you like a sherry before we phone the Foreign Secretary?"

Clayton Holyoake glanced at his watch as his driver, in a world of his own, nosed the Mercury onto the 14th Street Bridge, mind locked onto the target of the River Entrance to the Pentagon, (he was an Air Force man). It was just after 4 pm. He was damned glad that the Goldwater-Nichols Act of '86 gave him the authority to act alone, and get his 1600 staff to work directly for him. There'd be no time for consultations on this one. It was the toughest Jim Sunderland had ever given him, with the shortest time frame, since he became Chairman of the JCS and they'd just about started their jobs together. In fact, when the President went, so was he. He was retiring back to Seattle. He hoped it rained a lot. It helped the fishing, and that's what he was going to do for the rest of his life, make war on the fish. But this problem. What the hell was he going to recommend? The only real information they had was from a Goddam printer! Jesus!

"Sorry, Vanessa, I'll bet you're watching the Nine o'Clock News!"

"Fit. How lovely to hear from you! How are you? No, I was just clearing up, and then I was going to have a long, hot, luxurious shower and have a leisurely drive to the airport to meet JD."

"Oh Ness, sorry to bother you. It was JD I was going to talk to. He's obviously away then."

"Yes, he flew to Washington yesterday morning. On

that plant thing you were involved in too. He was working over the weekend too. All big-time stuff, Fit. He's been with the Chief and the Foreign Secretary and God knows whom else. I think he's feeling very important. He's certainly been quiet over the weekend, and you know that's not him! He hasn't even been for a run since last Thursday!"

"Ness, he'll be getting fat. Maybe then you'll see you'd be a lot better having an affair with me! Ronni would bless it!"

"Ronni will haunt you, you wicked man!"

She was so glad to hear him back to something like normal, though she knew instinctively that it must be an effort for him to sound like that.

"Look Ness. I won't take up any more of your time. You go and have your shower. I wish I could join you! I'll give him a ring tomorrow at the office, or you could ask him to call me."

"Of course, Fit. I don't think he's going into the office tomorrow. I think he plans to work from home again. He's flying out with the Chief on Thursday early, back to Libya."

"That's what I want to talk to him about, Ness. I've been involved in that as you know since the beginning and, to tell you the truth, I don't want to sit in here any more. I'd rather be doing something, you know."

Vanessa felt emotion wash her body. She felt so much for him. She could picture the house, and Fit in his chair with the mobile. There was almost a catch in her voice.

"Yes, I think I can guess, Fit. But only you know how it feels. I wish ... I'll get him to phone you tonight if you want."

"No, no, no need for that. I'll be in bed anyway. He'll be a bit pissed anyway, Ness. He's been on a plane for seven hours! You know how bored he gets!"

"I know how much he enjoys a drink, Fit! Still, he might be better if he's on his own. He always says you're the bad influence!"

Fit protested his complete innocence, cursed JD, and they bantered a little longer. She went for her shower hoping she'd made him feel a little better, feeling immense sympathy for him going to bed in that house of memories, alone, feeling grateful that she was going to meet someone who made her life complete, even if it was sometimes complete irritation. Still, she knew he loved her. He always came home.

Brandon Spencer picked up the phone in his suite at the Bayerischerhoff Hotel in Munich, and called his pilot.

"Captain, I've decided I am going to join you on Thursday morning. Give me the details again."

"Certainly, Chief We have to use the Executive side at Luton. Report 6 a. m., take-off 7 am. It's a distance of 1,640 miles, flight time approximately three and half hours. We should be there easily by noon their time, which is the scheduled time of arrival. We should take off again within 15 minutes for the return journey so we should be back in the U.K. by 2.45 GMT. That is, if I might say, Sir, rather sudden."

Brandon Spencer smiled to himself. The Captain must be extremely curious. He hardly ever allowed himself the latitude of a comment on their flight plans, unless it was purely technical. He'd obviously taken him completely by surprise. Not surprising, as it was only fifteen minutes since he'd told the Captain he wasn't going but staying in Germany and they were to pick him up on their return journey from Libya. The Captain wasn't to know that he'd had a curious conversation with Sir Julian Urqhuart since then. The Foreign Office obviously weren't keen on him going to Libya. Nothing could have ensured Brandon Spencer's determination to do so more than such a phone call. After all these years, they still didn't understand him.

"I hope I haven't inconvenienced you as far as filing flight plans etc are concerned, Captain? If so, I do apologise."

"No, not at all, Chief. I've done nothing about it yet. I will do so immediately." Anton knew he'd get no more information out of the Chief. It didn't matter. He paid, it was his plane, and he could go where he wanted.

Mary Matthews sat naked on the armchair in the warm and luxuriously appointed bathroom that Jonathan had planned and helped to build and finished drying her hair. She was aglow, hot in fact, from the hour she'd spent luxuriating in the shell-shaped Jacuzzi bath. She'd stay there and cool down a little before putting her bathrobe on and going back into the lounge. He was asleep anyway. He'd dozed off before she came for a bath. That was just before eight-o-clock, and she'd lain in the bath for nearly an hour! He'd be dead to the world by now. She'd let him sleep, and just wake him up around midnight to go to bed. She wanted time to think anyway. She felt fabulous. Yesterday had been wonderful. She'd been fantastic, everybody she'd ever wanted to be. She could hardly believe it. It was like an erotic, perhaps pornographic, movie running through her mind. She'd shocked him, she thought. She'd shocked herself! She almost laughed out loud as she pictured his face when he'd opened that toilet bag! She'd never really thought it would happen to her, that she'd be capable of all that. It should happen to everyone once in his or her life. Women had such power, if they only learned how to wield it.

But it wasn't about power. It wasn't about once in life. It was about something else. That was the problem. Maybe men could use women as little more than a masturbatory aid, but it was different for women. In fact, she thought it wasn’t really like that for men. Really good, deeply satisfying, sex only took place between people who felt deeply for each other. She felt more deeply satisfied than at any time since she last spent hours with him sixteen years ago. The serious problem was she also felt deeply as well. God, how she wished the two things could be separated. They could enjoy such times together. She needed to think about this. She was still hot, he was probably still asleep, she was still his wife, she was still a mother. Bloody hell, she was still 44, and she was still going through this again.

She needed to think.

General Sadiq Osman sat down to dinner in his large private house, behind its high walls, with the Rotweilers standing guard with the two soldiers, who stayed on the outside of the gates. The dogs didn't differentiate much after nightfall. It was so quiet on the Omdurman side of the river, and his land sloped down to the water almost in the shadow of the Nile Bridge, not far away from the confluence of the White and the Blue Nile, where the rivers ran together retaining their distinctive colours for a couple of kilometres before finally merging to make their way down to the sea so far away. It was late. 11 pm. His steward understood though. He always found it difficult after the end of Ramadan to get back into a normal eating routine. They should be used to him by now though. They'd worked for him for years, and whilst there were many months in the year when they didn't see him, they knew he'd always be back for Eid. The festival, in his mind, meant home, Khartoum, Omdurman, his sisters and their families, music and dancing. His nephews were wonderful lute players at nine years old! How his father would have loved to see them now. But, he thought, how he would have nagged him about getting married and having children of his own! He loved this house, and this time of year. This time, however, he'd been acutely aware of how little time he'd been able to spend with his family and he had no more time left on this visit. He was going back to Sirte tomorrow. But he was glad it was all determined, provided it was Allah's will. The Hanifs had been unanimous in their decision. More people than had gathered in Kabul a month ago had attended the meeting. It was obvious that the importance of the work attracted so much attention. He was now one of the most senior and longest-serving brothers in the movement. He was one of the most senior men outside the movement. How proud his father would have been of the little boy of seven he'd initiated. There was no doubt that his destiny now made him one of the most important members of the movement.

The decision had been made. He was to ensure the work in Sirte continued. The time had come to confront the evil that the unbelievers perpetrated in the world, aided by their money and their weapons. Their money would be used as the weapon against them. What Divine justice. The only aim of the movement was to bring the faith to all men, to bring peace and stability and decency to the world. Their guiding principle remained so simple, so perfectly voiced by the Prophet. "One Prophet, one faith, for all the world." He knew what he had to do.

General Belazir's door opened. Only the Colonel would come in without knocking so he didn't put the bottle away.

"I had to wake them up. They're obviously trying to maintain some sort of routine and they go to bed at 9 pm. because, they say, the Guards wake them up with morning prayers. That's probably by five each morning. That's too early for them! So, they'd been asleep for an hour when I went in. Well, they'd been in bed. I don't think they can sleep much. They're doing so little each day. They don't look too good, General."

"That's not surprising, Achmed. They've not seen the sun or even tasted fresh air for weeks! Did you tell them to prepare, and say absolutely nothing?"

"Of course and I don't think they will say anything to anybody. They realise, I think, in some way, that this is their best chance to get home. They won't jeopardise that. I've told them to leave almost everything, and we'll forward it on to them. I could tell that raised a little suspicion. It probably reminded them of how the Germans treated the Jews! I made it plain to them without telling them anything that it was simply because we expected the company to offer to fly them home and there just wasn't room for their kind of equipment on the executive jet. They know that's not true, but it seemed to calm them a little."

"I would think that was simply because you actually mentioned the possibility of them going home with

Dilworth in the plane. They won't have thought of that, so they'll probably think that for us to have thought about it must mean that we've actually arranged something."

"You're right, General, I think. They did, of course, ask about their families. I told them they were OK and that I didn't want any more questions on the issue. It shut them up."

General Belazir poured Annan a vodka. The Colonel took his cap off.

"Our plans ready?"

"Every detail, General."

"Then now we are in the hands of Allah. Perhaps we shouldn't drink this. . !"

They both laughed aloud and downed their drinks in one gulp.

£$£

Chapter Forty

He looked through the one-way bullet proof Mylar, over the Pentagon Parade ground, over the Tidal Basin with its pretty yachts, across the Potomac to the Capitol. He should have been tired, he'd been up all night, snatching just an hour's sleep between 5 and 6 am., but he wasn't. He seemed to have that permanent adrenalin rush coursing through him which had carried him through Vietnam as a Lieutenant when getting his patrol back to base had been the only, and most important, thing in the world. It had always made his mind crystal-clear. Fear had always had something to do with that too, and fear sat with him at his desk now. It might be expected to be different in this setting, but it wasn't. It was just the same fear as that engendered by VC ambush, landmines, poisoned spikes, snakes, the permanent darkness of not being able to see in bush, jungle, swamp, tall grass, bamboo, or a seemingly peaceful friendly village when what couldn't be seen was hidden behind smiling eyes. He'd learned to treat fear with respect. There was a good reason for it remaining in Homo Sapien after so many millions of years of evolution. Properly treated it was of immense benefit. It saved lives, first of all probably your own.

But now the fear was over other people's lives, ones that he was about to introduce fear into. It wasn't as easy as getting back to base. And it made it worse that it wasn't his life which was going to meet fear in adverse conditions again. Not that many people would believe that.

He swivelled round and looked at the wall behind his desk, lined with green-bound histories of the Second World War. Dwight D. Eisenhower's name was written all over those pages. In a few minutes he'd be walking down the Pentagon's Eisenhower Corridor to see the Secretary of Defence, to tell him why fear was sitting at his desk with him again.

He was glad the Secretary had been brought into the 10 am. meeting with the President. He liked and respected him. He'd served longer in this Administration than Clayton Holyoake. He'd been one of President Sunderland's first appointments, and he'd welcomed the new Chairman of the Joint Chiefs of Staff when he started the first of his three two-year terms. The Chairman was in his third term now, he was retiring in less than two years time. He'd done all right, it had gone well, until now. Now he had to tell the President the truth, and it was a pretty awful truth. But, he told himself as he looked at the books, as Ike said, "Bad news is only the worse for keeping".

He got up and walked to the Secretary's office. He was glad he could tell him first. It would break the ice, perhaps the taboos, just telling him first.

At 9.45 am. they stood waiting for the car in the River Entrance Parking Lot. The Secretary was quiet. As the car approached he turned to Holyoake and said, "Is it really the only way?"

"Mr. Secretary, yes."

"Let's go, Clay."

Everyone stood as the President entered the room at precisely 10 am. It was a sombre gathering and it seemed appropriate to observe all the formalities. There had been none of the usual small talk and banter that preceded many meetings. Perhaps Howard Cunningham's decision to attend, Clayton Holyoake's serious countenance, matched by that of the Secretary of Defence, told a story lethal to levity.

The President looked tense. He engaged in none of his normal pleasantries, little jokes. He was not trying to make anyone feel at ease. After a terse, "Good Morning, gentlemen," he launched straight into the business of the morning.

"I have to tell you, we have received no further contact from the Libyans. Reports from the CIA, FBI, State, the

British SIS, keep rolling in. What's going on keeps going on. It is, indeed, gentlemen, building, like Ravel's "Bolero". It is our job not to be distracted by the crescendo, the cacophony. It is our job to make the hard decisions. The British are with us. Indeed, they have their own vested interests, and job to do. I'll be talking to the Prime Minister after this meeting. I intend to tell him everything. I intend to tell no one else anything. Secrecy over this matter must be maintained. Total secrecy."

The President was speaking in a tone that few had heard. He switched his attention to Clayton Holyoake.

"General, Tell us what we can do. I will decide, with your help gentlemen, what we will do."

The Chairman of the JCS stood up. For some reason he felt better doing so.

"Mr. President, gentlemen. Our own information is scanty, inadequate. We have satellite and surveillance mapping and that's about all. Our main source of information is the British. You have to remember they fought over this desert for nearly three years sixty years ago. There are a lot of their graves there, then they "garrisoned" it 'til the late 60s. They know every inch of the place. They've even kept their maps up to date since then. They've got thousands of workers in the oil business in the field there. We have too, but we're not quite as cynical as the Brits with our companies."

Out of the corner of his eye he caught the slightly sour face of the CIA Director, but it wasn't the time for inter-departmental niceties. He went on.

"You know the British company, Daltons, built this plant. They are literally the only ones who know this base, who've been in it. They've done their best to describe what's there - but unfortunately they have no one with any military experience who's seen it. They do have an MD, though, who has a great interest in military history, all things military in fact, and he's done his best to note as much as he can. It's not so much, but it's all we have, and I think, fortuitously, it's enough for us to draw the most important conclusions.

Not that they're ones you'll want to hear."

He paused. The room was still with silent anticipation.

"John Dilworth, the Dalton's MD, has drawn a plan. It is based on the factual knowledge they have of the Press Hall, as they call it, the approaches to it, and what they know for certain lies alongside that hall from hear say and observation. It seems to us that it is probably accurate, as far as it goes. There is possibly much more. We can only concentrate on what's known. It is enough to illustrate what I have to tell you next. I've done copies for all of you."

He was taking the A3 sheets out of his large map-case as he spoke. He walked over and gave the first one to the President, then left the others on each side of the table to be passed round. He returned to his place and stood with his fingers resting on the plan.

"There is, of course, a full-size military air-field at the base, all weather, concrete. It is surrounded by a high wire fence that we presume to be alarmed, and probably electrified to keep animals off the runway. There is one main gateway, permanently guarded. We presume the perimeter is likewise guarded. We estimate the underground site is not far short of I million square feet..."

The President interrupted him.

"That's a hell of a size, General. Are you sure?"

He hoped this wasn't a foretaste of how the meeting was going to go. Of course he wasn't sure. Hadn't he just told them so? He reminded himself he was talking essentially to politicians. More patience, Holyoake, more patience.

"Sir, the estimate is based mainly on the size of the Press Hall and the corridor running up to it from the elevator, together with the size of the elevator. Plus the size of the building we have observed which is above ground and which we have accurate details of from our surveillance."

He was glad to hear the President's response.

"Of course. Sorry, General. I won't interrupt again."

If he didn't, nobody else would. The General was keen now to get it all out.

"The Press Hall is 200 yards long by 100 yards, the corridor leading to it from the elevator is 200 yards long, the elevators themselves, we're pretty certain there are two of them, one at each end of the complex, are 66 yards long. So the total known length of the complex is 466 yards. Let's say 500 yards. Let's presume that the aircraft "bunker" is the same size as the Press hall. That gives us a width of 200 yards, that's 100,000 square yards. That's 900,000 square feet. Allow for "unknowns", that's why we're postulating one million square feet. We don't know how deep the installation is, but we do know it is built with seemingly top-class materials, and superb facilities such as air-conditioning and communications. It has been openly stated that it is a "nuclear bunker", a match for the Nato Strategic Strike Command HQ at High Wycombe in the UK. In fact, it is claimed to be bigger than that, and that is the biggest in Europe. The base is obviously self-sufficient as far as water and we presume food-stocks are concerned. It is heavily guarded, with most of the troops being underground, with, we estimate, about 1000 men, including staff. We know little of the weaponry on site, except that at least two Mig-25 "Foxbat-As" have been seen, and are kept in the underground bunker. We postulate that up to eight may be in the flight. It would make sense, for internal transport and travel reasons, for there to be helicopters also kept there. They usually use Meridionati Vertol CH-47Cs. They would be housed, of course, with the Migs. Only small arms have been noted at the base, but these are the latest AK-49s, and it is also noted that the guards are all older men, obviously time-served trusted soldiers, not conscripts."

The Chairman was feeling more comfortable. He was talking about purely military matters, something he'd lived a lifetime with. It was the next part of his presentation he wasn't looking forward to.

"Mr. President, it is access to the base which is most impressive, or should I say most problematical. From all we know, there are only two ways in and out - by giant elevators at each end of the complex. At one end this "elevator", we guess, will be little more than a "platform" which will carry up to two planes at a time, with a shaft protected by a retractable bomb-proof cover, at the "Personnel Entrance" end the elevator is obviously a bomb-proof structure which also doubles as a "loading bay" by dint of having a type of retractable roof. We're not unfamiliar with this type of arrangement at some of our bases here in the States. The "Personnel" elevator is protected by an automatically activated system of enfilading machine guns designed to cut anything and anybody inside the elevator to pieces. It is also equipped with a similar system of anti-tank weapons. No conventional force could survive in that elevator. We must presume that the aircraft platform is similarly protected. To get into this base a force would have to neutralise the elevator defensive systems. Or create a new shaft, with explosives, of digging gear, or "bunker-busting" bombs, as they're popularly known. To guarantee success such a force would have to consist of three to four thousand men, heavily armed and well equipped for the excavating task. We could possibly drop them in, using airborne troops. Our difficulty would be getting them out quickly enough to prevent the raid turning into a land war."

This time he did pause for effect. He looked slowly around the table, then directly at the President.

"But even if we got a force into the zone we couldn't do any of that. Because they've protected the base with something else which is specifically designed to prevent such an assault. They have rigged the elevators, and we have to presume other areas of the complex, with gas that would be triggered by an assault. It has possibly been done in such a way as to eliminate the defenders if it's used, but that would be a quite probable cynical calculation. They would be expendable. It would certainly render the base unassailable by conventional methods. The gas is the deadliest known to man. It is VX."

Everyone at the meeting was familiar with VX. A spot on the skin would result in an awful, extremely swift death.

Originally a British discovery, which'd since destroyed all their chemical weapons, it had been refined and stockpiled by the US Military. They always claimed the Soviets were doing so during the "Cold War". Two milligrams would kill a person. It had even been "improved" upon, they now had ZV which killed "better". It only took two milligrams to kill 100 people.

The President stared at the Chairman of the Joint Chiefs of Staff. He said slowly.

"Are you sure, General Holyoake? How can you be sure it's VX? What makes you think its VX?"

"We're pretty sure, Mr. President. It's the only gas which fits the description of lethality which the Libyans described to the Dalton's MD."

"But he has no military experience. Were they not just bull-shitting him? They could have been."

"Correct, Mr. President. But there is one other major reason for believing that this is the case. In 1997 the UN Arms Inspectorate estimated that Saddam Hussein in Iraq had 200 tonnes of VX. You'll remember how the Iraqi's vehemently denied it, then admitted they had four tonnes, which was destroyed, then more was found and destroyed, then more, and so on and on. Finally, a total of 199 tonnes of the gas was located and destroyed. One tonne was never found. Intensive investigations failed to reveal its whereabouts, though God knows we tried, or should I say, the UN tried. The one tonne was enough to kill 100 million people if used in a densely populated area. So it had to be found. It wasn't. But, in 1998, another senior member of the dictator's family defected and he stated quite clearly that it had been sold to Libya. It made some sense. The Iraqis had sold Scud missiles to the Libyans. It also made some strategic sense. The Iraqis were hardly likely to sell such weapons to any of their close neighbours for obvious reasons, they're not exactly popular, nor to Arab nations they consider pro-Western. But the Libyans? Yes. They'd given the regime support at times when no one else in the world had. Since then, there have been persistent reports from our own intelligence, from the British, the Egyptians and the Israelis that Libya was the recipient of this gas. Where better to store it, and to use some of it, than at their most secret base, their nuclear defence bunker? We are convinced it's there."

The President continued to stare at Holyoake.

"So what are you saying, General? We can't send a Special Forces team to "take out" the base, we can't send a larger conventional force and we can't even bomb it to neutralise it because of the risk of loosing this deadly gas. We're impotent, we can't stop them carrying on printing and ruining our economy, or we can only stop them by revealing to the world what they're doing and still doing great harm to our economy. Jesus! There must be something we can do!"

"Mr. President. Whatever we do, I urge you to do it quickly and I stress, we cannot allow what's happening to get out. That's as bad as letting it go on." Howard Cunningham spoke firmly. The President looked at him like a grub on a salad plate.

"Howard, that's what we're here to do. Decide what to do. I haven't heard anything yet that we could do, have you?" The President's tone was terse.

The Chairman of the Fed. returned the President's glare but said nothing. Clayton Holyoake spoke again to break the tension.

"Mr. President, there is only one thing we can do. Use B61s."

The President's face tightened. Again he spoke very slowly.

"General. They're nuclear weapons."

"Correct, Mr. President. Tactical. Low-yield. Designed to penetrate the deepest bunkers and incinerate germ warfare agents. They generate heat up to 20,000 degrees Fahrenheit, 7,600 degrees Centigrade."

The Secretary of State couldn't help it. He blurted out.

"My God, General. You're proposing using nuclear weapons against an Arab state?" He was obviously aghast at the myriad of consequences he could see arising from such action.

"I'm afraid, gentlemen, that our conclusion is that to do so is the only effective way to neutralise this base, to prevent it operating. Our only other suggestion is to blockade the country, prevent anything getting in or out."

"Blockades never work. They take ages to take any effect anyway and you always need the co-operation of a vast array of allies to ensure even moderate success." The President spoke matter-of-factly, as if there was something much more important on his mind, which there was.

Bruce Teitelberg spoke again, almost as if he were speaking to himself, just voicing his innermost thoughts aloud.

"A conventional attack would be an invasion of sovereignty which would be considered an act of war."

"Bruce, you don't need to tell me!"

The President sounded sharp and irritated. He realised no one could help him. This soldier, who he liked and respected, had told him the truth. He didn't like the truth, but it had to be faced.

"General Holyoake. You're absolutely sure this is the only way?"

"I am, Mr. President. We have never tested the B61 on chemical weapons, only germ-warfare material, but we're confident it will be effective."

"You mean you can't be sure."

The President interrupted the Secretary of State's incredulous question unceremoniously.

"What are the downside risks of doing this General? The nuclear fall-out'?"

"There will be minimal fall-out, Mr. President. But there is a risk. The possible escape of some of the gas."

"Jesus Christ! I thought it would all be destroyed and the base is in the middle of the desert anyway, far away from any main centres of population, isn't it?"

"We consider the risk of an escape of gas is highly improbable but not completely impossible. Yes, the base is a long way from any really densely-populated areas, but, at this time of year, the wind and the currents don't help us."

The President's teeth were clenched and his face taut, but he controlled his voice.

"Wind and currents, General? What the hell does that mean?"

"Sorry, Sir. I should have been more explicit." Clayton Holyoake could see the President was extremely tense. He didn't want him to lose his cool. The man was in the most unenviable position he could imagine anyone being in at the moment. "Unfortunately, although most of the Westerly winds miss this part of the North African coast normally, in January and February two regular winds sweep East-wards from Spain and Tunisia, and turn North-eastwards from about just where the base is situated, carrying across the Med. Only the Fohn winds off the Alps moving south would counteract them, and there would be a danger that they'd cancel each other out, leaving the air "hanging" over the Med., Southern Turkey, Greece, Yugoslavia, perhaps even Sicily and Italy."

"Good God, so anything released from the base would possibly be carried by these winds and disperse over these countries?"

"Yes sir, and over Egypt. Likewise with the sea currents. They flow in the Med. from the Straits of Gibraltar eastwards along the North African coast, up the Levant, then move westwards along Southern Turkey etc. back to Spain."

Everyone in the room felt the weight of the burden on the President's shoulders, everyone wanted to lighten the load, but didn't want it on their shoulders, no one wanted to be the first to speak. The President did, after a long pause.

"General, gentlemen, I'm taking the decision to use the B61 option. It is, in my considered opinion, the only one we have which can be used effectively and swiftly. Speed is of the essence here. There could be an international out-cry. We all know that. But this is in the crucial interests of the United States of America, and some of our most important allies. They can all argue about it in the future, if the

Libyans ever reveal that something has actually happened. I'm gambling on them not doing so. How would they explain what they are doing at the base? If I remember correctly, a small tactical nuclear explosion will not register on any seismic monitoring systems. God knows I don't want to harm the poor people in that base, but committing our own troops would be condemning them to death as well. The greatest risk is the release of any of this gas. That is my responsibility. I can only pray to God that he is with us and that this does not happen. I'm exercising Presidential prerogative. We're going ahead with this. It will be undertaken as a covert operation, regardless of our obligation to submit such operations to Congress in advance. In my opinion this must be treated as one of the rare exceptions that the Act allows for. I am conscious that there may be some amongst you who do not wish to be associated with this action. If there are, you need only speak now and it will be recorded and committed to paper by the end of this day."

Jim Sunderland was moved by the silence. It would have been easy for any of them to dissociate themselves. They were a good team. It made him even more resolute.

"General, it is essential that this operation is carried out before tomorrow night."

That took Clayton Holyoake by surprise. His mind was racing. Where the hell were the nearest B61's? How could they get them to the Med.? What delivery systems did they have there? Before he could reply the President carried on.

"The timing, gentlemen, as I'm sure you've guessed, is dictated by the arrival of the Russians. They'll be here by early evening tomorrow. I believe it is strategically vital that the action takes place whilst they're in the air, and before they arrive. That way, we have the advantage if the Libyans do scream murder internationally. I've already said I don't believe they will, but let's protect ourselves as best we can. I do not want to give the Russians any excuse to call off this summit. We're drifting too perilously close to getting into a full-blown Cold War again under the new leadership. We have to stop that for our sake, and theirs, and everybody else in the damned world's sake."

The President had given Holyoake time to think. The B61s were with the Stealth Bombers at the Maimstrom Air Force Base at Great Falls, Montana, the aircraft carrier USS Columbia was with the Sixth Fleet in the Med., not far from the Gulf of Sirte. Their F-15s could deliver the laser-guided bombs. It could be done in time. He told the meeting this. The President nodded then said.

"General, I'll confirm this later, after I've spoken to the British Prime Minister, but the Brits have a little show of their own that they want to undertake. Their schedule is set for 12 noon to 12.30 Libyan time, that's right, Bruce isn't it?" The Secretary of State said it was. The President carried on. "We'll make I pm. Libyan time our zero hour. OK?"

"Of course, Mr. President."

"I'll brief everyone else, or Bruce will, as to what the British are doing, after my call to London. There isn't time now. Let's break up, gentlemen. Let's get to work."

As the Chairman of the Joint Chiefs of Staff was putting his papers away he was calculating what time it was in Montana, and what time it was in Libya at this precise moment. He figured he had 19 hours, maximum.

£$£

Chapter Forty-One

It was dark and silent in the little village, not a light anywhere. Not surprising at 4.45 am. Fit thought. The moon was full and bright though, painting trees and houses and parked cars with a pale blue-white wash, the touch of frost like the glitter-dust on a Christmas card. The stars coruscated gently behind every roof, over every tree, lying like a mantle down to the very road he was on as it dropped down off the escarpment on its way out of the village. He turned into the quiet tree-lined road and he could see JD's house, seemingly every light on, looking like an all-night diner on Route 66. As soon as he nosed into the drive the security lights snapped on, bathing the whole garden in a bright white light. He expected a UFO to land, or at least loud voices shouting "Achtung!" with huge dogs barking in unison as the guards came to get him.

Instead the front door opened and Vanessa stood there in a dark green dressing gown, the open door throwing warm yellow light into the cold white glare.

"Hello, Fit. How lovely to see you. Come in and join us for a bite of breakfast. Come on, it's chilly standing here!"

He'd tucked himself in by the lawn so he wouldn't impede any of their cars, and he walked briskly towards the door carrying his briefcase. He reckoned he didn't need anything else. They'd be in and out in the same day. Should be before evening.

"Ness, darling. How are you? Nobody can look as good as you at 4.45 in the morning!"

"Come in, you old flatterer. It will get you everywhere! Don't stop…"

He stepped through the door and he kissed her on both cheeks. He could feel the warmth of the house, and smell bacon grilling. It was all so welcoming. But, as he'd thought all the way across in the car, nothing seemed the same, nothing even looked the same. He knew nothing had changed. Only him, and his life.

JD came thumping downstairs with all the grace of an ageing rugby player with a touch of arthritis. Immaculately dressed and smelling like a Moroccan bordello, but with hair un-groomed as usual, looking like a bedraggled military out-post on a hill waiting for the last assault of some overwhelming assailants, bedraggled but defiant.

"Morning Fit. Fancy some breakfast?"

"Sure, JD. I wouldn't say no." He certainly wouldn't. He hadn't really eaten anything since brunch the day before. There seemed no point in cooking anything just for himself. And he hadn't been hungry since that day the Oncologist gave him the real prognosis.

"Smells delicious. As good as you look, Ness."

"Bacon, scrambled eggs and tomatoes. Do you want toast?"

"Yes please."

"I'm so glad you could come Fit, seriously. I think with you there there'll be less chance of any fuss or argument from Belazir or Osman. The Chief is too. He's decided to come. Anton phoned me yesterday to tell me. He'll be pleased to see you Fit."

They sat round the circular pine table at the end of the large kitchen. Ness poured coffee.

"Ness, he is lucky to have such a lovely wife who'll get up at 4.30 am. just to cook him a breakfast before he goes out into the wide world."

"I always do, Fit. I always make sure he's pampered. Even if he's just catching a train to have lunch in London or… "

"You little liar! You're usually zonked when I set out! You stopped getting up with me after we'd been married for less than a year!"

"That's because you're such a demanding, exhausting lover JD. How could a young innocent girl like me keep up with you, without at least 14 hours sleep a day..?"

Fit watched and listened and smiled. But it hurt. Like

everything else did.

They did everything they could to make him feel comfortable and welcome, and in this house he knew he was. But he felt better talking about business, so he changed to that subject as soon as he could. JD filled him in on details he hadn't gone into during their telephone conversation the previous day. He'd said he would.

“What do you think the Yanks will do, JD?”

“Don't know, Fit. But I'll bet there's some pretty intense top-level diplomatic activity going on, even as we talk and we've not got long to talk. It's 5.45. We're going to be a few minutes late. It doesn't matter. Take-off's only 7 am. That's why we're at Luton, amongst the Portakabins under the wings! It's the nearest business side that would let us set off so late and the Libyans are pretty adamant we've got to be there spot-on noon. Flying time is about three and a half hours, maybe a bit longer. They're an hour ahead of us. We should get there by 11.45. Anton says he'll lose a bit of time if needs be.”

“The Chief won't let him do that! He'll find something else to do!”

“Yeah, you're right. Anyway, all I want to do is get the engravers out. No arguments. They're coming with us, home. The Chief agrees. The Libyans won't argue with him.”

JD got up from the table.

“I'm just going upstairs to clean my teeth again. Use the downstairs bathroom off the hall if you want to do the same, and then let's go. Ness is driving us.”

Fit looked at Vanessa stacking the dishwasher. She caught his eye and smiled.

“I'm going like this. Well, just with a coat over my housecoat. No one's going to see me. I'm not getting out of the car, so don't you try to introduce me to anybody when we get there JD or I'll kill you!” He laughed and patted her cheek. She pretended to take a swipe at him.

As they were leaving Fit watched Vanessa help JD collect his papers and pack his pilot's case, before ushering them both out of the house and waiting until they were in the car before putting the burglar alarm on. He desperately wanted to take JD to one side and say to him, "Treasure every moment. Tell her you love her. This time is precious, every second of it. Drink it in. Savour it." But he knew he couldn't. It would embarrass them, and he'd sound foolish, maudlin, over dramatic. If only people could appreciate what they'd got, if only….

President Sunderland hadn't slept much. He looked at his watch. It was 5.45 am. It was unusual for him not to sleep. But it was unusual for him to have ordered what was going to happen in just over an hour's time. It was that which fretted away at him all night. Not the summit with the Russians, that was only to try to get them to agree to do something about the mafia-type organisations that were now running their damned country. They had to realise what was going on. They did, of course - but nearly all the politicians had a hand in it anyway. Russia was now one vast corporate gangster state, its violence and corruptions spreading like poison gas across its borders to every country in the world. Like poison gas, that is what he was really worried about. That's what had stood beside him, lain beside him, straddled his chest whilst he was asleep or nearly asleep. The spectre of the poison gas. Like a foul demonic beast, like one of those paintings by Herronymous Bosch or whatever the damned man's name was. It could kill millions and millions of people. And the bomb, the nuclear bomb. The first to be dropped in anger since Nagasaki. How could he justify it? Who'd listen to it being "only a tactical device"? Who'd believe it was the only weapon to stop the gas? Who'd agree it should be used just to protect a currency? No lives at stake, who'd listen to the stories of how much misery and death could be caused if it wasn't dropped? How could we be sure the Libyans wouldn't scream to the rest of the world? God, he'd be better outside in the cold, jogging. He'd told Security he was jogging at 6 am. It was too cold to swim. Better get out.

His man was waiting for him on the terrace of Aspen Lodge, the Presidential home at Camp David. He looked at the Catoctin Mountains, serene and seemingly unchanged, around him, below him, a world unaware of what was going to happen in just one hour nearly five thousand miles away. Something that might change that world forever if it all went wrong. What if he was wrong? What if…?

"How far, Mr. President?"

"Just a couple of miles son. I'm getting old!"

He wanted to be back in Aspen, showered and waiting when the final call for authorisation came through at 6.45 am. It somehow only seemed right to do it dressed in a suit.

The two girls had learned to lean on each other a lot over the past few awful months. They'd cried a lot at first, with anger, then frustration, then fear. But it had settled down now to a dreadful monotony. They were fed well, their clothes were laundered, their homes were cleaned, and their children received regular tuition. They had absolutely nothing to do. They were constantly told not to worry about their husbands, not even when the phone calls stopped. They were constantly being told that their husbands would be "back with you next week". They knew now that they were prisoners. They supposed their husbands were. But if they were being treated as they were, it was a strange kind of prison. Both women were intelligent. They both realised their husband's skills were the reason they were all on "captive holiday". They knew those skills must be being misused. What happened when they were no longer being used?

They both felt dreadful, but the regime of outdoor games with the children, outdoor meals, outdoor tuition had left them all with super tans, hiding the pallor of worry. And they both lived behind a carapace of normality for the sake of Daniel and Laura. As far as those two were concerned their only complaint was that they didn't have anyone else to play with. With the natural stoicism of children they just got on with it and played with each other.

Sometimes, the young guards, who were all friendly and forever smiling and loved children, would join in. They could hardly speak any English, but it didn't seem to matter, and they went out of their way to see that the mothers and the children didn't want for anything. The only English they seemed to know was, "don't worry," and, "husband home soon". All delivered with smiles. Everybody smiled all the time, except them.

"We'll have lunch out here again, shall we Bronya?"

Bronya looked at her with mock surprise and said, "No, Lisa, don't be silly! Let's just drive into town and book a weekend in Cyprus. We've got loads of money, girl. And with tans like this, and an island full of frustrated soldiers, all fit and under 25, even you and I could score."

They laughed a little, and seriously launched into the discussion that would be the most important, the most serious, of the day. What would they have for lunch this time?

It was nearly noon.

Three CH47 Chinook helicopters landed on the vast deck of the USS Columbia. Two, with British Royal Air force markings, landed aft, and were greeted by a party led by the Captain. The CEO and a team of technicians met the other, landing well forward. It bore USAF markings. The three Chinooks had followed each other from Malta. The only other craft on deck in the bright Mediterranean sunshine were two F15 Fighter-Bombers and three UH60 Blackhawk helicopters. The F15s were obviously in a state of readiness. Around the carrier the languid blue of the sea was disturbed only by the wakes of warships of every shape and size, visible seemingly to the horizon on every side. From the air the Sixth Fleet looked awesome.

The Captain of the carrier met the two British craft because they were foreign guests, close allies, now landing on U.S. territory. He was also curious because they were two British SAS teams, 16 men in total. Dressed in shabby-looking DPMs, with Browning Hi-Power automatics their only visible weapons, they wore no distinguishing badges or other insignia, but they were accompanied by a Major in Para uniform who immediately shook hands with the Captain. No one had any time for niceties, so after the briefest formalities they moved off for final briefing. Communications arrangements between the U.S. Navy, Royal Air Force and the Special Air Service were top of the agenda. They might be vital in the next hour. There had been no time for any of it to be done before this moment. The first orders about the operation had only been issued 18 hours earlier. The SAS men had been in Hereford eight hours prior to landing on the Columbia. They stayed on deck in the sun. The 'copters had not closed down.

At the other end of the flight deck the rear door of the Chinook was open and scissor lifts were being used to load two long steel cases onto automated bogeys. The large copter contained nothing else, except a few sacks of mail thrown in at the last moment for the Fleet. The bogeys were driven to the F15s.

It was 11.15 am.

General Youssef Belazir blew smoke rings towards his friend, and leaned back in his chair. He looked relaxed and happy, though a little tired.

"I know I've been blessed with a beautiful family, Achmed, but at times like these I envy you being single. You wouldn't believe the trouble I had in getting them to go to Morocco. You'd have thought Marrakech was a hellhole! I've still not told her she's going to be one of the richest women in the world, she just thinks it's a bit over the top to take a holiday just to celebrate the end of Ramadan! Anyway, they're away now. She'll go hysterical when she finds out I've left everything behind, and we can't come back for anything, but I'll send her all over Europe, or wherever she wants to go, to buy everything she wants. That should keep her quiet. What about your brother and his wife?"

"They're at their place in London, General. Both boys, you know, are at Brunel University. I think myself they'd planned to stay there anyway. Nabil's work is almost exclusively in London or Geneva. They've got a beautiful house there. I think I'll buy one close by, with my pension!"

They both laughed.

"I've instructed Saif to discontinue all operations here from midnight tonight. He just grunted as usual, and asked nothing. But I think he was a little surprised. This...", Belazir picked up a document from his desk and held it upright, "is his written confirmation. You know Mahmoud, he insists on everything in writing!"

They laughed again. They were two old friends looking forward to a very affluent future. They'd certainly keep in close touch with each other.

"What about our helicopter, Achmed?"

"Standing by. All arranged. It is by the Mig ramp. The pilot is Khaled Aliah, totally trustworthy and it will secure his pension, too, of course! He's expecting us from 11.55 am. onwards, ready for immediate take-off. We're supposed to be going just down to Suknah for an inspection."

"Right, Achmed. It's 11.45 now. Time to get the Englishmen. You do that. I've got to see Osman at 12.00. He's just requested it. I'm almost sure it will be about the closure of the operation. Another bloody message from the Hanifs pleading with us to save Islam! Mahmoud will have told him about my verbal order. He'll be trying to persuade me to delay issuing it in writing. Too late, eh! I'll use the helicopter schedule as the excuse to cut the meeting short. I'll tell him I'll see him later. He can wait forever! I never realised he'd got so mixed up with the bloody fanatics. Anyway, one thing's for certain. After getting the written order, Mahmoud will stick to it like a limpet mine. There'll be no more banknotes printed here!"

Colonel Anan stood up and made for the door. Belazir said. "Achmed. Be careful. You've got the only delicate bit to do, getting those young men to the Dalton's plane. Don't take any risks. We don't want any delays through getting mixed up in a row with Osman or Saif about letting them go."

Anan slipped into the familiar. It seemed appropriate in the circumstances.

"Don't worry, Youssef. I'm looking forward to the cold in London. I'll buy you a lunch at Simpson's on the Strand. We'll look like just two more old rich Arabs…!"

They parted smiling.

£$£

Chapter Forty-Two

They'd looked at each other and suppressed, 'I told you so,' smiles when the Chief told them he'd drop them off, 'just a little early', then fly down to Az Zahrah to the new oil concession. It was, 'only 15 minutes flying time', he was having a, 'quick look,' and be back for them by, 'about 12.30'. He'd meet Belazir and Osman then if there were any difficulties about, 'the boys', coming home with them.

Anton landed and taxied towards the Monolith, but stopped about 500 yards away from it. JD slipped on the jacket of his Cannelli lightweight suit and picked up his case, Fit was already waiting at the door of the galley.

"It will be a pleasant walk in this weather. Look," the Chief was pointing to the cabin display, "it's 72°F out there. Like a lovely English summer day. Good luck, boys. I'll see you in a short time. Give them my best."

They turned and waved as the G4 circled and girded itself for take-off. Within seconds Anton was up to speed and the graceful white craft soared like something from a sci-fi movie in a steep climb. Anton was playing at Luftwaffe pilots again.

When it was gone, they were left standing in the silence, broken only by the diminishing noise of the Rolls-Royce engines. The sun was warm, there was no breeze. They instinctively started to walk towards the terminal at a gentle pace. They knew they were a few minutes early. They didn't slacken their pace when they saw the dark Mercedes pull out from the Monolith and head towards them. As yet no sound reached them from the car. They didn't speak. They were enjoying the stroll.

Bronya was carefully pouring olive oil onto the tomatoes and cucumber slices in the large plastic bowl, Lisa was re-reading a Maltese English-language newspaper, which they got about three days after publication, the kids were trying to dig in the hard earth of the garden, or compound as it really was. They were tired of the swings the guards had put in at the end of the "lawn". It was a lovely day, all the better for being cooler. She wished, on a day like this, that they could wear their bikinis. It was perfect sun bathing weather. They'd soon realised that wasn't allowed. The young guard they'd nick named "Tom Cruise" was sitting on the low cast-concrete border-wall watching the kids, "Burt Reynolds" was round the front.

When she first heard the sound it sounded just like her washing machine at home when it started to spin. Laboured, but gaining in power. But she hadn't got a washing machine here. She looked up. She saw it, very low, heading straight for the house. She stared, straightening up, the plastic salad fork still in her hand. It grew bigger, very quickly. Lisa stared at it over her paper. The kids kept digging. The noise was very loud now, and a cloud of dust was billowing under the helicopter. The 'copter looked very big. It was almost in the garden now. It slewed sideways, and she saw the markings. It was still twelve or so feet off the ground when the first men jumped out. She knew instinctively what was happening. She dropped the fork into the bowl and twisted her head towards the guard, who was sat, transfixed. Just staring.

"Run! Run!" She shouted wildly. She waved her hand, pointing behind him. "Run!"

He stood up slowly, seemed to hesitate. She looked back at the 'copter. Three men were running towards the low fence. The first one took it in his stride. They were armed.

"Run!" She was almost screaming now. "Tom" looked at her and then at the running figures then back at her. It seemed to take him minutes to comprehend what was happening. Then he took her advice, doing a scissor leap over the fence and ran. As if in a farce on stage, as he disappeared into the sparse bushes hedging the compound the other guard appeared from round the side of the house.

He pulled up short, registering just the right emotion of open-mouthed shock the stage director of the farce would want. He had his gun, unlike the first guard. But it was slung round his back, and he made no move to swing it around. She stared at him wide-eyed. She was about to shout when three panting soldiers invaded her space. One was in the process of scooping two children up, the other was reaching down for Lisa. The third spoke to her in a broad Lancashire accent, his face not four feet away from hers.

"Mrs Clay? Please, you're coming with us. Please. Now!"

Inexplicably, she found herself saying.

"Yes, and this is Mrs Rogerson."

He grabbed her arm. She could see the other soldier was pulling Lisa away and the third had the two kids under his arms and was heading for the fence. For the first time she saw more soldiers lying and kneeling at the other side of the fence, all pointing guns at the house. She frantically turned to look at the other guard. Two soldiers had him pinned on the ground. Where had they come from? One was pulling his gun from round his neck.

"Don't hurt him, please! Don't hurt him!"

Her soldier kept pulling her. The Lancashire accent said, "Don't worry yourself, Mrs Clay. There'll be no need for that. Just come on, love, quick! Quick!"

They were nearly at the helicopter. The noise was awful. She couldn't hear, but she could see Laura crying. She wanted to get to her to comfort her. Daniel just looked dazed but curious. Lisa was on her stomach facing into the 'copter where she'd been pushed and she couldn't see her face. Her soldier pushed her in. She was shouting at him but no human voice could possibly be heard in that racket. She kept trying.

"My purse! I've left my purse and my passport!"

The 'copter lifted. The door was still open. She could see "Burt Reynolds" get up and sit on the wall. He was looking round. He was obviously wondering where "Tom

Cruise" was. She hoped they wouldn't get into trouble. The soldiers were shouting at each other and laughing. She jerkily moved a couple of yards, jolted by the yawing movement of the helicopter as it turned sharply and climbed at the same time. She just wanted to hold Laura and stop her crying.

The Sergeant leaned back, sweating and elated. Job done! Not a shot fired! He was really proud of his lads. They'd performed perfectly. They'd done just what he told them. Even in all that excitement nobody had sworn in front of the kids.

Belazir was surprised to see Saif with Osman and he was a bit early, Osman spoke as he came through the door.

"Youssef. You didn't tell me Daltons were coming. They've just landed, a few minutes ago. Mahmoud says Colonel Anan only gave the landing clearance instructions this morning."

"Those were my instructions, Sadiq. I only told the Colonel this morning." He said it sharply. He wanted no argument or even conversation about it. It was nothing to do with the Sudanese General anyway and he was running out of time.

"Sadiq, I'm quite sure Mahmoud has also informed you about my other instruction. This plant closes down at this base at midnight tonight. Completely. There will be no more banknotes printed here from that time. I presume you wanted this meeting to try to persuade me to change my decision. Am I right?"

"Yes, General, you are. It is not in the interests of the greater good of the Islamic world for us to close down. I have received very clear instructions, from the Council of the Hanifs, to continue with our programme. I have…"

Belazir jumped to his feet as he slammed his chair back and threw his lighter on his desk. He was angry. He wasn't simulating it. He shouted.

"Instructions! What instructions? It has nothing to do with them! This is a Libyan plant, this is my plant! It has fuck-all to do with the fucking Hanifs, or you for that matter General!" He was stabbing his finger at Osman's face. "We close! Tonight!"

Osman sat, unmoved, one hand in his tunic pocket, the other easing a cigarette from the gold case he'd placed on Belazir's desk. He stared up at Belazir, eyes cobra-cold.

"I must ask you to re-consider, Youssef. Please."

"The decision is made, General. The order has been given. That's it, end of story."

To emphasise his point, he turned to get his cigarettes from the filing cabinet behind him, signalling that the meeting was over. He heard Osman's voice.

"I'm afraid not, Youssef. General Saif agrees with me. The work must go on."

He froze for a split second, then began to whirl round to confront the insubordinate mutinous bastards when he heard what he thought was Osman's cigarette case snap shut, and felt a light punch in his back. He turned to see Osman, still seated, with his Walther Pistole 38 and silencer pointed at his face. He felt a warm sensation just below his sternum and looked down to see a dark stain spreading on one of his best uniform jackets. He was incredulous. When he looked up he heard the sound again. The next sound, which he didn't hear, was a large part of the back of his skull hitting the metallic wall behind him.

The blood and brain were sliding slowly down the wall when the phone rang. Osman was dismantling the silencer. He nodded to Saif to take it.

Saif remained as impassive as ever as he listened. He watched Osman, after a few seconds he said.

"Radar has picked up a force of aircraft heading this way. Close. Looks like fighters and bombers. There's been a raid to release the English families."

Osman fastened his holster and said with icy sarcasm tinged with brusqueness.

"The Christians have launched a crusade, Mahmoud. Scramble the Migs. Let's get down to the Comms. Centre."

Saif gave the order.

Osman looked at the mess on the desk and against the wall.

"Leave him. We'll just lock the door."

It really was pleasant in the sun. They wouldn't have minded walking all the way to the Monolith. Fit spoke.

"They are, JD. They're in the car."

Fit's eyes were better than JD's. Fit always told him to forget playing golf, stick to rugby. The ball was bigger.

"Yes, I can see them now Fit. That's good. But I wonder why they're bringing them out here. Suits us, though."

"It's Colonel Anan driving JD."

They were still about 400 yards from the building when the car pulled up in front of them. Anan got out. The engravers stayed in the back, as if they'd been told to do so.

Anan greeted them courteously, but with all his usual formality. They responded. JD was staring at the men in the car. Anan made no move to invite them to get into the car, and the engravers made no move to get out. JD thought they made an odd group, two men in business suits and a third in full uniform, standing next to a gleaming Mercedes in the middle of a runway in the sun in the desert.

By simply taking JD's arm, Anan turned them to face away from the car. He spoke firmly, but in an oddly conspiratorial manner.

"Mr. Dilworth, Mr. Thomas. Your men are here. We want you to take them home with you. Their work is done. I don't want to go into any more details, but I can assure you it is important that this is done."

JD responded immediately.

"Colonel. That is fine by us. That is exactly what we'd like to do. That's what we were going to request of you."

"Good. They are here for you. Take also my word for it when I advise you not to spend any time at the base. Just re-board and go your way. Where has the plane gone?"

His voice sounded anxious, not just curious. JD was trying to figure out what was going on, because something was. He answered the Colonel's question.

"Oh, they've just flown down to Az Zahrah. They'll be back in about half an hour now."

Anan looked concerned. He hesitated, then turned to the car and looked at the engravers. After a few seconds he seemed to make up his mind.

"You may as well meet your men here. They've not had much sun lately. They've been so busy. Let's get them out." They moved towards the car. "It's a pity the plane didn't wait. You could have taken off right away."

"Well, we were conscious of being a bit early when we first landed, and the Chief..."

He stopped. Anan had opened the door of the car. Simon Rogerson slid out of the rear seat first. Paul Clay moved to that side of the car. JD was shocked by their appearance. They'd both lost weight, and grown beards. But it was their pallor that shook him. They were grey, no, colourless. Pallid wasn't a strong enough description. He instantly saw what had happened to them. They'd been kept underground, nose to the grindstone until the Libyans had got everything they wanted, whatever that was. Poor buggers and they looked so, crushed. As if....

"Excuse me, please." Anan broke away from them, making for the front of the car, he was staring at the Monolith as he did so.

JD followed his stare. He couldn't see perfectly, but he could see enough to realise that what had fixed Anan's attention were two Migs appearing out of the desert floor. They emerged like an illusionist's subject as if from nowhere, not far from the Monolith. One of them, at least, as far as he could tell, was firing up its engines. The noise was just reaching them. Anan was speaking loudly and rapidly, in Arabic, into the car phone. The five men stood staring at the sight. Suddenly, they were aware of another sound, growing louder, as loud as the jet engines being started up. Then they saw it. Coming into their line of sight after previously being out of it behind the Monolith was a large helicopter. It was flying low, passing over the Migs and heading straight for them. It kept on coming. Anan put the car phone back and looked as if he was in shock. The helicopter plainly had the markings of the RAF.

It seemed to JD then that all sorts of things took place either simultaneously or in some hideously choreographed action ballet. The helicopter was landing near to them, soldiers were jumping out before it landed shouting at them, one of the Migs near the Monolith moved off the ramp and onto the runway, from behind them, from the direction none of them were looking in, two more Mig-25s screamed in, just above their heads it seemed, and in the split second it took to grasp they were there, the other Mig on the ground next to the Monolith exploded in a fireball of white and crimson flames. The smoke-trailing debris from the explosion was still arcing through the air towards the floor when the air was filled with heavier throatier jet engine sounds that blanketed all the other noises. The earth and the air and their bodies seemed to tremble like the surface of a mountain lake during an earthquake. Three huge jets flew low overhead. Without anything seeming to pass between them and the Monolith it suddenly began to erupt in flames and bricks and dust and smoke. It was being bombed into obliteration.

Even those without military training were flat on the floor, with their hands pressed over their ears. The ground bucked under them. It seemed to go on forever. If anyone had looked up they would have seen the three Tupelov "Blinders" circle tightly and make a return run. The earth erupted again. What was left of the Monolith disappeared after the second run. A lot of the bombs and missiles simply threw the already shattered rubble into the sky again for a second trip. The reverberations went on for several seconds. Dust and small debris rained down on them and swirled in the air. The dark-blue Mercedes was brown-grey. Before it died away another sound lashed into the maelstrom of noise. The Mig that had moved onto the runway roared over their heads, only a few feet above them. It appeared to be flying away from them. After a few seconds the human voice could make itself heard again for the first time in what seemed like many minutes, but which was in reality probably only a couple.

"Out! Out! Get out!"

It was one of the soldiers. He was yelling at the two pilots of the helicopter. He was waving and pointing madly in the direction of the Mig that had just taken off. He was the only person standing at first, but he was joined within seconds by some of the other soldiers.

"Rubble! Get to the rubble!" The shouter was yelling now, pointing to the pall of smoke and dust that had been the Monolith. At almost the same time he was yanking at the door of the 'copter, still screaming. The pilots seemed to suddenly understand him. They bundled out. They all started running towards the dust cloud. The shouting soldier pulled Fit up, and JD and the engravers followed them. They'd covered about three hundred yards when there was another huge explosion behind them. Everybody threw themselves down. They heard the scream of a low jet again. JD looked back momentarily as he scrambled to his feet with the rest to continue running. The Chinook was smashed. Still recognisable, but obviously hit by one of the Mig's air-to-air missiles. It had come back to do the job. JD understood why the shouting soldier had been shouting.

There was a large bomb crater, shallow and surrounded by rubble, like a hole dug in the sand by a child at the seaside. They followed the soldiers who scrambled over the rubble and threw themselves into it. Their professionalism was superb, second nature. Shouting to each other ceaselessly they were no sooner in than they were half-way out again setting up immediate vantage and defence points. The civilians, the RAF men and Anan lay where they'd thrown themselves when they got into the crater, panting and sweating. JD realised that his heart was drilling a hole through his chest and attacking his spine at the same time. It had only been about 400 yards, why was he in such a state? He was bathed in sweat, utterly breathless. He was never like this when he'd done a five-miler. He knew the answer. But he let his mind stay on auto-scrambler. It blocked out, for a moment, the horror of the situation. One minute he's sat in luxury on an executive jet, next minute he's in a fucking war! He was scared. That's why he was panting and sweating. He was terrified scared. Shit scared. His mind kept straying to odd things. Where had he left his pilot's case? Would this suit clean? Why in Jesus Christ's name were the Army here, the SAS it looked like, when the bloody Air force were bombing them? Whose bloody air force, anyway? A cock up between the Brits and the Yanks? Why were the boys so pale? What was Anan doing here?

It had been quiet, eerily silent for a couple of minutes. The shouting soldier finished speaking rapidly into his radio and slid down from the side of the crater, carefully keeping his head below the height of the rubble. He lay next to the "civilian group" at one side of the crater, resting on one elbow. He spoke calmly. JD noticed he wasn't breathless, and hardly sweating, even though he seemed to be carrying enough hardware to equip a battalion of Third World soldiers.

"SAS. I'm Patrol Leader. Angus. Call me Gus. Who's John Dilworth?"

JD said he was

"Where's your fucking plane? 'Copter's gone. It's the only way we're getting out of this shit!"

JD said, unconsciously mimicking the staccato military style.

"Should return by about 12.30. Gone down to Az Zahrah."

"That's less than 10 minutes. How many will it carry?"

"Everybody here."

"Thank Christ!" Gus turned his attention to Anan.

"Colonel, can you tell me, please, what the fuck is going on here?" He sounded genuinely puzzled and aggrieved, but only like a man who's got home to find he's been given the wrong video. Jesus, thought JD, why isn't he terrified like me?

Theoretically, Saif was Senior Officer, but everyone in

the Communications Room, including the Libyan General, deferred to Osman. Belazir had instructed that it had to be so, and the two of them had been like Siamese twins for months.

The young officer turned from his screen and spoke to Osman.

“Confirmation from the Mig pilot Sir. The attack was carried out by “Foxbats” and “Blinders” with Libyan Air Force markings. But he also confirms that he disabled a British RAF Chinook on the strip, and that it did drop its party. He doesn't know whether he accounted for any of them. He's awaiting your instructions, Sir. Do you want him to engage the Air force Group. They're heading west, on a course for Tarabalus Base, he's fully-fuelled.”

The officer was obviously in shock, and baffled. Osman reacted swiftly.

“It is a trick, Captain. The British are attacking us. There'll be more. Tell him to sweep the area to the coast and simply observe and report what he sees. Do not engage. Await further instructions. Keep in close contact.”

“Yes Sir. Shall I contact Tarabalus?”

“On no account. Maintain radio silence, except with the Foxbat. What's the external damage?”

“Don't know Sir. All external cameras destroyed. No contact with the Gate. Two companies are moving in from both ends of the perimeter. They're about three miles from each other, both about one-and-a-half miles from Base. Not mechanised. E.T.A. 10 minutes. They can't see anything yet. Just smoke and dust, Sir.”

“Tell them to keep us posted. Especially for the troops dropped from the helicopter.”

“Yes Sir.”

Osman spoke in English to Saif.

“They can't be working in collusion, Mahmoud. They wouldn't attack simultaneously with the incursion of a ground mission. They're acting independently. Tarabalus just wants this place out of action, certainly doesn't want us to launch any more of our Migs.” He didn't need to say any more. Saif obviously understood.

"Well, they've achieved that, General. The ramp is blocked by surface rubble and debris from the Mig they blasted." Saif's tone was sour, then a note of suppressed anxiety crept into his voice and onto his normally impassive face. "But, the gas, General. Is it .... will it be alright?"

Osman looked slightly contemptuous.

"Of course, Mahmoud. You know that. This place is impervious to conventional bombing, it's a damned nuclear bunker! The defences are only activated if the bunker is breached, either by special device, nuclear device or human intervention. Without one of the keys there can't be human intervention unless they land a force which can excavate its way into here, and the Air force have no bunker bombs that I know of, and certainly no nuclear devices, do they?"

"No, no. Of course not, General. Of course not." Saif was relaxing a little. It was really only the gas that terrified him, so impersonal, so deadly, so indiscriminate, so pervasive, and so final.

"But, Mahmoud, We should be worried. Think of the scenario. It seems to me they've sent a "snatch" team in to get the British workers out, our own people have unknowingly simultaneously decided to render the base inoperable, the British must be working with the Americans, from a carrier I presume, or from Egypt, but I can't believe even they'd be that craven or stupid, and the Americans will still want this base destroyed, not just closed. In fact, unless the British outside tell them, or they've got surveillance at this precise period, they won't even know of the attack. That worries me like hell. The next thing we might expect is an American attack, they'd surely co-ordinate with the British, with deep penetration bombs. Their "bunker-busters", that would be a nightmare. That would activate the gas throughout the Base."

Saif felt his stomach turn. He'd seen the effects of the gas on "dispensable" prisoners. An awful death. Osman continued in English, not altering his tone, "There is little else we can do here. This place can do no more for our cause. We can continue elsewhere."

He became coolly businesslike.

"Is there any way out of here other than the two elevators?"

The implication was immediately obvious.

"Yes, there is." Saif retorted quickly. He'd already been thinking of it, way ahead of Osman. "There's a manual escape chute, which leads straight to the surface. Not far from the Personnel elevator and from the shower room in the corner of Belazir's office. It's the only one."

"How convenient." Osman said with heavy sarcasm. He switched to Arabic. "I suggest we pay the General a visit, General Saif."

Saif nodded, and swiftly informed the Communications Officer at the central console loudly that they were going for a briefing with General Belazir. He told him to hold all communications until they returned. They'd be less than 10 minutes. The young officer saluted. The two Generals smartly returned the salute and left them, to do their duty.

£$£

Chapter Forty-Three

JD's mind was racing, slightly hysterical, disconnected, as if he had a mild fever. There was a constant repetition of an image running through the vacuum that used to be his brain. It was a black and white cartoon in one of his history books. It was from the First World War. It had been published in a London newspaper at the time. There was an old soldier with his steel helmet on, in a shell-hole, scowling grumpily at a younger lad who'd obviously just jumped in with him. The caption read, "Find yer own 'ole." Looking around him, he wanted to grin inanely at the mental image. He was shaking now, and his sweat was cold. He felt it was all happening to someone else, strangely removed. He couldn't be here.

He heard but hardly registered the intense discussion. The Colonel was just lying:

"The base has been taken over by rebels. They're miss-using it. General Belazir and I are trying to stabilise the situation. I was trying to engineer the escape of the only foreign workers. These two young men." He indicated the engravers, who were staring hard at him. Paul Clay made as if to speak. He was obviously agitated. Gus shut him up. He was speaking urgently.

"Later. Listen. How much gas is in there?"

Anan hesitated only fractionally.

"One tonne. It is rigged to flood the base if the defences are penetrated, and if the elevators are mishandled. It's deadly. It's…."

"We know what it is. In just over 20 minutes time the Americans are going to bomb the base, and they will penetrate it! They're using a tactical nuke bunker-buster. If that plane's not back here in a couple of minutes we've got to leg it as far away from here as possible. The nuclear blast will kill us, or we'll get bloody radiation poisoning, or, worse, the Yanks don't know whether the nuke will destroy the gas! If that gets out, Christ help not just us, but half the fucking Mediterranean!"

Fit interrupted him even though the SAS man gave him a fierce look.

"Are you serious? Could deadly gas be released'? That would spread? How far?"

"I've just said, half the fucking Mediterranean!"

Fit looked shocked. He was shocked. He shook his head in bewilderment. He'd had enough of war in his lifetime. It had frightened him when he was young and robbed him of some of his best years, years he could have spent with Ronni.

Gus turned back to Anan.

"What's the status of perimeter guards? They could count us as hostiles. In fact, I'm bloody sure they will!"

"Two companies, one each end of the perimeter, which is a rectangle about three miles long, ten men in each, usually. They'll be on their way, for sure."

"Shit! What about forces inside the bunker? Will they come out?"

"No. Doubt it. Standing orders are to remain below ground ready to repel possible incursion."

"Good." Gus looked at JD, who stared vacantly back at him. "Where's that fucking plane?"

JD looked at his watch as if he was checking the time for an appointment.

"They're a bit late." He frowned a little disapprovingly, and then looked up into the sky, still vacant.

The SAS man cautiously stood up, reassured by Anan's comments. He swept the landscape round 360 degrees. Others joined him. Fit stood and walked the few paces to where JD still sat.

"JD, you'll never believe it! The bloody elevator we use is just sitting there in the middle of the rubble, absolutely unscathed! All that's happened to it is some of the paint and plaster on the outside's been knocked off!"

He was trying to regain JD's attention. He'd seen men

like this in Malaya during the Emergency. They either snapped out of it or they snapped completely. JD moved his head as if he was a robot and slowly stood up, looking at the elevator. It looked as if it had been deliberately stripped down to it's sanitised "steel". The sunlight now beginning to shaft through the dust was reflecting on it. It reminded him of what he'd first thought about the main gate when he first saw it now. So incongruous, just stuck there in the middle of the desert. He slowly rotated his head to look back at Fit.

"Yes. Strange isn't it?"

Anan was next to them. He accepted it as a normal conversation.

"It's supposed to be nuclear-proof. It's certainly bomb-proof."

Fit took JD's arm and led him to the side of the crater.

"Let's sit down a bit JD. I'm getting too old for this!" He was using his golf club captain's voice.

There was a faint rattle, hardly audible after the ear-splitting explosions of the last few minutes. Gus suddenly yelled.

"Down! Where?"

"South, 500 yards!" It was a soldier on look out at the crater rim.

"Keep down! Everybody! Just stay low! It's a perimeter company. Must be. They're firing. Jesus! Al, Dave, join Tich. Return fire. Keep 'em where they are. We need the space for the plane, and if it doesn't come, we're going that way! Andy - watch north. There's another patrol on the way!"

The three soldiers moved swiftly into their positions.

"All of you, here!"

Everybody crawled to Gus. Even JD. He was coming out of it a bit now. His mind was stopping whirring. He was thinking and seeing, not much, but some.

Gus put his H and K. MP5 down and unslung a Mini-Uzi from his back. JD, recalling his favourite reading, began to notice how lightly armed the group were for SAS men. H and K.s. Browning Automatics, Mini-Uzis, only a small amount of spare ammo, one of them had a 203 combination automatic rifle and grenade launcher, one radio that he could see. No heavy machine-gun, no GPMG, not even a Minimi. They'd obviously classed this as a lightweight mission. Nothing much more than escort. Gus gave the Uzi to one of the RAF men. He motioned, without speaking, to the other three SAS men to do the same, and called for the men on the rim to throw their spare weapons across. He handed them to each man, with a brief instruction.

"Fire like this. Short bursts. Spare mag. under the barrel. 32 rounds per mag. The plane's not come. We have to get out of here. We're going towards them, the bastards shooting at us. We know where they are, they know where we are. We can take them. No trouble. Looks about 10 of them. No heavy weapons. We'll just out-gun 'em. We don't know where the other patrol is. We don't want any surprises waiting for us if we go in the direction of the building. That's North. When we've sorted this lot out, I'll call for a pick up. But we've got to go right into them. Just keep running, keep low. Stop and drop when you hear me shout to do, or if I'm laid out, any of the others. Point and shoot when you can, and don't fucking hit us! Follow me!"

Crouching low he made his way to the south side of the crater. They followed. Fit suddenly said to JD.

"JD, You got the pen?"

JD realised immediately Fit meant the elevator "key".

"Yes. Why?"

"Just give it to me. Please, quick!"

JD reacted automatically. Everybody seemed to know what they were doing better than him. He gave it to him. Fit moved forward faster until he was alongside Gus. He put his hand on the SAS man's shoulder. Gus turned, a little surprised.

"Gus. Can you call off the nuclear strike?"

Gus stared at him as if he was crazy. Fit repeated his question.

"Well, we can contact the ship, but I'm not sure." He looked at his watch. The F15s would be taking off about now. Then he suddenly checked himself. Why was he talking to this old geezer about calling off an American mission? Jesus!

Before he could speak Fit said, "I can get into the elevator and disable the base completely. I know how it works. Believe me. Trust me, I can make sure that nothing and nobody comes out or goes in to that base for years. Swap me my Uzi for your Browning."

Gus looked even more wide-eyed at him. The silly old bugger was playing games now!

They were interrupted by a raucous shout. It was JD. He'd jumped up and was shouting at the top of his voice like a madman.

"The plane! The plane!"

"Get down, pillock!" Gus screamed. But he looked up and there was the G4, at about 500 feet and a mile away, heading their way. There was no doubt it was coming in to land. God knows, thought Gus, what the pilot must think when he looks at the remains of the building and the dust haze. But he kept on coming. He must have had a grandstand view of the little contretemps going on below. But down he came.

The SAS man weighed up the situation in an instant.

"Covering fire! Work your way towards the plane!"

Two more SAS men joined the three on the rim and blasted away at the patrol. Gus led the group left to the rim of the crater closest to the runway. They all lay on their sides while he shouted instructions.

"When it lands, you go! We'll cover you all the way, and follow you. You'll see us doing it in batches of three, who'll stop and fire while the others make ground. We should all make it. Those poor sods don't really want to fight. They're keeping their heads down and not moving towards us at all. We can keep them that way. When I say Go - **GO**! And don't stop for a chat or a shot. We want no fucking heroes!"

To JD's surprise, and even more to Gus's, Fit grabbed him by the arm again.

"Swap guns! Call it off! Please! Do it, Trust me, I was in the Ghurkhas!"

Even Fit thought what a stupid thing it sounded like to say, but it had a salutary effect on the young SAS man. He grabbed Fit's Uzi and gave him the Browning.

"Stop the strike. Stop it. There'll be no need for it!" Fit patted the SAS man on the shoulder like a reassuring sports master.

With that, some of which JD couldn't hear above the din, exacerbated now by the G4 engines, Fit turned and ran back across the crater. JD stared, totally puzzled. The world had gone fucking mad.

President Sunderland thought the world was going mad. He'd been sitting with the phone in his hand since 6.35 am. The reports were coming in thick and fast from the carrier. But they weren't always making sense. The British families were out, the British Special Forces team was lost, the RAF helicopter was destroyed, but everyone was still alive and fighting at the base. The Libyans had bombed their own top secret base to ashes and attacked their own aircraft. Jesus! Why couldn't someone just give him a clear picture? He'd given the go-ahead for the B61 raid at 6.45, now the captain was screaming for permission to abort! Jesus! And now they were telling him they didn't even know whether they could contact them in time to abort, even if permission was given. The pilots were observing strict radio silence. They were within ten minutes of target. But why abort? How could the base have been destroyed or immobilised by conventional weapons by the Libyans themselves? It was nuclear-proof, not just bombproof and what in God's name where they doing bombing their own base? His head was whirling. He tried to rationalise. He'd order abort. If all the confusing information turned out to be incorrect or not enough to achieve that aim that he was absolutely determined to achieve, well, they could "go" again, within the hour. And God knows he'd do anything to avoid taking the risk of spreading that gas to how many millions. He didn't even want to think about it. But he had to. He was the President. He prayed there was enough time.

"Abort, Captain. Presidential permission. Abort."

JD knew what he was doing, what Fit was doing! A fleeting panic hit him, but he punched it back. He leapt up and raced after Fit. He was yelling Fit's name. The bastard kept running straight for the elevator. JD cleared the top of the crater. He was vaguely aware of the SAS man screaming at him and following him. But his eyes were fixed on his old friend. He was going to stop him. He had to stop him.

What happened next was like a dream, a surreal dream. The ground opened up, and General Osman appeared, between him and Fit. It was like a genie in a child's cartoon. He just came straight up out of the ground. He took one step and another genie appeared. Christ Almighty! It was Saif. It had taken JD about three steps to perceive this. It took only one more to see that Osman was pointing a pistol at Fit's back, who was only about 10 paces from him. JD started shooting as he was running. Not in bursts. He just pressed and kept pressing. Osman never turned. His back suddenly went black and his head exploded as more than twenty bullets raked him from between the shoulder blades upwards. JD kept running. Saif stood wild-eyed and immobile as he lurched towards him. He was still shouting at Fit. His momentum prevented him re-aiming at Saif. But Saif's face exploded like Osman's head. JD automatically ducked and slowed as if to avoid the pieces of gore, but it was really just an instinctive realisation that someone behind him was shooting in his direction. He was hoarse with screaming at Fit and breathless because he wasn't breathing but shouting. He staggered a little through lack of oxygen, even though he'd only run 50-odd yards. Fit was coolly stepping into the elevator. He stood framed for a second in the doorway as it closed. He was smiling and waving that wave JD had seen so many times, as if to say, "See you later", his standard phrase on parting. He was mouthing something but the door closed completely, and JD's hoarse gasps as he tried to draw air into his burning lungs filled his own ears. He reached the door, and almost slammed his head against it due to his momentum and in desperate frustration. He stood there, leaning on the metallic door, his forehead pressed against his arm, the Uzi dangling down in front of him. He was gone. He'd have done it by now. That's why he wanted the pistol. A bloody sub-machine gun is a bit awkward to shoot yourself with and he wouldn't wait for the gas.

"Get down you stupid bastard!" The SAS man almost thumped into him and pulled him down. "They're still shooting at us you pillock!"

JD was getting his breath. He began to think. The Libyan patrol, still shooting, yes; Gus shot Saif, yes; the bastards had been getting out of the bunker leaving all the other poor buggers to die! Yes. Oh Jesus! Fit! He'd bloody killed himself neutralising the base, bloody killed himself!

"He bloody killed himself killing this fucking base. Hear me?" He was shouting at Gus. The SAS man grabbed him and yanked him round, pushing him back to the crater, in the direction of the plane.

"Run, or I'll fucking kill you!"

They both ran. JD could see that there was a semi-circle of SAS men about 20 yards from the plane. They were firing everything at the Libyan patrol, including grenades. There was no fire from the patrol. They ran past the lying men. Gus was shouting at them. They got up as one into a crouching position and started moving backwards in the direction JD and Gus were running. The G4 engines were screaming. The door was open and to JD's astonishment the Chief was standing there, in an immaculate white shirt and tie, waving them towards the door like a very genteel old-fashioned traffic cop. It was something else that seemed surreal, absurd. He dived on board. Gus nearly slammed on top of him. He scrambled on his hands and knees up the galley. He heard the others crash on board. The engines deafened them and Anton was airborne almost as fast as a

Harrier VTOL fighter.

He kept thinking of Fit. In that elevator, as the door was closing. What was he saying? He twisted round and grabbed Gus by the shamag round his neck. He was shouting as loud as he could to make himself heard over the noise of the straining engines as the pilot pushed them to their limits.

"The raid! The Yanks! Did you stop the raid'?"

Gus nodded vigorously, and pulled his head towards him. He put his mouth close to his ear.

"We radioed the carrier. Tich also used his TACBE, on their special frequency, to tell the pilots of the F15s to abort. That's all we could do. Only the President can give the final order. I hope it's got through. It should do, from the carrier especially."

JD felt exhausted. He felt close to tears. If Fit had done what he did and then the bloody Yanks couldn't stop it. Oh Christ! What a waste! What a balls-up the whole business was, had been.

He was still panting, gasping in air in excruciatingly short bursts, enough to hurt his throat. He looked up from the floor as he turned on his side. Every seat was full. People lying, sprawling on couches and arms of the armchairs, sitting in the aisle. Even the SAS men were slumped breathless, looking weary. It must always be like this after an action, JD thought. Weariness, but a joy to be in one piece. Intense relief. That's what he felt. And he felt guilty for feeling it because of Fit. Anan, still in full uniform, was sprawled backwards on the last armchair seat in the cabin, head laid back, one leg over the arm dangling in the aisle. He thought of Mary lying just like that in that chair at the Savoy. Lying in the aisle, in his filthy dusty ripped suit, still panting with fear and relief, he thought of Mary as she was 72 hours ago. For some reason that was beyond the limits of his limited mind at that moment it all fitted into some kind of pattern. It was all part of some other design, something to do with his life. He closed his eyes and Ness in her dark blue coat over her green dressing gown without make-up was blowing him a kiss as she drove away.

Suddenly the Co-Pilot Pierre appeared at the door. He was shouting.

"Look! Look out of the windows - that side. Quickly"

JD hauled himself up. Everybody was craning to see out of the right-hand windows. There were two jets below them, on a diverging course.

"They're F15s. They must be from the carrier. We're heading North west. They're heading due North. It's 12.55."

Pierre could sense as well as see the incomprehension.

"They're heading straight back to the carrier. They're travelling in exactly the opposite direction from the base. They must have been recalled. Zero hour was 1 pm!"

JD felt an enormous relief sweep over him. If he'd been able to analyse it he would have had to admit it didn't have much, at that precise moment, to do with saving tens of thousands, or millions, of Arabs and Greeks and Turks or sailors from an awful death. It was because Fit had done it. He'd succeeded. God, he'd done it.

There were a few grins amongst the SAS men. The professionals were quick to recover. The rest of them just slumped back.

The Chief stood at the door of the cabin, with his back to the galley.

Anna-Greta appeared behind the Chief. She was smart as usual, her make-up perfect. She smiled.

"Would anyone like tea, coffee, mineral water, or perhaps a beer?"

JD didn't know whether to laugh or cry.

£$£

Chapter Forty-Four

There was an Exchange of Letters.

The Secretary of the United States of America Department of State wrote a letter, passed on by the Swiss Ambassador in Tripoli, to the Minister of Foreign Affairs of the Great Socialist People's Libyan Arab Jamahiraya Republic. In it he praised the action taken by Libyan forces in the Desert of Sirte, reiterated the inviolable right of the ships of the United States to sail in the waters of the Gulf of Sirte, and warned of the lethal danger of the gas they had excellent reason to believe had been released in an underground facility in the area. This gas was of the deadly organo phosphorous ester class. The only possible action to be taken was to seal the facility for at least one year. The United States would then be willing to place facilities at the disposal of the Libyan Government to help in neutralising the gas in any planned cleansing operation after that time.

The Libyan Minister of Foreign Affairs replied to the U.S. Secretary of State, via the same channels, in a strongly-worded letter denying that any action had taken place on Libyan territory except the shooting down of an armed British helicopter which was illegally operating in Libyan airspace and obviously on a spying mission. No such gas as referred to in the American communication existed in Libya. The country rigidly adhered to International Treaties prohibiting the manufacture and storage of such illegal weapons of terror and mass destruction, unlike the United States of America, which was now the only nation in the world which continued to refuse to do so. The Gulf of Sirte was Libyan Territorial Water. International Waters commenced 100 miles from the Libyan coast, and they protested in the strongest terms over the incursion of hostile U.S. warships in the Gulf.

The Libyan Minister of Foreign Affairs wrote to the

Foreign Secretary at the British Foreign and Commonwealth Office, using the offices of the Cypriot Republic's Ambassador to Libya in Tripoli, protesting in the strongest possible terms about the armed incursion of Libyan air space and territory by a British Royal Air force helicopter on what was obviously an illegal spying mission. The Libyan Defence Forces had had no option, after repeated warnings, but to counter-attack against the hostile aircraft. Assurances were demanded that no such incursion would ever occur in the future.

The British Foreign Secretary replied to the Libyan note via the Cypriot Embassy, stating that the aircraft had accidentally flown into Libyan air space whilst on a routine Joint British-U.S. Naval Exercise. There was no question of the aircraft being involved in any illegal activity. This was totally rejected. However, the British Government deeply regretted the incident, and thanked the Libyan Government for allowing the crew of the aircraft to be flown out by the civilian jet fortuitously engaged in legal business in the area at the time. Tragically, it seemed that one civilian passenger on the aircraft, Mr. Frederick Ian Thomas, had been killed in the air-crash, and it was respectfully requested that his body, or ashes, and his personal effects, be returned to Britain at the earliest opportunity for proper internment.

Mary Matthews wrote to John Dilworth at his office, on her special blue speckled notepaper:

Dear John,

See! That's another first you've introduced me to. I've never written a "Dear John" letter before!

But I've never been unfaithful before. Until I first met you 18 years ago I wouldn't have believed it could ever happen to me. I've never been unfaithful since I last saw you 16 years ago - until I met you again last week. At the risk of making you even more conceited that you are - if that's possible! You made me feel like a complete woman again, like you did all those years ago. Can you believe I was still in my twenties then! Even you were only 32! Mere kids weren't we.

I remember something you said then, when you were bathing me in that wonderful huge shell-shaped bath in that hotel in Scotland (Do you remember it? I've had one installed at home just like it!). You said the problem with our society was monogamy, and our obsession with it, bred into us because of centuries of religious belief. You and I were happy atheists! But you said it was the root cause of such heartache and hurt because no-one would accept that people could truly love more than one person, or at least that's what they were forced to pretend to believe. You believed that there could be one "other person." Only one, though. You said that I was that other person. I believed you then, although I thought I was being stupidly naive. You proved I wasn't. I still believe you.

But it's the world we live in. And if you love more than one person it only works if it remains a total secret. And that's impossible. Everyone in my office knew we were having an affair 16 years ago. They knew almost as soon as I did! I can tell you now that I was as glad as I was sorry when we lost touch. It would have got out of the office, and found it's way into my home if it had gone on any longer.

If it had, I couldn't have faced Jonathan. He's been a wonderful husband. Loyal and devoted. A true friend when I've needed one. We've shared, and built, a life and a family together. The years have made us one living entity, though we're separate beings (Lord! I'm beginning to sound like you when you're rambling!). You must feel the same. You know you love Vanessa and your family. Think, seriously, what you would feel like if she found out you loved me as well. I know you do, and I'm not being conceited. I believe you. But think of the heartbreak.

What we had, I'll always be grateful for. What we have now I treasure. But it's so precious I'm locking it away in a safety deposit box of isolation. I don't want to see you again. No, correction. I do want to see you again, to touch you, enjoy you, and laugh with you. But I'm not going to.

Our last meeting was our last meeting.

I've agonised over this. I long for you. But I also long for permanence and stability and the love of a husband and a family and all the things that make life worth living in the society we have to accept because we live in it. There is no other way. We're both incredibly lucky. We still have, I hope, many long years to appreciate it.

How I wish, JD that we could have met in another time, in other circumstances. What we could have done together!

You know I'll always love you. You were that "other person" for me. Goodbye.

John Dilworth wrote to Mary Matthews.

Dear Mary,

You're right and every single word, I believe you. I'll always love you. JD.

It was probably the shortest letter he'd ever written. It reflected a truth he'd only learned at 48 years old in a hole in the desert. And in dirt-encrusted clothes on the floor in a plane. The truth. The only truth a man can ever really know. About himself.